M000117005

WRITINGS ON THE WALL:

ARLISSA'S Story

GODDESS A. BROUETTE

WRITINGS ON THE WALL:

ARLISSA'S Story

WHAT GOES UP, MUST COME DOWN

WRITINGS ON THE WALL: ARLISSA'S Story

This book is a work of fiction. Names, characters, places, and incidents are the product of the author's imagination or are used fictitiously. Any resemblance to actual events, locales, or persons, living or dead, is coincidental.

Copyright © 2021 by Goddess A. Brouette

All rights reserved.

Cover Design: Enchanted Ink Publishing
Editing: Enchanted Ink Publishing
Formatting: Enchanted Ink Publishing

ISBN: 978-1-7374147-2-8

Thank you for your support of the author's rights.

Printed in the United States of America

Inner
Child
Publishing
SINCE 2021

TO MY SOULMATES, WE FINALLY DID IT.

GODDESSABROUETTE.COM

Prologue

"I'm sorry, I'm so fucking sorry, Xavier. Just please for the love of God come back!" I shout as I straddle the lifeless being that causes my entire lower body to make friends with the blood. My fists beat his chest repeatedly, hoping for a response, anything. As more tears fall, my fire-red cheeks start to sting from the aggressive rubbing and sobbing I've been doing.

"Fuck! Why are you doing this to me? What did I do to deserve this?" I shout, anger bubbling up inside me as I stare at a sickly-looking version of my lover.

No.

No. No. This can't be real life. I can't lose someone else, not here. Not like this. Why? Why does everything I love get ripped away from me like I did something wrong? I'm not the problem. I can't be the problem.

Pain flows out of every pore, and I can hear my heart shatter bit by bit. It's not a silent shatter, no. It's the kind that makes you want to grip your chest and rip that very organ out. I wish I'm looking down at someone else other than him. Anyone. It could be anyone else; just not Xavier. I rest my head on his still body, the blood on my hands beginning to dry now as I trace my fingertips down his chest. Is he breathing, or am I just shaking?

I'm numb; maybe if I just lie back down and close my eyes, I'll wake up and this will all be a dream . . . Right? I can wake up and none of this will be happening right now. He'll be smiling at me before running out the door for a meeting. It'll be okay. The pools of blood soak into my white nightgown. None of that concerns me.

At least wherever I go after this I can take a piece of him with me.

"You can stop joking now . . . " I whisper to what's left of the man I gave everything to. A laugh escapes my chapped lips while my melting brain tries its best to process what's happening in these four walls. "You won . . . You fucking won."

The sarcastic laughter continues as the guilt of my entire life piles up inside. First my sister, now this. I take notice of the sunrise coming up gently, shining light on everything that was once hidden in darkness.

"I did it! Okay? I fucking did it! I killed him. I killed her. I killed my daughter," I shout as if the sun is going to give me a round of applause for confessing. My vision trails off and so does my voice, cracked and going in and out from the countless screams I've been vocalizing all night. "This is all your fault, Lissa . . . You ruin everything you touch, you worthless piece of shit."

My spiral is interrupted by a bright light and heavy footsteps pushing through our bedroom door. I jump up, both hands covered in half-dried blood as I hold them up in fear.

"Arlissa Benson, I'm going to need you to step away from the body."

I vigorously shake my head, overwhelmed by the number of

armed officers that now surround me. Every time I blink, a new one shows up.

"What's going on?" I scream.

"Ma'am, please slowly get off the bed and step away from the body."

No, no, no! They are not going to take him from me.

"No—"

Before I can finish my thought, two large hands yank me from the sheets, revealing all the blood that I had let soak up in the fabric of my nightgown. "Get off me! You can't do this! You can't take him!"

"Calm down, Ms. Benson," one of the officers calmly says with what I'm sure is a gun pointed right at my face. But his flashlight is so blinding there's no way anyone could see anything clearly. The coat of one officer catches the light, revealing the three letters printed: FBI.

"I want to stay with him! Leave me alone! Let me stay with him!" I fight with all my might and scream until my throat burns, salty tears dripping onto my nose. I holler as if my brain is on fire.

I try kicking, I try scratching, biting. But before I know it the right side of my face is pressed against the stone-cold wall, and my hands are tied behind my back, a metal binding locking them together.

"Arlissa Benson, you are under arrest for the murder of Xavier Amari. You have the right to remain . . . "

Every cell in my body feels as if it's melting while I try to make sense of the words that are being sent in my direction. What did I do?

How did I even get here?

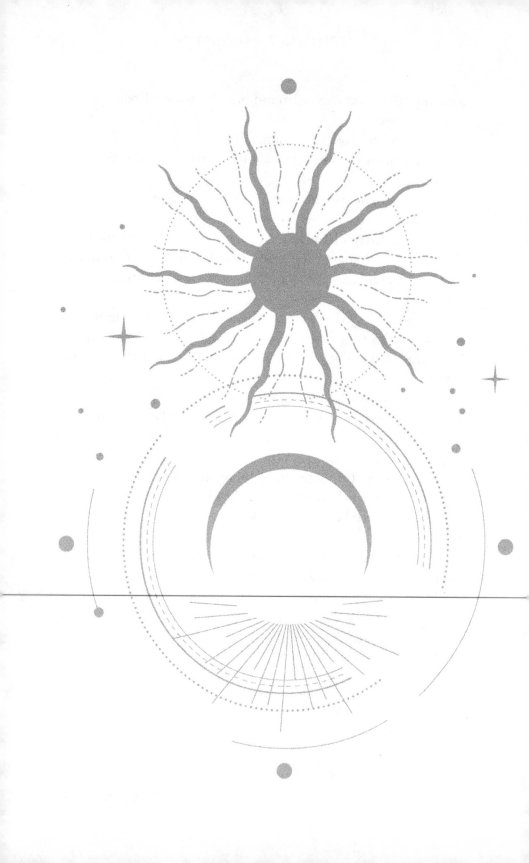

PART ONE

Sunrise

ONE

*H*it me with a fucking car, please. No? Well, why not? It'd finally give me something to update my family with during all those spine-curdling Thanksgiving silences. At least when you're paralyzed you have something to talk about. But, hey, my whole life is ahead of me after graduating high school. I get to meet my college sweetheart and chug kegs on campus like my parents did. And most importantly, I'll finally discover who I am.

Who the fuck is Arlissa Benson?

She's the boring friend. The one with no deep desires or achievable dreams. She's the one who only wants to go to an online school simply because she doesn't have that annoying itch to dorm with a stranger and argue about the thermostat. On the bright side, at least I can pass a drug test. I guess what I'm trying to say is I've just never been one of those people, the ones who drool at the idea of this future they've visualized for years. I've never wanted anything that badly. Never. Ever.

My world, my life. It's all black and white. It's not like I'm sad or anything, because I'm fine. I live a good life with a good family who will love and support anything I choose. We even used to take typical family vacations to Disney and watch *Elf* every single Christmas Eve. And every Sunday night, mom would make an authentic Jamaican meal to remind us of where she came from.

Life has just been quiet since— anyway.

I guess when you're living on borrowed time you don't have the energy to create a ten-year plan. Instead, you spend every day waiting for the reaper to remember he left you behind and come to collect.

I'm nineteen years old, and I've never even had a minor fender bender. I've never had a guy break my heart. There have been a few boys and a lot of sex, and most of those experiences were my own pitiful attempts to break my own heart. What is love, anyway? Of course, I've experienced the emotions of sadness and happiness and the waves of things in between. It's just never been anything to go write home about.

I just want to feel something. But there's always nothing.

Sitting, staring, pulling out the thin hairs I skipped over while shaving my currently exposed thighs. With every pull, my tawny skin began to turn light red. Maybe if I wasn't being rushed, I wouldn't have skipped over a whole patch of leg hair that had been begging me to hack away at it since last month. But, come on, who actually shaves when they're not going anywhere?

The air conditioning keeps the goosebumps on my arms well and alive, reminding me that it's either sitting here in silence or stepping out into the hot California sun. This is it; this might just be Alejandra's life for the next few years.

"Excuse me, do you have an appointment?"

I didn't even notice the secretary hovering over me with freshly poked lips. I shake my head feverishly. The bun my hair was in completely comes undone shortly after.

"No, no." I stammer over my words, trying to collect my bouncy brown tresses as they fall. "I'm here waiting for a friend, Alejandra. She's just right in there." My chin tries desperately to point her to the direction of the record label logo that's placed in the center of the double doors that hold my best friend.

"Oh . . ." The woman steps back a bit, clearly realizing that I'm in no condition to be bothered right now. "Well, we have water over there if you'd like some."

I smile awkwardly as I watch her walk away. Rolling my eyes, I finger comb my hair and pray that it doesn't look like a hot, curly-ass mess. There's no time to go into the bathroom and try to redo my bun now. Alejandra could be out at any moment.

Maybe if I sit here and really focus, I can hear whatever is going on in that meeting. This means so much to her. That's the only reason I'm here. And honestly? I hadn't prepared a speech if she didn't get offered a record deal.

My chocolate orbs focus on the immense glass door that stands tall, intimidating me like I'm the one talking to my idol. I can see Alejandra's raven hair swinging back and forth with every word she says. Amy's bright blue eyes give me the chills from six feet away.

And just like that. It's over. I watch the pair give each other a goodbye hug.

"I'm now the brand-new mentee of *the* Amy Fucking Montana!" Alejandra comes bursting out of the room, voice first, body second.

I shoot up in an instant, ready to take on the taller girl's body weight as she flings herself into my arms. "I—I'm so proud of you!"

"I did it! I fucking did it!"

9

"I'm so happy for you, Aly."

"You've got a talented friend here." Amy's voice roars, but her presence is even louder.

Slowly, Alejandra and I release our grip on each other. I wonder if I look as frazzled as I feel. "I don't think we got a chance to meet earlier."

"Uh, no. No we didn't."

Aly nudges me, whispering in my ear. "Shake her hand. I may, or may not have set the bar high for you in there."

I clear my throat, forcefully putting my hand out. "I'm Arlissa."

"Yes, yes. She told me you'd be joining her in my guest house during the length of this mentorship."

"Huh?"

The brunette steps in front of me, cutting off any chance of my mumbling ruining this for her. "Yes! I can't write a single song without my sister here with me. She's my walking inspiration."

Amy pouts. "Aw, it's nice to keep your loved ones close during these moments."

"Closest thing to family I have, let me tell ya."

"And just to double-check, you're all okay to move in tonight?"

"Yes!"

"Arlissa?"

I gulp, still trying to process what the hell Alejandra got me into this time. "Yes. I practically have my whole life packed in that backseat already. Aly's too."

"You guys were prepared."

Aly lets out a soft giggle. "We weren't taking no for an answer."

"I like that. It's settled then. I have a lunch scheduled and way too many meetings lined up today, but you two should take a look around LA, then meet me back at the office at six, and we can head over to the house. It was so nice meeting you, darling." Without hesitation, Amy wraps my friend in another hug. "Also,

Aly, I like that. I think we're going to keep that. How do you feel?"

"If you like it I fucking love it!" Alejandra exclaims, still in the embrace of her idol. "Sorry, sorry. Didn't mean to cuss."

"No, no. Don't apologize. You've got personality. I like it, and I would like to see so much more of it, hon. I'll see you girls tonight." And in the blink of an eye, she's off to do more of whatever billionaire icons do.

Alejandra turns in my direction, pulling me as far from any lingering ears as she can. But of course, that's hard to do when we were standing in a building where celebrities are practically birthed. I think, who knows. Alejandra is the one who kept up with all this shit and I never knew the difference between Brad Pitt and Leonardo DiCaprio.

"Stay with me, whore."

"I mean, do I have a choice?" I aggressively whisper.

"We all have choices, so technically yes. But . . . I want you here, and I already said you'd stay. Plus, you know I can't drive."

"Right, and what about the diner? Why couldn't Christian stay with you?"

"Christian and I broke up, and you can quit your job at that stupid diner."

"Hold on, hold—broke up?"

The Latina sucks her teeth before yanking me out into the stale Californian air. "Christian and I are done. Finished. Finito."

"Why?"

"I just—I'm starting something brand new here, and I don't think he wanted to be a part of it. Anyways, please, please, please. We can take on LA together! You and me—we're a power team. With you behind my back, I'll be on the cover of *Vogue* in no time."

"Yeah, and I'll always just be behind your back."

"Lissa—"

"I could be home working on getting enrolled in school and the diner and—"

"And you'd be miserable."

"You have a future here. I do not."

"But you can! Just give it a shot. Give me a shot."

"I—"

"Lissa, you can be whoever you want here. We have a chance to do this life shit over. Do you know how much content you'll have in your journal entries being here?"

I roll my eyes. "I haven't written in my journal in ages."

"Yeah, like I didn't see you pack it in your bag. Come on, just do this with me. For me."

It's always so difficult to say no to her doe-like eyes. They're a beautiful dark brown that is almost mesmerizing. Nothing anyone with a sane brain can say no to.

"Fine!"

"Ah!" Alejandra squeals before jumping up and down like a high school cheerleader. "Now let's go get something greasy and disgusting."

"Okay, but promise me this . . . "

"Hm?"

"We won't become one of those LA girls who eat celery for lunch and drink broccoli for dinner."

A giggle escapes Aly's lips as she nods. "Okay, new tradition. It's Friday, right? Every Friday we have an insanely gross dinner. Calories on top of calories. Grease on top of grease. We'll never become LA that way."

"Deal." We begin making our way to my rusty old car, hand in hand. "So what happened to you and Christian, anyway?"

"I told you. He wasn't down for palm trees and Instagram blogs suddenly knowing his name."

"Sucks. He seemed so happy for you."

"Yeah."

LA is going to be new territory. So much more than I'd ever experienced in the small town we both were born and raised in. But no matter how uninterested I am in the good, the bad, and the ugly, I agree to try.

TWO

The sun slowly makes its exit as my 2007 Volkswagen Jetta enters the property. The greens of the grass beckons us through the property. I follow Amy's car while the glowing home slowly but surely reveals itself to me. The house is surrounded by water as glass atriums call me to the entrance. The property screams "I make millions," and for a moment, I get so stuck staring at how the setting sun reflects on the windows that I don't realize Amy's car turning. I quickly adjust my vehicle and look over to make sure Alejandra is just as speechless as I am.

We pull into the private driveway before coming to a nice stop. Aly practically jumps out of the car—this is all finally settling in for her.

"You're both probably starving so we can start with dinner. My husband set up a nice authentic Middle Eastern meal for us all. I sure hope you girls don't have any dietary restrictions!" Amy says as she locks her Range Rover.

"Nope, none at all. But I think we might need some with the way we eat," Alejandra adds, her eyes still in awe of the property. I grab my purse and lock my car as well, waiting for Amy to give us the signal to follow her.

What the fuck has Aly gotten us into?

"Great. Where you'll be staying is right down that way, but I'll show you all of that after dinner." The woman points behind us, and our eyes follow her index finger. The little white house is more like a modern-day cottage than a mansion. The doors are made of glass and through it, I see a small couch but nothing more than that from the distance we're at. "As of right now, you guys can follow me." The tall woman runs her fingers through her curly blonde locks as she directs us to a much smaller door than the one we originally drove past. She steps to the side and beckons us through. We both take baby steps, unsure of how far inside we're even allowed.

How dare my $8.25-an-hour ass stand on this stone-cold floor right now? I'm sure the air alone costs more than I've ever spent.

The inside is just as mesmerizing as the outside. Stone and glass cover all of the walls. And instead of family photos, awards and trophies grace the sideboards. Suddenly, my senses are attacked by an overwhelming smell of paprika and meat.

"Aaron, I'm home!" Amy calls out, her silvery tone perfectly echoing throughout the home. Alejandra and I stand there, not too far from the doorway, hand in hand.

"Welcome back!" The words surf through the large space. There is still no face with the voice, but it's clearly coming from the left side of the home.

Unfamiliar footsteps derail my train of thought as it comes from behind me. *No one else came in after us, right? Don't tell me they have a damn butler because—*

"Ah, perfect. You're here, Ma. I was just—"

I turn to my right, my eyes locking with a man I know I've

seen somewhere before. His shaggy brown hair is in desperate need of a cut, and a white (partially stained) T-shirt perfectly displays a huge sun tattoo on his forearm. He's rich enough to not look homeless. He clings to a single black boxing glove.

Alejandra squeezes my hand tightly before her whispers fall on my ears. "Oh my God."

"Hey, I'm Xavier. You must be—" he starts.

Amy steps in front of us. "Excuse him, girls. He left his manners when he moved out." She turns to him, her tone lowering significantly. "I told you I was bringing my mentee today."

"I know. You called thirty-six times."

"It's not my fault I have to beg you to come see your mother."

"Ah, Mom. You didn't have to beg. I was coming over tonight, anyway. Which brings me to my original question—"

"No boxing tonight, Xavier!" Amy whines. "I'd just like this to be the one night where you and your father leave that stuff alone." Her eyes roll to the back of her head, taking the glove from her son's hand and placing it on a nearby counter.

"Leave the boy, Ams. That's how he wins—he's always thinking about the ring."

The husky voice from before finally clears. The older man appears from around a corner with a dishrag as he casually wipes off his hands. He's insanely muscular with salt-and-pepper facial hair and would scare the living shit out of me if he didn't have an apron on that said, "Kiss the Cook." "Nice to meet you, ladies. I'm Aaron, Xavier's father and trainer."

"And my husband, which he seems to forget on occasions."

Aaron smirks. "Isn't she a peach?"

"Alejandra Garcia! I'm the mentee." She quickly shakes his hand before turning to Xavier, who stands behind us. "Nice to meet you as well, Xavier." Their hands meet, but his eyes aren't on her. They're on me.

"I'm Arlissa—" I pause, trying to shake the burning feeling of his deep brown eyes piercing through the right side of my skull. "Arlissa Benson. I'm just emotional support."

Focus. I shake Aaron's hand fiercely but avoid his son's completely.

"You'll be more than emotional support, darling. This is California. We'll find a place for you," Amy adds as she put one arm around my shoulders. "Now, can we please eat? I'm starving."

Kefta. Apparently, it's some sort of Arabic grilled dish, and honestly, I've never eaten something I couldn't pronounce before. Chicken fingers. See? Easy to pronounce, easy to eat, an American delight. I chew slowly, trying my hardest to chime in on the conversation whenever I can.

"Cory Tubman said he's done boxing, I forgot to tell you—"

"Aaron."

"I heard, Dad."

"Xavier!" Amy whines. "You two are the worst dinner guests."

Aaron rolls his eyes, stuffing a fork full of food in his mouth shortly after. "We'll talk later, Xavier."

"Thank you."

"So, where are you girls from? I know my wife was doing this contest worldwide, but you look American to me."

Alejandra releases an awkward giggle before quickly wiping her mouth. "Carson City. Way more boring than any place you guys have been to, I'm sure. Probably never heard of it."

Xavier interrupts, "Nevada?"

My brown orbs meet Xavier's when he speaks; what was avoidance at first is no longer. He's directly across from me, but for some reason, the thought of us acknowledging each other sends a chill down my spine. "Yeah, actually."

"Cool, I've been there."

Aaron raises a brow. "What you doin' in Nevada, boy?"

"I have a friend there, Dad. No big deal." Xavier avoids eye contact with his dad like I avoided him. Suddenly, he rises from his chair. "Well, lovely seeing you guys, but I am out of here, family."

Amy stands with him. "Wait, leaving so soon? Dessert?"

"He doesn't need dessert, Amy, sit down. What the boy needs is some rest."

"Well, Xavier, before you go off, be sure to send S—"

"Whoa, whoa."

"Right, I forgot. Sorry. Well, before you go home, can you at least show the girls their guest house?"

The younger man slightly rolls his eyes before his attention goes to Aly and me. "Are you guys even done eating?"

My energetic friend jumps up. "Yup, sure am."

"Come on. And, Dad, can you please find my glove and bring it to the gym tomorrow?"

"I'll just get you some new ones."

"Alright, cool. Come on, I've got shit to do."

"Language!"

Alejandra and I get up and push our chairs in as fast as possible considering he's already started walking. We don't even catch up with him until we're completely outside.

"Sorry about that," he says in a gruff tone as he finally turns to face us, walking backward now.

"Parental issues, huh?" Alejandra never really speaks about her parents, mainly because there isn't much to speak about. "I know how that feels."

"So that's why you flew all the way out here to live with mine? You don't make the best choices, do you?" There's a forced cheeriness in his voice now as he juggles his keys between each hand.

"Your mom has faith in me, something mine's never had."

We walk in silence for about five more minutes, our guest-house being on the very edge of the property. The small home is gorgeous. There are even two entrances that are separated by a path of stone. It's completely see-through, so you can see that the main entrance holds the living room and kitchen and the second holds the bedrooms and bathrooms.

"I wish you could see this place with the sun out," he murmurs as he unlocks the door.

"I wish I could see this place with the sun out," I whisper to myself, basking in what maybe isn't the worst relocation in the world.

At the same damn time.

My stare immediately goes blank as my heart works a little harder to circulate oxygen through my body. I don't even have to look at Alejandra to know she has a stupid smug grin on her face. He doesn't flinch. I know he heard me. He had to have heard me.

"All right, all yours. I'll give this key to you." He places the key in Alejandra's hand, and that's when I realize he's probably over a foot taller than me. I mean, it's not that hard to be taller than someone who's five-foot-nothing, but wow. His attention shifts to me, sending a chill down my spine. And for a moment his twinkling orbs meet mine yet again.

"My mom has a spare key, so I'd get it from her in the morning if I were you." With that, he steps in between us and begins to slowly make his way back. "It was nice meeting you ladies. Hopefully, I'll be seeing a lot more of you." When the three-letter word drips from his lips, he just focuses on me. He's talking only to me.

Once Xavier is a good few feet away, I feel a tug on my arm and am yanked inside the house. Alejandra gently closes the door before letting out the loudest shriek ever.

"You just got hit on."

I roll my eyes, moving away from the door and throwing myself on the couch. "I did not."

"But you did. He was all like, 'I'll be seeing a lot more of you.' Come on, Lissa. I know you felt that."

Maybe.

Come on, you know he was.

"I don't know what you're talking about."

"You're fucking nuts. I hate it here. Fuck you! He's a legend-ary boxer in-the-making. I mean, he's only twenty-one, you know. And he's, like, super close to taking his own dad's title. I think that's what the blogs are saying. I don't know. I don't actually watch that shit."

"Oh . . . he's a boxer."

"You didn't know that?"

If I roll my eyes one more time they'd be stuck in the back of my head. At what point was I supposed to pull out my phone and Google this man and his entire background? I immerse my-self more in the luxury cushions. "I know nothing about these people. I'm here because you were yodeling on Instagram, and, well . . . Ta-da."

"Well, let me give you the rundown."

"Please don't."

"Hush. Amy is an icon, and she redefined country music while also redefining pop music while also marrying a legendary boxer and then giving birth to a very hot legendary boxer in the making."

"Right. You've told me this a million times, I'm sure."

"And you didn't remember?"

I shrug. "Guess not."

"Then you need to be memorizing these things so next time you know how to behave!"

"Well, I'm sorry. I'll curtsy next time."

"You suck."

"So?"

"So! You should care more that he was hitting on you."

I scoff, this entire thing is absolutely ridiculous. "You're nuts. Don't you have songs to write?"

"I have all summer to write these songs, baby! Look at where we are!"

We allow ourselves a moment of silence, a moment to really think.

"Yeah, look at where we are, Aly." My voice calms down and for once I'm really letting myself believe this is happening.

The couch shifts once Alejandra takes a seat by my feet. "You know, I always dreamed of days like this. I mean, no shit, you know. But it's so much better than the dreams already." The brunette pauses, taking a moment to enjoy the silence. "Coño. I'm tearing."

I lift my head, a smile creeping up on my face. "I love you."

"I love you more."

THREE

How's she doing?

Good, I think. But I'd rather worry about you.

At the sound of Aly's footsteps, I quickly pivot and stuff my phone in my pocket. Our gazes meet and when I see the bags in her hand my facial expression rearranges itself. "Another shopping trip? We're gonna run out of money, Aly."

"Just one more, and we'll be all moved in!" the brunette exclaims while adjusting a faux plant on the coffee table.

"With whose money?"

She pauses. "Right . . . Hey! Maybe you can ask Amy to help find you some work. Didn't she offer?"

"Barely. I'm sure she wouldn't even blink if I took camp as your shadow all summer."

"My God. That attitude of yours has really gotten sick lately."

"And why can't you get a job?"

"Because I'm occupied, you know—becoming the next Amy Montana. Hello."

"Right. So the singer can't take an order anymore?" I question, a bit annoyed that she's putting the work of getting a job all on me.

"Right. I have to keep focused, or we'll both be right back at the diner." Finally, she stops fiddling with that damn plant and prioritizes the issue at hand. "Look, I'm just trying to help."

"Help with what?"

"You haven't been happy since the day we got here, and it's been like . . . a week."

I release a deep sigh as I take a few steps over to her. "I'm just trying to get used to things. This is your dream, not mine."

"Lissa . . . "

No. Not the tone. She's using the tone she always uses when she's about to bring up the thing. Okay, I lied earlier. I haven't had a completely boring life, and my family isn't completely normal because we—

"You have to let yourself have a damn dream again."

My eyes are glued to the floor, freshly painted toes being the only focus of my eyesight. "I don't like talking about that." Dreams are overrated. And so is love. What's the point of trying when bad luck follows me around like a virus?

"You were a kid. I'm just asking you to live a little. You haven't even had a boyfriend since . . . Ever? And don't say Emmett because that shit did not count."

If this was a perfect drama I'd already be in tears talking about how my best friend is right and maybe closing myself off to feeling absolutely anything is pure stupidity. But it's not a perfect drama, and none of that is correct.

Alejandra's parents basically beat the hell out of each other every night of her entire childhood while she muted the sounds with "Because of You" by Kelly Clarkson. Having a daughter

ended up being something they forgot, and when I met her she was on an all-cereal diet. Somehow, she still sees hope in people. She still has dreams. I had a stupid dream once, and I promise I'll never have one again. Or even get close to anyone else, because for some reason bad things happen to really good people.

Yes, I'm bored out of my mind, and I'm envious of everyone who can wish upon a star even after their childhood is violently ripped away from them. How in the hell can I go out and find love when I'm the reason that my very first best friend will never get to walk down the aisle? So tell me, wise guy, how am I going to experience life when I'm too scared to learn anyone's name?

"I'll ask Amy if she has any idea what I can do here while you focus on your EP. Promise."

"Sneaking up on a woman in her fifties is quite rude," Amy says softly, bending over what seems like an endless garden of roses.

"These are beautiful," I mumble, taking a few steps closer.

The sun beams on my shoulders as I try my best not to make it obvious that the heat is cooking my skin at three hundred and fifty degrees Fahrenheit. Sunblock? Definitely didn't pack that. But it's hard to complain when a sea of red keeps my eyes in awe.

Amy rises, adjusting her sun hat over her blond tresses. "Thank you. They're my proudest creation. I never had a green thumb, you know. But I just kept trying until I got it right. Wait—my second proudest creation after my son."

"Well, I hope one day I can be as dedicated to something as you . . . " My words are purely for conversational purposes but it doesn't make them any less true.

She raises a brow. "Are you settling in well here, Arlissa?"

Honestly? No, say that. "I mean, it's amazing. I'm so grateful that Aly finally gets to live her dreams and—"

"What about you?"

"I'm just here."

"Go on."

I shrug. "I don't know. I think that might be the problem."

"Ah, I see. Have you ever been out of your town before?"

"No. I mean, yeah, for vacations. But never here. Never like this. Just three weeks ago I was waiting tables, and now you're housing me just because I picked the right best friend."

Shut up. You're talking way too much. But something about her just—I wanted to. *No. Focus. Employment, money, something to do, hooray!*

"I see. Can I tell you a quick story?"

I nod and give her a soft smile. "If we can step out of this sun."

Amy releases a light chuckle before beckoning me over to the porch, where we both take a seat.

"When I was slightly younger than you ladies, I wanted someone to hear me sing so bad. I'd pray on it, I'd write little notes to myself saying someone is going to take me seriously. Someone did."

"Yeah?"

"My husband. We've known each other forever and—" She shuffles in her seat a bit, twisting her ring as she speaks. "His family owned this restaurant, and he believed in me even though we were kids. Begged and pleaded with his momma to let me sing for them on the weekends and after school. I did that for a long time. Then once he decided to take boxing seriously he took me on the road with him. I sang a song in every state in this country before the right person heard me. I guess what I'm trying to say is, be easy on your friend. I created that contest because I'm tired of this industry just as much as anyone else my age. But I wanted to give another girl that chance. Teach them what I wish I knew. I formulated a mentorship program that was closer than just manager and client. You live here with me, I teach you not only how to write but how to deal with this life in ways no one ever taught me. She brought you because she loves you. She won't even stop talkin' about ya! Enjoy it. Okay?"

I sit there in silence for a minute. Did she just call me ungrateful in a monologue? I think she did. The truth sucks, stings even. But I'm a grown woman now, so I guess I have to handle it the "right way."

"Thank you. I think I needed to hear that, and I promise you she's so grateful. I'm—grateful."

"You're special, Arlissa. Don't ignore that."

My soft lips curve into an even wider smile. "Um, I do need to ask you something, though."

"Shoot, sunshine, I've got all day."

"I need a job, like, badly. I know Aly has her music thing so I just—"

"I have the perfect thing for you, buttercup!"

"Oh?"

"My son."

"Oh."

"Oh?"

"No! He's great—well, cool. I don't know, I don't really know him."

"Mm-hmm, well, he's a—very kind boy. He just expressed to me this morning that he had some problems with his previous assistant. Something about leaking information? I don't know, we didn't get to talk long." She holds back, messing with her ring once again. "Never mind the details from me, I'm sure you can ask him. He's having a gathering tonight with a few friends to celebrate—whatever he's celebrating now. Very quaint, nothing too much, I'm sure. He trains like a dog, so he can't afford to party much. But he is in need of an assistant, and if you want I can give

26

him a call, and you guys can talk about it tonight. But please go. It'll do both you girls some good." She ends her sentence with a smile, one of those smiles that makes you want to immediately say yes.

Live a little, right? This better be worth it. "Thank you so much. That would be awesome. I'll let Aly know."

"Of course, I'll let him know you're interested and send the address to Alejandra."

Fabulous.

FOUR

*A*lejandra forces me to straighten my long brown hair instead of running it under a faucet and letting my curls do their own thing. Honestly, for something that's supposed to be casual, I don't understand the need for me to squeeze into my favorite shorts because they cup my butt in a flattering way. Or even the burgundy crop top Alejandra insisted I wear because you never believe when someone over thirty calls a party a "quiet get-together." Part of me knows she's right, yet a dominating part of me can't believe Xavier would be okay with me going to something that was more than just a job offer.

I'm nobody. And if what Alejandra says is true, he's a big fucking deal.

The whole process of getting there, the elevator ride up to the condo, was the longest period of time Aly had gone without complaining about my lack of enthusiasm. Her usual rambling about how well I would do in LA was now replaced with her excitement for being invited to what she described as a "premature industry party."

Text me when you get home safe. I'll be up.

Kk.

"Are you gonna knock?" Her tone takes me out of whatever trance I was in, and for once I don't even comment back. I just knock. The muffled music makes its presence known through the walls, causing my stomach to repeatedly cartwheel. Seconds turn into eternities before we're rescued by a cast of light coming from the door.

"Well, well, well. I made a bet with a friend saying you guys wouldn't show. Fuck, I guess I owe someone twenty bucks." Xavier's words spew out a mile a minute like he's ready to run a marathon. And am I crazy, or are his pupils dilated like a puppy thats eye-fucking a bone?

His tall frame stands there in the doorway, a short-sleeved shirt showcasing enormous biceps; accompanied by another tattoo. Yet, unlike the first one I noticed, I can't identify this one. He towers over me with a Solo cup in his hand, yet my eyes are attracted to what's behind him.

People stand on couches, share drinks, and one girl even rips her top off in real-time. The last party I went to had streamers, cake, six-year-olds, and Paw Patrol balloons. This time, there are sweaty bodies humping on top of each other and alcohol being sprayed around the room like it's rain. The floor is soaked in it, and I'm almost positive he's going to have to get his tiles redone after this.

But to bring it all together, the immense speakers resting on each side of the milky white home bar blare the current Hot 100.

"Some small get-together . . . "

"Told ya so!" Alejandra sings before snatching Xavier's drink and pushing past him.

I follow her footsteps, the smell of his cologne completely overtaking my senses for a moment. My eyes continue to take in the living room and bar area that we walked into. It's barely midnight, and the place is already trashed. Empty bottles and shoes are scattered all over the floor, just waiting for someone to fall face-first onto a heel.

"My parents would shut this shit down if I told them otherwise." His voice is directly above me, his breath sending a shiver down my spine as he ends his sentence. I'm so focused on what's going on around me and who's hovering over me—that I forget to keep following Alejandra.

"Lying to your mother? To think she thinks you're the sweetest boy ever."

He smirks before stepping in front of me. "You've never lied to your parents?"

Once. "Nope. I tend not to be a shitty person."

"Ouch." He lets out a chuckle, his pearly white teeth practically blinding me. "How about you have a drink? You look like you need one more than I do right now."

"Is that how you get the girls?"

"When you're Xavier Amari, you don't need to get anyone drunk. Come on, is that attitude your only personality trait?"

"Is it yours?"

"You are failing this job interview."

I smirk. "You haven't even asked me about my availability yet."

"Have a drink. I'm high as shit and drunk so this isn't fair."

"You smoke?"

"You don't?"

I've never seen brown eyes twinkle like this before. "I'll take that drink."

"Well, all right! Finally, she decides to act like she's at a party." He makes strong strides through the crowd, everyone parting for him. He doesn't even have to say "excuse me" or adjust his body awkwardly to the side as most people do. They just know he needs his space, so they move out of the way for their king. Xavier reaches over the bar and grabs a bottle of something I don't recognize and pours it into a cup.

"We don't do chasers here, so you better chug until there's nothing left, shorty."

I grab the cup; my hesitation to chug it is very much present, but I can't back out while he's staring at me. Something about him challenges me, makes me want to do what he says.

Come on, live a little.

As I chug, my eyes focus on the stubble that's wrapped around his chiseled jaw to make it easier to ignore the burning sensation traveling through my petite body. There's a sense of security in his eyes as our gazes meet, but also something there that scares me. Is he scared of me too? Does he feel it? There's a tiny string pulling us together, but if I touch it my entire body will electrify. This isn't the kind of electricity that I can look past, no. It's the kind that turns every cell in my body into blazing pieces of amber. It seems like the longer I analyze the more complex my assumptions of him become.

The cup is empty. I wipe any spilled contents off of my chin and slam it on the bar. "I have a feeling you assumed I would back out."

Xavier clears his throat with a flustered look on his face. "You're a trooper . . . Arlissa, right?"

Forgetting your name already? Nice. "Right."

"Stick around, meet some people. I gotta go, uh, host this party, but I'll catch up with you later." He goes off into the crowd, and suddenly I remember where I am.

I had completely tuned out the music while in his presence, but now it's almost unbearable. He left me unattended, and Alejandra is somewhere with someone, anyone. That's just what she

does being the social butterfly she is. Except, most times I'm right behind her. There's an overwhelming feeling of disappointment over me. I want more. But more of what?

With an eye roll, I pick up the same bottle he used and pour another cup. My stare goes blank while I watch the clear liquid flow like a rapid waterfall, droplets jumping onto the floor. Leaning against the bar for a moment, I scan the room. No one seems inviting. No one seems like they want to do more than touch my hair or spill their drink on me. I release a pitiful sigh before deciding to head down the hall. Maybe if I find the bathroom I can not only find some peace but also shamelessly take these agonizing heels off for a moment or two.

Maybe I should text— no. I already talk to him more than I should.

"Excuse me. Excuse me. Excuse me." I shuffle through the drunk girls and even drunker guys, sounding like a broken record as I go. God, I need to get out of here. *No, no you don't.* I let Xavier distract me and make me think that maybe this environment is a decent place, but spoiled rich kids walking around this drunk? That can't be a good idea. I anxiously push open the first door I see, my eyes catching the whiff of the scene before the rest of my body.

Oohs and *ahhs* fill my ears as I stand frozen in place. The worst part though is that they didn't even stop. A huge bare ass moons me, front and center, just all out there. And to add to the trauma, some chiseled dude is snorting something powdered off of her lower back.

It takes a few moments, but they finally realize I'm standing there. The girl first, shrieking as if she isn't in her birthday suit getting drugs snorted off her body at a party that has a population of at least one hundred. The guy didn't even get a chance to tell me to get the fuck out because an alarming scream alerted all three of us.

32

The blood-curdling sound sends shivers down my spine, but the intensity of it all still leaves me stuck like a statue. The girl is struggling to get her clothes off the ground, probably wondering why I haven't moved yet. But that's when it hits me. That scream was familiar—it's Alejandra.

"Get help! What the fuck, man!"

The sounds grow intensely as I finally gather the strength to move my legs and get that disturbing image out of my head. With each step, I can hear every sentence with more clarity.

"Can someone get some help?"

"Move!"

"Okay, party over, guys. Get your shit and get out."

"Call 911!"

But what's laid out on that living room floor is even worse. No, not again.

The crowd of people disperse (only after getting a glimpse of what's going on), making it possible for me to see what's going on myself. Xavier is nowhere to be found, but I'd recognize those raven tresses anywhere. Alejandra, like the superhero she is, is bent over another curly-haired woman whose body vibrates on the floor.

"Come on! Everyone, move out! You don't have to go home but you can't stay here. Did anyone call 911?"

The voice comes from behind me, then suddenly I'm being pushed to the side by the same guy I just walked in on. Except, this time he's clothed. The unidentified man hovers over Aly as they both try their best to get a handle on the situation. Spit, foam, and whatever else begins to cover the woman's cheeks as her mahogany skin gets paler and paler with every trickling second. With the lights on everything gains clarity: Aly's flushed face from the stress of what's happening, the tanned guy with alarmingly bushy brows, and the people still trying to get a snapshot of the scene.

My body remains frozen in time while I observe. I want to move forward, but gravity weighs down on me like a ton of bricks. Moving isn't an option. There's a girl dying on the floor, and I can't even function properly enough to help. My heart bangs at my rib cage as catching my breath proves to be harder to do. It's all settling in now. It's all making sense.

People in this town don't have any decency; if anything, the only thing they have is audacity. They don't even give enough of a fuck to take care of themselves. Is this what they do? They party with no regard of who might miss them, or need them later on in life? It's selfish.

It's all too much.

Shaking my head feverishly, I mouth "no" a hundred times as I push through the crowd and out the front door. With shaky fingers, I'm torn between praying that I didn't just watch another person die and attempting to focus on sending Aly a "had to go" text.

My heart runs a mile a minute and scattered thoughts follow its lead. There's no amount of fresh air that can help me now.

See what happens every time you try to "live a little"?

FIVE

think I tossed and turned a million times when I got home that night—and a million times more throughout the last few weeks. Sleep has become a stranger to me, and so has Alejandra.

By Sunday morning I thought I would forget that party entirely. I'd wake up and somehow just as my energy was replenished, I'd be able to get back to embracing this new life I was dragged into.

Did I ever attempt to embrace it, though? I mean, I did. Or maybe I just want to embrace one thing—one person who just so happened to live here. I don't know. What I do know, though, is that when I go out of my way, when I get too excited about something, bad things happen. So what's the point?

Something else did happen that night, though. It wasn't the negative feelings that I'm trying so hard to shake now. Instead, part of my time has gone to ignoring that fluffy, child-like feeling

in the pit of my gut. But these things are sneaky. There's no avoiding them when they creep up on you. It's washing your hair and remembering how his cheekbones lift oh, so effortlessly when he smiles. It's being in the middle of a conversation and wondering how it'd go if it was him on the phone instead.

He sent me a text, a few hours after I walked out of that condo: *this is Xavier's number.*

I wanted to know how the hell he got my number, I wanted to text back, but my main concern was where the hell was he? A girl was dying on his floor, and he wasn't around. What could possibly be more important than someone's life?

The whole night sticks with me, like gum on pavement. I don't know if that girl survived. I don't know enough about her to even try and find out. Maybe Aly did.

From the glimpses of her that I've seen, she's been working hard on new music, so I guess that's a good thing. She's doing everything right: meeting the models, writing the music, building her reputation in this scum of a city. So, no, we haven't spoken about it. And we probably never will.

Tonight is one of those nights where she sends a "*luv u xo, won't be home till late. pls come out with me eventually u hermit*" text. My brown orbs meet the clock, the glowing numbers letting me know it's only eight. It was just noon. I turn over as the blankets swallow me whole. This bed is slowly but surely becoming the only thing I can depend on these days. The blankets, the pillows, they all hug me in a way no human ever has. Not for a while, at least.

Restlessness. The cause of time flying but your thoughts somehow managing to keep running in place.

With all the things circling my mind, there's always been one common factor—Xavier. He's running circles around my head rent free, and it's causing a migraine. Where did he go? It wouldn't be so bad to find out, right? It's not like I want to see him or anything because trust me I don't. I'm just . . . curious.

My fingers, in desperate need of a manicure, trace over his contact name. To send or to not send that pride-crushing text. He's been waiting long enough, right? Shit, he's probably forgotten about me by now.

You won't know until you try.

With one eye open, I quickly press the letters on the keypad and hit send. *Busy?*

What a stupid text. He's not going to reply to that. I wouldn't acknowledge it either if I was him. Of course he's fucking busy. He's an undefeated boxer and, well, he's kind of cute.

Stupid, stupid, stupid.

Nine p.m. My favorite chef went home.

Midnight. I'm pretty sure I can make the perfect appetizer from a mystery basket of ingredients.

Two a.m. Did Casey Anthony actually kill her daughter? I guess I can watch this documentary.

Four a.m. The sound of stumbling and the front door slamming occupies my attention. My best decision would be to pretend to be asleep, right? Alejandra's muffled tone comes across as annoyed, her voice going up and down as she tries to control the volume in which she's speaking. I turn the TV off. *Get up and see what's going on, or sit here in silence?* If she wants to tell me, she will, right? Can I even count on that these days?

Wait—there's a second voice and heavier steps. This one I can't make out, no matter how hard I try. But it doesn't sound like this person is over the phone. Are they physically here? Like right now? The voice is deep, almost familiar—a man. Quickly, I rise, creep over to the door, and glue my right ear to it.

"Give me one good reason!" The thick Australian accent fills my ears and that's when I know—Christian.

Why didn't he tell you he was coming?

"I do not want you. Okay? Point blank fucking period. Go home," Alejandra spits out in a hushed tone.

Moments of silence follow her sentence. Heavy footsteps shake the oakwood floors before a slam of the front door follows shortly after.

My countdown continues. By five a.m. I've given myself a homemade mani-pedi and learned all the words to "All I Want For Christmas Is You." I guess I can take that one off my bucket list. My body is jolted with energy now, completely unfazed by my lack of sleep. Suddenly, the vibration of my phone alerts me, sending my heart racing as Xavier's name pops up on the screen.

Up?

It vibrates again.

I can pick you up if you are.

With a deep sigh, and one eye open, I quickly type *okay* before raiding my closet for something that screams, "I'm not trying too hard, I swear!"

Time slows down for the first time in days. But my heartbeat hasn't. To go with a man who lives a life where people openly perform sexual acts in *his* home and overdose in *his* home. To go with a man like that will probably go down in one of my dumbest decisions in history. But I can't stop myself.

I want to stop when I'm brushing my hair. I want to stop when I'm slipping my Crocs on. I want to stop as I put both arms through my sweater. I want to stop when I tell him I'll be right outside. I do, I promise I do. But maybe curiosity doesn't always kill the cat. Maybe, I've still got a few more lives left.

SIX

*B*eing nervous is a weird feeling. You either get the butterflies that further ignite the fire in your belly, or that annoying feeling of having to take a shit. With my luck I always get a combination of it all.

"I'm surprised you were even awake." His voice breaks the silence as he turns the wheel of his jet-black Range Rover.

I sit there in silence for a moment, a bag of greasy food occupying my lap, wondering what the right reply might be. "Oh."

He chuckles. "You're making this hard for me."

"What? Eating French fries at six in the morning? Oh, don't look at me like that!"

With a smile, he reaches over and grabs a fry out of the bag, his hand just slightly brushing my arm. "Usually these trips are solo, but . . . felt like you could use it."

"Well, what made you think that?"

The car comes to a graceful stop. We are on a hill somewhere, engulfed in trees and overgrown grass. Yet, the rising sun is in perfect view. The waves of blue in the sky had turned into ripples of oranges and golds like ballet slipper laces that had just come undone.

Xavier adjusts in his seat, eyes glued on the view before us. "My party didn't end how—how most parties should, I guess."

"Are you apologizing?"

"No. I mean, I can, if that's what you need." Finally, he completely turns toward me. "Look, I do want you to work for me. I've been having a hard time finding an assistant I can trust, and honestly, you look like you don't care about anything. That's the kind of person I need—"

"Following you around every day?"

"That's part of it."

"I don't know about that."

"Why not?"

"A woman almost died on your floor."

He releases a deep sigh as he runs his fingers through his freshly cut locks. "Maya's okay, I swear. I even sent her flowers last night. She's good. If that's what you're—"

"Look. No disrespect or anything, but that wasn't the only thing I saw, and if I have to be around people who behave like that—"

"Whoa, whoa. I can't control my friends. Shit, I can't control anyone. I learned a long time ago to take people for who they are. I mean, we're all a little fucked up. And we all deserve to have a good time, right?"

"I guess."

"And that's what I give 'em. Plus, I don't fuck with the heavy shit."

"Oh?"

Another chuckle leaves his lips. "Fuck no, I'm an athlete. Are you crazy? I'd lose my career in a heartbeat."

"Fair."

"I'm sorry, though. Seriously. No one should have to witness that, and I'll admit it was an awful first impression. I wanted to talk to you right after it happened but . . . shit came up."

The sun continues to rise, following the same escalating rhythm of our conversation. But if he's going to convince me to work for him I need to know one thing first.

"So, where did you go that night?"

"Huh?"

"When she was on the floor and everyone was freaking out. I—it's not like I was looking for you or anything, but I just realized, you know, that you were nowhere to be found."

"Oh . . . " His gaze drops to the dashboard, his demeanor shifting from a single question. "Uh, I can't be around when things like that happen."

"But it was your house. I'm sorry, I'm confused."

"Yes, and my roommates. But, again, I'm an athlete. I also have a brand, a name, a family to represent. When things like that happen people pull out their dumb-ass cell phones. If there's no evidence of me being there, there's nothing to tarnish the image."

"So you just run when people get hurt? That's what you celebrities do, right? You just bolt because it's more than you bargained for? Because—"

"Who do you think called the ambulance? It's not running. It's protecting the brand, short stack. We'll have to put you through a crash course of that if you'll be working for me." His hand hovers over the gearshift.

Make him stop. You don't want to go back yet. "Should I believe you?"

"Do you want a job?" He moves the gear to D.

No, we can't be going back already. I don't want to. "I'll work for you." The words slip out of my mouth before my overthinking mind can catch them. "Just—just no more of that, okay?"

With every syllable that slips out, his body goes from preparing to leave to relaxing once again. *Good.* "Deal."

A wave of relief showers over me as I lean back in my seat as well. "So . . . why are we out here? Gonna pull a Ted Bundy or something and off me?"

"Hell no. I just, uh . . . I kind of have a weird obsession with—"

"Taking girls on hills?

He rolls his eyes. "Sunrises—especially when I was little. It was fucking crazy, I mean . . . I was always waking Mom up to see 'em."

"That's cute."

"You know what my favorite part was, though?"

I shake my head.

"It's constant. You can always look forward to a sunrise or a sunset. You can always depend on it happening even if you're not watching." His voice trails off, eyes shifting to the view in front of us.

I wonder if he feels the comfort between us. It's as if we've known each other from a million lifetimes before. I have no idea what his favorite color is or when his birthday is coming around, but I feel like I know him. Maybe it's a silly thing to do, to follow that white rabbit leading me to only God knows where. But as we sit here with the seats leaned back all the way down, I'm okay.

"In your line of business I guess consistency is important, huh?"

A chuckle falls from his lips as he reaches into the bag and pulls out his burger. "Yeah. More than you'd think."

"So like, is that why you're up in the middle of the night?"

"I work out around this time. It's quiet. Then I get my ass up again and train some time during the day with my dad." When he takes a bite of his burger, there's a smile forming on his face.

"Twice a day? Every day? Fuck, that's some commitment."

"Yeah. I really shouldn't be eating this," he mumbles as he

wipes the grease off of his chin. "My—" His pause is long and unnecessary. Almost like he doesn't mean to bring up what he's about to say. "Dad. My dad would kill me."

"Your dad is your manager, right? I think I heard something about that." The topic of his career keeps him talking. I like hearing him talk.

"Mm-hmm. He's been training me since I could walk." Xavier sits up a bit more. "That's when I became obsessed with sunrises. We would workout at, like, four in the morning and by the time we were done we could watch the sunrise. No matter how bad the workout went, something beautiful came after."

"Bad?"

"Well, you know. If I didn't get something or whatever... Boxing shit."

Quick. Change the subject. "Does this make me a bad influence?" I ask, stuffing a few more fries in my mouth. "Because if you can't eat like this usually, I don't wanna mess you up, sir."

A laugh echoes through the car when he shakes his head. "No, no. I do this all the time. A friend and I used to make this a thing but, uh ... Now it's just me."

"Well! Considering you have the best assistant in the world now, I will be more than willing to do these early adventures with you."

"I'd like that..." Those chocolate orbs are on me again, this time giving me a look that's almost too inviting to resist. "Speaking of." He places his hand on the wheel and begins to pull out of the space we're parked in. "I'll call you. I lost track of the last few days, a bunch of work shit ... So, tomorrow. We can get a start on what the job is and all of that."

"Okay ... that's cool. Thanks for all of this, by the way. It feels like I've been losing my mind lately."

"I understand. Just try to get some rest. Something tells me

you had no reason to be awake this morning." Laughter fills the space between us as the sun sings a silent good morning.

"Yeah, I think I'll start getting dark circles soon if I don't get my shit together."

"Real shit."

SEVEN

The movies lie, and the porns do too. Being the assistant of a gorgeous rich kid isn't all butterflies, rainbows, and spreading my legs to a one-hundred-and-eighty-degree angle. Not that I want to, of course.

It's been constant talk about sunrises and shopping. I have one consistent task so far—mail out this envelope to this specific address on time every week. I never know what's in it; I just know it's important. Maybe he owes money to the mob or something. Anything is possible with these self-centered celebrities, right?

But, hey, this is better than chasing Aly and her new friends around. It's embarrassing to even think about, honestly. They all have careers or sugar daddies—or both. I'm just the tagalong with mousy brown hair who doesn't have a name for herself. Is she just using me for my driver's license?

No. That would be utterly ridiculous. No one loves you more than Alejandra does.

"I'm thinking purple. Like an eggplant color." Xavier paces back and forth on the marble floor. "No homo."

My eyes follow, hip bones sinking deeper into the tile as I sit crisscross-applesauce. "I think eggplant and a . . . a moss green, you know? That would look good on you," I chime in with a smile.

"I don't know what the fuck 'moss green' is, but good idea. Go ahead and text T with the color I want for my suit so she can let Marc know."

I nod, doing as I'm told immediately. It's not like I have anything else to do. I have a business phone; it was Xavier's "welcome to the team" gift because he felt like it'd be too overwhelming for me to use my own. I agreed, until I realized "business" was just a handful of contacts and a notes app list of his go-to order for almost every restaurant in Los Angeles. I guess having the assistants to high-end designers in my contact list is something to brag about. But these people never fazed me to begin with. At least if Alejandra ever needs a gown I have the inside scoop.

"Done."

My voice causes a clear look of shock transferring from him to me. He pauses pouring himself an entire glass of vodka and pivots in my direction. "Are we done for the day? Can I take a fucking nap now?"

"Gonna drink yourself to sleep?" I ask sarcastically before finally picking myself up from off the floor.

"Gonna drink yourself to sleep?" Xavier mocks before taking a sip. "No, short stack. I'm going to drink and sleep. Two different situations. That's why you should join me."

That's not a bad idea . . .

I roll my eyes as my fingers quickly scroll down the calendar to make sure there's nothing else. He never keeps up with his emails or important dates, so getting that organized gives me something to do with all my free time.

46

"Oh!" I gasp, landing on an upcoming deadline. "You need to RSVP for that charity dinner with your mom and sign up a plus-one if you have one."

He falls silent for a moment. His eyes focus on the floor as he rubs the back of his neck. "RSVP yes and add yourself to the list." Xavier continues to drink the alcohol until it's gone—the contents not even fazing him, like it's juice.

"Me?" I ask tentatively.

"You heard me."

"Yeah, I think that's the problem. I'm the assistant. I say yes for you and go home. I don't go to these things."

"It's in the fall. You got time to put your big girl pants on."

Why me, though? There are a million girls in this world with D cups and lip filler who would die to walk a carpet and pretend to donate money to the less fortunate. This isn't my crowd. It's not my life either.

"I don't know . . . "

"What are you so scared of?"

Becoming someone like him. "This just isn't my kind of thing."

"So what is your kind of thing?" He steps closer to me, causing me to take a step back.

"I'll let you know when I find out."

"Yeah, let me know." His voice is deep as he continues to move toward me. His pupils are pulling me in, stopping me from taking any more steps back. The organ in my chest goes from a calm rhythm to an EDM beat, and all I can do is stare.

"I—"

The sound of keys jingling in the door causes Xavier to jump back like he's been caught red-handed. Saved by the bell, the lock, or whatever. Point is, I'm left shaking on the other side of the room. And someone who was hovering over me just a second ago, whose breath I could smell as strongly as his Spice & Wood cologne, has turned back ice cold. I'm left here to wonder if I'm making it all up in my head. I guess nothing is ever this good.

He makes it back to his post at the bar in record time as the door swings open, revealing someone I hadn't seen since that awful party.

"So, yeah. Make those arrangements and I guess we're done for the day." The echo of Xavier's voice startles me a bit, loud and assertive as if we weren't just laughing a bit ago.

Right, I'm just an employee.

The other guy steps in and passes me, heading straight for Xavier to dap him up. "'Sup."

"Yo. Oh—right. This is my new assistant, Arlissa." Xavier's still avoiding eye contact as he introduces me to the man with the caterpillar eyebrows. With every second I look at him, I'm adding another three years to that memory of him sniffing coke out of some poor woman's ass being stuck in my brain. Does he remember me?

"Greyson. Have fun working for this guy, though. He's a fucking nut."

No.

They both share a laugh as I stand there in silence. The only person who's a 'nut' in this room is the one who does cocaine. *And that would be you, Greyson.*

"Nice meeting you," I force out before hiking my purse onto my shoulder. "But I think I'm gonna go now."

Xavier nods. "Before you head out, can you find that ticket and pick up my dry cleaning sometime between today and tomorrow? Shit, where'd I put it?"

"You, uh, gave me the ticket when I walked in. I'll see you tomorrow." My brown Michael Kors bag rests on my hip as my legs carry me out of that condo without even waving goodbye.

The LA heat is beaming, causing me to speed walk to my car to get as close to an A/C as possible. With every step I take, I might as well blend into the concrete. People walk past me, not even attempting a second glance. Yet, when Xavier walks around there's at least some hesitation. They recognize him. They always recognize him.

It's times like these that I feel alone. LA is a huge city, and no one is concerned about what little Arlissa Benson is doing. My best friend is here, and somehow I'm still alone. Xavier's handy to pass the time, but he has this jumpy hot-and-cold attitude that reminds me what reality actually is. What my reality actually is.

I find myself glancing out the window and realize I'm on Rodeo Drive. Intrusive thoughts had completely overtaken me. Rodeo Drive was never on my route from Xavier's condo to home.

Louis Vuitton, GUESS, Chanel. I look out my window again. Louis Vuitton, GUESS, Chanel. I'm driving in circles. Louis Vuitton, GUESS, Chanel.

My car doesn't belong here. I'm surrounded by sports cars and fully paid-off Ferraris. Holy smokes, I'm sure that's Lady Gaga leaving a store and jumping straight into a truck with windows so tinted it has to be illegal. Paparazzi are everywhere, and I'm sure they wouldn't hesitate to run me over to get their Gaga photo. I'm just a small factor in a world full of very important people.

In a world full of people who seem important, you're the brightest star.

The voice echoes deep in my brain, getting fainter as I get older. It seems like the more years that pass, the more I'm beginning to forget what she sounds like, and that only makes it hurt worse.

When I was a kid, I would always come home crying because we couldn't afford cable or new clothes at the time. Being the odd one out is something I eventually got used to. Yet, my sister always told me I was important, that I was meant to do something.

I wish she would have told me what that something was.

It takes me an hour to get back to the guest house. The sun is fully set, and my energy went with it. All those nights of staying up and allowing this place to run my mind wild is catching up with me.

Walking through the front door is a more exhausting task than it's been any other night. As I make small steps throughout the space I realize that this tiredness can only be cured by a long rest.

I didn't even bother taking my hair down or my shoes off. There's no need to check the time or wipe the mascara off of my eyelashes. My bed is waiting for me, and for the first time in days I crave it.

My fingertips make friends with the thick comforter as I pull it aside and allow the mattress to swallow me whole. There's a sense of safety that comes from getting in bed. If there's anything on my mind, the idea of falling into a deep sleep easily trumps that. Eventually, I give into the quiet call of my dreams.

Lissa, I really don't think we should go . . .

Come on, Sammy! I really wanna meet her! Please.

My body is jolted back into reality due to the sudden ring of my work phone. I always leave the ringer on, but I never expect any calls at random hours of the night. With foggy vision and scattered thoughts, I reach for the purse and pull the phone out. My eyes finally pop open as the contact name flashes on the screen. Xavier Amari. There are so many questions I have, but my tired brain is incapable of answering them all.

"Hello?" My voice sounds pitiful, almost like it's begging to hang up.

"Hey . . . did I wake you?" He sounds wide awake and his breathing is heavy, almost like he's jogging in place.

"No shit."

There's a chuckle, and then a pause. "I want to see you."

When those words process in my head, all I can do is sit up. Part of me wants to remember that he has a tendency to be hot and cold. Well—lukewarm and cold. But the other part is tempted.

50

I clear my throat, looking at the glowing numbers on the nightstand. 5:05. "How long will it take you to get here?"

"Give me thirty minutes."

A small voice inside of me screams *no, bad idea.* But an even louder one pushes the negativity to the side.

"I'll be ready." Just like that, that feeling of exhaustion has passed and been replaced with the energy bursts I've become accustomed to.

As soon as he hangs up, my brain tries to process the recurring memory that made its way into my dream space. I shake my head. Quickest way to ruin a mood? Thinking about the one time you allowed love to fail you.

"The shit is overrated," he utters, his high energy slowly disappearing before my eyes.

"You say that because you've had this your entire life. That financial cushion has always been there for you. So . . . duh."

"That's the thing, though. Everyone sees it as a financial cushion. That's all fine and shit, but money ain't—it can't fix everything."

"I'm surprised you didn't say buy happiness," I add with a smirk.

He pauses, copying my smirk with his own. "That it can do. Come on, what's one thing you want?"

His question is taunting. It sends me back to an internal conflict I've had for years. What do I want?

An idiotic answer spills out without giving my mind a chance to approve it. "To belong somewhere, anywhere. Shit, here, even."

"Money can buy that. LA is full of opportunities. Just gotta pick one. Plus, you have me. That's leverage enough."

"I do not *have* you. I work for you."

"You have me." The words fall off of his lips like pure gold. They're so valuable, yet there's nothing rare about it. When he speaks it's like he's rehearsed it time and time again.

Coyly, I say, "I do not."

We've been hanging out for a bit now, but most of it is for "work purposes only." Sure, we go off into a few conversations as I drop off his laundry and Thai food that he can't bother to pick up himself. But the words he speaks make it seem like so much more. It can't be that, though. That's ridiculous.

"You do. More than you think, actually." His eyes haven't left my direction. What does he mean by that?

Throughout this whole conversation we miss the sunrise. But I don't think I mind.

"And if I wanted to be more than your assistant? I'd still have you?" My heart sinks, realizing how thirsty the question sounds. "You know. What if I decided I wanted to act or be on Playboy." *Nice save.*

Within a moment, his fingertips are dancing with the stray hairs that have escaped my ponytail. I'm being teased—tempted. "You're far too beautiful for Playboy." His whispers only amplify the enticing energy he holds.

It's so natural for Xavier. He knows how to make a girl crumble, and he does it well. He has an energy so captivating it keeps you coming back, wanting to drain him for whatever else he has left. I wonder what he's like to the girls who aren't as ordinary as me. The ones who stand tall on their own and put their curl routines first, skin care next, modesty last. Wait, no—I can't actually be crushing right now. A few car rides conversations, and I'm melting?

Oh, hell no.

EIGHT

had a friend in ninth grade who was really into astrology—I mean, *really* into it. It was almost comical, to be honest. But she told me one thing that I never really forgot: *pay close attention to your dreams.*

Now, I'm not saying I keep a dream journal or anything, but recently . . . I've been suffocating. Every dream feels like someone's wrapping their hands around my neck and squeezing until there's no air left to depend on. I wish I still had her number. Maybe I could ask what it means.

"Rise and shine, my little buttermilk muffin princess."

Aly's radiant voice fills my ears. Still half asleep, I smile. "Breakfast?"

Slowly, my body slides up and leans against the headboard. She stands over me with a plate in one hand and a glass of orange juice in the other.

With a gleaming smile, she speaks again. "I woke up this

morning, and I said, Alejandra, we're making Lissa breakfast. Look, it's a chorizo egg and cheese sandwich. Oh, and I threw some bacon on the side because I know it's your favorite."

Grabbing the plate, I begin to devour the contents with no hesitation. "And what did I do to deserve this?"

Seriously, what?

She sits down next to me, scooting herself as far onto the bed as she can without sitting on my lap. "I've been an awful friend— sister. Person. Whatever. And I am woman enough to admit that."

"Right."

"I was hoping for a 'you're not a bad sister, Aly!' But okay." She releases a deep sigh, unimpressed by my inability to feed her ego right now. She's right, she has been an awful friend. Well, maybe not awful but to be distant from me in a town where I know no one? Dick move. "I got so wrapped up in Amy and—"

"Amy was never the problem. I knew you would be spending time with her. She's your mentor."

"Yeah. The girls I met at that party have just been making me feel so . . . like I belong here. And there were times I wanted to ask you if you wanted to go but you were never home."

"I'm sure I was here. You just never actually wanted to ask."

"Not true!" she exclaims, pushing a strand of her thick black hair behind her ear.

"Aly, you've never left me in the dark before. In all the years we've been friends. So, yeah. This is weird. But if you have new friends that make you feel just *'so LA'* I can go home."

She rolls her eyes before crossing her arms over her chest. "You can't have breakfast like this at home."

"I'm serious, Al. These last few weeks have fucking sucked."

"And I'm serious too! I'm sorry, okay? Punch me about it later. But there's something else . . . "

I raise a brow. "Mm-hmm . . . "

"I met someone else. At Xavier's party." Suddenly there's an

GODDESS A. BROUETTE

energy change. Alejandra rises, beginning to pace around the room with a small smile plastered on her face. Just the thought of whoever this guy is makes her undeniably jovial. "Never mind the new friends. This new guy he's—just so gentle and sweet. He's in the industry too, and said he could help me, you know? I can't tell you his name, though. It's too early to jinx it, I'm gonna wait a few more weeks."

How is she already into someone else after *just* dumping Christian?

"So I don't even get to know anything about him?"

"My friends said it's very important to, uh, what's the phrase . . . protect my energy? Whatever. Jinxes are real, you know! Once you start blabbing your mouth to anyone—boom! Romance over."

"I think that's only for people you don't trust and like—social media and shit."

It's at this point that I decide not to say a word about Xavier. But it's at the same moment that she decides to ask.

"Anyways! You've been spending a ton of time with Xavier. What's that about?"

"Define a ton."

"Well, Amy said his car is here more, but he never comes in, so . . . I assumed he's here for you, smart ass."

"Oh!" I shift a bit in bed. "I got the job, so . . . I just follow him around and spike his coffee with steroids——reg shit."

She sits again, stealing a piece of bacon from my plate. "Go on . . ."

"I mean, yeah, he's an interesting person. I don't know. He's so hot and cold. Like I'll go do something for him, and he's super appreciative and easy to talk to. But let his roommate come around, and he's all like, 'you can go now, Arlissa.' Like who even calls me that?"

"I think I know why."

"Huh?"

"Well, I decided to do a Google search on your friend after Amy mentioned him coming around a lot."

"No." I push the plate off of my lap before quickly rising from the bed. "You are not about to tell me a bunch of TMZ gossip about my boss."

"It's not gossip."

"It is if he didn't say it himself!"

"Well, if you would listen, you'd realize he did."

I freeze, temptation creeping up on me slowly but surely. "No. I don't wanna hear it."

"He has—"

Quickly, my hands cover my elf-like ears. "La-la-la-la-la!"

"You are a fucking lunatic."

"*La-la-la-la-la-la-la!*"

"Well, can you at least come to lunch with me today?" she shouts over my obnoxious voice.

I shrug.

"I want you to meet my friends, c'mon. You'd fit right in."

I just don't know if I should tell you, I'm already stuck between a rock and a hard place with talking to you . . .

She doesn't know?

You knew this. But I have been meaning to ask you something.

Shoot.

Why'd you stop by the other night? Miss her that bad?

"My loves!" Alejandra exclaims as we enter the cozy coffee shop. In front of us is a five-person table already seated with three

56

girls. One has honey blond hair and lip filler I'm sure was done right before this lunch date, thanks to the obvious bruising.

Maybe she's a sweetheart. Be nice, Lissa.

The second is another blonde, but this time it's bleached to the extent that her hair is visibly dry—like cotton candy. The last girl is beginning to head in our direction. She's tall and slender, her skin a sepia, reddish-brown. Her plumped lips are smothered in gloss as she gives Aly a sticky kiss on the cheek. The best part is, when she smiles she has the same "bunny teeth" as me.

In the middle of me admiring the mystery brunette, she turns her attention to me and waves. "Hiya! I'm Jerrica."

I wave back, immediately feeling a warmth from the other woman. "I'm Arlissa, but you can call me Lissa."

The honey blonde chimes in, "Welcome to the club. Alejandra would not stop talking about you. I'm Megan."

The bleached blonde is finishing a martini before smiling and inserting herself as well. "Oh, is it my turn? Olivia. Nice to meet ya."

Alejandra and I take a seat at the table, and almost immediately the girls begin to talk to me like I've known them forever.

"I'm thinking of trying a juicing diet, but I don't know . . . I fucking love cheese." Megan pouts, her focus glued on the glass of water in front of her.

Olivia rolls her eyes. "So don't fucking do it."

"So, Lissa, what do you do? I know Aly makes music, but you?" Jerrica's voice holds an inviting tone as she gives me a place to speak at the table.

"I'm an assistant—"

Aly interrupts. "For Xavier." The way she says his name sends a chill down my spine.

"Yeah, he had some issues with his past assistant, I think. His mom figured I could fill in since I was here with Aly."

"Yeah, he had some issues, all right," Olivia mumbles, followed by a smirk that comes from Megan.

"He had issues figuring out what position to fuck her in."

"He was sleeping with his last assistant?" I blurt out.

"What's the tea?" Alejandra asks, raising a brow.

Megan raises a brow as her eyes piercing a hole into mine. "Do you know anything about him?"

Aly chimes in, "She lives under a rock."

"I'm friends with Xavier's girlfriend," Jerrica starts.

"Ex-girlfriend," Megan adds.

"Whatever. We've been friends since, like, high school."

Olivia gulps her water before adding to the conversation. "Savannah's in rehab right now."

Alejandra leans over before whispering in my ear. "I tried to tell you earlier."

This is what she wants. She wanted me to know all this shit before, but I wasn't listening. There's no real intention for me to be friends with these people, right? She just wants to put me on the fucking spot.

My emotions are mixed. My blood isn't exactly boiling but there's a layer of discomfort toward Aly for sure. Maybe a hidden part of me wants to know all of this. But a bigger part of me feels a rush of disappointment over the fact that Mr. Amari is taken.

But does it really count?

No. No Lissa. This is the last thing we need right now. You're sitting at a table full of networking opportunities. Get it together.

"What's she in rehab for?"

Olivia chuckles. "Do you want the media answer or the real answer? The girls a drug addict, but her billionaire daddy told everyone she's been going through, uh, mental health issues."

"O! That's my friend." Jerrica's tone is stern enough to make me want to shut my own mouth.

"Anyway, Xavier is just bad news, okay? He, like, pays for her rehab but he only does it because—he just sucks."

"He pays for it? Why would he do that if—"

Olivia cuts me off. "If he's such a bad guy? Because he's the worst kind. I've known him long enough to know he's the biggest drug addict I've ever met, and I've met a fuckton."

This is bullshit. They clearly have no proof and are only speaking on the things his drug addict ex said. Olivia is accusing him of being on drugs, but that doesn't make sense. Xavier doesn't even drink coffee, let alone snort some shit up his nose. Maybe he drinks a little, but who in his position wouldn't? One person is in rehab, and it's not him. Hollywood rumors are fucking brutal.

"Xavier just isn't shit," Megan chimes in. "I've had a few friends that were so certain he was going to leave Sav for them, and it literally never happens. They have this weird codependency thing. They had just broken up—when? How long has she been in there?"

Jerrica whispers, "End of May."

"Whatever. So, they broke up, and the story is they both overdosed that night. Xavier needed to clean up his image but couldn't miss a match so he shipped her off to rehab, all expenses paid. And the next day it was like it never happened. He looks like the hero, and he's in interviews talking about how he's behind her every step of the way in her recovery. But ask him who was into drugs first. What about your recovery, dude? He's just concerned with saving face."

This is the Savannah fan club, and I'm sitting smack in the middle wearing an "I heart Xavier Amari" T-shirt.

Jerrica sighs before finally making eye contact with me again. "Just watch him, okay? Savannah doesn't deserve another heartbreak."

Olivia gasps. "She doesn't? She knows what he does, how

about all the girls he mind-fucks. Whatever kind of dick game he has, I want to be far away from it."

Part of me wants to see Google's side of this story. But the other part can't go through with it. It's not my business—and everything he's being accused of doesn't make sense. If anything, this Savannah girl should be grateful that he's willing to pay for her to get better. That says more about him as a man than anything else does.

NINE

I have a bad habit of not being able to keep people's secrets. Ever since I learned how to talk, I couldn't stop running my mouth. Samantha was my last victim.

My mom was always super strict about dating, but surprisingly, my dad wasn't. I knew my sister; I knew she wanted to date someone. She was the only one in her class who hadn't had her first kiss by the time she was freshly thirteen. Or at least, that's what I remember her whining on the phone about.

Anyway, she went on a date once. A bowling date, I think. My dad helped her lie to my mom, and he agreed to pick her up. In order to make it look less suspicious he took me with him. To make a long story short, I told on them both, pioneering my exile from knowing about any sneaky activity until I was the one begging her to keep a secret with me.

I lean back on the leather couch as I lazily scroll through my business phone. Xavier isn't a normal boxer who does little fights in cities around the world that no one really goes to. I guess. I don't know that much about boxing, but that's my point—neither do 85% of his fans. He's a celebrity, and I'm just beginning to understand what that word means. He's treated like a king. Commercials, interviews, magazine shoots, events, big Hollywood parties he's invited to just for being him.

With perfect timing, he comes out shuffling his feet across the polished floor. Shirtless, he dances over to me with the largest grin on his face. "Dance with me."

I giggle, pushing a loose curl from in front of my face. "Hell, no. There's not even any music playing!"

"Use your imagination, Benson."

I didn't know my name could sound so beautiful.

He makes it to me, still swaying slightly as he holds his hand out. With an eye roll, I connect our palms and follow his lead. "This is stupid."

He laughs. "do you ever just . . . smile and be fucking ridiculous for once?" He spins me around.

"No, because what happens when someone walks in?"

"Then we just look like the happiest couple ever." His whispers are coated in vodka.

The words freeze my entire being as I take a large gulp and part from him. "We have that ESPN shoot in the morning, by the way. Am I going with you to that?"

"Of course. They contacted me this morning, actually. Speaking of, where is my phone?"

"Did you check your pocket?" I peer his way, unimpressed by the fact that I can literally see the phone print in his pants.

He quickly pats his pockets before shaking his head. "Nah."

Oh, that's not his phone.

"There it goes. Left it on the fucking bar." Xavier shakes his head and chuckles to himself while I'm left desperately attempting to regain focus.

"Stupid," I mutter with a smirk.

"Ay, I can't be on top of everything, all right?"

"So I've been told."

The conversations from the other day wrack my brain intensely, leaving no room for any other thought to form. If Savannah is so important to him, why hadn't he mentioned her by now?

"Oh, before I forget." He speeds off to his room, only gone for a second before his voice enters my space again. "Could you please mail this check for me? I haven't found the time to do it." He hands me the envelope with a smile and all I can think of while reaching for it is the possibility that this check was going to the rehab center.

"Yeah, but Xavier . . ."

His brows furrow, worry overcomes him as he hovers over me. "Shit, not that tone. Okay, lay it on me."

"Lay what on you?"

"The gossip, the burning questions, the chatter that somehow made its way from point A to point you. This isn't my first rodeo, I promise."

The way he delivers his words is confusing. You can never tell what he's really feeling. Is he annoyed or just joking around? I have to tread lightly. I'm probably already on thin ice.

"I'm, uh, not someone who gossips or anything, but Aly—"

Xavier rolls his eyes before taking a few steps back. "Oh, I'm scared."

"I'm serious! Aly had me meet some of her friends the other day, and I told them I worked for you, and—"

"Let me guess, they're still spilling that old tale about that creepy-ass suicide pact they think my ex and I had?" He runs his hands through his loosely curled locks and heads over to the bar to do what he does best—drink.

"No, I didn't hear it that way but—"

"Well, I've heard it a million fucking ways. Each way more ridiculous than the last."

"I just want to know who I work for, that's all. And it's weird you haven't been more open about your girlfriend."

There's a silence as he gulps down the remnants of his beverage. "So ask me."

"Well . . . was she actually in rehab?"

He nods, his eyes fixed on mine without even blinking.

"Oh? Okay, and—don't roll your eyes at me!"

"No, I don't do drugs. I can't do drugs. My dad would wring my neck." He pauses, placing the drink down and taking two steps toward me, both of his hands grabbing mine. "Ms. Arlissa Benson, the hardest drug I do is pre-workout. You don't have to worry about me. Those girls are people that show up to my parties sometimes and are cool with Savannah. They want my head on a stick. Nothing more, nothing less."

Exactly! I knew they were just bitter about their friend.

Always trust your instincts, Lissa. They're always right.

"Why, then?"

His hands start to warm up in mine, the feeling of us having this much skin-to-skin contact slowly melts the doubts away.

"I said I didn't use. I didn't say I didn't fuck up with her."

"So your last assistant . . . " I mutter.

He shrugs, a cocky smile plastered on his face. "Like I said, I fucked up." Within a moment his lips are pressed against my forehead—but not the sweet kind of kiss you'd see in the movies. Well, maybe if we're watching *Air Bud.*

My lips release a light sigh in annoyance as I pull my hands away from his. "Well, that's all I wanted to ask."

"Savannah and I are finished. With Greyson here I can't handle another addict in my life. I'm helping her, but that's about it."

"Greyson?"

"He drinks—mostly. At least now. Sometimes he slips, gets

into the hard drugs more than he should and, well—he can get scary. But he's my best friend. I'm just trying to keep an eye on him. Look, leaving her was hard. But, knowing she did that because of me was even harder. So her friends come up with all this shit to make me the bad guy. But I'm the only one who's fucking helping her. Haven't even asked her dad for a dollar, and he has way more than me."

My heart sinks. He doesn't deserve his name to be slandered by a crazy ex-girlfriend and her friends. All Xavier wants to do is help people. He helped me, he's helping Greyson, and who knows who else he sticks his neck out for. There's a purity in his actions, a purity that deserves recognition. I can give him that. I can see him.

I use all the strength I can muster and pull him closer to me, both arms wrapping around his midsection. A warmth overcomes me as his large arms embrace me back. Not only do I feel protected, but I also feel like for once I'm protecting someone else. It's a simple gesture, but one that means way more than just a boss to assistant relationship. I can do it for him. I can protect him from everyone else.

I know it's your day off, but if you're going to do anything this morning can going out with me be one of them?

I stare at the text, wondering what the hell I did to deserve a date proposal from Xavier Amari. The hug from yesterday has burned its way into the memory motion picture of my mind and has been on replay for hours on end. My thoughts run in circles, wondering what would've happened if I hugged him tighter.

Live a little. Those were words that had been thrown my way

since I entered high school. Being disconnected from the world and anything that could ever hurt me has yet to prove to be fun. Watching your best friend chase her dreams and live through her passions while your heart yearns for nothing is even more of a slap in the face.

Maybe I do yearn for something. There were moments where I'd try to fall asleep and my pillow would suddenly smell like how I'd imagine someone's lips to taste. Someone. Anyone. Or my blankets would feel like an arm wrapped around me, guiding me to a better place where the world stops for me, temporarily. I wonder sometimes if falling asleep feels like dying.

I wanted to die once before. I enjoyed sleeping all the time because even as a kid I liked that it felt like I was dead too. I could see Samantha in that dark space, and she'd tell me to go in her room and watch one of her DVDs and pretend she's still there. I did a few times. My mom would never let me before because they were inappropriate, but after Samantha died, she let me. I watched the guy and the girl. I watched the guy change because the girl begged him to, I watched them take on the world together and beat the odds. I witnessed all the modern-day fairytales that my sister swooned over.

No amount of touch from any guy could fill the hole in my soul from missing her. But it could patch it up. Xavier could patch it up, because when he hugged me, his hands felt like the Band-Aids my wounded heart needed to become fully operational again. The electricity dripping off of him is unlike any I felt before. I almost felt it once, but that feeling was a forbidden fruit. This one is mine, ripe and ready to be picked.

So why keep running? Why keep running away?

For years I've been driving ten miles per hour, using yellow and red lights to keep people away instead of just pressing on the gas and running through them all.

There are guys like Xavier in those movies. The ones who

have seen hell and have a rough exterior because of it. All they need is a chance, all they need is one of those girls from the movies. Girls who always got the guy and made everyone eat their words because she was there for him. Because she was kind and patient. The guy might have been dark and mysterious and had a couple issues, but in the end he was a prince who everyone else painted as a beast.

Samantha loved those kinds of tropes. She'd want me to say yes, she'd want me to hit the gas right now.

Yes. Send.

The process of getting ready is effortless. I even decide to do something different with my hair. Wash it so it's curly, and then put it in a ponytail. Skin that once lacked glow had taken to the LA sun and gifted me a more bronzed look. Skip the foundation and ignore the strumming of my heart strings. Oh, I do still need blush.

Put it at the right spot to showcase those dimples.

Okay, I'm content with my jeans, crop top, and combat boots. Shit, he's here. Aly not being here makes leaving a lot easier. There's no questions. No wondering why I'm heading out on my day off when she knows I don't know anyone but her and her friends.

Swinging open the door to a Range Rover I'm way too familiar with, I step inside. It smells of pine, the culprit being the green air freshener hanging from his rearview mirror. My gaze falls on him. He wears a blue T-shirt, black pants, and a pair of black Chelsea boots. Every time we're together he's usually in workout gear. This is a nice change.

"Yo, yo. Hey, gorgeous."

"Hola, hola!" The cheeriness in my voice is as transparent as his car windows.

"So." He takes his eyes off me, beginning to drive. "We're

going to one of my favorite spots. It's pretty close. About five minutes from here."

"Is that why you're so close sometimes when picking me up?" I blurt out. Curse this inability to keep my mouth shut.

He chuckles. "Yeah. I like to hike in the mornings but today I thought, why be stingy? So I'm going to show you something dope since you're my favorite person now and all that shit."

"Favorite, huh?"

"Don't get too excited." A wave of laughter fills the car as we start to go uphill.

"Oh, I'm not excited. You're not even my type, honestly."

"Yeah, so what is?"

"Excuse me, sir. I only date rappers who fuck me while also fucking my friend," I tease, laughter following the sentence.

"You have been watching way too much reality TV. I need to get you out of that house."

"You need to?" I raise a brow, a smile remaining on my face as he parks the car.

"Yeah, because you're clearly not doing shit."

"Excuse me, I am booked and busy!"

"Yeah, doing what?"

I pause, lightly biting my lip to think of some sort of excuse. "Mind the business that pays you, Amari."

It seems as if mere seconds had passed before we're parked in what appears to be a California wonderland. My feet slowly guide me out of the car as the breathtaking view knocks the wind out of my lungs. If I look behind me, all of Amy's acres are down below. The main focus is what's in front of me, though. The trees are a rich shade of green, and there's a rainbow of flowers growing all around. I take a few more steps, A picnic blanket is laid out over the grass with a basket neatly placed in the middle.

"I wanted to say thank you . . . For being so understanding when all that shit came up and, you know, not quitting." A light chuckle fills the air as he stands behind me. "A lot of people here are bullshitters. They talk shit and only fixate on a story if it entertains them. You've been a breath of fresh air for me, honestly. Real talk."

I look up at him, completely speechless. "You didn't——"

He cuts me off, grabbing my hand and walking me over to the blanket. "I did. And I think this goes without saying, but I fuck with you. You're not afraid to say whatever's going on in that head of yours, and you're pretty fucking funny too." He smiles, revealing pearly whites.

"You're sweet. Thank you . . . And——" For the first time in a while, I'm nervous.

Green light, Lissa. Step on the fucking gas.

"I've never been good at whatever these things are, and maybe this is so out of bounds for us both, but I don't see myself going anywhere. There's not really anything anyone could say that would make me think differently of you." I freeze. Maybe I'm not interpreting this correctly. "You're stuck with this assistant for a while."

Xavier shakes his head, still smiling. He leans in closer, our lips being a breath away now. "I don't think you get what's happening here," he whispers.

"I was never the sharpest tool in the shed."

"You're good. I'm a shower, not a talker, anyways."

Before I can pull back or muster up a stupid response, his lips brush across mine before formulating into a full-blown kiss. The world completely melts away as the softness of his lips make an agreement with mine.

"I'm hungry," I mumble, lips still against his.

The eyes that were glued on me just a moment ago are taken away by his need to suddenly look up. "Chemtrails."

"What?"

He steps back, guiding my chin up so that I can see the rows of white in the sky. "Chemtrails. It's a theory. Science says it's just condensation or some shit, but some people believe it's chemicals. Shit that they put in the air to fuck with our brains."

"Do you believe it?"

"In chemtrails, or the crazy part?"

"Both."

He takes a moment to think. "It'd give me a good excuse for the shit going on in my head for sure."

Cheeky banter and flirty comments filled the rest of our date. I tossed some food in his mouth, he attempted to toss some in mine, but I never caught it. We debated *West Side Story* and how his favorite character was probably the worst ever. But most importantly, I laughed. I was in a world of happiness that I couldn't imagine leaving. If flowers could sing, I know they'd be singing to me. Telling me how running those red lights is the best thing I could have ever done. The drive back kept the same energy as well. We were both on cloud nine with each other and it showed. I'm his assistant. This much is true. But I'm also a girl who's able to connect with him in a way no one has before.

"I'll call you tonight!" Xavier shouts through the car window as he pulls off. All I can do is wave.

This is the only thing I've ever had faith in. I have to tell Aly.

My feet move as fast as they can take me as I swing open the door and kick off those god-awful boots.

"Alejandra!" I exclaim, heading straight for her door and practically kicking it open. "Girl, do I have news for you!"

I stop in my tracks, wondering if my eyes are playing a trick on me. She's there. But she isn't alone. The tanned skin, light brown eyes, chiseled jaw, and cheekbones—Greyson. He's lying there cuddled up with my best friend and as much as I want to scream, I can't. The big guy upstairs didn't even give me time to tell her what Xavier told me about him, yet here he is. All that information I know about him now, and somehow this is who she described as 'gentle.' He's an addict who I literally saw sniff cocaine out of some girl's ass crack. Now, he's three feet from my bedroom, being man of the year to Aly. He has her cuddled up in his arms, and I want to vomit.

When I come back to earth, I realize they're both looking at me like I have two heads.

"What's up, Lissa?"

I can't tell her now. I saw how she lit up when she spoke of him. Who am I to ruin that?

TEN

"Sorry, guys," I mumble hastily before pivoting until I'm completely turned around. One foot in front of the other; the only goal is to get out of this house.

I call Xavier, praying he's still in the area. How could this be? How could she do this to herself? How could she not see right through him like I can? Alejandra came here for a better life and after what I saw Greyson do—she'd end up just like her parents. Just as angry, just as selfish, just as inconsiderate.

He can get scary.

Thorn-covered words cut through my mind as I stumble out into the fresh air, praying for the wind to stop the bleeding.

Fifteen minutes had to have flown by with me sitting on this porch, and neither of them had even bothered to come out and even check if I was still in the house. It's not like they're obligated to, but it would have been nice. Especially considering that Aly knows me well enough to know something's wrong. Does she care? Is this the start to a series of events where I'm put to the side for Greyson? Does she even know about his bad habits? I mean, I just learned about them, and she can be a bit impressionable sometimes. Yet, here he is, pushing up on the most stable person I know.

I miss you. I miss home.

What happened?

I'd hate to be the one to tell you, C.

Slowly, the black Range Rover comes into sight, causing my entire being to let out a sigh of relief. My emotions paint an unaesthetically pleasing picture of the entire ordeal. It feels as if I don't know up from down anymore. Is this clenching of my jaw or the racing of my heart justified? Does all of that even matter when there's an overwhelming feeling of worry hovering over me like a rain cloud? I've had a small taste of how Greyson behaved at parties, and now the woman I care about the most is infatuated by him. How could that possibly be fair?

Plus, what did Xavier mean by scary? Is Greyson capable of hurting her?

Without a word, I swing the door open and get in the car.

"So . . . " Xavier is trying desperately to break the silence already. It's almost like he can feel the volcano beginning to erupt inside me.

"Greyson and Alejandra. Your new Hollywood power couple," I spit out, an eye-roll effortlessly following my words.

"Oh . . . right. I didn't know you didn't know about that."

"So no one thought to fucking tell me?" There's instant regret as I realize I'm being harsher than he deserves. That isn't his responsibility; it's Aly's. I just wish I had five more minutes to tell her what I knew about Greyson. "Sorry, it's just weird to see especially after what you told me. And then that party . . . "

"Look. Grey isn't a bad guy. He—he does shitty things when

he's out of his mind, but who doesn't? I promise you, he won't hurt your friend."

"I can list about twenty people who don't do shitty things when they're drunk, Xavier. What kind of excuse is that?"

"I'm just saying. She could have picked worse, trust me. Like I said, he's working on it."

I raise a brow in his direction. "Does snorting coke off a girl's ass count as 'working on it'? Because it doesn't look like he's working on shit. This is my *sister* we're talking about." The word alone has the ability to collapse my lungs, but the best I can do is swallow it and move on.

"I understand, trust me. I know you walked in on him at the party, he fuckin' told me. I spoke to him about it, believe me. He shouldn't have been wildin' out like that, anyways."

"She just got out of a relationship—something else she won't really tell me about, and I think . . . I think he came to see her recently."

"Oh?" Xavier pauses, uncertainty entering his tone. "I didn't know all that, though. But I knew Grey was thinking of seeing her seriously. I just assumed you knew."

"Nope. She told me it was a 'romance jinx' or some shit if she said his name out loud." The anger continues to build up inside me as I speak. "But you know? I think that's bullshit. I think she had a feeling I didn't fucking like him, and she just didn't want to tell me. I'm sure she told Meg or whoever the fuck. I just can't even look at them right now. I need a goddamn nap."

Caring about the ones you love is exhausting. Ten out of ten would not recommend.

"People are going to do what they want, Lissa. There's no controlling that. The best thing you can do is decide if you're going to let it get your blood pressure up or not."

"Well, I surely wouldn't want that," I mumble.

74

"A heart attack at nineteen? That's unfortunate," He replies with a smirk.

"Go to hell."

He places a hand on my thigh, his touch being the ankle weights that bring me back down to earth. "Look, I, uh, have a house I own for, um . . . " He swallows. "When I just want to get away from things. You can stay there if you need to."

"I'm not staying in a big old house by myself. That's fucking creepy. Ghosts kill people. I've seen *Supernatural*. You know, I should tell her. Fuck him. Where's my phone?" Immediately, I begin searching my pockets and purse for my device.

"No!" Xavier exclaims, catching both of us off guard. "I mean, it's not your place. You should let him do that. We're all adults here, right? Look, I can stay with you. I'll just leave earlier for my workouts and shit. I won't mind the longer drive for a few days."

"I-I didn't mean—" I stumble over my words, feeling awful for him automatically feeling obligated to watch me. "I mean, you don't have to if you don't want to."

He smiles slowly as he peers over at me for a split second. "I don't mind. Plus, I think your friend is capable of watching Grey for a few days."

Xavier is a hero. He watches over and cares for the people he loves deeply, and even the ones he doesn't. He's a bigger person than I could ever be. Especially since you wouldn't catch me paying for anyone's rehab who slandered my name like his ex did. Or covering for my screw-up of a best friend if I ever had one. Greyson's a mess, but because he's so close to him, Xavier does everything in his power to make sure he's safe and okay.

Then there's me. He had a job offer on the table before I even knew I wanted it. Everyday I'm with him I feel a little bit more okay with pressing the gas on this weird timeline we all live in. Not only did he give me a well-paying job just for keeping him on track and taking phone calls, he gave me the support I needed in a place where I didn't belong. His spirit is warm and comforting in a place where everyone else is chilling to the bone.

I just run from people. I guess that's what trauma does to you, huh? I've been living in fear of love and people since I was seven years old. My life has been a nineteen-part highlight reel of nothing. Nothing to show for, nothing to feel, nothing to wake up to in the morning and daydream about. I think about her all the time. I think about how it's my fault all the fucking time. If I wasn't such a stupid little kid, I'd have my sister here. I'd be able to call her and let her give me advice on what college courses I should pick. A few weeks ago, I thought being a department store manager at thirty would be my peak in life. Oh, and I'd never move out of home—it's safer there. But recently I allow myself to see things a bit different when it comes to the future.

The forty-five-minute drive passes pretty fast and before I know it, we're in the store debating over toothbrushes for our spontaneous slumber party. He's really into the ones that spin and run for about sixty bucks. I don't see the point in spending more than five dollars for something that I'll toss out when I get home in a few days. We went with his choice.

The house is smaller than anything I would ever expect from him. In fact, I think his condo is a lot flashier than this. There's a pebbled driveway that leads to a two-car garage. The lawn is the perfect shade of green that complements the teal color of the cottage. Just from standing outside I can tell that it's going to be cozy and maybe all of my complaining was for nothing. Well, not for nothing. I got him to stay with me, didn't I?

"I know what you're thinking," Xavier starts as he unlocks the door. "Dope bachelor pad, right? But if you want to go incognito in this city you need to go where no one would expect you to be."

When the door swings open, I'm amazed by how nicely decorated everything is. It keeps a cottage-like vibe, kind of like someone's modern-style grandma lives here. There's a white fireplace up against the wooden walls. The kitchen, dining room, and living room all share the same space, but it doesn't feel crowded. Casual clutter decor occupies the counters and small area rugs make their place known on the wooden tiles.

I place my bags on the snow-white kitchen counters and look up at the man next to me. "This place is so . . . nice." Somehow, I'm more impressed with this small cottage than Amy's house. It just feels like a real home. The smell of wood chips fill my nostrils and for someone who's never stepped foot in the country, it feels familiar.

"Thank you. Took some time to get the right vibe, but I like it."

"And how long does 'sometime' imply?"

He takes a moment to reply, occupying himself by putting some of the TV dinners we picked up in the freezer. "Six months?"

"Hm. Sooner than I expected you to say."

"Well, shit, I have some kind of sense when it comes to designs, okay?"

I giggle. "I can tell."

My feet carry me around the area as I try my best to find anything to compliment next. Yet, the events of the night overpower any positive thoughts I can muster. I take a seat at a bar stool and watch him.

Xavier's been an outstanding distraction over the last few weeks, but this time it isn't working. I glance down at my phone. No notifications. I look around the home. No distraction there. Nothing seems to be working. I can't put a finger on why Alejandra and Greyson are bothering me so much. Is it all just worry? I don't know. Imagine dating an addict, and a "scary" addict at that. I truly would never.

"I just don't want her to get hurt . . . " I blurt out as the volcano bubbling under my ass begins to erupt. The tears come next as they stream down my now blood-filled cheeks—how fucking embarrassing. My hands quickly try to wipe away any evidence of emotions, but it's too late.

"Hey . . . " Xavier whispers, making his way around the island and wrapping those comforting arms around me. "I'll talk to him if that makes you feel better. But trust her—I'm sure she can handle herself if he picked her."

The cotton of his T-shirt soaks up my tears as I try my best to calm down the waves of emotions that crash along my shore. This isn't just the fear of losing Alejandra to a man who isn't good for her; it's something else. There's way more going on in this fucked-up head of mine that needs to be addressed. But not now, not at this moment. Before I can think of the words to say, we're interrupted by a soft vibration coming from his pocket. At first, he tries to ignore it, but once we realize it's not stopping, he backs away and picks it up.

As nosy as I am, I make a failed attempt to listen to what the voice on the other end is saying. His responses are short and sweet. He even smiles a bit. The tone he uses is the same one he'd use whenever someone was in the room with us. His "business voice."

The whole energy changes when that conversation is over. He's more fidgety now, like he's trying to figure out the best way to beat down on my spirit some more. Remember when your parents would promise you something, then something more important came up, so they had to cancel? Yeah, that kind of fidgety.

"You're going to hate me."

"Not more than I hate today."

Xavier returns to my side, slowly stroking my back. "That was an important call. I need to head out somewhere for a few days, but you can stay here. I'll send you some money for some more groceries. Whatever you need." He pauses, retrieving the envelope from his jacket pocket and placing it in front of me.

"Uh, keep up with my emails, and mail this off. Let me know of anything I need to do when I'm back in the city. I'll be back in, like . . . three days."

He's leaving? Of course, he has no choice, and his life is demanding—but was this supposed to feel like a kick in the face?

"Yeah, okay." I want to protest, beg him to stay, maybe.

He plants a kiss on my forehead. "I better head out now. I have to head to my place and pack. I'd—I'd stay the night if I could. I'm sorry." When the words "stay the night" leave his lips, he uses one hand to cup my chin and make direct eye contact. Just his gaze alone is enough to send shivers throughout my body.

"It's okay." My mind is blank. It's like he has the ability to completely hypnotize me and mute any negative thoughts I could ever have about him. The way he exercises his power over me is effortless.

His lips press against mine and just as quickly as the kiss begins, it's over. Leaving me with my eyes closed, begging for more than I'm getting. I'd get on my knees for him. All he has to do is ask.

"Call me if you need anything. I'll leave this key with you." He places it on the table after detaching it from the key ring and takes one last look at me. His large hands hover over the doorknob as a grin appears on his face. "I want to see that million-dollar smile of yours when I get back."

"You will. Be safe, okay?" I have no idea where he's going, yet I don't care to know. I trust him enough to know if it's important, as his assistant I would know.

"Always," he says simply before swinging the door open and leaving this quiet house all to me.

ELEVEN

*M*en who live on their own aren't the cleanest—I guess until they are. They aren't forced to learn how to cook or dry their dishes perfectly so nothing rusts or creates mold. They normally don't learn to keep an array of seasonings in the cabinet because salt and pepper just don't cut it. Plus, take-out gets old (and expensive) after a month of it. From my experience with men, they're cradled until they get tired of having to fuck quietly because their parents are trying to sleep. Men don't have the pressure to be the Superman of our generation because someone's bound to pick them anyway. Glasses on or glasses off, it doesn't matter. Just smile pretty! Me? Well, I have to be a jack of all trades.

I actually hate dating because it's an awkward moment where we both stare at each other and list our best qualities.

Hi, my name is Arlissa Benson. I'm nineteen, and I turn twenty in the fall. My mom taught me how to make jerk chicken when I was sixteen because

I begged her, so at least I have that skill going for me. Considering I'm only nineteen, I don't have a clue what I'm doing with my life. Somehow, I managed to find my way into a cushy job where I scribble things down in a planner and make sure Xavier has his pre-workout restocked monthly. If we're being honest, I'd love to have sex with my boss but I'd rather not rush things. You know, gotta make him respect me as a woman and all. Oh! And I see my dead sister in my dreams at least once a week. So, date me?

There—the truth is out. Dating is fucking stupid.

To return to the point, every guy I've dated has issues with the basics, like keeping their nails clean or brushing their tongue. Yet, Xavier's bathroom has fresh towels and a lifetime supply of Dove soap under the sink.

During my tour of the house I realized everything is in perfect order. It's empty for the most part, though. The only thing occupying the closets are a few gym outfits and a bathrobe. The kitchen is also stocked with clean silver and porcelain china waiting to be used.

Eventually, I realized that there's an extra room by the master. The door's closed, so I didn't think much of it when I was snooping after Xavier left. In fact, it's been a full two days since I first discovered the door was even there.

No longer in the mood to binge anymore TV, I rise from the bed, my freshly painted black toes meeting the floor once again. Even though I'm alone, I feel like I have to be cautious. Something about snooping around a house that isn't yours doesn't sit well with me. But, in nosy Arlissa fashion, I have to look anyway.

My hand meets the doorknob, and I jiggle it a bit—locked. The weird thing about it is it doesn't have a normal turn button knob like any other home. It has a keyhole.

Well, now I'm intrigued.

The great thing about wearing your hair up all the time is that you almost always have a bobby pin somewhere in there. My dad, being ex-military and a detective, used to put my sister and

I through random "if you get kidnapped" situations. "If you get shot at" situations would have proved to be much more useful. I learned how to pick a lock with a bobby pin by the time I was six.

After straightening the bobby pin, I bend down a bit, sliding my tool into the hole. It takes a few seconds of maneuvering the pin before that joyful clicking noise fills my ears. Locked doors always equal secrets, right? Walking into this room broke a lot of rules, but how bad could it be?

I cautiously push the door open a bit, taking one step inside. A breath of relief escapes me when the empty room opens itself up to me. Letting the door completely open on its own, my careful feet guide me throughout the space. For the most part it's an empty room. Except there are a few cans of paint and a moving box in the furthest left corner. My eyes land on one of the walls, noticing a splatter of pink paint. It's as if someone began to paint, but suddenly stopped. That could have easily been at fault of the previous owners, though.

Baby steps. Just take a quick look in the box, and then go.

I crouch down to examine the box for any obvious giveaways that it's booby-trapped. Thankfully it isn't taped; the flaps are just folded down. A scattered pile of pictures make themselves known to me as I peel open the flaps. When you think of going through a celebrity's personal belongings you think you're going to find the hottest Hollywood secrets or three pounds of cocaine. I found pictures.

Most of the pictures are framed and vary in size. I pick up the first one I see, wiping the dust off in order to get a clearer picture. It feels so wrong. Maybe I should put it back. But curiosity can't kill this cat. A picture of a blond girl on a beach. She looks happy, really happy. She has one of those floppy beach hats that look great in pictures but are a pain in the ass to actually wear all day. Carefully placing that one on the floor, I move on to the next picture. This one is of Xavier—he's younger, though, maybe about five years prior to today. The same blonde in the first picture is also in this one, looking younger as well. The two are holding each other in the middle of an empty street. She's holding him tighter than he's holding her.

One more picture, and I'll put everything back where I found it. A larger frame—the portrait is of the two of them and looks like it's been taken this year. It seems like something out of a couples' shoot due to the high quality and white background. Her hair is frozen in the air, his arms wrapped around her. The woman's eyes are a gorgeous green, something I didn't notice in the other photos. Her plump pink lips no longer smile, just assist with the striking stare she's portraying. That's when it clicks. All of these pictures, this whole box, is an altar to a dead relationship that he still worships. A gravesite, and the name on the tombstone is Their Love.

While putting the pictures away, a loose piece of paper catches my attention. One peek won't hurt, right?

Right.

Carefully, I unfold the paper and realize that it isn't a random document. It's an ultrasound. The creases from the folds are practically permanent at this point, marking an X across the smallest child I've ever seen. The baby is about the size of a small chicken wing. "Savannah Middleton" and a date I can't make out is printed at the top. My once steady breaths come to a sudden halt, and the conversation I had with Alejandra's friends returns to the forefront of my mind.

How could someone put their baby at risk to do drugs? It all makes sense now why Xavier is paying for her rehab—she's pregnant. Oh my God, she's pregnant. And where does that leave me in this twisted game of *Family Feud?* I swallow hard, trying to wrap my brain around what's happening. That realization is enough for me to pack everything back up and close the door behind me in record time. I fish my phone out of my pocket, wanting to get to the bottom of this Savannah girl once and for all. Hesitantly, I type her name into the search bar, my breath moving faster than my fingers. He doesn't deserve to have his privacy invaded, but there's no turning back now.

I hit the news tab and begin to scroll through a few articles about fashion and the top ten models in California right now. One blog article specifically catches my attention: "Boxer Xavier Amari Seen on Romantic Beach Date While Savannah Middleton Sits in Rehab." My fingers begin to shake as I check the date the article was published. Today. I click it, my eyes glued on the paparazzi image of Xavier lounging on a beach with some brunette.

Read before you react, read before you react.

My inner thoughts begin to disrupt any lingering piece of sanity I had left. I close my eyes for a moment, squeezing them tight as a ringing sound puts my senses into overdrive.

Calm down, Arlissa.

I breathe the best I can, counting to four while my eager fingers scroll down the page for some useful information.

> **Xavier Amari has found himself in the arms of yet another woman. After leaving ex Savannah Middleton to rot in rehab, he's had no issue moving on. The mystery woman has yet to be identified but sources say they've been enjoying each other's company for quite a while.**

Throw it.

Without a thought about actions having consequences, I'm watching my phone fly across the room. The ringing continues, but this time it's accompanied by a pounding at my forehead. In a quest to find out more about this Savannah girl, I end up realizing

84

that the man I went to for comfort left me with a migraine so he could have a hot body and a tequila sunrise.

I guess being here with me is just too fucking boring. I guess I'm just too fucking much.

My body is hot, my mind is scattered, and my emotions are fragmented. I'm jealous. Damn right. I have every reason to be too. He made leaving sound so urgent, like it was life or death. Instead, it was just him jumping at the idea of getting his dick sucked.

Hi, my name is Arlissa Benson, and I fucking hate dating.

TWELVE

If I come home just say you're gonna be there.

Lol, where else would I be? You good tho?

Xavier comes back tomorrow, and I'd be lying if I said I left the house as soon as my brain processed that blog post. No. Even though it wasn't my home, it was still the one peaceful place I had. The guest house probably has Greyson's DNA all over it by now, and home is just too far of a drive. So I took advantage of the alone time I had.

Did I wallow in self-pity for twenty-four hours straight? Damn right I did. The anger that I felt when I saw that article is still very much present, but as I rode an Uber back to the guest house I had no choice but to get over it.

My initial thoughts were right. I don't belong in this city. I refuse to sit here and watch someone else disappoint me. Or, in Alejandra's case, disappoint themselves.

When the vehicle makes its stop, I say my goodbyes and head

straight for the door. Alejandra is sitting on the couch—by herself. A deep sigh of relief releases from my lips before I make my presence known by walking inside.

She looks up like an excited puppy. "Where have you been? I've texted you like fifty fucking times!"

"Nowhere," I mutter, shutting the door behind me.

"It's clearly somewhere if you weren't here."

I roll my eyes before attempting to head to my room.

"Hello! What is wrong with you?"

"I'm going home." The words pour out of my mouth as my feet remain nailed to the floorboards. My back faces the person I could express my emotions to just a few weeks ago. Yet, those emotions don't feel safe in her vault anymore. It seems like time has gone on and the longer we've been here, there's been a wall building slowly between us. Brick by unnoticeable brick. The thing about a wall is the longer you give it time to build without stopping it in its tracks, without finding the reason why, the longer it takes to tear them down. And the more threatening they become, transforming from a single wall to a room with no exit. First you can't see them, and then soon you can't hear them, either.

"Are you joking? My EP isn't even done!"

"I said me. Not we."

"Well, what the fuck? Not everything is about just you."

I pivot. She's standing now, her eyes piercing through my entire being. I don't have time for this. I need to get my things and go.

"Honestly, Alejandra? Nothing would be about me if it was up to you."

"Huh? Are you having a fucking moment or something?"

If my eyes roll behind my head one more time, I'm sure they'll get stuck. A sarcastic chuckle escapes my lips before I conjure up a reply. "I'm going to pack. I can't right now."

"So what the fuck am I supposed to do?"

"You have your new friends, your new career, your new boy-friend. I'm useless here." These words are more than just words. They're the foundation that helped build the wall between us, and I wasn't even aware it existed until now.

Alejandra raises a brow and takes a slight step back as if she's trying to figure something out. "Are you jealous?"

"For fuck's sake, get your head out of your ass, Alejandra! You dropped everyone before you came here for no real good reason except me because you needed a ride, I'm sure. You had a whole boyfriend who I swore you were going to marry or some shit. And now you're all cuddled up with a druggie? You have these friends who just like to fucking gossip, and you know what? You were all right. Xavier is a fucking asshole, and I guess I know that now. But, you wouldn't have ever noticed that this was more than someone I worked for because you don't notice anything that doesn't benefit this delusion of yours. And you know what? For so long I was jealous of the passion you had, but it's turning you into someone I don't know. So, congratulations, but this shit show isn't what I signed up for."

Strangely, it feels good to get that out. The words had danced around my mind for so long that letting someone hear it feels like a mountain is getting lifted off of my shoulders. The silence is heartbreaking. The more seconds that pass, the more I come to terms with the fact that in that little monologue I may have said some unforgivable things.

Her heavy gulps break through the thick veil of silence, but I don't have it in me to look her in the eyes anymore. "You should go, Lissa. Because you're right. So . . . just go."

I let out a laugh, the only thing I can do to let her know how ridiculous she is before walking off.

There's nothing more to say, and honestly, I think she broke my heart more than Xavier ever could. Alejandra was some-one that I could depend on for so long. We had had so many discussions about how strongly we felt about things like this. It only took one summer in LA to ruin it all. How could she forget we're sisters?

She's the only sister you have left.

As I pack, I want to cry. Not one of those silent cries where you just sniffle and wipe your tears. It's one of those cries where you ball up in a corner and scream as loud as you can. I crave one of those.

Once both of my suitcases are packed, I drag them outside and toss the contents in the trunk. It's windy tonight, the moist air letting me know weather is not going to be on my side if I don't leave as soon as possible. With one hand on the car door, I look up for the final time. Amy's house, the mountain behind it. And ironically, the sun's setting.

Xavier shared something with me during my time here—a sunrise. I never noticed them before, and now it seems like he owns them all. For the rest of my life I'll see them and his name will be neatly written across the glow. I just hope that's all he owns. Truthfully? It was a schoolgirl crush. Yet, it was one strong enough to tattoo his signature on every gradient of orange and red I see.

As I drive off of the property, the sun continues to set. Xavier wasn't consistent, and neither was Aly. Hell, I wasn't consistent, either. But one thing always is. Sunrises and sunsets. The world could end, and those two things would remain constant against all odds. You can count on them both, and where there's a sunrise there's a beginning. Where there's a sunset, there's an end. But you see, one always comes after the other. So whatever ending this is, whatever relationship is leaving along with this California skyline, it's okay. Sooner than later the sun will rise again and something new will begin.

And while driving I finally understand why he found peace in them—why he loved the sun enough to tattoo it on him. Maybe

I could have used the comfort of the world around me to better deal with what happened to Samantha. Maybe, but I don't think the sun can bandage a wound that old. It's just been too long, too many times of picking at the scab and watching it bleed. There's just nothing left to pick at anymore.

THIRTEEN

"Checkout is at eleven!" the man shouts as my feet drag throughout the brightly lit hotel. My room—so close yet so far away. It seems as if I had blinked and my palms were already pushing on the big oak wood doors.

I throw myself onto the queen-sized mattress, my purse hitting my hip as it follows my paces. In a desperate attempt to take the accessory off, some of its contents begin to fall to my feet. A white envelope floats slowly onto the ground and immediately catches all the attention I have left. Wait—*fuck*, I was supposed to mail this for Xavier. Well, I can keep it, but I'm sure that will put me in prison. I guess I can do him one last favor (just to avoid jail time) and personally drop the letter off if it isn't too far, right?

Right.

I squint, trying my best to see the address on the front of the thin piece of paper.

MORGAN KENT
342 PALMS BAY AVENUE

Who the hell is Morgan Kent? With the letter in one hand, and my phone in the other, I begin to type what I can see of the address.

A rehab facility.

I sit in my uncertainty for a moment, trying to piece together everything I had learned about these people within the last few weeks. *Savannah's in rehab right now.* The voice echoes in my head and suddenly the lightbulb goes off. Morgan Kent has to be Savannah, right? They're celebrities; no one would want to use her real name. I've been the one sending checks to his ex this entire time?

Well, excuse the fuck out of you.

My heart stops. I know she's in rehab, I know he's helping her. Yet, I feel like something is missing from the story. I get told one thing from Savannah's friends and another from Xavier himself. If I'm going to leave, I might as well leave with the missing puzzle piece—Savannah's side of the story.

The facility's only a thirty-minute drive from this hotel, so why not go? Why not ask Savannah herself? Not that she would be willing to talk, but if I was holding her money she would.

Oh, this is getting good, just like the movies . . . Good job, Lissa.

As my heartbeat brings my energy levels from zero to hundred, I pace around the room. I have my sister's approval, so this can't be wrong, right? She'd be so entertained right now. I know it because I can hear her with every move I make. I couldn't hear her much before, especially during high school. But as of late she's been getting louder and louder, guiding me throughout the way. If we were in an alternate universe, I'd be on the phone, and we'd laugh about how interesting my life has become.

Get yourself to bed, Lissa. Big day tomorrow.

I nod to the empty hotel room, not sure where she could be but it doesn't matter because I know she's somewhere. Somewhere close to make sure she's watching over me. Quickly, I rip off my clothes and jump into the bed.

Deep breaths.

I follow the command, breathing in and out as slow as possible into the darkness of the room. In and out until the control over my body is no longer mine.

As the warmth of the sun wakes me, the first thing I think about is what I have planned for the day. Slowly, excitement begins to fill my veins while I make quick movements to the shower. My curly brown locks fall onto my shoulders, only getting curlier as the sticky humidity in the bathroom increases. Getting dressed takes about ten minutes since I only have but so much in my duffel bag, anyway. My outfit: a striped crop top, a pair of jeans, and brown sneakers. I sprint out of that hotel room and into my car; there's something about the ridiculousness of what I'm about to do that's lighting my ass on fire.

I grab my keys out of my bag and start the vehicle. One of my many keychains sways back and forth. The only keychain I hope to never catch my attention. It's the only reason I have so many, anyway. I wouldn't dare throw it out but I also can't stand to see it. Two halves of a heart—one for my sister's keys, and one for mine. Of course at the time the only key I had was to the front door so I could get into the house after I got off the bus after school. In an alternate universe Samantha still has the other half. I wouldn't have to keep the "Sisters Forever" all to myself because the other half would be in the possession of the person who deserves it the most. I still remember when I gave it to her. I still remember

when my mother ripped it off her keys and gave it back to me. I remember when she didn't realize there was still a bit of blood on it. I never wiped it off.

The drive goes by like the speed of light. I pull my rumbling car into a parking spot and gaze at the facility before me. The stone building looks small; nowhere I would expect a celebrity to be, at least. I grab the envelope before getting out of the car and making sure it's locked. As I walk toward the entrance there's a nurse sitting outside smoking a cigarette.

Fuck. How the hell are you going to get inside?

"Good morning!" the cheery woman calls out to me, tapping the ash into a nearby trash can. "The sun's shining real bright today, ain't it?" Her smile reveals coffee-stained teeth.

"Good morning." I return the smile, keeping a tight grip on the envelope as I walk a bit closer to the older lady. "Yeah, I think we're going to enjoy the weather today."

"I know one thing for sure, the patients really need more bright days like this . . . " She puts her cigarette out and tosses it in the trash. "Are you here to visit someone?"

Lie. Lie. Lie.

Hush, Samantha. Wait—maybe you're onto something.

"Uh, yes! I'm here for Morgan Kent. She's my sister. Uh, I miss her a lot and, um . . . It's hard knowing she's not here, you know? I just want to see her." I pause, emotions that are unrelated to Savannah beginning to coat themselves in my lies. "I also just have a payment for her stay here."

"Well, I've never seen you here before."

"Yeah, we usually mail them in because we had a huge fight before she—left. I just wanted to surprise her."

The silence; unbearable. But eventually she sends another smile in my direction. "She's actually been expecting some family. I can take you to her. I'm about to head back in anyways. It's

94

nice seeing someone other than that boyfriend of hers come and visit." She turns and begins walking into the building.

I quickly follow. "Boyfriend?"

"Do you not know him? I'd assume so because you're sisters. Great guy brings those little caramel candies for me every time he comes. An angel. And easy on the eyes too. I just wanna bake him some sweet apple pies whenever I see him. You know, I'd date him if I was about twenty years younger." She laughs. "So what's your name, sweetie?"

"Oh, yeah! He's a great guy for sure. I'm so glad he's been with her throughout all of this." I clear my throat, the discomfort in my tone becoming obvious. "Abby," I blurt out.

"Well, Abby, I'm Marie. It's nice to meet ya. I love caring for the patients here, you know. But getting to know them is really my bread and butter."

We make a few turns, go down a few halls, but finally we end up at what looks like the backyard. She slides open the glass door, a gust of wind introducing itself to me, and allows me to step through. The trees are a gorgeous green, and there's even a pond in the middle of all the acres of fresh grass. If I look hard enough, I can see the tiny droplets of dew on each blade of green. People are walking around, one girl is even jogging. To my left, two men are playing chess and look really fucking happy to do so.

What I said earlier sticks with me as I look upon these people. My sister. A wound left untreated. But it's still a door I'm not willing to open just yet, no matter how often she haunts me. Some pain is meant to be forever. Because maybe if I treat it, I'll forget what she sounds like. What her presence feels like.

Marie points to a brunette whose back is facing us. I guess there's no bleach in rehab. Her body rests against a dark brown bench, her figure remains covered by a blanket. "She's right over there . . . but I'm sure you recognize your own sister."

"Thanks."

I take cautious steps as I get closer and closer to the bench. What am I even going to say to her? I don't have a clue what I should mention first or what I should avoid. How do you ask someone you don't know to honestly talk about their ex? Or boyfriend.

"Savannah?" I whisper, finally getting close enough to walk around the bench and into her view. The woman jumps in shock, her green eyes piercing through my soul as she furrows her brow.

"Excuse me?"she whispers. "My name is Morgan. How did you get in here?"

"Um." I stumble over my own feet in a pitiful attempt to take another step toward her. My eyes fall first onto her greasy roots and then to the glowing "S" chain on her chest. "My name is Arlissa. I worked for Xavier." At the mention of his name, I watch her body tense up.

"Oh, so Xavier sent you?" The brunette snatches the envelope out of my hand.

"Hey!"

"Is that not mine?"

"Yeah, but—"

"Okay, so go. What else are you here for? And don't tell me Xavier wants you to recite some stupid love poem to me or something. I'm not in the mood today."

"No." I point to the empty spot on the bench. "Can I sit?"

You have to get her to talk to you.

"I don't see what's stopping you." She has a sultry voice, every word falling perfectly off her lips.

I push a bit of her blanket out of the way and take a seat. "I came on my own. I wanted to talk to you about something. I know, I'm prying. I know this isn't my business, but I can't continue to work for or trust Xavier if I don't know him."

"Let me stop you right there." A sarcastic chuckle falls from her lips as she glares at me. "Leave that kiss-up bullshit out of this,

96

okay? I know who you are. That replacement assistant he hired. Now, what I want to know is why are you bothering me?"

"Um . . . " I clear my throat, wondering how I'm going to word this. She's coming on so strong, and I'm completely unprepared. *Samantha, help me.* "How was your relationship with him?"

She hesitates for a moment, leaving me to draw on my own wild conclusions. "He . . . " The way she looks off into the distance makes me believe she has the answer hidden deep in her mind. Either that, or no one ever asked her that before. "He's the greatest motherfucker in the world. Wouldn't trade him for a Snickers and a wine cooler. Can you go now?"

I roll my eyes, her attitude beginning to really annoy me. "I just want to know if he's as shitty as everyone thinks. I can't work for him if—"

"You don't care if you work for a shitty person. I know him, and I know how weird bitches get when they get a little too close to him. You care if he's a shitty person so you know if you should fuck him or not. Stay the hell away from him," she hisses, her energy clearly escalating by the second. "I'm not going anywhere, in case you were wondering."

"Huh?" I utter.

Savannah chuckles. "Are you stupid? I see that puppy dog look in your eyes. He's sunk his teeth deep in you already, hasn't he?"

It seems like with every word she says my fire is ignited even more. I'm not scared of her—*right?* But for some reason I can't do anything other than let her dig into me.

Shaking my head, I slide over a bit to make some space between the seething woman and me. "None of this matters anyways. I fucking quit. I don't even know why I'm here."

She rolls her eyes, a sinister smile gracing her face as she rises from the seat. "Just don't let him get you pregnant too."

My eyes immediately drop to her stomach. I'm pretty sure

she doesn't have a bump. No, I'm one hundred percent sure. As Savannah stands there I drown in a sea of confusion.

"I'm sorry." The words slip out of my mouth before I can even fathom what's going on.

"Don't be there when I get out of this place." The taller woman bumps me as she swiftly walks back into the facility, leaving me with the wind and a shit-ton of guilt.

Okay, so maybe I was wrong. Maybe I had no business showing up and asking questions. Bad idea, I get it. I don't know what was going through my mind or what is even going on in my mind now. I have more questions than I came here with.

I sulk in my car for about an hour. The way that conversation went made me feel small, just confirming that I have no place in this twisted universe they had created. Every word she said runs marathons around my head. Is she still in love with him? Are they still together? Do they plan on trying to have another child when she's released? Was she telling me she still loved him or not?

None of this is my business. None of this is my life. The only thing that makes sense is that I never need to step foot in LA ever again. These problems don't belong to me, it belongs to them. I don't need to feel bad or carry these things on my shoulders like I own them. There is no future for Xavier and me. Even through these concrete walls she's still calling the shots. I guess he's just passing time until she gets out.

They deserve each other, and this whole city deserves them.

FOURTEEN

It's hard adjusting here again.

But I thought you weren't doing alright there anyways?

Yeah but, being here again feels weird too.

Let me fix it.

Doesn't feel like a good idea . . .

Because you're actually just five miles away instead of 500? Give me a chance.

OK.

"So . . . fall semester's starting soon. Will you be registering for school since you're back?"

My mother's question causes an immediate eye roll from me. I've been home for like, a week and a half and somehow it still feels too soon. Too soon to do anything concrete, at least.

I stand there, accompanying her in the kitchen as she goes back and forth between cabinets.

"I don't know."

There's a presence looming over me, and every time it's silent it whispers, *you don't belong here either.* My mother's long brown hair is now in a short curly cut. My dad started going to the gym more for reasons I have yet to understand. And my sister's room—well, it's not locked anymore. It's the little things, I guess, the new china cabinet or the brand-new flat screen TV.

Even when you're gone, the world just keeps spinning. And the sun keeps playing its role as the center of our universe. Consistently. How many times has it spun since I've been gone?

"Your father and I think it would be a good idea. Get you out of that diner and into the real world, you know?"

"Mom, I haven't even gotten my job at the diner back yet."

"Yes, Arlissa, and you shouldn't. That's my point."

A deep sigh releases from my lips in annoyance at the topic. "Can I please just . . . get some room to exist?"

"You've been existing all year. It's time to get serious about your future."

"I am."

My mom raises a brow. "Are you? Because if you want to exist in this house I'm going to need you to start bringing in some money, Arlissa. You're an adult now."

"I know. It's just been hard to focus."

"It's always—"

Our conversation is interrupted by a soft knock on the door. Mom and I stare at each other, my face full of confusion and hers looking way too excited for her own good.

"Gonna go get that?" she asks, pointing to the door with a dirty knife that she's just beginning to wash.

My eyes immediately dart to my Bratz pajamas that I've been wearing since middle school. "Like this?"

"Girl, if you don't go get that damn door . . . "

I roll my eyes, tucking the unruly brown tresses behind my ear before storming off to our front door. It's probably the mailman or something, nothing worth stressing over. I pull on the knob and allow the door to swing open, and my present attitude immediately vanishes at the sight of him. For a moment he isn't a man, he's a rush of secret text messages sent behind the blanket of "do not disturb" and turning my screen brightness all the way down.

Within the last few months he's gotten bulkier, his body resembling someone's MTV Man Crush Monday. His brown hair is a bit messier than I remember him keeping it, but it goes well with the new, insane amount of facial hair he's grown. His gray eyes peer into my soul, and this time, Alejandra isn't here to remind me that he's hers. But that's the thing—he's not hers any longer, and honestly? Within the last few months, he may have become mine.

Was it always this way? Catching his gaze across rooms and answering his calls for her when she was in the middle of something. Did I ask to be in such a treacherous position? There was a night last summer when he and Aly were on a break, and she had yelled at him so loudly he had to pretend to go on a run just so he had an excuse to cry like a baby in the park. I was only in that park to do the same, but not for that reason. We skipped rocks that night. I got his number that night. And that morning I met them both for breakfast.

"Hey, Christian! What are you doing here?"

When I thought of Alejandra's future and my place in it, I always included Christian in those imaginary scenarios. Yet, here he is, reminding me of when he first transferred to our high school and was fair game for everyone.

I was too late.

"Oh right!" His shining smile leaves me weak as I step to the side to allow him to come in. He's hesitant at first, making me think he might be just as nervous as I am. But why? We've been friends for a while, family even. Where on earth is this emotion coming from? There's one thing that's out of the equation—Alejandra.

"Your mum, I saw 'er at the post office yesterday and she, uh, asked me to stop by. I would've called you first, but I felt like a surprise was a bit more charmin'."

"Oh, did she," I mumble as we move toward the living room, glaring at my mom on the way. "Why so early?" I question with a joking tone as I plop down onto the couch.

"I've got to get to work in an hour. Your place is on the way and I, uh, just couldn't wait, I guess. Ya packed up and left without saying goodbye, ya know?"

"You can say you missed me. I won't blame you, I promise. But, hey! I did not. I didn't even know I was going anywhere. You know that! I just thought I was the chauffeur."

"Yeah, Alejandra's funny that way." His voice trails off for a moment. "But anyways, I just missed having someone small enough to pick on around."

"Oh, fuck you. I swear I've grown an inch since I left."

"Not at all, love. Your hair, maybe. But are we shocked?"

I roll my eyes, playfully swatting him on the shoulder. "I can't believe you're seeing me before I've even showered."

"You threw up in my car once. I think that's made every boundary completely disappear," he jokingly adds.

"Not every boundary!" my mother shouts from the kitchen, a cackle immediately following.

"Right, Mrs. Benson. Not everything," Christian calls back before turning his attention back to me. "I also thought I'd check on you."

"Check on me? Why? If anything, I should be checking on you. You're the one playing 'pop up' on both Alejandra and me."

"Ah, I'm good. I fought for it as hard as I could, you know?

But I think you were right. There's better out there. Showing up that night was stupid."

"What about showing up now?"

"A smart move, love. Smartest I may have ever made, eh?"

"Maybe. Well, I guess neither of us will be hearing much from her, then."

"Hey, now that we're in person and not sneaking texts at three a.m., I'm seriously sorry she tossed you out like that. Want to talk about it? I've got time."

"You don't have time." My voice softens, a smile finishing my sentence for me perfectly.

His attention falls to his watch before he slowly rises from the leather cushions. "You're actually right. I've also got to go pick myself up some lunch but, uh, don't hesitate to text me, yeah?"

"Do I ever?"

He smiles. "No."

I get up, following him to the door with the intention of seeing him out. "We should do something soon. Uh, catch up. Like old times?" I ask, pulling the door open and watching him take a few steps out.

"I like that. Just let me know when. Have a good day, Mrs. Benson!" he calls out before turning and heading back to his car. The door shuts behind him.

My heart continues to race, and I'm almost positive it's loud enough to hear. I release a deep sigh and give myself ten seconds before heading back to the kitchen.

"You could have at least told me to change."

My mother smiles, drying her hands before walking over to me. "That wouldn't have been fun, now would it?" Her smile is sneaky enough to make me want to slap it off of her. She begins to make her way upstairs, completely content with her actions as I'm practically melting into the floor. "I always liked that boy."

"You're awful!" I exclaim as I watch her disappear upstairs.

Seeing Christian on different terms, for the first time in forever, makes my heart flutter. Not only that, but it also causes a lot of emotions to come back to the surface.

When I see him, I think of Alejandra. In times like these she'd tell me to get a grip because I know he thinks I'm pretty. Except, she isn't here—and for the past few days I've been seriously trying to figure out if I was ever an important factor in her life. Hurt people hurt people. So maybe that explained why Xavier and Alejandra hurt me. Why she hurt Christian. They're both two very hurt people who don't see someone standing right in front of them who had no intention of hurting them. But if the cycle continued, if hurt people *really* hurt people, then who was I going to hurt?

FIFTEEN

"You can go ahead and take your break now, Arlissa." The words sing like music to my ears throughout the empty diner.

My job is pretty cozy. Low-hanging lights, ripped-up red leather seats, peeling brick, and stills from *Grease* hang up on all the walls. It's family owned and has been around for generations. The only issue is, as more big chain restaurants come in, the fewer customers we have. Whenever a new takeout eatery moves in down the street we'd have a couple of weeks of steady emptiness, our few loyal customers being the only ones we see. This is one of those times.

I'm just glad I can be here with Courtney. I know her nerves skyrocket whenever she even thinks of being the one who let her family restaurant die. She isn't just the owner—she's a friend. Something like an older sister, I guess. The brunette reminds me of every 2010s starlet, actually. Somehow after two kids she still has an amazingly fit body. Added to that, the almond shaped eyes that sit under her blunt-cut bangs are a captivating emerald green.

"Do you need anything else before I go?"

"No, you're fine." She pauses, placing her hand on her forehead and releasing an obnoxiously loud sigh. "Actually, you can take an hour break. Hell, maybe even two."

It's just Courtney and me here. The cook and another waitress only come on weekends when we have a few more customers to handle, but that's about it. The business is failing; anyone can see that sad truth in her eyes. Or, in the way she drags her body around this place all damn day.

I nod, giving her a reassuring rub on the back before removing myself from behind the cash register and making my way out the door. The end is coming for this place. Her husband tries religiously to get her to just sell it—especially after Alejandra and I left for what was supposed to be the entire summer.

Usually, I would take my break in the restaurant. But the tension can be cut with a knife in that place right now. So my car is the next best option. I sit down in the vehicle before reclining the seat and beginning to scroll through my various social media accounts.

Boring, boring, boring.

My rapid scrolling is put to a sudden halt due to a recent picture that Alejandra uploaded to Instagram. I haven't unfollowed her yet. Truthfully, I don't have the heart to. Yeah, part of me has no interest in seeing her bound-to-fail relationship with Greyson, but another part wants to keep up with her. At least just a bit.

She looks happy. She's in a desert somewhere with her hair blowing in the wind. I swipe to find another picture of her and the models she's been hanging out with.

They all look so happy. Alejandra has on a moss green jumper—I told her green was totally her color. Glad she finally listened. *Swipe.* This picture is of Greyson in the same desert. He's kneeled down with a camera in his hand and the lens is pointed toward whoever's taking the picture. She's having the time of her life in LA, and I'm sitting here thinking of fifty new ways to sell apple pie before my boss is out of a job.

My thoughts continue to take over the better part of my break. I try to fight it, I promise I am. But it doesn't take long before I'm entering "Xavier Amari" into every search bar available. His Instagram hasn't moved much. A few workout videos, inspirational posts, mostly boxing-related things, and your occasional selfie with captions about how the boxing ring is his "one true love." His Twitter is basically the same thing, except, when I check for tweets with just his name—my heart feels like it's been kicked right in the center.

Xavier Amari getting his girlfriend from rehab and bringing her home is the entertainment I needed tonight.

Not Xavier and Savannah back together. I'm screaming.

Yeah okay, I still don't think Xavier is innocent but sureee.

I need a Xavier Amari in my life bc wow, guys never hold it down these days.

Savannah is so lucky to have a guy like Xavier Amari omgggg.

Savannah's pictured entering the same house I left. Her blond hair has made its return as if they stopped at the salon before going home. Priorities, I guess. Block-shaped black sunglasses cover her eyes as Xavier covers the rest of her body with his.

All the emotions I'm enduring, the fiery pit of anger that makes a home in the bottom of my stomach, it's sickening. The worst part about it all—she was right. He ran back even though he told me he wanted nothing to do with her. I'm a fool, an idiot even, to think someone who had that much history with a person could ever fit me in their heart. It was a stupid, dumb, childish dream.

Part of me wants to kick and scream, feeling like I've lost something that belonged to me. Maybe if I stayed quiet, maybe if I didn't lash out at everyone and didn't act so damn dramatic— maybe I'd be there instead of her.

That's possible, but look now. You fucked up for both of us. And here you are, back in this stupid little town. I've never been more disappointed in you.

My head begins to pound as I rock back and forth in my beat-up seats. "Shut up . . . " I mumble, trying my best to ignore the echoes that are making themselves known in my brain. I close my eyes, only making it worse as an image of my sister appears before me in high definition. Curly hair that was just bleached, prominent eyebrows, and lashes that I always wished were mine.

You're nothing without them, you know that. What is wrong with you?

"Stop. They weren't good for me, you know that." The pounding of my head intensifies, feeling as if someone is beating against my temples.

The vibration of my phone manages to interrupt my entire train of thought, bringing me back down to earth. In a split second, I'm cured. My senses are turned back on and my body is acting as if it wasn't just fighting against me. The words that light up my screen seem to have more than perfect timing.

It feels like a day for Chinese and Hennessey if ur up for it.

If I don't deserve anything else in this life, I at least deserve a friend. If anyone could put an end to this wave of irrational emotions, its Christian.

It took Christian a little over an hour to come get me since he had to work as well. It's fine, though. That gave me enough time to take another shower and change into some comfortable sweats.

There's no need to do more than pull my hair into a ponytail. He's just a friend. But pulling out a few wet strands won't hurt, right?

We arrive at a red stone townhouse. It's a cute little place with some yellow mums potted right out front. The air is still, drier than I remember it being before I left for LA. I follow him quietly, my body swaying back and forth as he unlocks the door.

"I got everything set up. Felt like that was easier, ya know?" His intoxicating accent breaks the silence as the door swings open and invites me in. "Welcome to my humble abode."

I smile as my crocs make friends with the off-white carpet. "It's cute."

There's an immediate smell of chicken and fried rice that fills my nose, only getting stronger with every step I take. My curious eyes begin to scan my surroundings. The kitchen area is right in front of us, along with the living room and two doors that I can only assume are the bathroom and bedroom.

"Ah, you don't have to lie. It's a bit small, but gotta start some-where," he adds before closing and locking the door. "Oh, would you mind taking your shoes off? Cleaning this carpet is an abso-lute bitch."

Nodding, I hold my purse to my stomach as I bend down to pull my crocs off. "It is cute! Shut up." My delayed response is accompanied by me taking a few more steps into the home. Sud-denly, a small dining table with some Chinese takeout cartons, a bottle of Hennessey, plastic utensils, and more fortune cookies than necessary catches my attention. "You weren't lying when you said you set up. And you got extra fortune cookies!"

He approaches my side, letting out a chuckle. "No, no I was not. And I did I remembered you always used to steal mine when we ordered before so." Christian pulls out a chair, his twinkling pupils directing me to sit down. Seeing him this way is strange. It was easy to evict any unfriendly thoughts about him from my mind when Alejandra was dating him. But now? There's nothing stopping me.

If Alejandra was here she would say we couldn't start eating until there was something on the TV. It's my turn to control things and Christian's voice is enough entertainment.

Step one: reach for the alcohol. "So, how are you doing? Seriously."

"Um," he starts, his mouth full of noodles. "I mean, with what exactly?"

Step two: get the awkward subject out of the way.

"You know . . . " My eyes are focused on pouring just the right amount of alcohol in the cup. "With her."

"What about you with him? How are you doing?"

"I told you about that?" I manage to cough out, the alcohol in my system causing every part of my upper body to burn.

He rolls his eyes, reaching over to grab the bottle and chugging it immediately. "Me mum told me everyone falls in love like what, three times in their life? This was just one of those times. Maybe it was like that for you too."

"Oh, please, I did not love him. But . . . What do you think about that?"

"What?" He finally puts the bottle down, replacing it with an eggroll now.

"Love. Like, the whole idea of it."

"Have you ever experienced it?"

I take a moment, unsure of how to answer that. "I mean . . . I love my family and friends."

"Well, with more than just ya mates."

"No. I don't think so."

"Really? That's surprising."

I raise a brow. "How the hell is that surprising?"

"Well, you're fuckin' beautiful. Someone had to have swept you off ya feet by now."

The way the words fall off of his luscious lips causes all the energies in my lower body to scatter.

Close your fucking mouth, Lissa. You're probably drooling.

I see what Alejandra saw in him, and she's stupid for letting him go. Greyson's a lost cause, Christian isn't.

"Oh, you're just being nice. I promise there's no one."

"Not even in the big fancy town of LA?" His question strikes me for some reason. There was someone. Lord knows there is someone.

"Nope. Not a soul. They're all living off of trust funds and up each other's asses." I smirk, stand, and take small steps around the table. He's so fucking beautiful. From the newly acquired facial hair to every vein under his skin that outlines his muscles. My small fingers make their way across his shoulders as I reach over him to grab the bottle.

"Try to share next time, yeah?" I whisper with a smile.

He returns the grin, eyes focusing heavily on my petite figure. "Trust funds, eh? Well, how will I measure up to that?" He's partially flirting, partially speaking on his own experience with being left for a trust fund baby. He's hurting, I'm hurting. We deserve each other in this uninterrupted moment.

"You don't have to measure up . . . " I start, pausing for a quick break to take a few sips from the bottle. "You just have to be here." My eyes seal the deal with his lighter colored ones.

Our focus is only on each other.

In a split second his hands are wrapped around my waist, awakening every fiber of my being. It's the excitement of being with someone we know we shouldn't be with that makes the touches more electrifying. When he plops me on his lap and presses his lips to mine, I completely bow down to every action.

It doesn't take long for my sweats to be located elsewhere while my body is sprawled over the carpeted floor. He hovers over me, planting small kisses across my chest and neck. His breath

smells like Hennessy and Chinese food, yet it doesn't ruin the moment in the slightest. In fact, it makes my body crave him more.

I close my eyes as I succumb to his touch. There are rushes of thoughts and emotions going through my mind, none of them being guilt.

The only issue is, when my eyes shut, I only see Xavier.

SIXTEEN

I wake up to his smile and watch him breathe with his eyes closed. The posters and paintings that cover his walls are slowly being revealed as the sun comes up. I roll over a bit, immediately alarming Christian's radar as he moves with me, his grip on my waist only tightening.

Enjoy it, Lissa. There's someone here who wants to hold you through the morning—he's always been right here.

I allow the blankets to engulf my tiny frame as a sigh of relief escapes from my chapped lips. I listen to Christian's breath. It's just as peaceful as I had imagined. Is it bad that I imagined this before?

How many secrets can I keep? Because I know for sure if I were to ever befriend Alejandra again, I'd never be able to see a Pink Floyd shirt without thinking of the way I opened myself up for the Aussie. I just have to cross that bridge when I get there.

I tried to get here that night at Parkway. I was on the cusp of leaning in to kiss him but—did he feel the same? I don't think so then. I think his mind was still on Alejandra, which is understandable. But I dreamed about him nearly every night for days. I didn't speak to her much that week.

"Rise and shine . . . " The grumbly voice fills my ears, perfect timing. I look down as his head rests on my chest.

"Hey, sleepyhead. How hungover are you?"

He smirks, finally opening his eyes a bit and looking up at me. "Not as much as I thought, honestly. You?"

My hands shake as I lay there, refraining from touching on him some more. But he's sober now; is the feeling still mutual? "I'm perfect."

Our smiles meet before he raises his upper body a bit, our lips only a centimeter away. I wonder, while staring into his ice-cold eyes if he sees me or—her. Because even though it's morning, I still see him.

"You are."

I smirk. "You're not just saying that?"

He furrows his brow before lifting himself up off the bed completely. "I'd never just say something to say it. You know me."

I remain in the same place, not wanting to leave the comfort of a bed that's not mine. It dawns on me, like a meteor striking the ground, none of this is actually mine. This bed, this situation, this man. It still has the person I once called my best friend written all over it. My eyes scatter the floor for my clothes as I watch him pull on a T-shirt in my peripheral vision.

"Chris—"

He pivots, facing me as he puts another leg into his boxers. "Wait, before you say anything. Stay the rest of the weekend. I feel like . . . We never—"

"We never got the time to do this?"

His eyes soften. "Yeah. I want to—do this."

I sit up a bit, resting my back against the headboard. "Do you remember that night . . . It was your first date with her, and I had to come because I had to drive since she didn't trust you enough yet to be in your car alone."

He chuckles. "Yeah. And she spent the first thirty minutes in the bathroom. So, to pass the time, you and I ordered the 'mystery shake' and got brain freeze trying to see who could drink it faster."

I can feel my face lighting up as I laugh along with him. "Yes! And when she finally came out she couldn't figure out why we both didn't have an appetite anymore."

Christian nods, the redness in his cheeks becoming more and more apparent. "I should have known then."

I run my fingers through my curls, hoping they don't look like a lion's mane by now. "Known what?"

"I mean . . . " He sits at the edge of the bed. "Like that night at Parkway. Every day after that I think I was still with her to see you."

"Chris . . . "

"Look, let's not pretend we're doing a good thing here, but she's gone, right?"

My heart skips. *Is she?* I don't want her to be if that's the case. She means more to me than this or him but—I'm useless to her. "Right."

He leans in, placing his rose-petal-textured lips on my forehead. "I'm going to head out and get some groceries for breakfast. You can stay here, shower, do whatever makes you happy."

"Breakfast?"

He stands, grabbing some sweatpants off a nearby chair and slipping them on. "Yeah. You like pancakes?"

I nod.

"Perfect. See you in a bit."

I sit there for a few moments, letting the sounds illustrate every action he's taking until I finally hear the front door shut. My

entire body relaxes, every joint, every muscle, just melting into the blanket.

Well, this is a turn, isn't it?

Shut up. I do not want to talk to you right now.

Now, is that how you talk to your sister? the voice in my head continues. *I bet he still has a drawer dedicated to her and everything. This isn't where you're supposed to be. You know that. And now you might have fucked up your one ticket to a more interesting life. Do you want this? This boring life? I didn't die to sit up in heaven and watch you roll around in Carson City for the rest of your life and marry an electrician.*

I sit up, ripping the covers from my chest and begin trying my best to collect the clothes that are scattered around the house. Bra, underwear, one croc, pants, other croc, top. While I grab my shirt from under the coffee table, I notice a glimmer of something that's been collecting dust. Curious, I pull what appears to be a chain from under it. I take a moment, analyzing the crystal encrusted outline of Australia that's hanging from the rope-like chain.

I remember going with Alejandra to buy this for him. It was his twenty-first birthday, and she knew he missed home. I remember standing there and waiting in line as she tried to debate with me about the fact that Australia is a country, not a continent. I remember dropping her off that night so she could give it to him, wrapped up in a sleek black box. The excitement on her face, the card she wrote, the love she felt. I remember knowing he wasn't much of a jewelry guy but he'd take it because it was from her. I didn't want to tell her because I knew she'd just tell me she knew him better. I still don't believe that. And I never told her Australia's a continent.

Does he still have her picture in his wallet?

I sigh, blurry vision becoming the immediate effect of my guilt finally rising to the surface. The necklace falls from my hands and onto the coffee table. I leave it there. These emotions are going to

116

run me dry if I let them. Quickly, I throw on my clothes and pull out my phone.

Mom called. Won't be here when you get back. Sorry.

I take a cab and cry the whole way home.

SEVENTEEN

Guilt isn't even the strongest word to describe the rain cloud hovering over me. This doesn't make any sense. This isn't supposed to bother me. She deserves it, right? I am not in the wrong.

My bloodshot eyes begin to flood. My fragile hands hold onto a small throw pillow that's soaked in a mixture of snot and teardrops. I'm not crying because I regret it. Hell no, I surely don't regret it. I'm crying because I never thought I'd do this to her. I've spent all this time judging everyone else around me for becoming "one of those LA girls," yet, I might have fit right in if I allowed myself to.

My eyes analyze the bits of baby blue paint that I can see from the cracks of light escaping from closed curtains. The day we painted those white walls blue, I convinced my dad I would never get tired of it. I practically begged him to take me to Home Depot and pick out the perfect swatch. Just one of the many times me begging for something I didn't need turned out to be a stupid idea. Honestly, I don't even know if I have a favorite color anymore. Baby blue represents innocence. Or at least, that's what my mother says. Purity, honesty. None of these words means anything to me anymore.

God, you're gonna hate that color when you're older.

Samantha's voice echoes through my mind, a voice at this point I'm hoping to forget. That memory's been stuffed in the back of my mind since it happened. She was there at Home Depot too, shaking her head at a younger me and wishing I would just pick something regular like white or gray.

Arlissa . . . Arlissa.

I want to take control of my thoughts, stop them from being so chaotic. "Take the wheel" as some people would say. Yet, every single time my mind calms down, a new wave of destructive sentences take over. As much as I try to hold it in, there's no way to stop myself from the ocean-like tears that are beginning to overflow.

I'm sorry, if I knew it'd be like this, then I would have never let you convince me to take you to that movie. I'm sorry, okay? But you need to stop blaming yourself.

My body rises in shock. "Samantha?" I whisper, my tired eyes trying to make sense of this dark room. "Samantha?"

That wasn't a memory. That wasn't my thoughts. My sister is talking to me. She has to be. She has been this entire time. The voice, the thoughts, the back-and-forth arguments in my head are from her, not just me. I'm not going crazy, right? She's here.

A bright light coming from the front of my room practically blinds me. Thanks to my eyes quickly adjusting, I can rule seeing heaven out of my list of options. A figure is coming from the slowly opening door, allowing more and more light to shine through.

"God, it's so dark in here." The familiar voice speaks. Her words are sweet, coming across as a whisper. "Your mom let me in," she continues, my vision fully understanding who the figure is. She looks exactly as I left her. Long black hair, squeezable cheeks, a sun-kissed tan, and brown doe-like eyes that make you want to forgive every bad thing she ever did.

"Yeah, I was sleeping," I say, utterly taken aback by the fact that Alejandra is standing in my room right now.

"Oh, well, sorry about that."

I clear my throat, trying my best to process the last fifteen minutes. "Nope, it's cool. What're you here for?"

"I—"

"How did you even get here? You don't have a car."

"I'm going to explain those things in a minute!" Her voice heightens a bit as she takes a few more steps toward me. "Are you okay?"

I shrug. "End of season allergies and, um, like I said, just woke up."

She's inching closer and closer to my bedside. "Right, right. Sorry. Can I sit?"

"Go ahead."

"Look." Here comes the speech in 3 . . . 2 . . . 1. "I'm sorry. I was overwhelmed, and honestly, the last thing I wanted to hear was that you were fucking leaving. I don't want to throw you aside and no, I don't think you're jealous of me. I was just being a damn idiot. I just want you to come back. My EP is done, and I can't imagine releasing it without you. There's just so much that I cannot imagine without you. My entire life, every plan, every manifestation, every dream . . . you're there somewhere. Not a stupid guy. Whether we're teaching the kids how to swim at the country club pool or skinny dipping off of John Legend's yacht . . . you're there. I'm sorry, okay? Coño, I'm sorry. And I know you're sorry too, so we don't have to go through all that. Can we please just kiss and make up now?"

Sure, I would love to. If only I could admit that your ex-boyfriend's se-men might still be crawling around my walls as we speak.

Her rambling continues. "I just really fucking like Greyson. And I can promise that whoever you met at that party isn't who he is. Just please let me show you that."

A deep sigh releases from my lips. She's the missing link, the only sister I have left. I can't lose this one too. "I missed you, superstar."

Maybe, if I try really hard, this time will be different. The possibility of putting the last few months to the side and giving into this new life instead of pushing it away is tempting. Plus, it's not like staying in this little town and running into Christian (again) is on my bucket list.

"So, does that mean you want to come back with me?"

"Sure—yes. I will."

A smile slowly appears on my face as Alejandra wraps me in her arms. One of those hugs is the exact medicine that I need. That feeling of warmth and acceptance. Just knowing someone has your back.

Maybe I'd sound crazy saying it out loud. But I'm certain now that Samantha sent me Alejandra. We're going to fight, but we're sisters.

EIGHTEEN

*F*all in California isn't anything special. Within the last few weeks that I've been back in town, I managed to find a tolerance for Greyson that I never would have obtained if it wasn't for Alejandra's begging. We finally moved out of that lovely, rent-free guesthouse and into an apartment that Greyson handpicked for us. Since, there's no possible way we could have found an apartment on our own, right? Whatever. We're tolerating him. Right?

Anyway, he's always here, and while that's cool and all, I'd love it if he'd help with a bill or two. Or all of them. What's the fun in dating a trust fund baby if he only brings doughnuts? The real kicker, though, is that Jerrica lives with us as well. I guess that's a better pick than dealing with Megan's obsession with new trend diets or Olivia's constant attitude.

Jerrica is a breath of fresh air. Every Saturday night we all sit down and watch some stupid cartoon that's only funny when we're drunk. Sure, she makes green juices every morning, but I'm actually beginning to appreciate those.

Unemployment's been a bitch but following Alejandra around is taking up a shitload of my time. So—whatever.

Today's event is one I'm more than proud to accompany her to, though. It's finally time to shoot the EP cover. There's a super small budget—it only covers the photographer and the rental space. Everything else is out of pocket. Thankfully, Jerrica knows a really good MUA who owes her a favor. And of course, it takes me five "how to use a curling iron" videos on YouTube before I get promoted to her free hairstylist.

"Lissa, red lip or nude? Wait, wait! Or pink?" Alejandra asks with a stone-cold expression while the makeup artist makes a painting out of her face.

"I think pink would be best. But like a nude pink."

The last time I saw Alejandra getting her makeup done was by my mom on prom day. We never had these glamorous experiences. In fact, we were probably pros at doing it ourselves and making it look like we spent the money.

Watching her now makes me beyond proud. She sits in that chair like a princess. Raven curls sit calmly on her chest. Her eyes remain closed as the woman makes gentle strokes across her face. Alejandra is stunning. The girl was truly born to be a superstar.

But if she's that, what does that make me?

"Hey, guys!" The overly cheery voice comes from the entrance as Greyson begins to walk toward us with a guitar case in hand. Yet, the greeting doesn't come from him. It comes from the person behind him.

"You didn't tell me Brandon and Bailey were doing your shoot today." The words slip through slight spaces between Greyson's teeth. Sliding past me, he places the guitar case near Alejandra's seat, giving her a kiss on the forehead.

Alejandra opens one eye, inspecting her surroundings. "I don't even know who's in this room right now."

Watching Alejandra light up due to the sight of Greyson almost causes an eye roll from me. *Jealous? No, of course not. He's repulsive.*

My mind begins to drift to Xavier. And how the only time I'd ever eye roll in his presence was in response to a stupid joke. No. Not allowing that. Because whenever he swarms my thoughts I remember that he's building a life of his own. I need to find a distraction ASAP. In desperation, my eyes scan the studio until they land on a woman setting up a camera. A beanie occupies her head with long, curly black hair creeping out the back. Without giving it a second thought, I inch away from the lovebirds and head over to the woman in the baby blue pullover.

"Are you taking the photos?" The words fall out of my mouth like a chaotic waterfall, but I hope I stuck the landing.

Smile, stupid.

The woman looks up at me, her brown eyes meeting mine. "No, that's just my brother. I come for, uh, artistic direction." A light chuckle leaves her lips as she slowly stands.

"Oh." I nod. "Well, I'm Lissa."

"Bailey. Nice to meet you. Are you friends with Aly?"

"Yeah! I'm just, uh, emotional support."

"Well, that's no fun. I know how you feel, though. I used to be like that when my brother started getting these photography gigs. But you know what the trick is?"

"Hm?"

The woman smiles, stuffing her tattooed hands in her sweatpants pockets. "Make a spot for yourself."

"Right." I let out a nervous giggle before tucking a few loose strands behind my ear. "I don't think she needs any artistic direction from me."

"So what do you like to do?"

I shrug.

"Come on, there has to be something."

"I don't know, I never really had the time to think about it, I guess."

Our conversation is cut short by a loud shriek coming from behind me. "This cheap shit fucking ripped!"

I turn to see Alejandra stomping out of the changing room, which is really just a corner with a makeshift door, with the gold fabric only halfway on. Before I can say a word or even attempt to run to her rescue, Greyson's already beating me to the punch.

"Hey, hey. Calm down," I hear him say. "I can get you something else, and it won't come from a damn thrift shop."

"How? What am I gonna wear? We only have this place for another hour! There's no time to buy something new," Alejandra whimpers.

Greyson stands there for a minute, clearly trying to conjure up a solution. "Uh . . . take it off, then."

"What?" I exclaim, finally walking over to the pair. "No way."

"You can do the shoot naked," he boldly adds.

"That's ridiculous," I fight back.

"Wait, he might be onto something. Sex sells. It's the fucking twentieth century, right?"

Wow. "The twenty-first, dummy."

"Whatever!"

Greyson rolls his eyes before quickly grabbing the instrument he had brought in. "We can use the guitar. You can put it in front of you and cover all of—that."

"No, I can see it," Bailey chimes in. "You can lay down with it in front of you and kind of hug it. You know? I can direct you on it. It's cool. Brandon! What do you think?"

Her brother looks over from the other side of the studio before giving a silent thumbs-up.

Alejandra's face illuminates, and she begins to nod aggressively. "Get this shit off of me," she mutters as she kicks off the ripped dress and is left in nothing but her heels and underwear. "It's go time, people!"

I'm out numbered. But that isn't what shocks me the most. I don't think I've ever seen Alejandra this eager to put herself out there. Anything for a dream though, right? I watch as Bailey and Greyson help get the guitar over her body. Brandon begins to get the camera together, and now the main focus is on her and her bare skin.

"Hey, can you click on the fan?" Greyson says in my direction.

I look around, wondering if I'm the only one in this area because he's never addressed me before. Since that night we've pretty much stayed out of each other's way. That's how it should be, I guess. Alejandra's the apple of his eye, and I surely have no business getting to know any more of her boyfriends.

"Got ya."

"Hey, Arlissa! Can you turn some of those lights down? I don't think we'll need 'em," Bailey calls out as she steps back so that she's shoulder-to-shoulder with her sibling.

I nod, walk to the other side of the room, and flick the lights off. As I turn back to face everything around me, I slide down against the wall and sit there. I'm invisible now. Bailey and Brandon have their backs turned to me, completely focused on her. I mean, what did I expect? She is the superstar.

Greyson's as close as he can be without getting in the pictures, looking proud as hell. Then there she is. She has her leg wrapped around the instrument now, the light perfectly detailing those toned soccer calves. The fan aids in complementing everything she is, blowing her hair in the opposite direction. Her plump lips and doe eyes innocently bow down to the commands of the camera. She's just so good. She isn't just good with music, the guitar, soccer, cooking, but she can take a picture like nobody's business.

Every task thrown at her she's mastered effortlessly, from men to pressing her vagina up against a cold instrument at the last minute.

I watch. I watch every click that camera makes. I always knew Alejandra had a way of grasping people. I just wasn't aware I was capable of feeling a fraction of that power.

"You look extremely bored."

My thoughts are interrupted by the deep whispers coming from my new friend's mouth. Was I in that much of a trance that I didn't even see her coming?

"What gave it away?"

Bailey smirks before taking a squat beside me. "Oh, I don't know. The fact that you're sitting all the way in this dark-ass corner, maybe."

"Well, shit, you got me."

We giggle quietly.

"You're new to town, right?"

"Pretty much, yeah."

"And how much of this city have you seen?"

"Um, not much. I just kinda got back."

"Yeah? Why'd you leave?"

I wallow in the silence for a moment, unsure how to word this. "Just had to tie up some loose ends at home."

"I get that. I know a cool place I can take you if you don't mind. Whenever you're free, of course. You just seem like shit like this doesn't excite you at all."

I scan the room for a moment, unsure of how to answer this very random proposal. "Uh . . . "

"Don't sweat it if you can't."

"No! I just—yeah. I'm cool with that. I'll give you my number."

"Yeah, I'd like that."

NINETEEN

*W*hat would my mom say?

Wait—that doesn't matter because this isn't a date. Women don't just ask other women out on dates in the middle of the day. They like, meet on Tinder or something, right? Exactly. Yet, why does it feel like someone has their hands wrapped around my stomach, and giving it little squeezes every day?

Wow, Lissa. Look at you assuming. She's probably not even gay. Women are allowed to dress like tomboys, look at 2002 Avril Lavigne!

But what if she is? Well, she is cute. But what would Alejandra say? Lord, I'd have to explain this to everybody.

I'm still going to put on a push-up bra, though. No doubt about that.

I chose the only lace pushup bra I owned and allowed it to lay nicely under my white blouse that I paired with black jeans and nude pumps.

Bailey did a surprisingly good job at keeping in contact with me throughout the week. In between answering texts from her and dodging texts from Christian, I found myself using the power of jealousy to stop me from Googling Xavier again. It's funny, really, how my brain can focus on more than one person at once.

My freshly manicured nails reach for the only purse in my closet that doesn't look worn out, yet. I think I'm getting the hang of this LA thing. I'm leaving an hour early to get to a location that's about thirty minutes away. With every step, the heels of my shoes make an unnecessarily loud clicking noise that only makes me want to get out of the apartment even faster.

I'm almost out of here. I just have to pass Jerrica in the living room and bolt for the front door. I don't mind her, don't get me wrong. But the idea of chatting about something that's literally making me want to nervous-puke isn't on my to-do list.

She's sitting on the floor, crisscross-applesauce, her cheery voice filling the air around us. Her yoga mat is laid out under her as she holds her phone camera at the perfect angle. Maybe if I step quieter I won't catch her attention. She can focus on whoever she's talking to and I can make a run for the door.

A few more steps.

"Lissa! Are you in a rush?" Her words send a shiver throughout my body. Suddenly, the door feels so much farther away.

I swipe my still-drying curls from over my shoulder and shrug. "No. What's up?" I need to stop lying.

Just tell her you don't want to talk right now.

"Actually, I have to head out right now."

"Right!" She rises from the mat effortlessly. "I just want you to meet someone real quick!" Her small hands shove the phone in my face before I can even object, causing me to realize exactly who she wants me to talk to.

Savannah curves her lips, her green eyes saying more than her fake smile could ever translate. "Hey! We were just talking about you." Her words ride from the speakers to my ears, and all I can

do is stand there in shock. She knows me. She fucking knows me, and the last time I checked we are not this friendly.

"Oh?" I start, flashing an equally fake smile to her as well. "I'm Lissa. I honestly haven't heard much about you—honestly."

Jerrica turns the camera to herself. "I'm just glad you're back in town, Sav. I really want you to come over sometime and meet them in person!"

There's a silence.

"I'd love to meet them, especially Arlissa."

I never said my full name. She's toying with me, and Jerrica's too ditzy to realize it. But fine. We'll play that game if that's what she wants. The brunette turns the phone back to me, allowing me to see the sea-witch on the other line.

Her face is different from when I first saw her. She was stunning then, but obviously tired. There were designer bags under her eyes, and her hair was in dire need of a dye job. But, as she sits on the other side of this call, she looks like the model everyone expects her to be. Her lips are way plumper than I remember. In fact, I'm sure if you squinted you could still see the injection marks. Her brows are freshly waxed too. Surprisingly, between being a total bitch and slobbing on Xavier's dick, she found the time to redo her lash extensions as well.

"Well, Savannah. Our door is always open. I do have to go, though. Bye! Tell Xavier I said hi, by the way!" I exclaim, smile intensifying as my bunny teeth made themselves known. "Bye, Jerrica. I'll see you later." I adjust my purse on my shoulder and make my way to the door, not even sticking around for her response.

The drive to the address given to me was hectic. Somehow, the way the other cars chaotically cut me off and beeped their horns with no remorse mirrored exactly what was going on in my head. Saying what I said to Savannah wasn't like me. Well, was it? These days I don't even know anymore. Yet, part of me wants to interact with her more. I like saying petty little things that get under her skin. I like watching that cocky smile fall from her face as she realizes what I said.

That feels good.

As large apartment buildings and Aston Martins begin to fade, I find myself in a quieter part of town. A part of LA I hadn't even experienced yet. There's a Roscoe's Chicken & Waffles with a hoard of people scattered out front—normal people. These people don't have designer bags or undesirable body measurements. I keep driving.

Eventually I pull into a hole in the wall kind of place. The outside is made of brick that's lazily painted a bumblebee yellow. The cars parked next to me are just like mine; old and unappealing. Ugh, Xavier would never invite me to a place like this. Maybe I should turn around.

My curious eyes fall on the glowing sign above the front door: Spoken Nights Café. I squint, trying to make sense of this mysterious address I was sent.

Well, here goes nothing.

My car door slams behind me as I make quick steps to the entrance.

Take a deep breath, and open the damn door.

The inside is dim, wooden chairs and tables scattered all around the place, with the stage being the main focus. The air smells of coffee and baked bread. It isn't packed but it surely isn't empty either. Nervously, I try to find Bailey before she can spot me looking like a lost puppy.

Wait, there she is. Her long hair is in a side part this time, accompanied by a button-up shirt and some jeans. She's sitting alone, scrolling on her phone.

Shit, this might really be a date.

I release another deep breath as I begin to take steps through the café, my shoes announcing me before I even can.

As soon as Bailey catches sight of me she jumps up and pulls out the chair across from her. "Hey, you're here! You should have let me know you were outside. I would have escorted you in."

"Oh! Well, I'm just full of surprises."

Why the hell am I blushing?

Just shut up and sit down, Lissa.

"So, do you know where you are?"

I look around—candles on the tables, people sipping drinks and whispering. No clue. "Red Lobster?"

Bailey lets out a laugh. "You're funny, new girl. Nah, Spoken Nights Café. Cool little place Brandon and I used to come to before he got too booked and busy."

"Why this place?"

"I have a few friends who do poems here all the time, including myself. You write?"

"Not unless I'm getting graded for it."

"Try it. You look like you got some pretty important shit to say."

"Hmm . . . do I? And what do you write about?"

She shrugs. "Everything. I really want to direct a movie one day and work on this screenplay I'm writing right now. But doesn't everyone in this city have big Hollywood dreams?"

"Not everyone."

"You don't?"

"I wake up most days and don't even know why I'm here."

"But you show up—that's enough right there."

"That's the rumor."

We're interrupted by small taps coming from a microphone feed. There's a lady, an older one, standing up there with a grin on her face as she takes in the twenty or so people sitting below her.

"I think it's time for our first poet of the night, don't you guys?" Quiet cheers fill the room. "Well, I'd like to bring up a house favorite—Ms. Bailey King!"

"That's my cue," the woman whispers in my direction before rising from her seat. I clap as she walks on stage, excitement filling my entire being.

I can't put my finger on it, but there's something—something intriguing about her.

"Hey, guys. Hey, Steve, glad you're out of the hospital." The brunette stands there awkwardly as her hands grip the mic. "I wrote something different for you guys tonight. Thought it'd be cool to share, if that's all right." The crowd roars for her like there's a hundred people here.

"Woo-hoo!" I find myself shouting. What can I say? The energy of the crowd is infectious. I adjust my top, trying to ignore the sudden chill in the air.

"I want love.

No, not the kind of love that has the whole world jealous because it looks picture perfect

But in the back of your mind you're wondering if it's worth it

I want the 'tell me your childhood stories' love

The 'tell me why you jump when I come through the door' love."

I sit there, mesmerized as every word her deep voice carries travels from the microphone to my ears.

"I wanted to be insightful and compare the love I want to rose gardens and calm seas

But those aren't the words that are coming to me

I'ma be real with you all

And

Hope you hear me loud and clear

I know the love I'm asking for
Well, I got it all right here."

As Bailey drops her hands to her sides and soaks up the cheers and snaps she's getting from the crowd, I'm stuck. Not for the same reason Alejandra left me stuck, but this is admiration. I feel moved by her words; understood, even. And I can't explain to anyone why even if they paid me, but the feeling grows inside me like ivy on a trellis.

TWENTY

find myself in a checkout line with about four different poetry books in my hand. I've never been much of a reader, honestly. But I could always start, right?

Bailey sent me some of her other spoken word pieces, and each one captivated me more than the last. There is one, though, that really caught my attention. One line that kept me on my toes and sent chills down my spine every time I rewound that performance.

My struggles are minimal because losing you trumps them all
I've never felt a pain like this before
But as for now I'll just drown it out in alcohol

With Bailey, I'm given a different perspective of LA, a more authentic view. I think I spent the last decade running from emotions, running from the idea of feeling things. What's so wrong with feeling things? Addressing them—what am I so scared of?

"So what'd ya get?" Bailey asks as I slide into her passenger seat.

"I got this . . . " My voice trails off as I pull my books out of the bag. "This. This. I thought this one had a cute cover and, well, you recommended this."

The brunette sits back in her seat as we pull out of the mall parking lot. I analyze her, olive skin peeking out of her tattoo-covered arms.

"You heard me?"

"Huh?"

A chuckle leaves her plump lips, flashing pure-cocaine-colored teeth. "Where to next?"

I'm not used to this, being asked where I want to go. Xavier—never mind. But, yeah, this is new. Maybe new is nice.

But could I ever be with a woman? No.

Shut up, Lissa. She just wants to be your friend, nothing more, nothing less.

"Um, hungry?"

"Oh, Benson. Are you asking me on a date? Wow, I never thought this day would come."

I playfully roll my eyes. "Maybe."

There's a silence. Partially because I'm in disbelief of what I'm entertaining, and I'm sure she is too. What am I doing? I can't date women. Well, can I? I've never tried it. She's pretty and sweet, and she introduced me to something I never even considered, but—I don't know.

"Well, where do you wanna go? We've got a ton of good places that I'm sure you haven't been."

"Do any of them serve green smoothies?"

"Oh, hell no. Don't tell me you drink those."

"I don't! I'm just hoping you didn't."

"All right, In-N-Out it is."

As she drives, I skim through my new books while a low hum

coming from the radio fills the silence. Suddenly, a loud gasp escapes Bailey's mouth as she reaches for the radio and turns the volume knob. A song I don't recognize at first parades through the entire vehicle.

"Come on! Tell me you know this song!"

A giggle escapes my lips as I shake my head. "I don't think I do."

"Do-da-do-da-do!" She begins shaking her head as she drives, curls flopping and flipping all over the damn place.

All I can do is laugh and in an attempt to enjoy the moment I begin dancing too. "Wait! I think I know it . . . 'And I need you'?" I mumble, trying to catch up with the beat.

I play the air guitar in my seat as she taps on the steering wheel enthusiastically.

As the song ends, we are both out of breath and laughing until there are tears in our eyes. The energy winds down, and the car follows suit by coming to a complete stop.

"So, tell me three things about yourself. Completely random," Bailey blurts out, the smile still plastered on her face.

"Three?"

"Tres."

"Uh . . . I don't really have any fun facts. You go first. Inspire me."

As the woman pulls into the parking spot, she playfully rolls her eyes. "Okay, okay. Well, I'm currently working on a screenplay, roughly. Brandon and I are twins, if you couldn't tell before. I think twenty-one is a stupid number, and that lesbians are top-tier human beings." A giggle escapes her lips before she turns to me.

"Now, how am I going to compete with that?" I joke. "Well . . . as a kid I used to eat goldfish for breakfast, or else I wouldn't eat. I was on the dance team in elementary school before I had to quit—"

"Why'd you quit?"

"Family issues. Oh, and I've never been in love."

"You're joking!"

"You have?"

"Una vez."

Thank God I let Alejandra teach me Spanish all these years. "What happened?"

"Her parents weren't good people. But, you know, you love and you lose."

"You're not afraid of losing?"

"Not anymore."

"Why not?"

"I don't think the universe would take away anyone I'm not meant to lose. Welcoming lessons is the best thing I've ever decided to do."

Chapter
TWENTY-ONE

Spending every day with Bailey is nice. Sometimes I just sit on her bed and attempt to write shitty poetry while she works on the screenplay she refuses to tell me anything about. I never rush her, though. Whatever she's comfortable with is fine with me.

She's fine with me. Everything about her. The more time I spend with her the more I learn about other people, and somewhere along the line—myself. She pays attention to me, how I bite my nails whenever she asks me about anything past last week. How I lose my mind whenever I see someone litter when the trashcan is literally right there. Bailey learned more about me within our short time together than people who knew me for years ever could.

But our alone time comes to a quick close when there's finally room for me in California.

"Get up, we have a meeting." Alejandra's voice rings from

behind me as I lay sprawled out on the couch like an exhausted puppy.

"Why am I just now hearing of this?" I ask, still refusing to move from the leathery seats as she appears in front of me.

"It's a surprise. Now get up, Lissa!" She tugs at my arm, causing an instant eye roll.

"Well, should I change?" I inquire, clear irritation in my voice. I glance over my ripped jeans and purple blouse.

"No, you look great. Maybe take your hair down?" Jerrica's voice comes from behind me while I rise from the couch. "I know you've been bored not working for Xavier anymore. For whatever reason. But I have a shoot in, like, an hour and my manager will be there. She agreed if I bring you, she'd take a look and we can get some headshots done and all of that right there!"

All of the information crashes into me like a wrecking ball. It's sweet of them to consider me, but I don't even know what you need to do to be a model.

With confusion on my face, I say, "I'm, like, five foot nothing. How can I be anyone's model?"

"I just feel like you need to worry about what you can do, not what you can't do," Alejandra chimes in as she heads over to the door. "Now, can you get your purse so we can go?"

I'm nervous, of course. Who wouldn't be? But I do as I'm told and stomp away to get my purse like a defeated toddler. The idea of modeling never crossed my mind, but honestly nothing ever does. I always thought the career I'd settle into would hit me in the face, and I'd wake up with the drive to do that specific thing. Long story short, nothing like that has ever happened to me. I spent my whole childhood watching my friends say they wanted to be astronauts or princesses and I always said, "I don't know."

What you up to?

I smile as I type a quick reply to the woman on the other line.

Becoming a model apparently, lol. Rather be writing something w/u

LA traffic kicks our ass. We arrive at a stone building with a ton of different rooms inside. Someone's taken the time to place potted plants every few steps, but other than that, there isn't a real consistent theme going on. We pass by one room that's completely blue with four girls and a photographer packed in there. We're directed straight to the biggest room in the building, I'm sure. This room is huge, completely white with immense windows across one of the walls. There's an even larger white backdrop surrounded by enough lights to blind me and one camera stands in the middle.

"Jerrica!" a woman calls out once she catches sight of us entering the room. "And these are your friends?" The older woman gives us all a nod, pushing her overgrown side bangs out of her eye.

"Yes, and this is Arlissa, the one I told you about . . ." Jerrica's voice trails off, her big brown eyes peering in my direction.

For some reason I'm nervous, unsure of how she's going to scrutinize me. Earlier today I didn't know this woman, or that she's looking for models. But I also didn't care for anyone to tell me if I was good enough or not—now I do. The woman takes a step closer to me. Now we're face to face. My feet are comfortably placed in boots with four-inch heels. Hopefully that helps with the height issue. In a matter of moments I care. I care if she rejects me or not. I care if I'm somehow on the cover of a magazine in the next six months.

"Hi," I blurt, waving at the woman practically grilling me right now.

"Hello . . ." Her voice trails off, eyes scanning me from my spiral curls to my black boots.

"I—I don't have any headshots or anything if you need those. I'm sorry about that."

She ignores me, turning to Jerrica. "I like her, good job," she simply says before her attention returns to me.

"I told you she was perfect," Jerrica adds, finishing her sentence with a high five to Alejandra.

"Well, honey. My name is Holly. I'm Jerrica's manager and also . . . her aunt." Giggles from both her and Jerrica fills the air. "I'd be happy to help you with modeling if you'd like." Holly's plump, cherry-red lips form a small smile. "We've been looking for a girl that, you know, had a more innocent, younger look to her. Somehow, that's been hard to find recently, so I'd be glad to have you on board with our agency."

"I . . . " I start, tripping over my words already. "That would be awesome."

"Perfect. We have some things to take care of, but I'll start with your number, email, all that jazz. With that height I can't promise you'd be a runway girl, but there's definitely a spot here for you." Her eyes are encouraging. They make me want to get up and dance. I don't care about being on the runway. I'm just happy to be doing something again.

For the first time in a long time I'm excited about something. The goosebumps on my skin have been awakened by a career I never knew I wanted until this very moment. No one understands the torture of being surrounded by people who know what they live for and you have no clue. I'm just lucky enough to have friends who are tired of me being sprawled across the couch all day. This might not be my true purpose, and I know for sure I won't be the next Naomi Campbell, but this is good enough.

TWENTY-TWO

hen you're not the person signing the dotted lines, stardom seems to come so quick. After deciding to sign my life over to that agency, I assumed I'd be complaining about how heavy my thirty-inch extensions were by next week. That's not how life works. No. But, eventually I did get the call.

My first motherfreaking photo shoot. An odd feeling, really. I'm excited because I can get paid for taking pictures, but the catch is scarier than the reward. I have no idea what I'm walking into. Fun, right? I mean, I know a bit from the emails Holly and I exchanged, but there's still so many question marks in my brain.

The studio where it's all happening is the same one Aly shot her cover at. Thankfully, it's some place familiar, because I have to do this one on my own. For Alejandra's first anything she had me or someone else for support. Now, it's my first shoot, and the only person available to go is Bailey. She offered, but I said no. Maybe I need to spend a little less time with her because when I start daydreaming about my future, she isn't in those feature films. Not yet, at least.

"Arlissa, you're here!" Holly's voice rings through the spacious studio as she forcefully wraps her arms around my bony shoulders. "We need to get you changed and into hair and makeup! Chop-chop!" Everything about her reminds me of a cartoon character. Or that chick from *The Hunger Games* with the gray foundation. From her voluminous hair, the way she sped up when she walked in heels, to the cheeriness in her voice. Everything is just so damn animated.

"Yes, where do I go?" I project my voice, trying to be as energetic as she is.

"This way."

No one told me my hair is getting spray-painted red for this shoot. In fact, it would have been nice to get a twenty-four-hour notice to avoid the shock of the hissing spray can that's way too close to my face. The heavy-handed woman pulls at every spiral, making sure the red completely takes over. My curly hair is now straightened for the first time in forever. But also—fire-hydrant red. The stylist tries to talk to me, ask me how old I am and what I'm doing in LA. But it's hard to reply to these things when you're getting a wine-red color plastered onto your naturally pink lips.

The makeup look for the day consists of a dark, smoky eye that on a regular basis I would never even attempt to pull off. When the manipulation of my face is over, my hair and makeup team leave to go get snacks or check their phones. I'm left in this insanely uncomfortable wooden chair to stare in the mirror that stands in front of me. Mirrors have a rude way of showing you everything. Not just the clutter or the cobweb on the floor behind you that wouldn't have been seen if it wasn't for looking into the enormous rectangle.

Truly, I don't recognize myself. I pull a bit at the pure red that my dark strands have become. My brown eyelids are now stained with this black and glittery silver color that should only be worn during Halloween. I rise from the chair, getting as close to the mirror as I possibly can. Who the hell is looking back at me?

When it comes to the wardrobe, I slip into a black bodysuit that has this immense pink bow on one of the shoulders that won't stop smacking me in the face. My small feet find themselves in these Lady Gaga-style platform heels that are almost impossible to walk in. If anyone asked my opinion, I'd say I look ridiculous. Yet, when I come out of that dressing room, everyone looks at me like a perfectly finished product.

I wobble over to where the sleazy-looking cameraman told me to go. What was once a plain white sheet is now a brick background with rusty old windows. In between the windows is a small blue bike that I'm almost certain they bought from Toys R Us. I'd have to squat down low to get on it if I wanted to. So, I'm praying they don't want me to.

Between the red hair, the edgy eye shadow, and the provocative version of Barbie's ballet costume, this isn't me. Added to that, the blush they put on me did nothing for my skin color. But I guess that's what modeling is about. Transforming into someone else. Making someone else's vision come true. I'm a puppet.

"I like the red!" Holly exclaims as she comes close to me and fluffs my hair. "We should make this a thing for you, no? Add some extensions too because, girl . . . " She pauses, eyes scanning my tresses. "Those curls of yours, but red? Give me *Loud*-era Rihanna. Don't worry, I'll make a hair appointment soon. This could be a look for you."

I shrug, unable to consent to this change before she's already getting out of the way and making calls. I stand there, analyzing the space around me. The draft from the vents above me sends a chill down my spine as smells of oak and dust fill my nose.

"Ready to go?" The deep voice projects in my direction as the cameraman takes large steps toward the camera on the stand.

I nod.

"Great. I'm going to need you to sit on that bike there."

This photographer isn't like Brandon. He's not tall, muscular, or even young. Instead, he's at least a hundred pounds overweight, his stomach spilling out of his grass-stained jeans. And he has a hairline that's so far back there's no reversing that without a transplant. He uses the back of his ears as cigarette holders; my nostrils recognize the smell of smoke and mold radiating off of his body.

I try my hardest to get onto the bike in these ridiculous heels, holding onto the wall in hopes that this stupid toy won't embarrass me. My knees let out a loud crack as I squat down and watch as the whole room shoots sympathetic looks in my direction.

"Today, please. You got it, you're small enough," the photographer mumbles as he watches me struggle with his ice-cold orbs. Holly is clueless to what's going on as she stands by the snack table with her phone pressed to her cheek.

"Sorry," I mumble, eventually plopping down.

No one trained me on how to do this. No one taught me how to pose within the time that I had spent waiting for a shoot—yet here I am.

At his cue I try my best to mimic the poses I've seen on billboards and Instagram.

He sucks his teeth, disappointment clearly written on his face. "No, no. Try to . . . slouch a bit, open your legs wider and spread them out."

I want to mention that if I open my legs, you can see the parts of me that are falling out of this leotard, but I'm sure he knows that. Maybe that's the point. I slowly begin to follow his instructions.

"Like this?" I whisper, my brow furrowing as it's impossible to hide my emotions.

"Wider."

"Okay." I try my hardest to follow his directions because the last thing I want is for him to walk over here and touch my skin with his slimy hands.

"They were right, you do have the perfect face for this, little girl," he whispers as he goes back to shooting. His sentence is accompanied by a sly smile that has the power to make my skin crawl.

I don't trust him, I don't trust where these photos are going. And the more he speaks and directs me the more I want to both cry and vomit at the same time.

"You look . . . No, just no," he mutters before releasing the camera and leaving it on the stand. Before I can process what's going on, object, or even fix myself, he heads over to me with heavy breathing and even heavier steps. He hovers over me as his fingers trace along my cheeks, causing my skin to burn until the rest of my body goes numb. His fingers drop to my neck, then graze across my chest. "Like this," is the last thing I hear while he continues to caress my body.

I black out, going anywhere but here. Instead of the insect-infested walls, and the Family Dollar-sponsored snack table, I'm back on the hill. The same hill Xavier and I went to more than once. The sun is beaming as it's finally risen, shining on my skin and highlighting his perfect features. The atmosphere is warm, like a comforting hug that radiates through everything around us. If only this was real life, if only I could hear him laugh because of me again. I can hear his voice in an echo; it's faint, but it's there. I don't know what's being said, but I know he's smiling while saying it. It's all I need to get through this. A sunrise is constant. I can always depend on that.

Everyone leaves before me. I insist on having it that way by giving them some bullshit excuse that my ride is late when in reality, my car is parked in the lot across the street. My petite fingers aggressively rub the paint-like foundation off my face until

my brown skin turns cherry red. The mascara and eye shadow leave me with raccoon eyes that won't go away without at least two showers. The hair is something I'll have to tackle when I get home, but is there even a point? According to Holly, I better get used to it now.

The mirror and I find ourselves together again. This time I'm near tears and completely alone in an old studio. As I analyze my face closer than I ever have before, the events of the last few weeks play through my mind. Maybe I'd be taken seriously if I looked older.

"Hey, you weren't answering your phone, so I parked and came in. You all right?" The voice comes from my left side as Bailey sneaks up on me, saving the day like she always seems to.

"Shit . . . " I mumble as I try to rub my eyes and look like less of a mess. "I forgot I even told you we'd meet up after this. I'm an idiot."

"Hey, hey . . . " She takes several steps toward me before wrapping one arm over my shoulders. "You okay?"

It's at this moment that I let it out. The tears I'd been hiding that whole shoot come down like a waterfall and don't stop until her sweatshirt is soaked. There isn't a moment in the silence where she asks me to get off her or complains that holding me is beginning to make her arms cramp. She holds me as if she knows how bad I need this. She holds me like she needs it too.

Bailey feels like it's best to cancel what we had planned and just take me straight home to get some rest. My bloodshot eyes are still flooding even as I make quick steps up the stairs and to my front door. After taking several deep breaths, my shaky hands finally attempt to pull my keys out of the purse on my hip. Yet, I'm too late. The door swings open.

Jerrica stands there before me, her normally ecstatic expression quickly replaced with a worried one. "I heard some shuffling at the door, and I assumed it was you." Her voice is light, her focus primarily on my irritated eyes and cheeks. My attempt at stopping my wave of emotions from making themselves known fails. I stand in that dimly lit hallway and bawl my eyes out once again.

Jerrica pulls me into a hug as if she's completing Bailey's charity work for the night. What had been slowly building up over time is now cascading down all at once. Every anxious moment I pushed to the side, every self-sabotaging thought, every disrespectful comment pointed in my direction. Would things be easier if there was a one-way road to everything?

"Your hair is pretty," Jerrica mumbles into my scalp as she slowly rubs my back.

A giggle escapes my lips as I continue to keep my face buried in her chest. "You think I can pull it off?"

"You can pull anything off, babe. It might kill your curl pattern, but . . . it's gorgeous." She releases the hug and guides me into our apartment, shutting the door behind us. "You don't have to explain . . . I've been there. I'm sure every model has." Jerrica's the kind of energy that everyone needs in their life, I think. Not only is her face kind, but she has the personality to back it up.

I remove my jacket, tossing it on the couch as I get used to the warmer temperature in our home. "How am I going to keep doing this?"

"Well, first you have to ask yourself if you want it."

Do I? Or am I just doing it in an attempt to distract myself from the fact that I'm falling behind while simultaneously falling for a woman?

Shit. "Yeah, I do. But I think I need to look older."

"Oh?"

"During that bullshit shoot he called me 'little girl.'"

You can become LA, and everyone in LA will want to be you. I swear it. And no man like that sleazy photographer will ever be close to you again. You'll be untouchable. Just listen to me.

"Um . . . Okay, well." Jerrica's taken aback by my comment as she trails behind me, grabbing my coat to hang it up.

"The whole time they kept commenting on how young I look. And I'm going to keep getting these bullshit bookings until I prove I can be an adult."

Jerrica sighs. "You can always do your makeup differently. But I think you're perfect just the way you are."

"Thank you, but you understand the situation, right? You of all people should get me."

"I mean . . . yeah."

"I'm a black girl who's five foot nothing with hair that everyone wants to straighten. I need to at least do something. Stand out."

"Okay, I hear you."

"I need something more permanent. Holly mentioned getting me hair extensions and keeping this color, though."

"I mean, I agree, I loved my extensions when I got them, and you can do curly or straight. Some lash extensions would do you justice too." She shrugs.

"Okay . . . lash extensions. Any other ideas?"

Jerrica let out a deep sigh. "I had a friend who had the same issue as you. She got lip filler and a brow lift. Some other fillers, maybe. Whatever worked for her. She started getting the kind of shoots she wanted after that. But, listen! I don't think you should let one shoot make you want to manipulate your face. You're beautiful."

"I think that's the best thing I've heard all day. Thank you." I shoot her a small smile before heading to my room.

"Lissa!"

"Night, Jer!"

Chapter
TWENTY-THREE

Personally, I don't think you understand women.
     Personally, I think you don't see us—personally.
     As people
Or someone worthy of a please and a thank you

I crumple up the paper I'm writing on before vigorously shaking my head. "I'll never be as good as you. This is useless."

Bailey smirks, her computer chair swiveling as she parts from her screenplay for a moment. "It's not about being good, my love. It's about what it does for you, remember?"

"I think I'm fine."

"I don't. I think what happened at that shoot really bothered you and you're trying to push forward because for some odd reason you think you have to. Come on, how long did it take you to even go get your car?"

I pout. "How is that relevant?"

"How long?"

"Like a week."

"Exactly. You literally told me you rather hitchhike than go back there."

I giggle before standing and placing a hand on her shoulder. "Come on. Can you just tell me what it's about?"

Both of our eyes are plastered on the screen as she scrolls to the top of the document. "I don't have a title for it just yet, but . . . It's about love and loss. Losing love, whatever."

"What made you want to write about that?"

"I think everyone deserves love no matter what, and there was a time in my life where I realized no matter what, there are going to be people who believe I don't deserve love, even if I do it quietly. Or anyone in my community, for that matter. And then I thought, why should I have to do anything quietly? So I started writing."

"Right."

"I mean, my entire life I've been faced with opposition, but there was one specific time—"

It's time for me to be here for her, like she's been for me since we met. I gently squeeze her shoulder as a signal that it's safe to share this with me. Every vowel she speaks, I listen. I promise her this through my frequency.

"My ex, the one I told you about."

"Yeah."

"Her parents found us in her room once, and they chased me out of their house while throwing anything and everything they could find at me. They didn't even give me a chance to get my clothes on. I was only seventeen, and these were people who called me their daughter, you know, back when they thought I was just the straight best friend. I decided that day I'd never be another secret again."

I stand there for a moment, reeling over the information that I just got. "And you're not angry?"

"No."

I scoff. "You're better than me."

"Well, I'm not ready to hold hands and kumbaya with homophobic-ass people, but what does being angry get me? I love who I love regardless. No one's changing that."

And it's in that moment that I let my guard down, allow myself to feel what my heart wants—what my head is blocking. She's such a gentle, helpful person. Someone who doesn't push me to do anything or feel any way. She doesn't want more than me just being here, and honestly, I feel the same.

Being here, thrown into this environment, wasn't planned. I feel like nothing is in my control but this—this I can control. This situation, these moments, I can decide how far I want to take them. How far I want to take her.

"You're so damn awesome," I mutter before quickly pressing my lips against her forehead.

She doesn't flinch under my touch like I would. She accepts it for what it is, her attention focusing on me for a brief moment before she goes back to the computer screen.

"I do want to tell you something, though," she blurts as I make my way back to where I was previously seated.

Oh no, let me guess . . . She has a wife in Jamaica who's about to finally come back home. "Hm?"

"You don't have to do anything you don't want to do to have a good life in this city, and anyone who makes you feel like you do is fucking insane."

"So I should cancel every consultation appointment I've made so far?"

Bailey spins around in shock. "Consultation for what?"

I shrug, releasing a deep sigh as I realize this is the only part of my sob story I left out. "I don't know . . . I want to look older, and Jerrica said—"

"Jerrica drinks spinach for breakfast and apples for lunch."

154

"Yeah! But she's a damn good model. A black one at that, something I want to be."

"Right. Something you want to be?"

The question stops me in my train of thought. *Yes? Of course I do, there's nothing I want more than to share a stage with my best friend one day.* "Yeah."

"Okay, well . . . Do what you want. I mean, I don't think I have much of an opinion."

"You do!"

"Come here."

I take small steps over to her, placing my hand in hers while she pulls me onto her lap. My entire body shivers as butterflies run rampant in the pit of my stomach. I sit on her thighs like she wants, the warmth of her sweatpants meeting my cheap, paper-thin leggings. This is brand-new territory for me, but if this was a movie, goddammit, I'd pay to see if we end up together in the end. Maybe we can.

In another world I guess we can run away together and live these lives in the countryside and I'd never have to explain anything to anyone. I wouldn't have to answer any questions about why I chose a woman instead of a man. It could all be so easy—in private.

"Are you listening?" she asks with a smile.

I turn to her, our faces just a centimeter apart. "Yes! Yes. I'm listening."

"You're beautiful, and I'm not just saying that because you're with me all the time now. I'm saying it because it's the fucking truth. Whatever you want to do is all you, man. But you're nineteen. You've got time. Don't let one sleazy guy make decisions for you."

"I know . . . "

She sighs. "If you want to do it, go ahead. I'm behind you regardless."

"Really?"

"Really."

"Even if I get botched and look like Kylie Jenner gone wrong?"

She smirks, her nose touching mine now. "I'd stop you way before then, I promise."

Suddenly, my smile is interrupted by her lips on mine. I don't push away, I don't do anything other than melt into her completely. A growing rhythm builds between us as we sit here, hands slowly finding themselves exploring the other. Her kiss isn't like anyone else's—it promises realness, and with it she communicates how genuine it all really is.

There's nothing to worry about—nothing but me.

TWENTY-FOUR

fter I scheduled my consultation it took a lot out of me not to call them and cancel. As of late, I've gone down an endless hole of YouTube videos showing exactly how the process goes. Most of them are filled with doctors shouting themselves out and coupon codes, but the point remains the same. To make a long story short, the idea of a needle going through my upper lip isn't settling well with me.

In a last-ditch effort to take Jerrica's advice, we filled a Sephora basket with expensive makeup (her treat because my broke ass still could never) to help me on my mission. During our shopping, we came across a pink gloss that gave me an unbearable tingly feeling that resulted in my lips being a bit plumper. I tried it, but I'd have to poison my lips more than six times a day to get the look I was going for. On top of that, it burned like hell. Jerrica even taught me how to properly apply lip liner to give the illusion that my lips were bigger. Still not enough. I needed more, so I got some lash extensions. The volume that they give me 24/7 is surely something to get used to. No, seriously, imagine waking up and rubbing the shit out of your eye and now your lashes are slanted to the left. Regardless, they're here to stay. Yet, I feel like my lips still have some catching up to do.

I'm keeping the appointment. Yes, I'm shaking in my boots but I'm keeping the fucking appointment. This will be good for my career, right? Right. Do I even want this career? Yes. Yes, I do.

Yes, you do.

I didn't ask you, Samantha. I can figure this out on my own.

Anyway, first thing first—hair. As I approach a cute little salon with a pink awning, a joyful Holly waves feverishly in my direction.

"Beautiful! Hello! Hello. Gasp, are you wearing makeup?"

"Oh, you noticed?" I coyly reply.

"Yes, keep it up. Now, come on, it's hair time!" She beckons me to follow her as we enter the salon. Everything is either white or marble, from the furniture to the ceiling. The smell of hairspray and blow dryers smack me in the face as I focus on the supermodels getting their ends trimmed and roots yanked by a rose-gold round brush.

"How much is this going to cost?" I whisper to Holly as she signs us in.

"Don't worry about that. It's on me," the woman whispers back, her red lips forming a smile.

"Are you sure?"

"Yes, I'll get paid back when you get better bookings and that percentage of mine increases." The enticing woman sends a wink my way before her attention drifts to a blonde heading toward us.

"Holly! So this is the client you mentioned?" This woman literally has the same energy as my agent. It's almost as if I've been thrown into some sick, overly happy simulation.

"Yes, this is Arlissa."

"Well, I've met a lot of women in this city, but never an Arlissa. How pretty. I'm Ashlyn."

"Thank you. Nice to meet you." I force a smile, giving her a quick wave.

"Still doing what we discussed?" She isn't speaking to me, the main subject of this whole ordeal; she's speaking to Holly.

"Yes, just as we discussed."

Listen. I've gotten my hair done before. It was years ago, but I've still been through it. This is so much worse. Between the awful smell of bleach and me finally getting my turn with the round brush gripping at my roots—I'm over it. I'm one hundred percent certain that my scalp is bleeding. But no one would be able to tell since I'm now a permanent red head. But at least Ashlyn's sweet. In order to distract me from this insane change my strands are undergoing she told me about her pregnant pit bulls. Yes, two. Princess and Diana (interesting name choices) were both impregnated by Buster, the next-door neighbor's dog.

As Ashlyn's veiny hands work on my head, I become acquainted with the growling of my stomach. To make it even worse, I get to watch the sun go down from the store window.

It's constant. You can always look forward to a sunrise or a sunset. You can always depend on it happening even if you're not watching.

The words creep into my mind like a thief in the night. It echoes and reminds me of a man I was once fascinated by.

The store window grants me access to nature's most consistent performance. Shades of purple and orange dance across the sky, reflecting on the buildings across the street from where I'm sitting. Since leaving my position as Xavier's assistant—and whatever else I was—I find myself intentionally avoiding this beautiful sight. He was right. There's something about the consistency of our planet that brings ease to my entire being.

Xavier. I wonder how he's doing. I'm getting better at forcing him out of my mind, or at least I'd like to think so. I'm sure, though. I haven't even Googled him or his relationship status in one whole week. Progress.

Pro tip: Deep thinking can get you through anything. Before I know it, my head suddenly starts feeling like it needs extra energy to hold up. My new Ariel-style locks are loosely curled and perfectly blended. Yet, when I look at myself in the mirror all I can think of is how much better I'm going to look when I get my fillers. I'm just saying, bigger lips would do this volume justice.

"Thank you so much," I say to Holly as I tighten my jacket. "You were right . . . I love it."

"See, sometimes you have to listen to me. I could tell you were scared, though." She giggles, swaying back and forth as she attempts to stay warm as the wind runs through us both.

"Maybe I was. I've just never done anything like this before."

"Hm, well, you're welcome. Speaking of firsts, I never asked for a review of your first big girl shoot. How did you feel when you got home? I mean, you looked pretty happy when I left."

Her words catch me off guard as I freeze. "I . . . I didn't really feel comfortable. It just felt like a joke—I felt like a joke."

"Why didn't you call me? Tell me? I'll always have your back in sucky situations like that. That's kind of what you pay me for."

"I didn't know I could . . . I just want to be seen differently. Taken seriously."

Holly smiles, placing her hand on my shoulder as she takes a step toward me. "Then we can work on that. I promise."

"I'm getting fillers soon. Just my lips, though. I think that'll help."

"Right . . . right." A suspenseful silence fills the space between us, sending a nervous wave through my body. Then, her lips curve into a smile. "I like that! In fact, I want to be at that appointment." Holly waves and walks toward her car. "Text me the details! Love the hair, doll. See you then!"

I'm left there on that boulevard as her car exits my sights.

Alone. The wind tugs at my sore roots; Ashlyn gives me a half smile as she closes up shop. Yet, Holly's words instilled a sense of comfort in me. If my agent is supportive of this choice, then clearly I'm on the right path.

Chapter
TWENTY-FIVE

"**I** circled the prices here for the amount we discussed. You said you'd be doing the payment plan, correct?" The woman on the other side of the desk slides the paper toward me discreetly.

"That's what she wants to do," Holly answers for me.

I'd complain about how she's here and probably shouldn't be, but that isn't how I feel. It's nice to have someone supporting me who doesn't just want to be at my shoots, but things like this as well.

"Yes," I clearly state, retrieving the thin material and stuffing it in my purse.

"And do you have a credit card on you right now that we can put on file?"

"Yes, ma'am." I effortlessly slip my hand into my bag and pull out the shiny piece of plastic.

"Amazing. We can do this today, then, if you'd like. Our next appointment slot is open, actually."

My consultation is supposed to be just that—a consultation. Thirty to forty minutes of me asking if their numbing cream is strong enough. Holly would then chime in to say something stupid like, "Beauty is pain." She'd tell me about the awful things that were extremely unlikely but could still happen. Then, we'd spend the last ten minutes talking about price stuff, and I'd go home and calculate how many doughnuts I could buy with that money instead.

But alas, within the blink of an eye she's guiding me down the hall in her Scooby Doo scrubs while telling me pointless stories about how she used to be a celebrity chef. *Sure, Jan.*

The room we enter is surprisingly warm. The lights that scatter around the ceiling creates a white glow, really selling that hospital feeling. The woman instructs me I don't have to take my makeup off for this and that I can go on about my day as if it never happened—until the swelling kicks in. Except, how can I do that? There's no way I can walk out of this room and not dread the shocking comments Alejandra will make.

Holly takes a seat in the corner, I take mine on the hospital bed that's pushed up against the wall. As I scan the room, I realize there are tons of abstract paintings scattered around the room. One reminds me of a beach, or a sky, or a shark eating a tomato. Another had a burst of colors centered in the middle on a gray background.

"Here you go," the lady states, breaking my train of thought. She hands me a small blue ice pack and walks away. I raise a brow, making eye contact with Holly as she lets out a small chuckle.

"Put it on your lips to numb them."

What the hell? I mouth. Why am I putting ice on my face and not a medical-grade numbing cream? But I listen, especially since I'm the only one here who's new to this. The sting of the ice first meeting my shriveled-up excuse for lips, makes me hesitant at first. But with Holly staring at me from across the room I suck it up and let the ice take over the whole lower half of my face.

The woman enters the room again, this time with a small blue ball. "Here you go. Squeeze this if you feel any anxiety, okay?" Her words are sweet, sincere, making this the first time I feel an ounce of comfort during this process.

"Does it hurt?" I blurt, unable to contain my childlike emotions.

She smiles softly. "It's a pinch. Plus, the actual syringe that I'm using with the filler in it has Lidocaine. So you might feel a few pinches but after that your lips will become number."

"Oh, thank *god*." My shoulders relax as I lean back in the seat. *This should be fine, right?*

We spend a few minutes talking about what I want my lips to look like. I'm too hesitant to really suggest anything past "use as little filler as possible," so Holly speaks for a majority of the conversation.

As she begins to lean my seat back, I swear I'm about to squeeze the ball to death. My knees are practically glued to my chest as I lie there. If I try now, I can make a run for it. Run for the hills—home even.

Holly clears her throat, rising from her seat. "Do you need me to hold your hand?"

I nod, unable to make words as my brain is scattered with a million different thoughts. Within a second she's by my side, her hand holding mine like I'm a seven-year-old getting blood drawn. The dermatologist says a few things as she swipes alcohol pads across my mouth. I give her automated responses.

"Keep your mouth steadily open. And eyes closed." Her voice begins to register as an echo while my mind drifts off.

I'm sent to a place of peace, colors, and positivity. I think about the two things that are always constant—sunrises and sunsets.

164

The pinch I feel isn't constant, and my nervousness isn't, either. All of these things will pass soon. I concentrate on something I can depend on. And for once, I fully understand why Xavier took these things so seriously. Any time I've found myself in any minor discomfort, I think of that. I think of the swirling blend of shades of orange. And it works, it fucking works.

"All right. bottom now!" she exclaims.

"Huh?" I question, feeling like only three seconds had passed.

"We're going to do your bottom lip, and then you're all done!"

"It already looks great," Holly adds.

I nod, closing my eyes again. The anxiety I had felt just a few minutes before has passed. I'm in control of my feelings and something like this isn't that big of a deal.

When it's all said and done, she massages my lips. A sigh of relief escapes my newly plumped lips. All that stabbing is over. At least for the next six months.

Holly releases my hand and takes a step back with a huge smiles. "I'm amazed at how good of a call this was. Holly, you've done it again!"

"Um . . . it was my idea?" I whisper as the doctor hands me a small mirror.

Holly says something else, but it doesn't fully get to me. All the attention I have is placed on the girl in my reflection. Her hair, fiery red and thick, resting behind a black headband. Her lashes, coated in another layer of false lashes that curl perfectly. Her lips, freshly plumped and perfectly pink. I flash a smile, my bunny teeth finally looking like they belong in my mouth accompanied by my newfound features.

I'm a new Arlissa now.

"I'm home!" I sing, closing the apartment door behind me. Both Alejandra and Jerrica's heads pop up from the couch. Just them. I let out a sigh of relief; no Greyson.

"Oh. My. Fucking. God." Alejandra's voice fills the spacious area as she jumps over the couch and meets me face-to-face. "Who the hell said you could go get your lips done without me?"

I let out a laugh. "I—I assumed you'd be busy."

She playfully swats me on the arm. "I'm never too busy for you, dumbass. But you look so damn good!" She pouts, her eyes scanning my face from every angle.

"Hey," I start, taking notes of the brown highlights in Aly's usually dark hair. "You dyed it."

She shrugs, twirling the strands. "Greyson thought it would be a good look for me. You like?"

"I do."

"You look really nice, Lissa. I mean, minus the obvious bruising coming in," Jerrica chimes in before giving me a quick side hug.

"Thanks, guys."

"LA really made a model out of you, huh?" Aly adds as she takes a sip from the Starbucks cup in her hand.

"I just—wanted something fresh. I turn twenty soon! Think of this as an early birthday gift."

"Shit, you're right," Aly says in between sips.

"What are we gonna do for it?" Jerrica inquires.

"Something will come up, I'm sure."

TWENTY-SIX

So I got a brow lift! Sue me. I'm a couple thousand dollars in debt over it; might've had to convince my mom I'm low on rent to cover the rest of the cost, but I fucking did it. It's fine. This will all pay off when I have ten million Instagram followers and I'm sipping Jamba Juice with the Hadids. Listen, my birthday is soon, and I have every right to treat myself. Talk about sculpted. I am giving bone structure realness, honey. All healed and ready to go.

With a duffel bag on my hip, I happily make my way out of the elevator. As I approach the door, the smell of baked goods smack my senses. The hint of cinnamon reminds me of a time when my family still had our Sunday dinners.

In a desperate attempt to push away my thoughts, I ring our obnoxious doorbell. I can hear some muffled words and then silence again. I wait, wondering if I should get my keys out anyway. Alas, the sound of locks clicking fills my ears and a smile creeps across my face. The huge wooden door swings open to reveal someone who isn't Jerrica or Alejandra. No. Not even Greyson. I stand back in disbelief as the tall blonde throws a cocky smile in my direction.

"You're a little late for dinner, but you made it for dessert." The voice is smooth and sultry, almost exactly how I remember it.

"What are you doing here, Savannah?" I question, my brown eyes landing on her green ones.

"For dinner, silly! I kind of just said that," she says in a high-pitched tone. Her smile expands, causing my stomach to turn.

"Arlissa, you're here! And you finally get to meet Savannah!" Jerrica's happier than ever as she widens the door and allows me to slip in.

I gently place my duffel bag in a nearby closet while also hanging up my jacket. There's no time to put things in my room when I have to keep an eye on Savannah at all times. My eyes quickly scan the area. Alejandra is nowhere to be found, so I'm stuck here with the devil herself and her lap dog. Amazing.

"I think the banana bread is almost done." Savannah heads over to *my* kitchen and opens *my* oven. Lord, don't tell me she's the one responsible for that scrumptious cinnamon scent.

"Shit, it's hot," she mumbles, kissing her ring finger. *No shit, dummy.*

It's then that I notice a gorgeous diamond on it.

"I'll help!" Jerrica squeals.

"No, I'll help her! You should find a movie for us." I put a strand of hair that's escaped my ponytail behind my ear before taking confident steps toward her. "Aw, you hurt yourself," I mock in a low tone once I reach the blonde. Swiftly, I grab a rag and step in front of her, removing the oven's contents myself.

"Oh, as long as my ring is fine, I'm great," she whispers back as her eyes focus on me placing the dessert on the counter.

"I'm sure you could buy it again if you wanted."

"I could!" Her tone is low still but sharp. "But then, Xavier would kill me considering it was a 'welcome home' gift."

That name has the power to bring me to my knees. Who knows why? I haven't spoken to him in forever. Plus, I'm sort of with someone now. Nothing she's saying should bother me. Just remain cool, that's all I can do.

"Speaking of home, you should finish painting that room of yours. That 'unfinished' look isn't too cute." I watch as her expression shifts, her brows raising in disbelief. I can guess what she's thinking, and maybe I went too far. Anyone with eyes knows that room was supposed to be a nursery. But if she's going to keep poking at me, then I'm going to bite back.

"You were in my home?"

Whoops. Had no idea she didn't know that part.

"I was in a lot of things while you were gone," I clearly state, body shaking due to the adrenaline rush that this conversation delivered.

"You wouldn't be the first. So please don't feel special. But can I ask how far you thought you'd get with my fiancé?" An empty laugh escapes her lips as she flips her freshly toned tresses over her shoulder and begins cutting the bread in slices. "Let me tell you, Jerrica. You were right, she's so funny!" she calls out.

My blood is boiling. I want to scream but for Jerrica's sake I have to keep it cool. This is her childhood friend, and I'm just someone she met a few months ago.

Savannah gets two pieces of bread onto plates and makes her way to the living room. Before brushing past me, she comes to a sudden stop. The blonde leans down to my ear and speaks in a soft tone. "Nice face, by the way."

My body is frozen. The old Lissa is holding me captive. I stand in that kitchen and wait until she's completely out of my sights to press play again. I need to shake it off. The night is still young, and if this is the game she wants to play, then so be it. The old me would have been drowning in an ocean of fiery tears right now, but this Arlissa turns fear into motivation.

I watched these movies before with my sister; I know how the girl on the losing team is supposed to turn it all around. She's supposed to tap into this inner strength she doesn't know she has and—win. I have to win.

"You didn't get any bread, Lissa?" my friend inquires.

"No, no. I really wanted to but Bailey and I got food earlier."

"Oh, come on. You gotta have dessert!" Jerrica pushes.

"We got cupcakes too! But maybe tomorrow, promise," I reply with a cheap grin.

"Okay, cool. Savannah makes the best banana bread, and I remember you saying you liked it."

Savannah chimes in, "She's right, I am quite the wizard in the kitchen."

"I wouldn't put it past you."

"But, yeah, Sav. You didn't finish the story you were telling me earlier."

"Oh!" The excitement on Savannah's face becomes apparent as she puts her plate down. "Right, right. So . . . Xavier and I were absolutely dating while I was away. I guess there was some confusion about that. Whatever. He was telling me that there was this girl who was so fucking thirsty over him. He kept throwing her pity invites and shit. But she was so fucking obsessed with him. She would do weird shit like text him at six a.m., and get this! She ambushed me at my rehab center." Her eyes shoot right to me when those words leave her huge lips. My anxiety raises as I try to process that the girl she's talking about is right in front of her.

"Are you serious? That's fucking sick."

Thanks Jerrica, I'll remember that when Christmas comes around. But that isn't how it happened at all.

"Right? And she's asking me all these questions about Xavier, and I'm like, dude! He doesn't fucking want you. So, I come home to everyone saying my baby cheated on me, but we both know that would never happen." She pauses, a sly smile sneaking up on her face. "He got rid of her, though. Finally told her he had a girlfriend, and she ran home crying."

"You should have gotten a restraining order."

Really, Jerrica?

"Shit, I still can," the blonde replies with a shrug.

"Well, I know it's all worth it. I mean, look at that rock on your hand."

No. No. No. She is not going to sit here and change my narrative like that. But what can I do? No one knew about Xavier and me. Or so I assumed. Was there even an Xavier and me? Is this his version of what had happened? I sit there, wanting my body to melt into the couch cushions as she waves her diamond around so that it reflects perfectly in the light.

"You okay, love?" Savannah questions, both her and Jerrica's eyes focusing on me.

I shake my head. "I'm great. I just . . . I don't think that food Bailey and I had is settling well with me." In reality I'm fucking starving right now, and that bread still smells so good.

"Is Bailey your girlfriend? That's so fucking cute."

Spare me. "No, I don't—I don't date women."

Jerrica furrows her brow. "Really?"

Fuck. "Yeah, we're just good friends. I don't think I'd ever see her that way."

"Oh."

Savannah winces. "Ouch."

I rise from the cushions, gripping my stomach like it's actually in pain. "Anyways, I need to rest."

Once I'm alone the thoughts and the emotions that come with them are overbearing. Old Lissa, new Lissa—they're both the same. They both got beaten by someone who had obviously been doing this to people for a very long time. But why me? I

haven't felt this small in weeks. The heaviness that weighs on my entire being is almost equal to the way I felt during my first shoot. The ultimate Barbie doll of Hollywood has gotten under my skin, and I can't let it happen again.

No one in this god-awful city is going to run me home for a second time. So I'll stay here tonight. I'll crawl into a ball, and I'll bawl my eyes out if that's what it takes.

But you will win this war.

TWENTY-SEVEN

I run my fingernails gently through my currently wavy hair. The wind tries it's best to take my vibrant strands with it; at the rate it's blowing, it just might.

"Is this your first outdoor shoot?" Brandon's friend asks as he adjusts the shirt on my body to his liking.

"That obvious, huh?" I reply with a smile, still struggling to keep my hair in one place.

"Kind of. But Bailey talks so highly of you, I'm sure you'll give me exactly what I need."

"You guys ready?" Brandon calls.

Here I am, standing with my toes in the sand because the girl I may or may not be with hooked me up with her brother and his friend.

"Yup," his friend mutters as he steps back and shoots a thumbs-up.

Before I can even reply, I catch sight of the main person on my mind since I got here. She's hopping out of her car with what I can only assume is a dozen donuts.

"Dope. You ready?" Brandon's eyes shoot to me, sunrays perfectly falling over his above-average, masculine figure. His curly black hair is now resting a bit over his forehead. He looks exactly like Bailey, but—a dude.

I nod, hands tucked into my boyfriend jeans. The rushing water occasionally meets my ankles with a sting, but a refreshing one. My eyes dart between Bailey and Brandon, two stunning people. Is that bad? That I find him as attractive as her? Maybe.

Effortlessly, my body begins to flow into several poses. I'm getting the hang of this modeling thing, if I do say so myself. I owe a lot of my practice to Jerrica for taking the time to give me pointers, though. Yet, a lot of it comes from my newfound confidence. I feel liberated for once, like I can do whatever the hell I want to. This new look gives me more than a slight advantage in a modeling career I already hold the short end of the stick for. My eyes are finally open.

I, Arlissa Kimber Benson, am capable of so much more than I'm giving myself credit for. I can do whatever the fuck I want. And I haven't gotten a smart comment from Samantha in a while—so I must be keeping her entertained.

The shoot consists of me changing into several shirts and even wearing a visor or two. It's quick; not much is expected from someone who's only offering me a hundred bucks. But I can't keep my eyes off Bailey, who's seated by Brandon with her eyes glued on me. I wonder how she thinks of me, or if she does at all. Is it obsessive like how I think of her?

"Can I see my pics?" My small feet attempt to carry me, trucking their way through the sand.

"Yeah, sure." Brandon begins to click some buttons on his camera as he waits for me to get to his side.

"Ay, Brandon, send me those when they're edited. Thanks

again, bro. But I gotta head out." Brandon's friend packs his spare clothing up in a rush. "Thanks as well, Arlissa! Keep the shirt!"

I nod in response and place my hand on Brandon's shoulder. "So let me see!"

"Yeah, let her see!" Bailey's voice sings from behind me as her touch sends a rhythm down my back.

I squirm, obvious enough for her to feel but lowkey enough for it not to embarrass her. When I look back at her, she looks confused, but doesn't say a word as she takes two steps away from me.

"Here, here," he replies with a laugh before clicking through the pictures. I look down at the images on the camera. They're more body-focused, but that isn't what I care about.

"Can you zoom in on the face?" I ask in a desperate attempt to let the awkwardness between her and I pass. "I don't know . . . "

"You don't like it?"

"No, it's a good picture. I just . . . don't think I really like my face. I don't know." I shrug.

Bailey chimes in again. "You're beautiful, and they look great."

I wince again, noticing all the people who are suddenly on this beach. "Thanks."

"Well, I'll send this to you. I guess you guys want some alone time, so I'll see you later." As Brandon begins to pack up, I awkwardly shuffle in the sand. *Please don't leave, then I'll have to explain myself.*

Before I know it, Brandon is in his car and Bailey has a burning question bubbling up in her throat for me.

"You okay?"

"Huh?"

"I mean, I just . . . You seem like you don't want me to touch you, so I just . . . thought I'd ask. Is it my brother?"

I feverishly shake my head before looking around and

grabbing her hand. "Come on, no! I'm just hot, and I've been standing in the sun all day . . . I'm just gross." I lean in, giving her a quick peck on the cheek.

"You sure?"

I nod. "Can we go back to your place now?"

"I'm fine wherever you want to be."

And maybe that's the issue.

TWENTY-EIGHT

"L . . . O . . . R . . . All done." Greyson springs up from the hardwood floor as he closes the cap on the marker. The freshly decorated banner lays there declaring: LIFE IN COLOR. Alejandra's dream—it's all coming true.

"It's done?" the Latina calls out as she takes struggle steps out of the bathroom in her six-inch heels.

Greyson smiles, his eyes glued to her. "It's done. Hey, Jerrica, can you help me hang this up?"

He's dressed simply, a white T-shirt and black jeans. The only thing out of the ordinary are his designer shoes that cost our rent money and his blinding chains and watch. As for Alejandra, she matches him with a fitted white dress and neon green pumps gift- ed by him. This is a celebration of Alejandra's first official proj- ect; it all has to be perfect.

I'm in charge of the cake. Thankfully, Jerrica told me about this small bakery down the street from our apartment complex.

Conflicted, I wasn't sure what to write on the cake. A simple "happy birthday" wasn't an option considering the occasion. But, when the baker told me she could put images on the cake it finally came to me. I decided to take an outtake from the EP shoot and place that on the cake with LIFE IN COLOR written beneath it.

Aly steps out of the bathroom again. "Hey, can you help curl this piece of my hair?"

"Me?" I inquire, feeling used to Greyson doing everything for her these days.

"Yes, you!" she says as she pulls on the straight strand of hair.

I nod, pulling the strapless dress over my chest.

"Shut the door."

Confused, I do what she asks before quickly reaching for the curling iron. "Is everything okay?"

"I want to say thank you," Aly says, looking at me through the reflection in the mirror.

My small fingers pick up her hair and place it on the curling iron barrel. "What did I do?"

"You were here. More than anyone else was, and I know it's been . . . a hell of a ride. I know you didn't want to be around me for some time. But . . . you came back. And that means more to me than anything else, you know? When you were gone, I witnessed what this life could be for me, and it was beautiful, but it was so fucking scary without you. You complete the vision for me, Lissa. You always have. Not Christian, not the damn fans, but . . . knowing I have you in my corner. That made it worth it. So . . . " Aly waits for me to pull her hair from the curling iron before completely turning to me. "There's a song on the EP that I didn't let you hear. It's for you, and you'll hear it tonight."

I try my hardest to keep my cool. My new makeup routine is forty minutes long now, and I do not have the time to redo it. I grab a bit of toilet paper and begin patting under my eyes. I cry for the friendship I missed. I cry for the decisions I made while she was gone. I don't deserve the song after what I did with Christian. Maybe I don't even deserve her.

"Say something!" she exclaims, playfully swatting me in the arm.

"I'm trying!" I whine back, a low giggle escaping my mouth. "Thank you. Just thank you, and I love you, and . . . if it wasn't for you I wouldn't be standing here right now, either, so . . . Thank you." Crumpling up the tissue in my fist, I wrap my arms around the taller woman and pull her into a hug.

Sometimes I dwell too long on the relationship I lost, a relationship I have yet to recover from losing. And because of that, it makes it hard to see what I have. I'll never replace Samantha, but I have a sister right here. A sister that I'm sure my angel from up above sent me.

Sisterhood is magical. The best part about it is that there's no direct way to go about treating it. There's no rule book on how to keep these relationships. Sometimes your sisters come from the same womb as you, but other times you meet because you went to the same school. The most important part is that you grow together, you get to know the ins and outs of each other. Lord knows I wouldn't be me without her.

Sometimes we die of laughter at memes or during really inappropriate moments in movies. Eventually we run out of breath and lie there in silence to recover. Never is there a time where I see my life without her either.

Sometimes I want to cut her hair off because she won't stop flipping it and hitting me in the face. Most times, I want to push her to be a better version of herself. And, well, most times she doesn't listen to me. But all the time, I love her.

"I just feel like you're fucking cheating!"

A roar of laughter comes from the island in the kitchen that we repurposed to play beer pong. Well, vodka pong, because Alejandra is not allowing beer through the front door. The music is on full blast, and I'm almost certain our apartment has managed to fit in over a hundred people. I don't know these people. Alejandra doesn't, either, but in order to have a successful party we left Greyson in charge of the guest list.

I lift the red Solo cup to my lips with one hand and use the other to fan my body that is two seconds away from being drenched in sweat. Pro tip: Don't wear latex to a house party with one AC.

"I'm gonna go get some air," I whisper-yell in Jerrica's ear before stepping away from the crowd. The brunette nods as she downs another full cup of alcohol. It's a task for my tipsy self to push through the ocean of wasted young adults. Once I finally reach the front door, the rush of fresh air smacks my moist skin immediately. Eyes closed, I take a deep breath and shut the door behind me.

"Well, talk about timing."

The voice startles me. It's deep, familiar, but a tone I haven't heard in a while. My eyelids slowly open to a tall figure stepping out of the elevator.

"I brought a gift," he adds, showcasing the small gift bag in his hand. It feels as if I've seen a ghost, yet I don't want to run from it.

"Xavier?" I blurt, feverishly blinking to see if the alcohol had officially fucked with my head and vision.

"In the flesh." He takes cautious steps toward me.

All I can do is stare. Did he get more muscular? Or is it just the leather jacket? Must be the jacket. He looks taller now, but I don't know how much taller you can get if you're already six-two. It has to be the hair. The worst part about it all is that he looks really fucking good.

180

"You look—"

"Different?"

He's so close now that I can effortlessly smell that obnoxious cologne he always used to wear. "No, good."

"Oh . . . " My eyes make contact with his scruff-covered jaw that immediately makes me want to melt.

But Bailey, fuck . . . Bailey. Wait . . . We're just friends, right? Right.

"How are you? Haven't heard from you since—"

It's at this moment that it all comes back to my foggy brain. Savannah, the blogs, the woman whose sheets I had been sleeping in, what was said to me, what I saw, what I read. It all comes back in waves and it dawns on me that he doesn't deserve shit.

"You don't care how I am." I step aside from the box that he and the front door put me in.

A look of confusion emerges on his face. He scoffs. "I don't know where you got that idea. You're the one who fucking vanished."

"Oh, fuck you Xavier."

"Don't threaten me with a good time."

"Go away."

"Look, I'm here for an honorable reason."

"I don't care."

He rolls his eyes. "Remember that gala we RSVPd for? Well, mi amor, that's next weekend, so I thought I'd give you an in-person reminder and let you know there will be an after party as well."

"Why are you telling me this?"

"Because you're my plus-one, remember? I'll see you there, and . . . for the sake of the flashy cameras and the nauseating questions, can you not show up like you hate me?"

"Does Savannah not exist anymore?" I slur.

He laughs, almost like he's mocking me for even mentioning

the other woman. "It'll be good press for that little modeling thing you have going on. I'm doing you a favor."

"I think I have my career taken care of."

"I'm sure, Lissa." He places a hand on the door knob, pushing it open a bit. "I'm going to go say hi to some friends and give this to Aly. I'll see you there, short stack."

Before I can even muster up a response, he's taken in by the loud music and crowds of people. When the door shuts, I hear a roar of gratitude toward him showing his stupid face.

Xavier is everyone's favorite. Shit, he's still my favorite. But he shouldn't be. He doesn't deserve to be.

Chapter
TWENTY-NINE

on't get out of bed too fast or your head just might explode. Get-up-as-slow-as-possible.

I trek my swollen feet through the hall, one eye open in a desperate attempt to get some Advil. It feels as if the world is moving in slow motion, but if I focus hard enough I'll eventually make it there. Once I turn the corner and enter the disastrous space we call a kitchen, someone already beat me to it. Not only does Jerrica still have her dress on from last night, her hair and makeup are an absolute mess.

"We have three more," she grunts as she slides the bottle across the island. Her eyes are heavy, as if she's fighting to keep them open. If she looks this bad, how the hell do I look?

"Never again." I shake out two of the three pills and dry swallow them. I don't care to get water, I have no time to. I just need the pain to stop.

Jerrica and I slowly turn our heads to see Alejandra, who literally looks like she just got hit by a bus. "I think Greyson's dead."

"I am not burying a body today," Jerrica groans, taking a seat on the cold marble floor.

Aly sighs. "Can I see those?"

"Only one left," I simply say before tossing the bottle.

"Goddammit," she whines. "I swear I was born to suffer."

"A literal drama queen," Jerrica adds.

Before adjusting her ripped dress, Alejandra grabs a glass for water. "I will say, I had a lot of fucking fun."

"How many times do you curse in a day?" Jerrica inquires, leaning her head against the wall.

"You'll get a way lower number if you ask her how many times she curses in a minute," I add jokingly.

Alejandra rolls her eyes. "Bitches."

"I had the weirdest dream."

Jerrica raises a brow. "What happened?"

"Xavier showed up."

Alejandra laughs. "That wasn't a dream, girl."

I take a deep breath, replaying in my mind what I knew felt too real to begin with. So it all really happened. Which means, I do have to go to this stupid gala.

"Then I have an itsy-bitsy problem."

Look, I spent the last few months running myself wild over this whole situation with Xavier—completely alone. Maybe it's time to open my fucking mouth.

Aly raises a brow before taking a seat next to me. "Right."

"I'm scared," Jerrica whispers as she rises from the floor and takes a seat as well. "Are you and Bailey okay?"

"Bailey?" Alejandra exclaims. "Are you seeing that woman and didn't tell me?"

"No!"

"She is."

"I'm really not. She's just a friend, I promise, Alejandra."

"For some reason I don't believe you." Her tone is softer, almost like she's hurt. But I don't have the time to decode this.

"Anyways, it's Xavier."

The confusion on both Alejandra and Jerrica's face is clear as day. "Xavier?"

"I wasn't just working for Xavier. I didn't know he had a girlfriend and . . . I was just lonely and bored, I guess. And when he offered me the job, we were just spending a ton of time together." I avoid eye contact with the girls, trying not to let their expressions deter me from my truth. "We kissed like . . . once? Twice? I don't know, and I thought things were going somewhere until he left me in his house to go play on a beach with some girl."

"There's a special seat in hell for you because of how long it took you to tell me this," Alejandra snaps.

"Excuse me! I didn't know! Why didn't you tell me before I invited Savannah over?" Jerrica pauses, a focused look emerging on her face.

"I don't know . . . I just didn't think shit would come bite me in the ass like it has been."

"Or like your lesbian lover has been," Alejandra mutters.

"I do not like her!"

"This is fucking ridiculous," Jerrica starts. "Xavier and I need to have a talk."

"Wait, why?"

"You're like the millionth friend I have that he's attempted to cheat on Savannah with. It's outrageous at this point. She doesn't deserve that, and neither do you." Jerrica isn't wrong, but it's just another reminder that I'm not special. Plus, I'm sure Savannah *does* deserve that.

"Okay, but what's the problem? You guys haven't spoken in ages, and you're riding the rainbow train, right?"

Clearly, this is bothering Alejandra more than I assumed from the first few comments. But again, no time to address her dramatics.

"Right, so. When we were working together I had to RSVP him for this gala next weekend, and he told me to make myself his plus-one. So now, I kind of have to go, and he said something about it benefiting my modeling or whatever the fuck."

Aly interrupts. "I mean, he's not wrong. The PR would be golden."

"At the cost of what? Her reputation? Savannah?" Jerrica argues.

Jesus Christ, I don't give a damn about that woman, Jerrica.

"If he cared about her he would have asked her to go," Alejandra rebuttals.

"Worst part about it is that it's Saturday, the day before my birthday," I add in.

"Crap," is all Jerrica can say now.

"I have an idea! I think Amy's going to that thing. I can beg her for a seat. Tell her I'll walk the carpet with you. Therefore, the most you have to do is sit with Xavier, but I'll be there too. All bases covered." Alejandra's eyes sparkle when she gets a new idea. Even hungover it's adorable.

"I still don't like this," Jerrica whines.

"Two words: Dress. Shopping. I won't let this douchebag ruin your birthday weekend." Alejandra finishes off her water and places the cup back down. "Now, I have a man to go bother until he wakes up." She flashes a smile at us both before skipping down the hall.

Jerrica rises from her seat. "Be careful, okay?"

I sit there, my brain scanning all the information of the past few days, looking for reasons to keep my ass home. There are a million; one being that I can't even afford a new dress right now.

186

But I want to go. I want so badly to feel his energy again since last night and every night before that. The man is magnetic, powerful, enticing. And if I can get five more seconds with him, I'll take it.

THIRTY

My pre-birthday prep consisted of redoing my roots, tightening my extensions, filling in my lashes, and painting my nails. Never in my life did I think I'd be walking a red carpet just hours before I turned twenty. But what was even more mysterious was the big black box that was left on my doorstep with my name on it. The immense rectangle held the black dress and shoes I managed to slide myself into just a few minutes ago.

"This way girls!"

"Smile."

"No this way!"

"Chin up, please."

"Move your arms out of the way!"

"I'm going to blow a fucking fuse," Alejandra whispers in my ear before giving in to the photographers instructions.

Truthfully, I'm shaking. The dress looks amazing on me,

there's no doubt about that. The faux feathers that ruffle over my upper body make everything come together. Plus, we paid actual professionals to do our hair and makeup for once. But, as I stand on that carpet, body shivering and all, I'm barely prepared for any of this. And the sheer thought of being here is enough to diagnose me with imposter syndrome. Who am I? How did I even get here? Because it definitely wasn't all the screaming I did until my lungs gave out that did it for me.

My heels carry me every step of the way as I hold onto Alejandra for dear life. She's wearing a fitted gold gown borrowed from Amy's closet. And even though it's someone else's, it fits like it was tailored with her body in mind. The golden goddess floats down the red carpet, capturing every stranger's eye, her features highlighted by the lights instead of drowning in them. And I, on the other hand, am trying to keep my pounding heart in my chest.

God, I'd do anything to run into the bathroom and send Bailey an SOS text right now. But I can't, because depending on her would make her think she could depend on me.

"Hey, ladies, could you come answer a few questions?" a woman a few steps away from us asks. She has a microphone in her hand and the camera that was once on her is now focused on us. Aly and I give each other a quick look before taking in-sync steps forward.

"Yes, always," Alejandra says with a smile, her hand now squeezing the life out of mine.

"You're Aly, the woman who won the Instagram contest for *the* Amy Montana. How did that feel?"

"Oh, Lord. I mean, I felt fucking grateful. I feel fucking grateful. Shit, sorry. I did not mean to cuss. Can I start over?"

"It's okay. Be you, girl!"

"This is all I've ever wanted, and she's been such an amazing mentor. I'm just grateful. Yeah." Alejandra is a natural.

Even when she's tripping over her words and stumbling over her thoughts as if this is a middle school spelling bee, she's a natural.

"What can we expect from you?"

"We have so much music that we're working on, I'm just shaking because I want to release it all already!"

They continue to go on and on about what she's wearing and why she chose to wear it. I stand there awkwardly as they speak. In a desperate attempt not to wear it on my face, I force a smile the whole time. Maybe the time will go by faster if I come up with a poem.

There's no comfort in knowing that tomorrow will be like today
Uh . . .

"Well, there you are, little red." The voice creeps up behind me, and instantly I feel two strong hands on my bare shoulders.

"Oh my gosh! It's Xavier Amari and . . . his date?" The woman speaks into the camera.

Great, it takes him to show up for you to notice that I've been standing here the whole time.

Aly shoots a look of concern in my direction. I know, the whole point is to walk the carpet with her and avoid a situation like this. Yet here he is crashing the party. But honestly? I'm grateful. He's the one person who's capable of making me feel seen.

"What's your name?"

Speak, idiot.

I put on my fakest smile as I lean over to the microphone. "Arlissa Benson," I simply say.

"And what are you wearing tonight?"

"Honestly, I have no idea. Actually, you can ask Xavier!" I look up at the man who clearly left that box at my front door. His eyes make it obvious that I caught him off guard, but he quickly recovers from it by flashing a sparkling smile.

"We're both wearing Valentino tonight." His voice is smooth, and as it travels over me I can already smell the traces of vodka escaping from his breath. "Doesn't it bring out her hair?" He casually moves a loose strand from my face.

"I don't know how to do this," I gulp, whispering for only Xavier to hear.

"Be cool. Just act like this isn't your first rodeo."

With shivers sent down my spine, his tone alone has stunned me into silence. So, I just keep smiling.

"Great! Thank you for having us. We better get to our seats now," Alejandra interrupts, keeping a strong hold on my hand as we walk away. Xavier walks with us, staying close for reasons I'm sure are related to making himself look good.

When we arrive inside the venue, the lights are dimmed, and everything is beautifully decorated. Lilac drapes fall from the ceiling, chandeliers accompanying them and reflecting the color throughout the entire room. There's a chill, a clear sign the AC is up a bit too high, but I can't even focus on freezing when I'm still shaking to my knees. My eyes immediately land on what I would describe as a high-end snack table. There's some chopped fruit, a chocolate fountain, and a few cheese cubes. God, my glasses would have been great to have right now. I don't have much of a chance to take everything in before both Xavier and I are being tugged into a corner.

"What the hell?" Alejandra whispers, trying not to catch the attention of the other people around.

"What?" Xavier nonchalantly answers.

Aly's eyes focus on me, waiting for a response like a cop during interrogation. There's nothing to say.

"You two clearly have shit to work out. I'm going to find my fucking seat." The Latina rolls her eyes and hikes up her dress a bit. I watch as she storms off, still unable to make any words. I don't know exactly why she had such a harsh reaction to Xavier. If anything, that should have been my reaction.

"Tough crowd, " he mumbles, that cocky grin still taunting me.

Finally, I speak in a low tone. "Why did you do that?"

"I was expecting more of a, 'You look great, Xavier. Thanks for getting me a dress, Xavier' response. You know, gratitude. Something you're not too good at." He pauses, turning to wave at some celebrities passing by before putting his attention on me again. Honestly, he does look great. His hair is gelled back like he was late for a *Grease* audition. His nails are freshly manicured, and his suit is perfectly pressed. "What did I do that was so bad, Arlissa?"

"I just—I don't want to hurt Bailey. That's why I didn't even want to come to this shit." The truth spills out of my mouth like an overflowing sink.

He makes a "shh" sound. "First of all, don't say that too loud. We're at a charity event. No one wants to be at these things. Second of all, I don't know who the fuck that is, so . . . I don't care."

I roll my eyes. "You're just a dick, and I am so over it."

"Well, maybe I would know who this Bailey person is if you weren't ignoring me."

"I have every good reason to ignore you, Xavier."

"Name one."

"Savannah."

"Name a more important one."

"Bailey."

"One that concerns me."

"You left me to go to a beach with some girl and just assumed that was okay. Plus, you leave me in Savannah's house and act like that's okay too—"

"Let me stop you right there, that's *my* house. Paid for with my money. I choose who stays in that fucking house."

I let out a sigh before continuing, "Anyways, you were taken, Xavier. You played me, and I trusted that everything *you* said to me was honest. You're a liar." I let out a sarcastic laugh as I clutch my hand bag a bit tighter. "And then this woman sits in my face and makes me feel crazy! You fucked me over and . . . I can't just act like it didn't happen like you are. Because you know what? It wasn't my fault, and I won't let myself think it was."

For the first time ever, he's completely stuck. A puzzled look sits on his face like a permanent mark. "Hold on . . . " he starts, before pivoting to make sure the coast is clear. I'm sure everyone has gone inside already, and we're five minutes away from being declared late. "That beach shit. I met a friend. Business shit purely. I put that on my life. We decided to have a beach day. Oh, well. The girl was my bros fucking girlfriend, and he was with us too. The paps. They pick and choose what they want to take pictures of. They make shit up. That's out of my hands, and seriously? I thought you were smarter than that."

Suddenly, a wave of embarrassment shadows over me. Maybe I am smarter than that.

You are.

Fuck, I knew I shouldn't have let those girls get in my head. There's no need to believe a bogus article, and if anything I should have talked to him. All of that aside, this still leaves Savannah.

"And the girlfriend? Oh, I'm sorry, fiancée."

"I was not with Savannah then. I was helping her out because of what happened to her after her parents cut her off. She couldn't afford rehab, Arlissa. Did I get with her after? Yeah. But you can't hold me to that. You left. You chose to do that."

"And how did she know anything about me?"

"You literally live with her best friend."

"Jerrica wouldn't do that."

"Then you don't know shit about shit."

"I'm sorry, but I just can't believe you, Xavier." This conversation is exhausting, and the only thing I want to do now is go inside. Whatever I see as the truth isn't the truth. Whatever I hear isn't the truth, either. Nothing is true anymore, and no one can be trusted.

No one except me.

"Can't or won't?"

"Won't."

"Then don't. But don't think I didn't care when you left. When you stopped answering my texts and calls. It was more than losing a goddamn assistant."

"Huh?" My voice cracks. "It was?"

"Yeah. It was, and if anyone should be upset, it's me."

I can't take my eyes off him, but every time I find myself impressed by Xavier I have to remember Bailey. *Bailey. Bailey.* "Um . . . we have to get inside now."

"Right. So are you going to sit with me like planned, or trip me on the way in?"

A soft giggle escapes my lips. "I'll sit with you, Xavier. Mainly because you're my way in."

"Great." His smile is wide as he wraps an arm around me and begins walking in the direction of the doorway.

"You're not off the hook, yet," I add.

"Shit, neither are you. But I know your birthday is tomorrow considering Alejandra hid your gift at my place."

"So, you're stalking me now?"

"Like you stalked Savannah? Yeah, she told me about that one. Didn't know you had it in ya, little red."

I deserve that.

"Anyways. Yeah, what about my birthday?"

We continue walking, slowly, not wanting to be interrupted by the likes of this charity event. "I got something for you. Can I pick you up in the morning? Early. Like we used to."

The devil on my shoulder is telling me to jump for joy and tell him yes. But the angel remembers every commitment I made with Bailey and my friends for tomorrow. *Early is fine, right?* "Okay."

194

Xavier leaves it at that and guides me through the doors. There are names on the tables and more celebrities than I can count surrounding me. They're all consumed with one another and their wineglasses, chatting away with the bottoms up. On our way to the table where his mom and Aly are seated, I spot a few people I recognize from TV shows and music videos. But celebrities haven't been able to faze me since—*yeah.*

Amy greets us with a smile as she points to the two empty seats. "You guys are finally here! Just on time. They're about to start with an opening performance."

"Sorry, Mom, I needed some help with my suit, so I asked Lissa," he replies before pulling my seat out for me. The way the lies slip out of his mouth like they were rehearsed is a bit frightening.

"Oh, what was wrong with it?" Amy explores.

Alejandra sends a glare in my direction. I have to help him out with this lie, but I truly have no idea how. "Um . . . " I start. "There was some string hanging from his cuff, and he was pulling on it and making it worse, so I helped him fix it."

"How nice of you, honey."

Xavier and I quickly sit down as the dimming of the lights prepares the audience for whatever is about to occur.

"Is everything okay with you two?" Aly whispers in my ear.

"Yeah, it is."

THIRTY-ONE

wenty feels the same. I mean, it's not like it's twenty-one or eighteen, but it's another year around the sun. To be fair, it's also four in the morning and my body is only half awake. I take quiet steps through the apartment, trying my best not to wake my roommates. They don't need to know I'm doing this. No one does. The last thing I need is Bailey canceling our movie nights because "I don't know what I want." I'm *just* trying to see what he got me for my birthday, that's all.

Still exhausted, I struggle to push open the double doors that lead me out onto the street.

"Need some help?" Xavier calls, leaning against a bright red vehicle.

"You switched out the Range Rover?" I whine, my sneakers carrying me closer to him. I decided to take it easy this morning—no makeup, just lashes. My hair is tied up in a messy bun to go with my leggings and oversized sweatshirt. It's way too early to throw on the birthday outfit I have planned, so hopefully he isn't expecting anything more.

"Happy birthday," he simply says once I finally get close. His breath smells of coffee this time, a refreshing smell I'd love to get used to.

"Thank you," I mumble before attempting to reach the handle to the passengers door.

"Aht-aht-aht." Xavier gently pushes my hand away. I give him a confused look, unsure as to why I can't get in.

"Are we not going anywhere? Because you cannot come in."

"You don't get in on this side." A sneaky smile graces his face before pulling car keys out of his pocket.

"Shut up," I blurt out, instantly covering my hand with my mouth, backing up to truly analyze the vehicle. She's a beautiful, cherry-red BMW with tinted windows. The rims sparkle and the polish glistens in the fading moonlight. The only thing I can do is spend my energy making sure I don't fall to the ground. "You're joking."

Xavier slowly walks over to me, the empty streets making his every step receptive. "Happy birthday to you. Happy birthday to you . . ." He sings in a low tone as he opens my fist and places the keys in the palm of my itching hand. "Happy birthday dear—do you have a middle name?"

"Kimber," I whimper, my eyes filling with tears as I take in this gorgeous car.

"Happy birthday, dear Kimber. Happy birthday to you."

"You didn't have to do this. I promise my car works just fine," I manage to get out.

"I'll take a thank-you, and I will personally drive that car to the dump if you need me to." He places his large arms around my much smaller frame in an attempt to stop me from letting out a scream of excitement.

"Thank you. I just . . ."

"Hey, I was going to put a big bow on it but I figured that wasn't the best idea. This isn't your only surprise, though. So you gotta get it together, little red."

"Huh?" I finally straighten my back and take a deep breath. This is actually mine. Ashton Kutcher isn't going to pop out and tell me I got punk'd. Right? I'm praying it's all paid off. Maybe that's the catch. But most importantly, this beauty is mine.

"I'll put the address in the GPS but we should go before it gets too late."

"You mean early."

"Get your ass in the car, red," he replies with a smile before playfully rolling his eyes and heading to the passenger seat.

I let out a small shriek of excitement before prancing over to the driver's side. The seats are leather and don't have dog scratches from years ago like my old one does. It doesn't smell like cheap perfume, and it damn sure doesn't have coffee stains on the floor. And when you turn her on, she purrs like a dream.

When we arrive at the older-looking establishment, the sun still hasn't completely come up. Xavier tells me to park in the back, so I do. To my surprise there's someone waiting by the door for us. Honestly, the whole thing feels like a set-up, and I'm wondering when he's going to cut me up and sell my organs. But I'm quiet, patient even. I follow closely behind the boxer and quickly realize this is a restaurant. It's small, probably family owned but completely empty. We walk past about twenty tables before treading up the wooden staircase. Once we get there, a huge sliding door with abstract paint is in front of us. The man pushes it open and reveals a spacious room with even more tables. This is private, though. Perfect for celebrities who want to dine without people prying, I can only assume.

"Your menus are already on the table, and I'll be back shortly to collect your drink orders."

"Thanks, Marcus," Xavier quickly replies as we both enter the room. Just like that, the door is closed and we're alone.

"What's this?"

He grabs my hand. "An apology."

"For?"

"Everything. It's your birthday, and I figured now would be the perfect time to do so."

It's like he has a radar on me. I mean, the timing is practically flawless. I was beyond ready to deep dive into Bailey a few days ago—I think. I was done with wasting days in bed and hovering over drafted texts for hours at a time. He's always fine, and I'm always a mess. I was finally at a place where I could let him go and forget that jelly-like feeling he brings to my ankles. Does Xavier know I almost got him completely out of my bloodstream? Is he going to stay this time? Or am I signing up for falling apart again? Damn, the man really has his timing down, because I'm right back at the start.

I scan the room, the peeling paint on the walls, the oakwood floors, and the cushioned seats giving off an old diner aesthetic. "This place kinda reminds me of Courtney's restaurant. I mean, it's called Baker's Diner, but I worked there back home. But, yeah, super similar, except with way more money, and geez . . . " I pause, realizing I got up and left that woman with no explanation. I knew her business was failing, and she deserves way better than that. Especially after giving me my job back when she definitely could have told my ass to kick rocks.

"You good?"

"My old job was going out of business and my manager— that's the main way she keeps food on the table. I grew up with that restaurant. It's like a staple in my town."

"Maybe things picked up. Hey, don't get all upset on your day."

"No, it's probably closed by now, and I—I just feel like I let someone down, that's all."

"Do you know for sure it's closed?"

"No."

"Then why not check?"

"I just haven't had time with everything . . . And—"

"Well, I can help."

"What?" He has to be losing his mind at this point.

"I'm sure I can help. Just tell me when, and we can go. I want to see this place if it means that much to you."

Just take the help. This is your ticket back to him. Don't blow it for us this time.

Finally, I release my hand from the soft grip of his. "I don't think we should be making plans like this . . . " I start, taking a few steps back. This whole situation can go bad at any minute, and I have a perfect person like Bailey trusting in me. She doesn't show up with cars or empty breakfast reservations with a large window so we can see the sunrise. But she shows up. She always shows up, and that is something Xavier isn't capable of.

"We're friends, Lissa. Just friends. And I'm doing this as a friend because I just want you back."

"As a friend?"

"As a friend. Relationships excluded. Now, can we please just order some food? I've been waiting all night for this."

So we sit, we talk, and we eat. We update each other about everything under the sun. Relationships excluded. He speaks about how he's been training for a big match soon, and I talk about signing with an agency. And to top it all off, I have the best breakfast burrito in all of Los Angeles.

THIRTY-TWO

*M*y birthday doesn't end with Xavier, although part of me wishes it did. Instead, my family drives to meet me for lunch. Our time together is full of refreshing conversations that for once have nothing to do with the trials and tribulations of finding the perfect hairstylist. Alejandra gives me specific instructions not to come home before six. This is an easy task, though, considering my dad has a bad habit of talking my ear off. He does that most times, especially since he associates awkward silences with wanting to bring up Samantha. We never bring her up on holidays or birthdays. It's just the polite thing to do.

"I hope I'm good to come in now," I call out, pushing the apartment door open slowly. Not a sound comes from my home; nothing at all. "Coming in now!" I exclaim before fully entering the space. My gaze raises from the floor to the group of people standing in front of me. Bailey stands proudly with Jerrica and

Alejandra on each side. In her hands is a huge cake that reads: "Happy 20th to Our Lissa." There are even small sparklers sticking out instead of candles.

"Happy Birthday!" they all shout.

"Thank you!" I exclaim with a bright smile before attempting to blow out the sparklers.

"I'll take care of that," Jerrica says with a chuckle before removing the cake from Bailey's hands and walking off.

"Happy birthday, pretty lady." Bailey's tone is low and sweet as she wraps her arms around me. My face rests in her chest, a fresh scent of vanilla radiating off her. As she holds me there, running her fingers gently through my tresses, the guilt creeps up.

Keep it down.

I have to. But it's almost impossible to act like the past few days didn't happen. Plus, I can see Alejandra side-eying me from the other side of the room.

Fuck.

Don't mind her.

"Thank you," I coyly reply before breaking our embrace. Hiding is going to bite me in the ass one day, lying coming shortly after, but now isn't the time to be morally correct.

Bailey smiles down at me. "I got you something."

"You didn't have to," I mumble, pouting a bit.

"But I did." Within seconds she's stepping over to the coffee table and grabbing a small book lying there. "You've got an amazing career ahead of you, and I know sometimes you get in your head and get insecure—scared, maybe? But I've watched you attempt to write, I've also watched your face light up when a line in a poem really hits you. And the day that we sat in my room and I told you to write how you felt, you told me it worked, right?"

"Right," I whisper, tears blurring my vision now. The cause of them being guilt more than gratitude.

"My point is, wherever you go in this world, I don't want you to forget what calms you. Look!" She opens the small journal to present me the first page.

Find serenity in every page whenever the world seems to be crumbling down on you. You're one of a kind, and your words are important. So, I saved every poem you thought deserved to be trashed. I also added some of my own. Xo, Bailey

"And in case that's too corny for you I also got this." The woman shuffles in her pockets and pulls out a small black box. "It's a necklace. Just an A. I know you're not a fan of super flashy stuff, so I tried to keep that in mind and go all sentimental."

Her speech is over, and I'm left feeling like my vocal chords have been ripped out of me. In what world do I deserve any of this? A few months ago I couldn't even tell Christian how I felt and would rather have choked on my vomit whenever Alejandra sat on his lap. And now, I'm being treated like the fucking Queen of England when all I've done is lie.

Look what you did to yourself. Don't get all tripped up now. Let's just see how it ends.

Maybe this can work. If I let it. She deserves for me to at least try.

Alejandra bought some alcohol for the occasion. We drank a little—okay, a lot. But it didn't feel any different than a normal day. Between that and the cake, I'm beyond stuffed and ready to head to bed. I look over at Bailey—she seems off. The smile that she usually graces us all with is slowly fading as the night continues. I mean, it's midnight. Maybe she's just as tired as I am.

I lean over to her. "Hey . . ."

"Yeah?" she quietly says, her attention on her phone.

"Can you stay over here tonight?"

"I—" Her pupils scan the room for an excuse—this has never happened before.

"What?" My pitch sharpens as I lean away from her. Maybe it's the alcohol, maybe it's the guilt. But I'm fucking offended.

"Hey, hey." Her voice remains calm and collected as she fills the gap between us. "Can we go to your room?"

I nod, unsure if I should be excited or frightened. I gather my belongings that are scattered around the living room, gifts included, and head to our destination. Bailey follows closely, shutting the door behind her.

"What's wrong?"

She sways back and forth, her body language proving to be uneasy. "I just think it'd be right to address the elephant in the room."

"Okay." I throw my drained body onto the bed, allowing the covers to comfort me.

"Are you listening?"

I roll my eyes, finding less of a tolerance toward her and these "conversations." "Yeah."

"Okay, I'm just going to say it . . . Are you even into girls? Because it seems like you're into me one second and the minute someone else is around, you go cold and—"

"I like you."

"Okay, look, I saw that shit with Xavier, and you didn't even—"

"Oh, come on."

"That's a brand-new car outside that you also avoid talking—"

"I was going to tell you. There was just no . . . timing. Timing was off." My words are falling out of my mouth like wearing flip-flops in the rain.

"You had all night. And I'm sure you haven't told anyone we've been seeing each other either."

Slowly, I stand from the bed and grab her hand. *It works when Xavier does it to you, so why not give it a try?*

"Love, they totally know. I just . . . PDA is weird for me, I'm just trying to get used to all of this—new."

"Arlissa . . ."

"I like you. I promise. Like . . . on my life," I slur, rubbing her hand with my thumb.

"Okay, you're right. I was worried. That's all. I'll let it go." With confidence, she pulls me into a hug. That's it, just a hug. Why are we still just hugging? Like an erupting volcano, a bubbling feeling of desire overcomes me. I want her even more than I did before this moment. And I want it all right now.

"You're fine . . . I promise."

"Promise?" she repeats.

"Promise."

When my lips crash into hers, it feels different this time. The magic I've been chasing this entire time is finally making itself known. Butterflies begin to grow in the bottom of my stomach. I know why. This is going to be so much more than a kiss.

It seems as if I had only blinked but within no time her warm body hovers over mine. Her soft hands caress my suddenly exposed thighs, giving me clear signals of what's next. I want it, I crave it. We need this if we're going to survive this. I need to be closer to Bailey than I've ever been before.

THIRTY-THREE

Waking up to Bailey was the shock of a lifetime. My body's natural reaction was to distance myself from her as much as I possibly could. It's not like I wanted to but sleeping with her just solidified that she's going to expect more while I'm fine just the way we are. The peace is the purest example of the word, the hidden giggles are music to my ears, and the texts that feel like passing notes in an eighth-grade chemistry lab are a thrilling secrecy. Her expectations of me are bound to ruin everything. I just wish I can pause time and shut everyone's eyes. Then, maybe, I can give her the public appearance she's begging for.

I can't forget the look on her face when she walked out the door and asked me a million times if I was okay with it. Of course I said I was and ushered her out of my apartment as fast as possible. I can't even forget the feeling of her hands over my drunken body. Just the thought of it alone sends static shock throughout my entire being.

Well, try. You know this isn't you.

Believe me, I am.

The glowing numbers on the clock across from me continue to change slowly but surely. I've been in bed ever since Bailey left, allowing a nasty hangover to ruin my day. My mind is active, and my body hasn't gotten the memo, either. Nothing is putting me to sleep, not Gordon Ramsay screaming at the lowest volume possible, not the floorboards creaking every time someone gets up to go to the bathroom.

My fingers dance across my phone screen. *Great, I'm out of Candy Crush lives.* Now there's no longer a wall between me and my guilty thoughts. The restaurant that I left in the dust is taunting me. And in the depths of my mind—my sister is pulling at me too. She's being quiet, but I think I could use her right now.

A deep breath escapes my lips before the thought slowly creeps up in my mind. I know exactly who's awake at this time. This whole moment promoted a sick feeling of déjà vu. With one eye open, I send the vicious *up?* text.

It isn't even a few seconds before my phone vibrates in response.

Yeah, what's up?

It shouldn't be this easy, but it is. It's wrong, but easy and if all the wrong things are easy, then maybe distancing from Bailey is the right thing to do.

The highways are vacant. We pass maybe one or two cars every thirty minutes, but that's about it. The smell of fresh air is something I missed when being held up in my apartment for almost twenty-four whole hours. It's nice, riding in the dark with Xavier. It's secretive, like none of this could catch up to us in any way. And it's nice knowing I'm on the same page with at least one person in my life.

"Want a Cheeto?" I ask, feet kicked up on the dashboard.

"Toss it in my mouth." His eyes are on the road, but he has a funny way of making me feel like I'm the main focus. I let out a soft giggle before attempting to toss the chip in his direction. Somehow, he catches it. "You were hesitant."

"Well, duh! One wrong move, and we were going ninety miles per hour into that lake!" I holler, interrupted by his phone ringer going off. It stops, then rings again, stops, then rings again. With one hand on the wheel, he uses his free hand to fish the phone out of his pockets. His eyes focus on the screen for a moment before transitioning into an eyeroll.

"You'd be doing Savannah a favor," he says with a deep sigh.

"Is everything okay?" My voice is soft. I'm terrified that he's going to jerk on the wheel and turn us around. But I'm sure his princess will love it.

"Do you really want to hear it?"

"Yeah, I mean . . . We're friends, right?"

"Yeah."

"So tell me."

"We're just not in a good spot. For real, though? I don't know why we keep trying. She's just a fucking liar, and when I leave her for it she's crying like I'm the problem. I can't take this shit anymore. Plus, I'm trying to sober up—"

I raise a brow, "Drinking . . . Right?"

"I'm trying not to drink anymore. And that's all her ass wants to do, man. I'm tired."

Wait, is he trying to leave her?

"Maybe you guys just outgrew each other." I'm petrified of stepping on any toes or crossing lines he doesn't invite me to cross.

"I mean, we're broken up now. Shit sucks, but she can't keep tossing her crap on me."

"I agree. She's grown. That's not your responsibility."

He lets out a concerning laugh. "Thanks, little red. I hope you and that Bailey person are doing well, at least."

"I have a hard time believing that. You know, I got in some trouble for accepting that car."

"Ay, I'm not trying to get in between anything. I promise. Just thought you deserved it, and if he really likes you, then I'm sure he thinks you deserve way more than a BMW."

"She."

Silence fills the car as he stops for a red light. "Oh. I see."

"It's nothing, though. I promise."

He chuckles again. "Hey, it's none of my business."

The floor is open for any kind of conversation, so why not speak on what's been raiding my mind lately? "Xavier."

"Kimber?"

"Stop calling me that!" I whine.

"It's your name. Plus everyone calls you some version of Arlissa. I'll pass."

"Anyways. Have you . . . " I linger on every single word, trying not to put this in a way that scares him the same way it scares me. "Ever not known how you feel about someone?"

"I've been with the same girl for six fucking years. What do you think?"

I gasp. "Six years?"

"Wild, ain't it?"

"How did you know when—you really—— loved her?"

Ask about the engagement.

No.

"You really want to know this story?"

I suck my teeth. "Don't roll your eyes! Yes, I do. Spill the beans."

"All right. Let me think. I was young. Uh, she . . . we were cool. Especially in high school." His eyes are still on the road but I can feel him getting more and more distant. "Anyways, I think we were like six months in when I came to terms with it. I was also fifteen, so I don't know what the fuck I was thinking. I can't remember how it felt but I remember how it just slipped out of my mouth. It's just one of those things where you just know, you know?"

"No. I don't."

"You've never been in love before?"

"When I love people bad shit happens," I mutter.

"I missed that. Did you say no?"

"No. Yeah. I mean, yeah, I said no. I just . . . I guess it's never hit me before. I don't know. I don't know how long it takes to fall in love, or . . . what kind of person it takes. I just thought you could help."

"I'm flattered you're asking me all of this, I really am. But the woman I love drained my bank account, so I don't pick well at all, I swear."

"Maybe you should pick better then, stupid," I reply jokingly, desperate to change the mood.

"I'd be happy to let you set me up on a blind date."

"I'd just show up alone."

"See, I knew I could trust your judgment."

I adjust myself in the seat, letting my big-ass head slowly find itself on his shoulder. We ride the rest of the way like this. We drive that jet black Range Rover miles away from our problems, relationships included, and it feels like total bliss.

210

Chapter
THIRTY-FOUR

I take hesitant steps into Baker's Diner, Xavier following my lead. My anxiety peaks as my feet make their way across the glossy tiles. My manicured fingers intertwine with Xavier's as I guide him throughout the space. Facing Courtney isn't pretty high on my to-do list at all. The idea of her knowing that I ran out on her for the second time doesn't sit well with me. My heart aches, and she deserves so much more. Her husband, her kids—they all do. Maybe everyone who ever met me does.

When my eyes catch sight of the exhausted woman, I can't help but sigh. The stress she's probably going through is written so well on her once youthful face. Her trademark bangs are now growing out as she wears them tucked behind her ear.

"Hey," I say once we get closer to her.

She looks up at me, her initial shocked expression quickly turning into a frown. "You got a new look," she simply says.

I nod. "Yeah, I just . . . I wanted to check in, see how you were doing." There's an elephant in the room—one we really don't want to address right now. She has customers and yelling about how I'm the most selfish person of all time would surely turn them away. "Oh! This is Xavier Amari. A friend of mine."

Xavier steps in front of me and holds his hand out. "She spoke very highly of this place, so it's extremely nice to meet you." He flashes one of his signature charming smiles, enchanting us both.

Courtney gives him a fake smile before shaking his hand. "Can I get you two anything?"

"Actually, I'd like to try some of that pie. That one, right there." He motions toward the dessert encased in glass.

"It's a peach pie," Courtney quickly responds before beginning to serve a slice.

"It's actually one of my favorites," I mumble to him, watching as Courtney glares at me.

"So, how long have you had this place?" he inquires before taking a seat at the bar. I follow.

"It's actually my grandmother's. I took it after my mom couldn't do it anymore, and now my daughter helps me out. Arlissa actually helped me as well." The way her eyes settle on me fills my heart with sorrow. Leaving her to start a new life in LA not once, but twice, knowing the conditions this place is under, wasn't right.

"I'm sorry," I blurt. My words catch the woman off guard as she stops cutting the slice.

"For?" she mumbles, avoiding eye contact as the piece of pie slides perfectly onto the plate.

"I left this place without notice. I left you after you gave me a job again when I left the first time. And for that I'm so sorry, and I can't help but wish I could fix things. I really want this place to stay open for you. I swear, Courtney. You're like a second mom to me, and I'm just . . . I know how ungrateful I can be."

The woman stands there on the other side of the counter,

almost as if she's frozen in time. Seconds later, she slides the plate over to Xavier before clearing her throat. "That'll be $3.75."

He looks at me, then at her, then at the pie. Without saying a word, he grabs the fork and places a piece into his mouth. The silence is tense, my mind partly focused on the both of them. He chews, in no rush at all. The both of us keep our gazes on him as I wonder what's going through his mind. His throat moves in waves as he swallows. The sickening silence is disrupted by the sound of Xavier shuffling in his pockets. It goes on for about fifteen seconds before he pulls out a folded slip of paper and hands it to Courtney.

"Would this work as payment?" he asks, taking another bite of the pie shortly after.

My old boss stands there in confusion before unfolding the rectangular slip. "Oh my God!" she shouts, quickly covering her mouth.

"What?" Then I see it. "Xavier."

"This is for you, and hopefully that's enough to get this place back in action," he adds in between chews. "This pie is fucking delicious, and you need to be serving this for the rest of your life. Sorry, beautiful."

"I—I—" the woman stutters, tears filling her almond-shaped eyes. "Thank you . . . This check can—thank you."

"If it wasn't for Arlissa expressing how important this place was to her, I wouldn't be here. So thank her."

Courtney turns to me and gives me the best smile she can manage as tears begin to stream down her face. Before I know it she's coming toward me from around the bar and pulling me into a warm embrace. I allow her in, feeling her overwhelming sea of emotions the longer she holds me. My eyes begin to tear as well. Not only am I happy for this place, but I'm also just as overwhelmed with Xavier's generosity as much as she is.

We talked, had as many slices of pie as our stomachs could

handle, and even took a picture for her to hang up on the wall later. It came around time for us to head out and as we shared our goodbyes, I couldn't help but tear up again. For some reason this feels like forever, like the last time I'll see this small town for a long time. So, I take a step back as Xavier closes the door behind us, taking in the little diner on the end of the street. The sign has been victim to some wear and tear, and the red awning along the building is in desperate need of another paint job. Hopefully she fixes all of that. I pay attention to every detail, the dim lights, the signs on the windows, the people still sitting inside.

"You okay?" Xavier whispers, his arm around me as he uses the other one to take a photo of the store front.

"Yeah, just gonna miss it." My lips release a deep sigh. "What's that for?"

"Ten k is great, but she's going to need some promotion, right? Just posting it as my new favorite spot. She'll get this place up and running again in no time." His bright smile makes it clear he's proud of himself, probably more than Courtney and me combined.

"Ten thousand dollars? Don't look at me like that! You didn't have to do that."

"It was important to you, so . . . I made it better." Xavier shrugs before placing a quick kiss on my forehead.

There's nothing left to say after that, mainly because I have no words left. For him to just come out of pocket that effortlessly because I felt a bit of guilt—it's intense. I don't know whether to feel even more guilty or just shut up and take all that he's showering me with. The only thing I know is that it's done, and if he's going this far that says more than whatever the past few months attempted to show me.

THIRTY-FIVE

"Things are going so well. This past month has been amazing for you, Lissa," Holly says as she hovers near me. I settle into the chair as a man continues to stroke my face with his makeup brush.

"Thank you, just . . . doing what I'm doing," I manage to respond without moving my face too much. My eyes remain closed, allowing the MUA to work with my features however he wishes.

"Right! Speaking of what you're doing. I have a tiny request."

"Okay, go ahead." Anything Holly requests is usually a good idea, so there's nothing to be worried about.

"I need you to rekindle that little thing you had with Xavier."

I freeze. Partially from the excitement of having the excuse of seeing him again, but also from the fear of losing Bailey completely. "Huh?"

"Hear me out, now! You trust me, right?"

"Always, but . . . "

"No buts. We just got this GAP shoot, and we need to keep the serious bookings going. This only started when you became Hollywood's 'little red.' On top of that he gave you some great publicity, correct?"

"Correct." There's no denying that our red-carpet charade effortlessly took me from one thousand followers to fifty-thousand. It also keeps Holly's phone ringing with people who want to use my fifteen seconds of fame to promote their own brand.

This needs to last more than fifteen seconds.

"So, talk to him. And I know you're worried about that lady friend of yours but tell her this is what it takes sometimes."

"She'll kill me."

Holly smirks. "Well, I thought you were just friends."

"We are."

"You don't have to date the guy, just . . . Share some pasta with him, on a balcony. In broad daylight. All I ask. 'Kay?"

I take a deep sigh. My body wiggles in the now uncomfortable seat in order to remain calm. "'Kay. I'll call him."

"Great. Now ciao! I have to run." In classic Holly fashion, she squeezes my hand gently before running off like an energetic puppy.

"Chinese date?" I take small steps into the dimly lit apartment.

Bailey closes the door behind me before wrapping her hands around my waist. But her grip isn't enough to calm me this time. The anxiety I felt the whole drive here isn't going anywhere anytime soon.

"Yeah, I thought, why not? We've both been pretty busy these days so. I got some takeout and bought a rom-com."

"You bought a rom-com?"

She shrugs. "I pirated—in good quality, might I add—a rom-com."

I let out a light giggle and allow my body to completely dissolve into hers. "I don't deserve you."

"You don't," she says with a smirk before placing a kiss on my forehead. "But I'm willing to go at whatever pace you want to. No matter what, I'm here."

"I know . . . And that's why I need to talk to you."

Bailey's wide smile doesn't budge, even with the possibility of news that could upset her. That's how much she trusts me. "Shoot."

My mind searches for the right way to put things, but she'll understand, right? *It's just business. There's no need to be so nervous.* "I need to start hanging out with Xavier more. For . . . press purposes."

The smile fades, completely, within the same second that the words fall out of my sin-filled mouth. "Oh?"

"Look, I'm getting these amazing opportunities, and I need to keep my name in people's mouths so that these things stick."

"So . . . you agreed to this already?" The voice being directed at me is calm, but her body language isn't. She begins turning the ring that rests on her index finger, something she only does when she's trying to understand what the hell is going on. I know what's going on. I'm letting her down—again.

"Yes. I just . . . I thought you'd understand."

"I do. You need a fake boyfriend with a big name, not a girlfriend, because, God forbid, another woman in this fuck-ass industry reps the rainbow flag."

"Bailey."

"No. If that wasn't true you wouldn't be asking this of me. How much longer do I have to sit on the sidelines for him? I won't do it, Arlissa."

"I've never put you on the backburner for him."

"Right. No, you put me on the backburner because you're too scared to admit you like girls."

"Bailey!"

"So what are you going to do when his real girlfriend makes an appearance? Does she know about this?"

"He doesn't have one."

"And how do you know that?"

I bite the inside of my lip, unsure of how to plead the fifth on this one. Yet, my fear of her being upset quickly shifts to rage. How can she only be thinking of herself right now? "You are so selfish. If we get this press you get a step closer to publishing whatever that screenplay shit is you want to do! He can work for the both of us."

She scoffs, running her fingers through her wavy locks. "Excuse me?"

"I—"

"Go home, Lissa. Just go."

"Call me when you can think about someone but yourself. And maybe, I don't know. Trust me for once."

Shaking my head feverishly, I push past the woman and make my way out of her apartment. A rush of chills populate my body as I storm through the halls, basically running at this point. I want to get as far away from her as possible, or maybe myself.

I swallow the anger and jump into my brand-new vehicle, adjusting my tight muscles in the leather seats. My head leans back as I take a moment to close my eyes and breathe. The continuous air escaping from my lungs manages to calm the firepit in my stomach, and for a moment I regret allowing it to burn the person I adore.

Once my eyes open, shaky fingers fumble with my phone to get to my contact list as fast as possible. *This is okay, this is justified.* I'm going to go somewhere great, and if a few people have to sit back and bear the kickback of my sins, then that's what has to happen.

When my gaze comes across the contact name, I quickly press the blue "call" icon. It rings for a few moments, and then a few more.

"Hello? Hey . . . When are you free? I want to talk to you about some things."

A lot isn't certain, but the smile on my face lets me know everything I need to.

Chapter
THIRTY-SIX

"Thanks for coming with me."

Keep your head low. Slide into the seat, easy now.
You're here. Thank God.

Outdoor seating is fucking stupid if you ask me. Why would I want to sit where the sun is directly assaulting only half of my face? Now I have half a tan, and my foundation won't match no matter what. On top of that, don't let it be windy or your hair is going to be dancing in your pasta. I won't even mention the bugs buzzing about. My point is, outdoor seating fucking sucks. And now, here I am, sitting in the blazing sun and praying my makeup doesn't melt off before the paparazzi shows up.

Sit up straight. People are watching.

"No problem. I got a thing for being wined and dined these days." Xavier's laugh enchants me, quieting the echoes of Samantha's return.

I gasp, "Who said I was paying?"

My stomach jumps with every breath he takes. I can't help but find myself trying to guess what he's going to do or say next. It's an exciting game. We're teetering on the tightrope of friendship and something a lot more dangerous. The guessing game is who's going to take the big leap first.

It better be you. Or that'd be disappointing.

He chuckles. "Wow. I promise I'm a cheap date."

"I've seen your takeout orders. You're really not."

"I believe a thank-you is in order, no? Plus you know you wanted to call. With or without your manager telling you to do it."

"You don't know that," I whimper pathetically.

"I do. I know that very well."

I raise a brow. "Hm? How so?"

"A magician doesn't reveal his secrets, or whatever the saying is."

"Hi! My name is Mary, and I'm your server today. May I start you off with some drinks?" The waitress interrupts us as she fidgets with the pen and notepad in her hand.

"I'll have water."

Xavier doesn't even glance at the drink menu. "I think . . . I'll start with a screwdriver."

"Alcohol? It's a little early for that, don't you think?"

"It's five p.m. somewhere, love." Suddenly, he pushes up the sleeves on his blue button-up, which is only buttoned up halfway. "Well, shit. It's a bit hot out here, yeah?"

Naturally, I find myself stuck on every feature of his forearms. The hairs, the veins, but then something else catches my attention. The scratches are still red, and if I squint I can see one literally about to bleed out right now.

"Is your arm okay?" I blurt, no courtesy whatsoever. The people sitting around us slowly and not so casually turn their heads—nosy LA behavior. With pure embarrassment in his eyes, Xavier coyly pulls his sleeves back down.

"Yeah, yeah. I'm fuckin' great. You know, I've been training real hard these days and got a little fucked up."

"A little? It—it looks awful."

"What?"

"Your arm, Xavier. Your arm looks awful."

"Oh, I'm good. It's a part of boxing, you know? Sometimes you get hurt." His calm exterior returns as his hungry fingers make their way under the table and onto my thigh. "No big deal."

"I don't know. I knew you were a boxer, but maybe I'm just realizing that it—no offense—kind of sucks."

A chuckle escapes his moisturized lips. "None taken. It's not being an assistant or anything—"

"Fuck you!"

"It's what I do, and I'm damn good at it."

"Oh, I know. The great Xavier Amari who took after his father and inspired young people all around the world to follow their dreams—if they have a trust fund." I playfully roll my eyes.

I don't understand the need to fangirl over celebrities. They're just people whose actions are glorified because they have the cash that the other ninety-nine percent of the world doesn't. But I guess when you run into a good one, you can end up with a ten-thousand-dollar check to save your business.

"Oh, wow! Tell me how you really feel." His replies are topped with sprinkles of laughter. "I get it, I do. But my dad's career—my mom's. It's only a fraction of my success—"

"'That's only half of who I am! Okay, Kiara.'"

"Huh?"

"*Lion King*. The second one? Ever seen it? Wow. What the hell was your childhood?'"

"Here are your drinks!" The waitress's tone is chipper as she places the glasses in front of their respective person. "More time to look at the menu?"

"Yes, please."

"Anyways. A fraction, that's it. I work really fucking hard, and honestly, a lot of people didn't take me seriously until I proved I could win. Shit, my own dad didn't. So, I get it. I have the cars and the last name and the mom who gets me a golden ticket anywhere. But I do think people should follow their dreams or whatever the fuck. Just know it'll take a lot of hard work to get there." His monologue ends with a not-so-graceful gulp from his cup. I can count the seconds on one hand that it takes for him to finish and return an empty glass to the table.

"I'm sorry."

"For?"

"I was being a bitch."

"Yeah, but it's fine. You're new to this—me." Slowly, he leans in closer to the point where his face is perfectly aligned with the middle of the table. It's only right I meet him halfway, right? In broad daylight, where men with cameras are posted across the street hoping for the perfect shot. Why the fuck not?

Do it.

"I don't feel new to you." I rise a bit from my seat. My body language is having a conversation with his. We're both hovering over the table, our lips just a hair apart.

"Then it's working," he replies in a low tone, a sly smile on his face.

"What is?"

"Everything." The electricity between us finally uses its pull to smash our lips together. The taste of his Chapstick dances across my taste buds. And for a moment, I forget where we are. I look in the corner of my eye, catching a glimpse of the camera flashes from just a few feet away.

Okay, this is fucking good. Get out of there, don't be stupid. Don't ruin this.

"Let's . . . go." Throwing myself back into my seat, I quickly gather my belongings in preparation to leave.

"Go where?" he asks, confused.

"Uh—my apartment! Aly's doing something with your mom until tomorrow, and Jerrica's visiting her parents."

"Shit, all right." He places a twenty-dollar bill on the table and follows my lead to a safer, more secluded place.

We make our way back to the apartment in record time. It's almost as if the universe wants this for me because traffic was basically nonexistent. The worst part about it is that those butterflies I got are only getting more and more intense. My eyes trace the veins on his arms. I daydreamed about days he'd visit this apartment and walk along those tiles like he is now. The way his deep voice would echo through the halls and make me crave his hand around my neck.

"Want water or something?"

"Got vodka?"

"Um, we might have a bit leftover from, like, forever ago."

"Shit, works for me."

Quickly, I head to the cabinet and pull out the half empty clear bottle. "Here."

"You're a lifesaver." Xavier makes his way over to me as his large hands remove the bottle from mine. My senses melt with every single touch he offers me.

"I try." Gulping hard, I can't help but wonder if he knows what he's doing. If he's aware that I'm shaking and thawing all at once.

"So, what's up?" he's standing in front of me now, bottle in one hand and my palm in the other.

"I just . . . wanted some privacy." If I bite my lip any harder I'm certain it's going to bust.

"I thought you wanted the whole 'hold hands in public' shit?"

"I lied."

His eyes wide. "I like where you're headed." The words slip out before he leans in to kiss me once again. My body presses itself against his, our lips dancing together as time passes us by.

Part of me wants to resist, fight it, because that's the part that knows it isn't right. But it feels so much better than what I'm used to. Gravity pulls us together; keeps our lips together too. The rush mixes with the dominance of his every motion, causing my addiction to only intensify. As his lips slowly part from me, a whimper of disappointment leaves mine. But no, he isn't about to let me down. His alcohol-coated breath makes contact with the pores on my neck, the tender brush of his mouth following closely behind.

I crumble. I completely succumb to everything his body asks for. From removing his shirt, to kicking off my own shoes. I'm electrified and as I pull off more clothes, the rushes of air continue to send chills throughout every exposed piece of skin.

It's in this moment, this very second of passion and secrecy, that I realize I'm his. No debate necessary. Sometimes you can just feel when a person owns every piece of you, and Xavier Amari has unlocked it all.

THIRTY-SEVEN

With the lights out and the blinds closed, I can still see the energy vibrating between us. Even without a blanket his body wrapped around mine feels warm and secure. It's one of those cozy moments where you spend the whole time wishing the world isn't going to find a way to rip it from you. My small hands grip his body as tight as possible, hoping he won't run off in a hurry. Xavier's strong embrace keeps me in a childlike position. I love it this way.

"Hey," he whispers, his breath sending chills down my back as his fingers brush gently against my soft red coils.

"Hm?" My heart begins to race. The softness in his voice only scares me more. I'm ready for it—the "I have to go," and it's going to hurt just as bad as the last time. Or even worse, because there's so much more on the line now.

Jesus Christ, calm the fuck down.

"I'm fucking starving." When he laughs, I feel my heart return back to its proper place.

"Oh," I simply respond, raising myself from the grips of both him and the mattress. "I can order something."

Xavier sits up as well, his messy hair falling effortlessly on his forehead. "Or I can cook something if the fridge ain't empty."

"It's not! We buy groceries, okay?"

"Then it's settled. Let me just, uh . . . get some clothes on."

"Ugh." I moan, pouting at the idea of him putting anything on at all. Now that I've seen him in his entirety, it's all I want for as long as I can have it. "Do you have to? I mean, we can just stay like this."

"Yeah, and have someone walk in?" He leans across the bed and places a kiss on my thirsty lips. "Not happening."

"Come on! No one's going to be home for hours." I continue to whine before getting up and grabbing my robe that hangs carelessly over my bedside lamp.

He pulls a garment from off the floor, "Shit, at least let me put my boxers on if you can wear a whole-ass robe."

"Fine, fine."

Being in this kitchen with him feels like a Lifetime movie. Time is at a standstill as we dance across the marble floors. My seconds have turned to minutes, my minutes into hours. It's such a wonderful thing to feel this way. It's like someone has encased us in a snow globe where all we can do is dance. Our laughter fills the space and I'm sure you can hear it from the halls. But the thing is, I don't care. Even when there's silence, there's something between us. The spaces without words aren't awkward or damning—it's comforting. We are enclosed in this tiny cubicle that I split rent for, and that's okay. As he cooks, I find myself doing the normal "girlfriend" things. I playfully pinch him, and we laugh at the seasoning that spills on the floor. My heart is pumping gold as our conversations carry on. Connections like this are once in a lifetime. Every relationship I have, every man I let touch me, it all felt so black and white. Yet, this is golden. This is something I have to keep at all costs.

We're interrupted by the sound of a few knocks on the door. We exchange glances before I tighten my robe and head over to see who it is. Without a care in the world, I unlock the door and swing it all the way open. "Ye—"

"I wanted to apologize," Bailey says, proudly holding a bouquet of Edible Arrangements in her hand. I stand there, frozen in time. Unable to say a damn thing. "You don't have to speak, I just want you to have this because I feel like we should . . . fix things. Maybe? Hopefully? I love having you in my life, okay? Talking—"

"Hey, Kimber!" Xavier calls, appearing next to me with nothing but his boxers on and a skillet in his hand. "I was going to ask for a spatula but I see I'm interrupting something." I can hear him gulping hard, but he doesn't back away. No, he just straightens his stance. And as I stand there with blank thoughts, at least I'm protected.

"No. You're not interrupting anything. Have a really great life, Arlissa." Bailey drops the arrangement on the ground, her expression going from hopeful and apologetic to completely shattered. I can see it all in her eyes alone. The disappointment, the betrayal, the heartbreak. It's not something I'm a stranger to, watching people look at me this way. But it is something I'm growing more and more immune to. I watch as she makes her way quickly down the steps, refusing to stand and wait for the elevator.

Xavier steps in front of me, dragging the slightly wounded arrangement into the house. "Mmm, good thing I'm a sucker for chocolate-covered strawberries," he happily says before pulling me out of the doorway and shutting the door. "What was all that about?"

"Nothing. She's just odd. Has this idea that we were a thing. Whatever, it's over now." I gulp, a false smile immediately appearing on my face as I pick the arrangement up off the floor and head toward the kitchen. "I'm good. But, hey, we have dessert!"

"Apparently we do." Xavier sends a sly smile in my direction before going back to tend to the food.

It's then that I notice a spatula on the counter right next to him. I place the arrangement on the island before raising a brow and handing the tool to the person who is clearly blind. "Hey, there was one right here."

"Shit, I'd lose my own head if it wasn't attached to my body. My dad used to say that all the time. Now I get it." A low chuckle escapes his lips before he turns back to me. "You sure you okay? If I would have known . . ."

"I'm great. Glad she's gone. Less for me to worry about."

My breath slows back down as he nods and places another kiss on my lips. *This is fine, this is okay. Because the right thing isn't always easy, right?*

Right. So, because this hurts now . . . it's the right thing. You're doing the right thing, Lissa.

Exactly.

THIRTY-EIGHT.

It's not every day that everyone I know isn't answering their phones. I get it; everyone around me has better things to do than binge *Top Chef*. Trust me, I understand. Jerrica's probably somewhere curled up with her parents like she has been for the past few weeks, hell, maybe even months. But, in all honesty, it's still odd. I'm sprawled out on this dingy ass mattress and watching as the time ticks on by.

Midnight. One. Two. Three . . . Maybe if I try really hard I can fall asleep. But where the hell is everyone?

The loud sound of a bang is accompanied by the waves of mixed laughter. I tighten my robe and slip into my dollar-nine-ty-nine house slippers. As I take hesitant steps toward the hall the voices grow in volume.

"You guys are fucking sick!" I hear Alejandra exclaim as I turn the corner to reveal Xavier, Aly, and Greyson all huddled together in the living room. I raise a brow in suspicion. When the hell did they become a trio?

"No, you really shouldn't have cursed that pap out, man," Greyson slurs, barely able to keep himself up.

Xavier stands there, laughing with the pair for another moment before catching sight of me. "Aw, shit, did we wake you up?" He darts his eyes to every shiny object in the room, only to then wipe his nose before separating the couple and make his way to me.

"No, I was awake," I whisper once he gets closer. "Where'd you guys go? Didn't you have to practice or something with your dad?"

He nods feverishly. "Yeah, yeah, yeah. I just . . . wasn't sleeping, and Grey told me he was heading out with Aly so I joined. I thought you'd be sleep."

"Nope. Wide awake."

Alejandra drunkenly jumps in between us. "Well! In that case, the party isn't over, yeah?"

"Shit, it's over for me. I need to fucking crash," Greyson whines, tossing himself on the couch.

"Oh! Let's watch a movie. You in, Lissa?" Aly suggests, a clear over-excitement in her tone.

"Yeah, let's do that." Xavier seems like the only calm one in the room, apart from me, of course, and that's pretty comforting. Well, he's calm, but his balance and attention span are completely wrecked.

"Okay," I mumble as I guide him over to the couch. He sits down first, me curling up in his lap. I watch as Aly and Greyson giggle and fumble all over the place for a few moments before getting settled. Even drunk, they're obsessed with each other.

"So, are you two, like, a thing?" Greyson's attention turns to us, eyes half open.

"Um . . . " I start, mentally guarding my chest for any heart-breaking thing Xavier might say.

"She's stuck with me, man."

"Fina-fucking-ly." Aly interrupts.

As my heart releases a sigh of relief, we all lie there, the only noise coming from Aly and Greyson smooching on each other as quietly as possible. It's either listen to them or allow some war movie to bore me to sleep. Yet, I decide on neither option. Instead, I lie there obsessing over the words that came out of Xavier's mouth. Did I finally make it? Am I finally good enough to be claimed by Xavier Amari?

"Oh my fucking *fuck!*"

The high-pitched words aggressively pull me from my dreams. I slowly rise from my position on Xavier's chest. He put the footrest up at some point but clearly went out of his way to not wake me up. He's sound asleep, his shoes and jacket still on. It's quite peaceful, actually, watching him in a pretty vulnerable state where he won't ruin the moment with a smart comment.

"*Fuck, fuck, fuck!*"

The shrieking continues as I fully snap out of my dreamy state. Greyson is sound asleep, but Aly's missing. I slowly get off the couch and look up to see her running back and forth throughout the kitchen. Her right hand covers her nose as she aggressively rips as many paper towels as she could off the roll. I take quick, cautious steps toward her, trying my best not to wake the boys.

"What's going on? Why is your nose bleeding, Aly?" My voice heightens as I watch the blood leak through the spaces in between her fingers. I grab some of the paper towels that had fallen on the floor and help the brunette apply pressure. "Lean your head back."

"Lissa, I'm freaking out," she mutters.

"I know, because your nose is like—exploding."

"No, my song. Okay, I woke up to pee and checked my phone. 'Forever' is blowing up on this dance app. Apparently it has, like, a million plays or something so far."

"That's the first song on your EP, right?" My hand continues to rest on her nose, hoping the blood would stop eventually.

"Yes! How do you not know that like the back of your hand? Whatever. Anyways. I—this is going to give me so much exposure. Do you know how many songs have blown up on the Hot 100 because of that app?"

"No."

"A fuckton. But the point is all the same—I need to call Amy. We need to keep promoting."

Offer something. Because if you don't, you're just going to be the person who used to be her best friend when she really gets big.

"You can shoot a music video, right?"

Aly's eyes sparkle as she slowly moves my hand off of her face and uses the cleaner edges of the napkin to wipe off her nose. "You're a genius, Lissa. And you say you don't know music."

That's my little sis.

"I promise, I really don't," I add with a giggle before cleaning up the mess she made. As I bend over to wipe up the tiny drops of blood, all I can think about is how far she's come from making me listen to her sing in her bedroom closet. "I'm proud of you."

"I wouldn't be here without you, and we have so much more ground to cover, man. We're just getting started." Aly bends down so that we're on the same level with a wet paper towel in her hand as she goes over the spots I just wiped. "Te amo." Her accent is always like music to my ears—truly something I can never get tired of.

I remember when she used to send me playlists. Songs she felt described how she viewed me and our friendship. I listened to them sometimes. Other times I'd just Google the lyrics because we never had the same music taste, anyway. She hasn't done that in a while. I mean, she wrote one, but I don't know . . . Does she still think of me that way? The same way she did when she sent love songs because they were the only songs that described how deeply she felt about me. I think that's what she said. Does she still think about our bond when she hears those melodies? Does she still think the best way to speak to me is through music? Or am I already playing the bench?

"I love you more. So much more."

"I promise you don't." Her brown eyes are focused on mine, the softness in them pulling me closer and closer to everything that encapsulates her.

"I heard we're celebrating?" a groggy voice interrupts us.

"Hey, babe. I was about to make some breakfast, actually." Aly quickly gets herself up from the floor. I follow.

"Food?" the second voice rises from the couch, a loud yawn following it.

"I'll cook," I offer. "You should shower and stuff, Aly."

"Whoa, whoa, whoa. Celebrations are in order, though. Are they not? Was I dreaming? Shit could have been . . . Someone say something in here about a million streams?" Greyson makes his way to us, holding his head as if he's stopping his brain from oozing out. "I say we go to Karma." A sly smile follows his statement and triggers an alarmed look from Aly.

"Um, that's not a good idea, because you know . . . and . . . Lissa." Alejandra attempts to whisper, but she never really knew how to do that.

"What do you mean?" I furrow my brow, unsure why things are being hidden from me.

Xavier appears behind me, his strong hands gripping my

234

shoulders. "Maybe they can go to Karma, and we can stay here," he suggests.

"No. Why can't I go?"

"I just . . . " Alejandra stutters, looking at the two guys for support but they're both mute.

Useless. "You what?"

"It's a pretty wild scene, Lissa," Greyson chimes in.

"Arlissa," Xavier corrects.

"Look, I just didn't think you'd be into that kind of place." Alejandra's tone is soft, like I'm a wounded baby bird.

Make them want you to go. Jesus, do I have to coach you through everything?

"Well, I want to go. So, we're going. Tonight." Their expressions are blank. "Now, can y'all freshen up or something. I'm gonna go cook." We all disband silently.

I can't imagine why they're keeping this particular club from me and that must have been why they've been hanging out privately lately. What could possibly be so bad about it?

Whatever it is, though, it doesn't matter now. It's a matter of hours before I'll find out.

Chapter
THIRTY-NINE

*T*he music is as loud as thunder. It makes my skin tingle in ways I'm not familiar with. The neon lights sporadically hit every corner of the club, perfectly illuminating what would have been a dark crowded room. I sit close to Xavier, taking in every person who tries to sneak a picture of us sitting in VIP. We've only been here about ten minutes and seven separate people have recognized Alejandra. So, she's stuck downstairs promoting her EP while people drool over her and perform an eight-count they made up.

I'm wearing an odd choice of clothing—at least to me. I had no idea what to wear and Xavier had taken it upon himself to tell his (new) assistant to pick me up something he'd like. So she did, and in record timing too. It was hours prior to our outing that I got a new pair of designer boots. They're knee-high and the tall heel was something I just assumed I'd have to get used to living in LA. The dress I'm wearing is more like an oversized tube top and way too revealing for the winter breeze LA is currently giving, but I guess it doesn't matter.

Over the roar of music, I can hear the distinct chatter going on between Grey and Xavier. The only thing I can make out is that Greyson is whining and Xavier is giving into whatever he's demanding. My focus goes from the sea of people below us to the man who's tapping my shoulder.

"Hm?"

He opens his mouth to speak but is interrupted by a bottle girl heading over to us. Greyson has a huge smile on his face as she places an empty bottle on the table. As the lady heads down back to wherever she came from, Alejandra arrives.

"Whew, that was fucking stressful. But woo! It is party time!" The Latina says with a deep sigh.

"There's more of that coming your way," Xavier replies. My eyes focus on Greyson, who's reaching over the table to pick up the bottle. What is he going to do with an empty bottle? I watch him peel off a small baggie that's taped to the bottom of it.

"I'm telling y'all, Fonty got the best shit in California," he mumbles as his eager hands pour the contents onto the table. I sit there, still as a statue, completely blown away by what I'm watching. It isn't Greyson that's shocking me, though. It's Alejandra hovering over him with eager eyes. "Xavier, you got that shit from Garret, right?"

Xavier looks at me, completely aware of the expression on my face. "Yeah. It's in my pocket."

"You didn't talk to her first, did you?" Alejandra questions, annoyance in her voice.

"I forgot!" Xavier explains as he reaches in his jacket pocket and tosses another baggy on the table. This time it doesn't have cocaine in it, no. It has about four different kinds of pills. As I watch all of them, and how they react to every substance on that table, I know why I wasn't invited before. "Lissa . . . "

"Xavier, I—" I start to think of excuses, reasons why I can't join their charade. This is wrong, this is *not* what anyone is supposed to do. But more importantly—he lied to me.

"Look," he interrupts, grabbing my hand. "It's just something we do. It takes the edge off. We all got a lot of shit going on, right? Loosen up, okay?" He pauses and retrieves a small tablet that kind of reminds me of the Flintstone vitamins my mom used to give me when I was a kid. Back when she cared about anything I did. "Take it." He waves the orange tablet in my face like I'm in hypnotic therapy. In the corner of my eye I can see Alejandra and Greyson already taking turns sniffing the white powder.

"You lied to me," I blurt, in a low enough tone that only he can hear over the roaring speakers.

He pauses, as if he forgot he said the hardest drug he ever did was pre-workout. "Kimber, trust me."

"How?"

"Woo!" Alejandra is standing on the table now, gaining an audience like always.

"I don't lie. This isn't an all-the-time thing for me. It's a party drug. No big deal. Those don't count. Come on, take it. Don't be the only one here not having any fun." His brown eyes burn a hole in my chest, and before I know it the orange tablet is making its way down my throat. Xavier quickly reaches over to the other side of him to grab a half empty water bottle. "Here."

I swallow the liquid quickly, feeling the tablet dissolve into my bloodstream. "What the hell was that?"

"Molly," Greyson answers for him, a huge smile on his face as he sniffs and wipes his nose.

"Now, you have to try the good stuff," Aly cuts in, looking down on me from her pedestal. Wide-eyed, I watch as she creates a row just for me. Xavier slowly places his hand on my thigh, squeezing it gently in an attempt to keep me on board.

"I'm here if you need anything," he whispers in my ear before giving me space so I can lean closer to the table.

"So, you take this dollar bill here. Or, if you're a pro like the king over there, you won't need it." Greyson lets out a chuckle before handing me the rolled-up piece of paper. "Just trace the line."

"The king, huh?"

Xavier coyly shrugs. "Stop fucking with me, man."

I sit there, legs crossed, wondering if this should be where I draw the line. I just swallowed a magical tablet that I'm sure was not given to me to help with my bone strength. Now, here I am, living like every Hollywood movie, and it's frightening. But I guess there's truth to every form of media, and this is exactly what I signed up for by agreeing to follow Aly.

She hops off the table, back into Greyson's arms. I close my eyes to stop from puking and put the bill slightly up my nose.

Just trace the line.

A roar of laughter fills my ears. I look up to see what could possibly be going on. Snorting coke is easier than I thought; it feels like nothing.

"Fuck, man. I haven't seen anyone do that in forever!" Greyson shouts over the music in between his laughs.

Aly rushes over to me and begins wiping my dress, trying to stop herself from laughing as well. "Oh, honey. You snort, not blow."

"Shit . . . " I mumble while Alejandra's hands feverishly wipe my chest off.

"Let me show you." Xavier kneels down next to me, his calm tone erasing every bit of embarrassment I'm feeling.

The feeling of betrayal quickly dissipates as I put my attention onto proving to my friends I can hang too. If this is their thing, I can learn to love it. I watch Xavier effortlessly make his way down the line, the contents going exactly where he directs them to go.

"Your turn." He doesn't immediately turn into the Energizer Bunny like Greyson and Aly, no. If anything his shoulders are less tense; he finally releases that clench in his jaw.

"'Kay."

"You got this, Lissa," Aly shouts before allowing Greyson to drag her down the stairs to the dance floor.

"It's just us now, no need to be nervous."

I lean back in, grabbing the rolled-up bill off the table and beginning to trace the white line.

Snort it, don't blow it.

Almost immediately my mouth begins to numb as the taste of gasoline overpowers my senses. I rise from the table, trying my best to feel out every change the substance is slowly giving me.

"You good?" Xavier stands tall next to me, like a bodyguard.

I look up at him, our dilated pupils making contact. "I'm fucking amazing." My body is being filled with a pleasant feeling of euphoria. All I want to do is take my hair down and feel the music. My eyes focus on Xavier, his physique, those daring features. It's funny—how we're standing in a crowded room but it just feels like it's us at every moment. As the music plays, I push my body closer to his and begin to slowly sway my hips. The confidence boost this gives me, the way all my worries escaped my mind—they're right. It's worth it.

FORTY

Success. The word itself I can't define with accuracy if anyone asked me to, but I think I can tell you what it might mean. Money—of course. But most importantly a life where I don't have to explain myself to anybody. Where I'm surrounded by likeminded people who want to indulge in the same things I want to indulge in. Success is when my biggest problem every year is figuring out what charity I'm going to donate just for tax purposes—even though I'd much rather buy a sports car. There. That's success.

At least that's how Aly always described it. I don't know what it means to me just yet.

"I'm gonna need this before we start shooting," Alejandra mumbles, revealing a small baggie in her hand.

I sit quietly, taking casual glances at my outfit in the mirror in front of us. For Aly's first music video she wanted to do something similar to *The Breakfast Club*. She said something about how people would want to watch it because of the tribute or whatever, I don't know. All I know is that Aly's sitting next to me with a jet-black bang wig on and I have to get my extensions removed and my hair straightened to give me that "Claire" look. Whoever that is.

Jerrica and Megan are also coming to complete the perfect music video cast, so that should be fun. She invited her hairstylist to be in the video as well. It seems like they had been friends for a bit; he's probably someone she picked up when I left. The dude's name is Noah. He's around our age, a pretty sweet guy so far. But the biggest thing I noticed about him is that his smooth caramel skin pumped out this thick scent of vanilla.

"Girl, you know that stuff is not good for you., Noah states as he combs through Alejandra's temporary locks. Her head is bent down, snorting the contents on the back of her hand since a flat surface isn't available in her dressing room.

"Nagging won't get you very far," the woman replies in a chirpy tone before her brown eyes quickly dart to me. "You've never done a music video before. Trust me, you'll need some."

"Well, neither have you! I've done shoots. It can't be that different," I quickly reply.

"Fair." She pauses and takes a quick look at Noah. "But not everyone has this guy's natural born energy. And I'm not taking any chances. Come on. Three scene redos too many, and you'll be begging for it." She quickly arranges another line of the substance on her hand while Noah lets out a deep sigh. My eyes go back and forth from him to her, then from her to him.

"Fine." I adjust my pink top before bending down to try my best at snorting the line off of my best friends skin.

Noah chuckles. "You are the perfect Alison, Alejandra. Corrupting good ol' Claire."

"I have no idea what any of these references mean."

"Look, I couldn't do *Clueless* or *Mean Girls*! It's been done one too many times. So, we're doing *The Breakfast Club*. Any more complaints?" Alejandra snaps, standing from her chair and heading toward the set. "Plus! It's innovative. We have girls playing guys. A gay guy as the jock. My beautiful ass. We're making history. God, I fucking love you guys!" the raven-haired beauty shouts as she continues to make small steps away from us.

"Love you too," Noah and I repeat at the same time before following closely behind.

We spend the rest of the video shoot continuously doing lines every hour or so to keep our energy up. We go from seven a.m. to twelve a.m. because it had to be *perfect*. If it isn't perfect, no one's going home. The time goes by quickly, though. I can honestly say I can go the rest of my life without listening to "Forever" and be perfectly fine. The song is everything a first single should be. It's a dance bop with an eighties influence, so I guess, *The Breakfast Club* theme kind of made sense. Most importantly, it's special. I'm flying high and selling the hell out of a character from a movie I've never seen before. Spoiler alert: drugs make it so much easier to learn an eight count in a skirt and boots.

Alejandra's right, being high made everything so much easier. I didn't yawn once. I didn't complain once. I sipped my grande latte and got back to work. So maybe, if I took her tips, my shoots would go easier as well.

FORTY-ONE

old morning air introduces a California winter that has no concern for a girl in a bathing suit. You know, they say it's always palm trees accompanied by a blazing hot sun, but whoever said that lied. They lied, and they need to be put in prison. I'm not saying there's full on snowstorms, but we own jackets too, okay? It's fine, though. The substances flowing through my system keep me distracted and my eye on the prize. My large pupils are focused on one thing and one thing only—the camera. That's the thing with modeling; you have to get that shot, and if you don't? Then you aren't going home.

There are nights where I watch my follower count go up simply because I took a quick supermarket trip with Aly or Xavier. Hollywood is easy. Well, it's easy for me. I'm blessed with all these high-profile celebrities around me, and now my followers are spiking from a small one thousand to two hundred thousand. It's funny how the right connections can bring this small-town, five foot nothing black girl to a freezing cold beach.

"All right, let's make sure we get the sunset!" the photographer shouts.

"Make sure it's my good side!" I shout back, the warmth of the upcoming sun making itself known on my exposed skin. My freshly manicured fingers quickly adjust the spirals that the wind attempts to ruin before consenting to the camera for another hundred shots.

The shoot goes on for another hour. By then I'm out of coke, my stomach is rumbling, and I'm as cranky as cranky can get.

"Here you go." The assistant drapes a warm white robe around me.

"Thanks." I adjust the garment to perfectly hug my body. "Do we have coffee or anything?"

You're crashing, don't embarrass yourself.

"I think—"

"Good morning, everybody!"

Xavier's charming voice seems to cause a quake throughout the whole beach. The crew, the random passersby, everyone turns to see the six-three man energetically walking toward us. He has his regular black leather jacket on, his workout sneakers, and a T-shirt that is still drenched in half-dry sweat, if you squint hard enough.

I push the stray strands out of my face before a gentle smile appears on my once aggravated face. "What are you doing here?" I speak in a soft tone as he approaches me.

He keeps one hand behind his back, a sly smile emerging on his lips. "I went out for a run this morning. Then I ran past—" He pauses, presenting a bouquet from behind his back. The flowers present waves of red and yellow, but what really catches my attention is the diamond necklace hanging around it. "I ran past this shop, barely open but I begged so she let me in. Anyways. This is for you. I thought you could use a new necklace. Get rid of that cheap shit what's-her-face gave you."

Speechless, the bouquet transfers from his hands to mine. The chain itself is a diamond tennis necklace that probably costs more than my rent. The pendant reads "Kimber," completely different from the "A" Bailey got me. I drape my fingers across the cheaper pendant hanging from my neck. I don't even know why I still wear it. "Xavier."

He says nothing for a minute, practically swatting my hand down before removing the necklace himself. Without a care in the world, he drops it in the sand, I don't dare to watch it fall. My neck is naked for a second, only to be replaced by the new one he just presented to me. It's cold to the touch for a moment, only taking a second to adjust to my skin.

"Look, you deserve it. And—" His eyes explore me from head to toe. "Damn, you look beautiful. Even in that Four Seasons robe."

Laughter escapes my glossy lips as I hold the flowers close to my heart. "You're an idiot. I'm standing with an idiot, ladies and gents!"

"Yeah, yeah. Shut up. Point is, I want to make this thing with you official. I'm tired of playing games, man. So, is this the time where I tell you to check yes or no if you want to be my girlfriend?"

"You'd need a piece of paper and a pen for that, but I already know I'd check yes."

"Fuck, yeah, cause a no would have been embarrassing as hell," he adds jokingly before pulling me into a hug and placing a kiss on my forehead.

"Ugh, okay, yay! But you need to go shower, like, now."

"Aw, c'mon. You don't like olives?"

I part from him, pretending to gag as he laughs. "You are so disgusting! What the hell did I sign up for?"

"Flowers and great jokes?"

I playfully roll my eyes. "I'm about to get out of here, so . . . coming?"

"You drove?"

"No, took an Uber. Didn't feel like sitting through the traffic by myself in the middle of the night."

"You could have called. You know I was up."

"I didn't, actually. Do you even sleep?"

Xavier shrugs. "Yeah."

I glare at him. "Sure."

"At least let me drive you." He pauses, pulling his phone out and typing a message or two to God knows who. "Actually, come to my place."

"All I have are the sweats I arrived here in and my purse. Plus, it's wash day, I have stuff to do at home . . . "

Xavier rolls his eyes. "Then we'll head to the store, get you a double of everything you have. I want you to feel at home at my place."

"I barely even go to your place."

"That can't change?"

"Touché."

He helps me change and get my things, my heart doesn't stop fluttering. Not for a moment. Even when I say my goodbyes to the crew and thank the photographer for cooperating with me; it doesn't stop. From now on it isn't Savannah and Xavier or Lissa and Bailey. It's Lissa and Xavier. Arlissa Kimber Benson and Xavier Steven Amari. This is how it's supposed to be. We look best together and feel better together too. I think this is everything I've craved, everything I've begged for. He comes closer than anyone else in terms of everything. In terms of making me want to do better, in terms of having the ability to open a closed heart.

Is this how Bonnie felt when she met Clyde? Did she see him and know that her whole future resided in that one person? Did she look him in the eyes and see the pathway to the rest of her

life? Were her butterflies constant as she struggled to breathe every single time he looked in her direction? All I know about Bonnie is that if she stood for nothing, at least she stood for him. And if passion was what I was looking for—I sure as hell found it.

You did. You found it.

FORTY-TWO

"Hello?"

The phone remains glued between my cheek and shoulder as I try my best to unlock the door. "Hey! I just wanted to check on you. You haven't been home in a bit."

Jerrica's voice whispers through the phone. "Yeah, I know. I've been meaning to talk to you about that. Can we meet for lunch, maybe?"

So, we do just that. I walk to the café a few blocks down from the apartment. Of course, I get there first. Thankfully, there's a booth unoccupied where I can wait for her. In no time she's illuminating the space with her energy, my smile intensifying with every step she takes.

"Hey, are you okay?" I blurt out, watching her take a seat.

Jerrica pushes some hair behind her ear before shaking her head. "I didn't know how to tell Aly or you this . . . "

Concern fills my expression. "What's up?"

"I'm moving out. I know you guys need the help with rent and stuff, and I feel so bad. But my dad is ill and I need to help my parents out right now. And you know, be there for him. Them. Be there for them." Her eyes water as she struggles through the sentence, word by word.

"Jerrica—"

"Please don't feel bad for me," she whimpers, falling apart in front of me.

"No, no. Just know that I'm here if you ever need anything." I reach over to grab her hand, hoping we won't catch the attention of people passing by.

"I know, and I'm so happy I met you. You're one of the few sane people in this shithole."

I let out a weak laugh. "I'm not too sure about that."

"Hey, at least you don't do drugs," she replies jokingly.

"At least."

"But, seriously, I'm going to miss you and Aly. I just need to spend this time with my dad. He doesn't have long."

"I promise you don't have to apologize. I love you, and I'll miss you, and we'll see each other again. Don't worry about it."

"Ugh!" Jerrica wipes the droplets from her tear ducts before forcing one of her signature big-bright smiles. "Can we eat? And talk about something else. Like you! I can't stay on this for too long."

"Yes, yes, we can. Me? I don't know, Nothing interesting there."

Jerrica is the last grip on reality I have here. Everything else in LA is fabricated and made out of distractions. She reminds me of what's real, what matters. It's not like I was grateful for that reminder when our mornings were filled with brewed coffee and "Happy" by Pharrell playing on repeat. But it's gone now, and I never got the chance to enjoy it, because she has someone else to save. Maybe one day I'll learn my lesson about appreciating something when you have it.

I rise from my bed and glance at the glowing numbers on the clock across from me. Eleven in the morning. Cute. I've been sleeping in a bit too much lately, especially with Jerrica not here anymore. The smell of chocolate coffee beans used to fill the apartment with its aroma and even though her healthy, get-up-at-six-in-the-morning lifestyle could get annoying, it was refreshing. It was refreshing to see a fellow model who didn't live the way I did. She didn't sleep in, she didn't care to watch her followers go up; she was different. She is different. Regardless, her light is officially gone from this dim apartment. It's just Aly and me. No complaints there, but still.

I take tiny steps into the hall, rubbing my eyes as I walk. When my vision finally starts to cooperate, I catch the view of two people sprawled out across the hardwood floor. Alejandra's raven hair is covering her face, and the other person who I can tell is Greyson, his face is completely planted onto the wood. I squint to get a better look at the pair.

"Guys, get up. This is pathetic."

Silence.

Are they even breathing?

In a panic, before this brain of mine can process my actions, I'm filling a glass with water. I try my best to aim, but when the water leaves its container a majority of it goes on Greyson rather than Aly. Everything happens for a reason, I guess. The one sprinkle that got on Alejandra causes her to wake up in an alarming fashion, though. So mission complete.

"What the fuck?" she exclaims, quickly jumping up.

"I thought you were dead."

Greyson repeatedly pats the back of his head where a majority of the liquid landed. "That—that could get your ass kicked," he mutters.

"Try it," I snap back. "A thank you would also be nice."

"Thanks for not leaving me for dead. My fucking savior."

Alejandra wraps her arms around me. "You're sweet for being worried, bunny. We just had a really long fucking night."

"What'd you guys get into this time?"

Greyson and Alejandra exchange looks. "Well."

"Well?"

It's at that moment that Alejandra adjusts her ripped up cocktail dress and slowly wipes her runny mascara with her left hand. A gleaming diamond ring is revealed, and all I can do is hang my mouth wide open.

"Surprise!" she shouts, running over to Greyson and wrapping her arms around him. "We decided why not! We're in this forever."

"You didn't."

"Vegas isn't that bad of a drive," Greyson chimes in.

"Shut up. What were you thinking?" My attention is on the groom now. I still don't trust Greyson as far as I can throw him. Who knows what he does at parties when she isn't around. But that's not my business, right?

"Lissa!" Aly stands in front of who I guess is her husband now, protecting him in a way that I can't wrap my brain around. "Be happy for me, please? For once. Don't do that thing you do."

"I'm just . . . I'm just wishing this decision made a lick of sense."

Greyson opens his mouth to speak, but instead just slides past Alejandra and me. "I'm going to give you two some time and go take a shower."

"Okie." Alejandra forces a smile.

I glare at the other woman. "So."

"Lissa, you're my sister. I don't have parents who talk to me, or even fucking care about me. I can't remember the last time we had a conversation, and I lived with them my whole life. Do you know how many times they contacted me since we've been here? Zero." She rolls her eyes while her right hand nervously toying with the rock on her finger.

"So this is about your parents? How does that justify marrying him?"

"No, I just . . . When it's right, it's right. What is *so* wrong with him? Maybe I'm ready to move on with my life."

"Maybe you just want to fix your parents' mistakes."

"Why is it so hard for you to just be happy for me? You had no problem with Chris! Or did you just accept him because you liked him too?"

"Everyone in that school liked him! I'm just saying if I went around trying to replace—But this isn't about Samantha. This is about you giving your life to someone we haven't even known a year."

"Maybe it is. Maybe you just don't believe in anything that's easy because you think everything is supposed to be hard to prove it's real."

I scoff. "Well, that's just bullshit. Becoming friends with you was easy!"

"Was it?"

I take tiny steps toward her. "I'm sorry . . . I just want the best for you."

"I know. And this is what's best. He's the best. Trust me. Just love me without the judgey eyes, please."

A small smile curves up on my face as I pull her into a hug. "I'll always love you, but I really would have loved to go to the wedding."

"There will be one . . . eventually." Aly giggles before pulling

away from me. "Now, I have a man to go join in the shower because I'm sure I smell like pickles and cigarettes. Did you know
they let you smoke openly in Vegas hotel lobbies?"

"No, I didn't."

"Well, it's awful. I think I have fucking lung cancer now." She
happily skips away from me. "Love you! Now get your ass up and
go propose to Xavier. We can have a double-date honeymoon!"

"Love you too."

I stand in that living room alone, internalizing it all. I can't
tell if I'm witnessing the beginning of something or the end. Either way, she's smiling and thriving, so who am I? It's just scary,
I guess. Seeing my best friend who was once glued to my hip
blossom into someone who doesn't need me. At all. She has other
people, she has her dreams, she has a husband, apparently. Did
she ever need me? Or am I holding onto her for a more worth-
the-read life story?

Maybe it's time to pen my own.

FORTY-THREE

*E*nvy. A funny feeling that you don't have any idea you're feeling until well, you're acting on it. No one ever sits themselves down and says, "Hey self, you're jealous.'

Yeah, and if you do that, then you're fucking weird.

I take quick steps toward the condo door, a bit irritated that I don't have a key yet. I'm sure Alejandra has a key. But before I can raise my hand to knock, my ears catch wind of a conversation just beginning to form into something worse.

"You are a monster, and it doesn't matter if you get——"

Savannah. Her voice fades out, then there's silence.

"Whatever you say, Sav."

Xavier. Calm, controlled—exactly what I'd expect.

"It doesn't matter what I say, does it?"

"Not really."

Muffles again. Dammit.

"Wow, just—you are unbelievable. After all these years you still shock me in the worst of ways."

His response, undetected for a bit until some words find their way through. "Love is funny, isn't it?"

"Go to hell, you sick bastard."

"Goodbye, Savannah. I'm sure I'll see you again."

Shit. She can be coming out any second. I run down the hall, as far away from his front door and the elevator as I can. At the exact moment that my body wraps around a corner, safe from anyone discovering that I had been that close, I can hear his door slam. I don't want to see her, I don't want to risk her seeing me. I stay glued to that wall until I hear the elevator ding and take her trifling ass as far away as possible.

I wait ten, maybe fifteen minutes before taking a deep breath and heading right back to that door. One knock, two—

"Hey gorgeous."

I smile, rising on my tippy toes to give him a kiss on the cheek. "Did I miss anything while I was gone?"

He shrugs before allowing me into the condo. "Nah, been quiet as fuck."

I roll my eyes and shut the door behind me. I want to tell him that I heard. But I can't ruin this. I won't. Because as soon as I confront him he'll push me away, I know that much. My focus lands on his tattooed hand. "What do your tattoos mean?"

"All of them?"

"Yeah."

"You've never asked that before."

"Maybe I just want to get to know you better. I don't know."

"Fair. Well, buckle up. It's show-and-tell time." He takes a sip from the drink in his hand before rolling up his sleeve a bit. Those scratches healed nicely. "The bird on my hand. Freedom. I use my hands to fight and, in a way, I guess, freed myself. I don't know. Saying it aloud sounds fucking stupid."

256

"From what?"

"What?"

"What did you free yourself from?"

"Nothing that you need to hear about now." He mentally scans his body before continuing. "The prayer hands on my triceps—"

"I don't know what a triceps is."

Xavier laughs and points to an area of his arm. "This part."

"Right! That one."

"My mom and I got matching tattoos forever ago so now I'm the boxer with two hands praying on his arm, but . . . anything for her."

"That's sweet. What about the sun?" Flashbacks of when I first saw him raid my memory. That white shirt he had on that perfectly showed the interesting choice of ink on his skin.

He smiles. "Come on, you know me."

"Sunrises and sunsets?"

"Sunrises and sunsets, baby girl. The only thing you can fucking depend on."

"You okay?"

"Peachy."

Fuck, I can't get Alejandra and Greyson's dumb-ass marriage out of my head. And now Savannah pops up out of nowhere? What if she's visited more than I'm aware of? Why can't I get a grip on anything?

"I want a tattoo, you know."

"Yeah?"

"Yeah, maybe we should get one together."

"Eh . . . it's a bit early for that. Don't you think?"

"Or something, anything . . . I don't know."

"I bought you a car. What else could you possibly want?"

"You can buy anyone a car. I—"

Xavier chugs the remains in his cup. "You matter, okay?"

"I know."

"Is this about Aly and Grey?"

"I just—"

"They are a special case, and they don't reflect us. Chill the fuck out."

"No, they fucking suck." And that's what I don't understand. How do the druggies reach a milestone before Xavier and I can even say "I love you"?

Calm down, little sis.

"Yikes."

"I'm just saying . . . I'm chill. I just think we need something. You know, to establish us, and it has nothing to do with them."

"Was the necklace not enough?"

"You know it was."

"Then what do you want? Because this conversation seems fucking pointless, and I've had a long day," he snaps.

"I thought you said it was a quiet day?"

"Yeah . . . just busy."

"I think I'm gonna head back home."

"You're joking," he spits, standing in the same place as the distance between us grows.

"I'm not. I just clearly don't feel well. Sue me."

"Well, sorry I don't want to move at the speed of fucking light!" he manages to shout before the door slams behind me.

Good job scaring him away, Lissa. I told you to calm down.

~~If this were a movie . . . I'd be leaving for snacks right about~~ now.

Days pass, and we haven't seen each other. It's almost as if every time he calls me he's just doing it because he feels like he has to.

The thought that I ruined it all creeps into my mind often but I have to remain positive, right? Xavier has the key to my heart in his pocket, and he's straying away. How can I ever do this again without him?

Thursday night, and that glowing text that I've been praying for finally comes in. The condo seems brand new every time I show up there. Mainly because he never invites me since for some reason he'd rather stay over at my shitty apartment. I quickly place a few knocks on the huge door before stepping back.

"You're here!" Xavier exclaims as he opens the entrance enough for me to walk through.

I raise a brow. "Yeah, I'm here."

"I've been thinking."

"Lord, you could have done this over the phone," I whine.

He places a quick kiss on my forehead. "No, I couldn't have."

"I'll be the judge of that."

Now he pecks my lips. "I wouldn't have it any other way."

"Are you high?"

"Maybe. Not the point, though. Are you ready?"

I cross my arms over my chest. "I have no idea what I'm getting ready for."

"So, Grey and Aly want to move in here."

"Why the fuck are you telling me this?" The anger comes out of nowhere. Is she ditching me again? She has to be.

Duh.

"No, but . . . look around."

I quickly scan the enormous space. "Boxes?"

"I'm moving out. And so are you. I bought the place right downstairs. I thought about what you said—"

"No." I quickly walk over to the gorgeous male and gently grab his hand. "You don't have to move in with me because I threw a fit."

"Well, then let's say I did it because I don't want you living alone. Plus, we're neighbors. It's like when Schmidt moved out on *New Girl*."

"I've never seen that show, baby."

"Then we gotta fuckin' watch it in our new place. Is that a yes?"

"Do I have any other choice?"

"Not really. You can't afford an LA apartment on your own, mi amor."

"Then yes."

The fear of losing him washes away as his lips meet mine once again. Once the negative emotions leave, the hope and optimism returns—butterflies included.

I can get used to this.

FORTY-FOUR

The first month living with my boyfriend was perfect. Xavier doesn't sleep much; in fact, his insomnia is so bad that he only schedules training at night. He'll stay out until morning, driving around and chasing sunrises. But I can always count on him to crawl in the bed at seven a.m. smelling like Sea Breeze and Head & Shoulders. And when the sun is well risen, he sleeps like a baby. And even though I have to pee most mornings, I'd lay there for another hour and let him cuddle me until I'm sure he's sound asleep.

He slept at a normal time once. Once being last night. Mainly because I told him we should try staying up for 24 hours straight to get his sleep schedule back on track. He tried to complain, whine, convince me it wasn't worth it. But I did it. We walked on the treadmill whenever we got tired, we played way too many rounds of Monopoly, and when things got really bad? We put on

horror movies. He finally passed out at around eight p.m., and I did the same.

A strange, muted noise woke me up while the moon was still high in the sky. When I searched through the darkness for the source, that's when I realized it wasn't a strange sound. Xavier was crying. I pushed aside the million pillows we had spread across that California King and revealed him lying on his back, still sound asleep. Yet, there were tears aggressively streaming from his eyes to his ears. There were quiet mumbles escaping from his shriveled lips as well, but it was nothing I could make out.

Slowly, I placed my hands on his broad shoulders and began to gently shake him awake. "Xavier . . . "

It took a few more shakes to get him to respond, but instead of screaming or falling back asleep, he just kept crying. The large man balled himself up in my arms and just cried. I didn't ask why, I treated it like it was seven in the morning. I sat there silently and let him dissolve into me. I don't know how much time had passed, but he fell back asleep eventually. I didn't, though.

Once the birds begin to chirp and the sun starts peeking through our sheer curtains, I slowly get out of the bed. Quietly, I grab one of Xavier's T-shirts and head to the kitchen. Whatever went on with him last night isn't going to be something he wants to talk about. I know him enough to get that. But the least I can do is let him know he's loved.

Loved? Is that what this is? Love.

I spend the better part of the morning burning pancakes and remaking them over and over so that I don't embarrass myself. He's an athlete, so he always kept his meal plans on the fridge (thankfully) because I have no idea how much protein to put in these pancakes. I add some turkey bacon, chop some fruit, and put out two glasses of lemon water. The creeks of the hardwood floor alert me that he's up and on his way. Something I realized about large empty spaces is that the floors always give you up before you can be seen.

"Morning," he grumbles, pajama pants barely hanging on.

"Hey . . . come! I made breakfast."

He approaches me as he feverishly rubs his eyes. "You made breakfast?"

"I did. You left your little protein pancake recipe on the fridge, so I decided, why not? Eat!" I give him a quick kiss on the cheek before placing his plate down on the bar where he can still be close to me while I clean this wreck of a kitchen.

Xavier grabs a fork before taking a seat. "I'm very fucking lucky, then."

"I'm glad you know," I reply with a smile. The question "how'd you sleep" wants to come out so bad, but I just know I shouldn't. "Any plans for the day?"

"Um . . . I have to go see my dad, actually. So that fucking sucks."

"Yikes. What's so bad about it?"

"You've met him."

"That one night when I met all of you, but he seemed nice enough."

"I'm sure," Xavier mumbles in between chews.

Come on, Lissa. Keep him happy.

"So. Rate my breakfast, one to ten."

"Maybe a solid three. These strawberries are cut in a ridiculous fashion—"

"X!"

He laughs, something like a deep roar coming from his still sleepy tone. "It's good, babe. Ten out of ten. Thank you, I appreciate it."

When my eyes fall on him, the circle motion my arm is moving in as I wipe down the counter begins to slow. His tired eyes, messy hair, and the smile that can light up a million rooms. He's truly beautiful, and I'm truly grateful to have him. Alejandra said she just knew with Greyson. She also said I have a habit of not appreciating the easy things. It's time I acknowledge what feels right and ride through that green light like I promised. I break eye contact in an attempt to ignore the bubbling feelings. I just can't.

"Xavier."

"Yeah?"

"I think . . . " I stammer over my words, wanting to force this thought back as far as I can. But when the warm fabric of his T-shirt hugs my body in an attempt to calm my shaking spirit, I know the truth. "I think I love you."

There's a silence after the word vomit leaves my lips. I'm shaking, unsure if that would be the thing to run him out the door. But it's my truth, right? I should be able to speak that. I stood here in this drafty kitchen for hours to make sure he was going to have a good morning. A bitch finally knows what love feels like, okay? What it makes you do. How it makes you jump at the thought of doing any and everything to keep that love in your life. Being with Xavier is like quicksand, but instead of being scared of how dangerous it could be, I'm willing. I'm willing to suffocate and stop breathing as long as my body is filled with every bit of him. I'm open and ready.

"I—"

"No, wait." I turn to completely face him. "I fucking love you, man." A heavy breath escapes my lips as the confidence remains. Xavier clenches his jaw. "You do?"

Everything else I had ever experienced I was just going with the flow. Xavier and I are friction. "I just thought you should know."

"I love you too."

The dangerous words slip from his lips and the butterflies that I had been feeling for months make themselves known again. Our lips press against each other, and a feeling of safety surrounds me.

My heart is pumping gold through my veins as I hold him. I'm here for him, and I'll be here until the end of time.

I pull away, but I just can't ignore the elephant in the room. "Hey, can I ask you something?"

He chuckles. "Way to ruin the moment, but shoot."

"Last night . . ."

Immediately, his defenses rise. His jaw clenches even tighter, his fists ball up. "Right."

"I just want to be sure you're okay. Please talk to me."

A deep sigh leaves his lips before he squeezes my waist a little more. "I've had nightmares since I was a kid. And . . . I'm sorry if I scared you, okay? I'm not all flashy cars and trophies. I need to know you're in this for the nightmares and every-fucking-thing else. I can't have another person tell me it's too much."

"I'm in this for anything and everything you decide to throw at me, Xavier."

He nods. "That's my girl. You know you talk in your sleep too, right? Since we're on the topic."

"I do?"

"Yeah. Something about a . . . Sidney, Sarah, S——"

"Samantha."

"Bingo!"

"Yeah."

"Wait . . . is something wrong? I just assumed you were having another gay moment."

"No. Not even close."

He straightens his stance a bit, "Now you've got some opening up to do."

I shake my head vigorously before pushing away from him. Not this. This is the quickest way to ruin the entire morning. "I don't want to talk about it."

"Woah, woah. If I can't do that, neither can you."

"It's just—" I try so hard to make it all make sense in my head, but I haven't explained this to anyone—ever. I never had to.

I take small steps away from him, the more distance while my brain spirals, the better. Jesus, someone save me from having to tell this man my fucked-up pity story.

Xavier's brow furrows in confusion, his hand grabbing my wrist again. "I need you to trust me like I trust you."

When his eyes meet mine, there's a feeling of security. I'm safe here, and maybe it's okay to finally say out loud the part I played in my sister's death.

"I was seven years old. Most people don't remember shit when they're seven, but how can I forget this? I was watching Disney Channel heavily back then, and there was this actress that I loved. I was so obsessed with her, I wanted to be her for Halloween every freaking year. Anyways, she had just done a movie—"

"It's okay. Continue."

"Um . . . I . . . The movie, right. And she was coming to do a meet and greet at, um, a theater not too far from me."

"Right."

"And I—" My eyes begin to well as I try my best to focus on telling the story.

Don't get worked up, Lissa. You've been over this a million times in your head already. Tell him. Do it for me. You owe me, remember?

"My sister didn't want to take me. Lord, she barely wanted to be bothered with me that day." A sarcastic chuckle leaves my lips as I wipe a few tears that had escaped. Xavier squeezes my hand, giving me the confidence to continue. "She took me. She took me after I begged and pleaded for literal hours. When we got there, everything was fine. We got popcorn, and the damn girl hadn't even shown up yet. Her meet-and-greet booth was set up and everything, so many little girls like me were waiting . . . We ended up seeing the movie, she ended up canceling, and . . . after that a man came in. Um, he had a gun. My sister jumped in front of me. She died instantly."

"Lissa . . ."

"No. Because, Xavier, if I hadn't forced her—"

"You were a kid."

"And she was smarter than me. She didn't want to go, because maybe she knew! But she did it for me. Because I felt like some stupid Disney star hosting a meet and greet was more important than whatever else she planned to do that night. She did it for me, and I never got to see her again. I never got to say thank you. The last memory of my sister is her lying there bleeding out and my gloves are soaked with blood because she made me put them on so I didn't get a cold. Samantha was my hero . . . is. And the most I can do with the life she gave me is sit here and fucking whimper about all the things that are going wrong. I just might as well say I killed her. Because I did."

As the tears fall, Xavier doesn't say another word. He just holds me and lets the time pass as I choke on saliva and get snot and tears all over his chest. It's okay, I guess. The good, the bad, the ugly. Because being perfect isn't what love is. It's being there for it all. And holding each other until your arms go numb because you know your partner needs it. That's it. That's love.

PART TWO

Sunset

Chapter
FORTY-FIVE

I blink, and two years pass me by without warning. I can't remember it all if I tried. If anyone asked me to recall the last
two years I'd just tell them to Google because the press has
done a better job accounting for my life than I have.

Wow, this is life.

I wake up and while I'm sipping on Kombucha, Holly tells me
GQ wants Xavier and me on the cover. I pretend I'm not excited,
just another magazine cover, but when the phone hangs up I get a
happy dance out of the way before Xavier rolls out of bed.

Xavier. He's . . . a dream. I mean, I thought a year ago waking
up to him would get old but since he travels so much for matches
and everything else under the sun, I'm never not missing him.
Work keeps me occupied, though. At least I try.

Aly released her debut album a few months ago, and it sold
so well they sent her ass on tour. Honestly? It's been pretty good
without Greyson coming to our place and raiding the fridge at

random hours of the day. I haven't spoken to Jerrica much, and her social media has gone from Instagram Model to "I meditate and pray for my dad every second of the day." But, other than that it's been pretty amazing.

Samantha would be proud. If she were here right now, celebrating New Years with me, she'd tell me how she knew my life would end up just like those movies. Like, *Fifty Shades* mixed with *After* and a sprinkle of that TV show *.Star*. Right? I think so. And she'd do it with a bowl of strawberry ice cream because that was always her favorite. She prefers that flavor more than chocolate or vanilla. I never order strawberry.

I grip the glass tight as I walk through our populated living room. New Year's Eve. I've come to realize that it's all fun and games when you're in someone else's house waiting for the ball to drop, but not when everyone is at yours. I keep myself smiling, waving as more guests begin to arrive with their deviled eggs and bottles of Mailly L'Intemporelle Rose Grand Cru.

"Where's your knight in shining armor?" Ellie creeps up behind me, a full glass in her hand. The woman's green eyes pierce through my soul as she reads every tiny action I make.

"He'll be here. It's his house, it's not like he can just . . . not show up."

The brunette rolls her eyes. "Yeah, he can. And you clearly don't believe it yourself because you're guarding the door like a bomb squad is going to come bustin' through."

"I am not!" I exclaim and move from the entrance.

"Well, call him or something, I don't know." Ellie suggests before squeezing my shoulder and heading into the sea of people. What she doesn't know is that I did call him. I've called him a million times, and he isn't picking up.

I've been planning this New Year's party for months, Xavier knew that. We had the conversation six million times, and it just doesn't make sense. This party is important to me. I'm twenty-two, and I don't have trust fund money to last me forever. I've pulled a lot of strings to get some very important people to show up and meet me. There are CEOs here of Fortune 500 companies who could give me millions for being the face of their campaigns. But I know they want to see the A-list celebrity I live with too. So, why isn't he here?

I take deep breaths as I adjust my passion twists and relax my grip on the wineglass. I grab an appetizer off the tray of the woman walking by and head into the crowd of people. They're all talking, sipping wine, making connections. Exactly what I should be doing. But my brain is too focused on if my drug-enticed boyfriend is on the side of the road somewhere. I force myself to mingle as much as I can to pass the time.

"Someone turn the TV up. The ball is going to drop soon!" a man shouts from the crowd as he points to our theater-size TV.

"Shit, is it really that late?" I whisper to Ellie before using the remote app on my phone to turn the TV up.

"Yeah, you feeling all right?"

My eyes won't stop darting to the door. Maybe, he'll come bursting in here with the widest smile and a million roses in his hand. Maybe I should be out looking for him and kick all these people out of my damn house. What the hell? Why the hell am I alone on New Year's Eve? "I'm great."

"Five . . . four . . . three . . . two . . . one! Happy New Year!"

The condo fills with roars of applause and confetti that comes from God knows where. People are kissing people they just met or the partners they brought. My heart feels as if someone is squeezing it as the thought of not getting my New Year's kiss dawns on me. I'm completely alone. Watching everyone's excitement, my eyes begin to fill with tears.

"Fuck," I mumble, hanging my head so low that if anyone is even remotely close to me with a camera they won't catch it. Before I know it, Ellie is tugging me through the crowd and to

the nearest bathroom. The brunette slams the door and locks it before her green eyes pierce my soul once again.

"He's not coming, is he?"

The tears stream down my face, holding it in has failed. "He said he'd be here, okay? He has insomnia and, like, really bad anxiety so sometimes he freaks out for social events, I get it. He's fine. I'm fine."

"Please don't cry. And please don't make these bullshit excuses for him," my friend pleads.

"It's not excuses. He really struggles, El."

"Lissa . . . "

"It's just ridiculous, you know? He helped with this, he knows I need this. I need to meet these people, and he just . . . I needed him here."

She places her hands on my shoulders. "Do you need him? Or do you need to shake it off and deal with that asshole later? There are millions of dollars in opportunities stumbling around your living room right now, and you're in the bathroom sobbing because your boyfriend is MIA. Come on, Arlissa."

I release a few deep breaths before grabbing some tissue and patting my eyes. "He should have been here . . . " Sure, I can shake it off but what do you do when the most important person on earth isn't there cheering you on?

"I got the perfect thing for you."

I already know what she means before she takes the contents out of her pocket and begins preparing it on the sink.

"I'm quitting that stuff, man."

"Yeah, okay," Ellie replies before taking a few more moments to create some lines with her credit card. "Come on, it'll give you that spark you need. You got this."

After another deep sigh, I lean down and begin to snort the contents. The initial rush is something that never gets old. "Okay, I'm fine."

274

She peeks up from snorting the rest and shakes her head. "Let me fix . . . " Her words drift off as she pulls some of my locs over my shoulder. "You're good to go."

"Thank you, you're—just thank you."

I catch the eye of one of the best photographers that California knows. "Ellis Mason! Arlissa Benson. I've been looking for you all night! Nice to meet you." I put my hand out, a bright smile illuminating my face.

Six in the morning comes quickly. As my brain sobers up, the thousand bodies begin to slowly make their way out the door. I watch as the huge space that's my condo empties. Empty bottles, confetti, crumbs, and business cards. My heart is in pain, and I've spent all night ignoring it. But as the sun rises I drop to the ground. The tears overcome me while the cold from the unforgiving floor touches my skin, completely dressed up with not a single person to impress. My red lipstick smears over the sleeves of my sweater dress as I aggressively wipe my face.

Keep it together, he can walk in at any minute.

My shaky hands pick my fragile body up off the floor. If I sleep it off, I can wake up from this nightmare and pretend it never happened.

A gust of wind makes its way through the living room as the door opens and shuts with a passion, revealing a man who's completely out of his mind. Xavier stumbles in. My eyes dart from him to the clock on my phone. It's 3:27 p.m. I sit there, on that large sofa and watch as he drops a piece of clothing with every step he takes.

"Where the fuck were you last night?" I blurt out.

Xavier freezes, his bloodshot eyes finally settling on me. "Don't. Not right now."

"Are you serious?"

"I said don't, Kimber."

I rise from my seat and follow him around our space. "No, we're going to do this right now because you fucking ditched me! You know how much this meant to me, and where were you? Did you even hear my voicemail?" Xavier is gliding across our alcohol-covered floors, turning over every book and ashtray in distress. "Nothing? Not an explanation or an 'I'm sorry'? Not even going to offer help clean this place up? You know, I don't know. I really don't because this is not—"

"Shut up, Arlissa! For God's sake, just fucking shut the hell up!" His fists are balled up as his cherry-red eyes focus on my completely sober ones.

"What the hell happened to you?" I whimper. Him yelling at me is new and frightening. I try my best to keep the tears back, but my heart genuinely begins to crack with every word he says. Maybe Ellie's right.

He goes back to searching the house. "I don't want to talk about it."

"You need to, Xavier! You don't just vanish for twenty-four hours and tell me you don't fucking feel like it!"

"What did I just say?" he snaps. "I have a fucking headache, and you're yelling at the top of your goddamn lungs."

"You know what . . . " Backing up from the person who I'm starting to see in a different light; I grab my purse off the bar and head toward the door. "I don't have time for this. I have a hair appointment."

"Wait." The tension in Xavier's body slowly starts to release, but I can't ignore how he still looks fresh off of the set of *The Hangover*.

"What?"

He reaches for my hand but I pull it away. "I'm sorry."

"You're not. So what do you actually want?"

"I'm serious. Don't walk out that door hating me."

"Then you should have *been* here. What else was so important?"

Clearly stressed, he takes a deep breath and runs his hands through his greasy hair. "My dad called, and we got in an argument." He shakes his head rapidly as if he's going insane trying to recall the events. "I was on my way, and he made me . . . Look, you know I wouldn't miss it unless I was completely out of my damn mind. I hadn't slept the night before—you know this. So I was going to handle some shit before the end of the night, and . . . I meant to be there. I just—I fucked up. He got in my head, and I fucked up."

"Xavier . . . "

"Please . . . just forgive me. You know how shit is." He looks absolutely pitiful standing in front of me. In a matter of minutes the over-six-foot man looks so small—helpless, even.

I shake my head. "No, I don't. Because you won't ever tell me."

His eyes dart from mine in a desperate attempt to escape. "Man . . . fuck."

"Xavier. Talk to me."

There's a silence as he walks over to the couch. I follow, wondering what would happen next. "My mom."

"Is she okay?"

"Yeah, but . . . before me. She was pregnant—with a girl. My dad told her to get rid of it ,and he'd keep making her until she gave him a boy. Girls can't fight or whatever the fuck, right? Girls can't carry the legacy. She had me—eventually." Xavier pauses, ripping off a piece of skin from his cuticles before continuing again. "After praying and praying, my dad . . . he did things to her, I think. That she won't really talk about. I mean ,when I came along things got better for her, but . . . that's because he had something to redirect his focus on." He pulls his collar down to show what looks like fresh marks that are slowly converting to black and blue bruises.

"Xavier, what the fuck?"

"It's not from boxing. It's from him. If I don't win, I never deserved to be born, right? It's more than just the fame and the trophies, I'm constantly fighting to prove to my mom that she didn't go through that shit for nothing and to my dad that . . . I'm worth the last name he gave me. Arlissa, I didn't want to tell you this shit because I already know you worry. If you knew about my dad—"

"What the hell . . . You need to stop boxing. How are you letting him control you? He's hurting you."

"He's my dad."

I'm stunned, unsure what to do with all the information that's been tossed in my direction. "Just let me help you like you helped me."

He nods, standing up from the cushions. "I love you, but no. I'm gonna go take a shower."

My hands grip tightly onto my thighs. "I love you. But you can't run from me, you know that right?"

"I know, little red. Wow, I miss calling you that."

"You do?"

"Yeah, but . . . I like the brown. I'd like it even better blond, though."

"Excuse me?"

"You need a new look anyways, right?"

"Yeah, but—"

"People are getting bored with it."

"Well thanks!" I reply sarcastically.

"Just trust me. Try blond or something. You'll get a refresh in attention with that."

I glare at him, still not fully sold. "My curls are going to shrivel up and die. You know what that red did to my hair back then."

"We should go on a vacation." A sly smile appears on his face. He knows exactly how to get me to agree to something.

I raise a brow. "Where?"

"Hm, let's see. Somewhere cold. Put those thousand-dollar coats to use. I got it! You can have your new hair then. Shit, I'm good. I should be your manager."

"Yeah, yeah. Manage yourself first." I roll my eyes before grabbing my purse and beginning to head out the door. "Fine! I was tired of this shit anyways."

I exit the condo to a filthy hallway, thanks to the party goers. You know, you would think rich people were better at not leaving their red solo cups all over the place. But nope, they're just as filthy as everyone else.

Chapter
FORTY-SIX

Brown coils are now platinum blonde. And I can't tell if it's thanking me for paying attention to it again or burning to death from the bleach. It doesn't matter, though. Xavier's happy, and I'm gifted a vintage Versace coat to take on our little trip to Colorado.

Never in my life did I think Colorado's a place worth vacationing to. We're staying in a pretty huge Airbnb that feeds into every "I'm rich and go skiing yearly" aesthetic. It's completely wooden with huge glass windows that allow the sun to peek in whenever it pleases. There's a basement, but instead of dust and cobwebs it has a hot tub, a fireplace, and more succulents than I can count. The home is fully equipped with a gym as well, because Xavier isn't going anywhere if he has to miss a workout. Every time I turn on a light, it isn't that annoying hospital-light brightness that would usually blind you. When I flick those lights on it covers the space with a candlelight-like glow.

The ski resort is everything the movies make it to be. Hot chocolate, ski lodges, ice skating, and sledding/tubing. But my absolute favorite would be the horse-drawn sleigh ride. Honestly, would I be me if I didn't kick and scream until Xavier got us at least an hour on one of those rides? No, I wouldn't be.

"What time is our ride again?" I ask, walking hand-in-hand with my lover on the property.

"Uh . . . " Xavier pauses, using his free hand to look for the receipt in his pocket. "Six thirty. You still good with that?"

"Mm-hmm. Just asking." I stretch up to give him a quick kiss on the cheek. "Thanks for this."

"Why are you thanking me?"

"I don't know. You do a lot for me, and sometimes I can't see that you're right. Like my hair. My Instagram impressions are already skyrocketing again."

He leans down to press his lips against mine. "I told you, babe. I've been doing this a lot longer than you have. Plus, I was trained by the best."

"I'm just glad I have you, that's all."

"And I don't know what I'd do without you, Minnie."

A giggle escapes my lips as we continue to trek through the snow. "Where are these nicknames even coming from?"

"The ol' noggin."

"I knew that big-ass head of yours had to be holding some kind of information. Who knew it was nicknames. Wait, does this mean you're always thinking about me?"

"Twenty-five-eight, Kimber. Does this make me a stalker, though?"

"Shit, if it does, just know I'm completely okay with that."

"Good to know. A little worrisome, but good to know."

My lips peel open to speak but are halted by a woman walking directly toward us, and Xavier's not moving out of the way. In fact, a smile forms on his face. It's then that I realize she's smiling at him as well. The woman has curly brown hair that's practically the same color as her skin. Her curls are highlighted with blond, and her big brown eyes are kind and inviting.

"Oh my God. Fucking Xavier Amari. What are the chances?" She's excited. Too excited.

Xavier releases his grip of my hand before pulling the girl into an embrace. "Willow fucking Ali. How've you been?"

"Great, amazing. Cold! Aren't we all, though. We're in goddamn Colorado."

"Shit, you're right. I'm just so happy to see you. It feels like forever."

"Has it been forever? My clock must be going slow."

He laughs. "Nope, it's been almost ten years since you bailed on me."

"No one bailed on you, Amari!"

"But you did."

I'm standing right fucking here. *Hello. I'm Arlissa, his girlfriend.*

"Yeah, I just . . . wow, you look great, man. Definitely didn't look like this at thirteen." They share a few more laughs.

Hello! Do something.

Okay, I've had it.

"Shit!" I exclaim after tossing my hot chocolate on the ground. "I'm a klutz, wow. This is so embarrassing."

Willow seems to finally notice me for the first time as she gasps and hands me a few napkins from her pocket. "You didn't burn yourself, did you?"

"Nope. Thank God, right?"

Xavier wraps his arm around me as the raging attitude emulates from my being. "You gotta be more careful than that, woman." He passive-aggressively squeezes my shoulder, causing me to wince a bit at the pressure. You'd think I'd get used to the "shut the fuck up" grip by now, but nope. "This is Arlissa. My girlfriend."

The face she makes leads me to assume she's shocked at the fact that he claimed my rightful title.

"Hi, Willow, right?"

"Yes!" she exclaims before briefly shaking my hand. "Nice to meet you, cutie."

"Mm-hmm. X, I think I'm not feeling too well. Want to get food before our ride tonight?"

"Oh! Are you two doing the horse rides?" she interrupts.

"Yeah, I thought, why not. She deserves it," he replies, still keeping me close in his hold.

"So romantic. I love that for you guys. Well! I'm going to head off to where I was going, but it was so nice to run into you."

"You too, man. Feel free to call me whenever you want."

What? No. She cannot call you whenever the hell she wants. What is wrong with this man?

"Oh! Right, also. Do you still live in that house?"

We were almost done with this, dammit.

"No, I don't. I live in a condo a bit away, but it's close."

"Fuck, good. I have to visit then, because I just moved back to California."

"Shit, really? No more Canada for you?"

"No more. But, yeah, I'll DM you or something for your number. Bye, Xavier. Bye, Arlissa. Nice meeting you again!" The tiny brunette runs off and takes a piece of my man with her, I just know it. But the last thing I want to do is argue. He's mine. I'm not going to turn into Savannah. I know how much of a headache she gave him, and that's the last thing I want to remind him of.

"So," I start as we continue down our path. "Dinner before our ride?"

"Anything for you." His eyes are distant, like he's stuck in thought and I'm just interrupting whatever process he's going

through. "Keep your drinks in your hand next time, though, yeah?"

"Yeah. Sorry."

Suck it up, Lissa. You guys aren't a repeat of history. You won't ever be. This is a whole new book.

Chapter
FORTY-SEVEN

"I'm fucking stuffed," Xavier blurts as he tosses himself on the couch and places the to-go box on the coffee table in front of him. I stand there, watching as he completely unwinds.

No matter what I did, or what we did, I can't get Willow out of my head. The way he was so excited to see her and didn't bat an eye at me for almost their entire conversation. The two of them were in their own world filled with rainbows and butterflies. I was just there. A bystander. I can't get that deep fear of karma finally coming to slap me in the face out of my mind. Willow had this ability to lock him into a trance, I think. I don't know. But that's what I saw. What I saw is justified, and I'm not fucking going crazy, okay?

It's fine, Lissa. Don't listen to the noise in your head. You're just being fucking paranoid. He's yours, he'll always be.

"You good?" His voice snaps me out of my thoughts. All I do is blink, and there he is, hovering over me.

"Yeah," I mumble, rubbing my arm with one hand. "Just a bit uneasy. I don't know."

Xavier begins to twirl his fingers through my strands. "You need sleep or something?"

"No, no. This is the only time where we're both not busy as hell. We should be having fun not sleeping." I try desperately to change the tone in my voice.

Be the upbeat, happy Lissa. The one he loves. The one that keeps him calm.

"Let's do something."

His ears light up like a puppy on Christmas morning. "Fuck, yeah. Let me see what I brought."

"'Kay, I'm gonna go change into something more comfortable while you do that."

I head to our temporary bedroom, half-melted snow falling off of my boots, thus creating a trail. Once I get to our gigantic chamber, my eyes set on the smaller duffel bag that I kept away from Xavier. He doesn't know why, and he doesn't ask, either. His trust in me is pure. He just knows I'd never do anything he wouldn't approve of. After tossing off the heavy coat and kicking my boots to the other side of the room, I bend over the bag and carefully unzip it. There isn't anything special in there, only four pieces of lingerie because I can't decide on just one. My excited hands graze the fabric as I pull at the black mini nightdress. I don't want to pull out the really sexy ones. *I'm gonna look like too much of a try hard, right?*

"Lissa!" Xavier's voice rings through the immense cottage as I struggle to pull the fabric over my big-ass head.

"Coming!" I shout before taking a quick look in the mirror. My black nails hover over the bows that rest perfectly to cover my nipples. The sheer fabric is completely see through, but who needs underwear right now? I fluff my freshly bleached curls to increase the volume a bit more. Perfect. The nerves in my toes jump as I quickly make my way across the cold floor (that should have been heated, by the way). My body releases one final breath before I slowly approach the corner. I've been with this man for so long and now, I need to prove why.

Xavier's eyes light up like the Fourth of July as he catches sight of me. It's the same look he gave Willow, but that's not good enough. He's hovering over the coffee table where the coke is laid out, acid, and a few pills I can't quite name. Slowly, he makes his way over to me and I swear classical music is playing in the background. Or maybe that's just in my head. My heart starts to flutter; like we're right back in our very first moments. Sitting in a car at five in the morning and arguing over caramelized peanuts and soggy tacos. Or when the sun was rising and we would watch as he went on about some stupid TV show he liked as a kid.

"You're beautiful." A sly smile appears on his face while those large hands grip my waist. "And if you would have told me I would have set out some wineglasses instead."

Chuckles leave both of our lips. "I just wanted to show you how much I love you."

"I'm in love with you." The words leak from his lips so effortlessly, like love is easy for him. I wish I was the same. But then again, no, I don't. Love being so hard for me is the reason why I appreciate him as much as I do. As I look into his eyes, I want to say I'm in love with him too. But it's more than that, and I truly can't put it all into words. Xavier Amari is love. I'm just the girl he chooses to share it with. And I know this because no matter how hard I tried to find love in different places, in different people, or different things, they were really just a million different ways of saying his name.

"Do you mean that?"

He nuzzles his head into the crook of my neck. "Of course I do. You're my best fucking friend."

"Greyson is your best friend."

"Let me be romantic, Kimber," he replies with a soft roar of laughter.

My eyes zone in on the dangling chain that sits eagerly over the dark hairs on his chest. The light coming from the chandelier above us allows the diamonds to glimmer. My focus goes from that to the tattoos on his arms and the veins that look like they're about to pop. I never noticed how his chin had a dimple in the middle before. I guess I was too focused on the jawline that can cut glass. But right now, while admiring him, I notice everything. I want to take this moment and put it in my pocket, I want to keep it forever. I wish life worked like that. I wish we could just put genuine moments like these onto a disc and play it on the big screen.

Thankfully, we have forever to recreate this over and over again.

"What?" he interrupts.

"You're beautiful." The words fall out of my mouth like a rush of raging water.

"I should be saying that to you."

We hold each other for so long I feel like the sun is going to come up at any moment. But no, it's still barely midnight. The next few hours are spent snorting more cocaine lines than I could keep track of and mixing opioids with cherry red wine. The norm.

"Let's dance!" Xavier's words slur as he rises from the couch and takes me with him.

"I am . . . I have two left feet. There's not even any music playing."

"Yet."

"I can't even feel my fucking face, Xavier."

He must have hooked his phone up to something but time

is moving faster than it takes me to turn my head. *You can call me selfish, but I want your love.* The lyrics blare through the home at an intense volume as I lay there and notice a headache coming on.

"Up, up," he commands as he pulls on my hand.

"My head hurts, Xavier."

"Then let's make it better." I know he's holding onto me and moving my body across the floor but there's no way I can physically be doing anything. Everything is moving in colors and not one object is clear anymore, not even him. Blurs have taken over my vision and I can't do anything about it.

"Tell me you love me."

"I love you." I think that's what he said. I hope it was.

I've just gotta have you for myself.

"Tell me a secret." The words leave my numb mouth before I can even process what's going on.

We stop and before I know it we're both laid out on the floor. "I have too many to count."

"Then tell me your favorite one."

"You don't even tell me yours."

"I think you know my only one."

"Right. But if I told you that, then it wouldn't be a . . . uh . . . uh . . ."

"A secret?"

"Yeah."

"Just tell me one. Like . . . " I want to stop myself, I know where this is going. "Who Willow is."

There's a brief silence. "That's not a secret."

"Oh . . ."

"I'll tell you one, though."

"Mm-hmm."

"I'd kill myself if I ever lost you. So don't fucking do anything to make me lose you. Ever. You're everything to me, and I'd die for you. Swear on my mother."

As soon as the words attempt to make their way to my clueless brain, a sharp pain from my chest immediately cuts that off. "Xavier . . ."

"Yeah?"

Shaky hands grip the lace that feels like it's suddenly suffocating my entire being. "My chest hurts." The breaths I'm taking begin to speed up as I try my best to calm down. Slowly but surely the ceiling begins to go from brown to completely black. "I can't see. Xavier, I can't fucking see!"

"Fuck." I can hear Xavier jumping up as the thud of his large feet makes the floor rattle—but I still can't see. All the feeling in my body has vanished and there's absolutely nothing allowing me to process what's going on. I know I'm lying there, but I can't speak. I can't cry, I can't scream. Am I dead? Am I dying?

Is this how Samantha felt?

"Lift her up, come on." This voice is unfamiliar ,and even though I can hear everything that's going on, I can't say a word. I can't feel them lifting me up and moving me. Suddenly, it's completely silent.

Chapter
FORTY-EIGHT

"I don't know how being a mother will affect me . . . I just hope it brings all the joy I know it will. I mean, it honestly already has. It's only been a short few weeks, but I'm not hiding it. I'm happy."

The words crawling out of the TV speakers are the first thing I hear as I come back to life, maybe it's what woke me up—who knows. I wake slowly. This isn't the feeling of waking up in a California king, it feels wrong. My skin registers the scratchy sheets. Raw and exposed. My toes wiggling first then my fingers feeling the rough cotton of the blanket on top of me. I notice the breaths I'm taking; in and out. My hearing comes back as well, the familiar voice being the only thing making a sound at the moment. I don't want to open my eyes. What will be in front of me when I do? I need a moment more, or ten more, to shake the sleep off of my brain.

"I'm in a very happy place." It's at that moment that I realize who's playing on the TV. My eyes shoot open like I've missed my alarm. An outdated TV hangs from the ceiling, showcasing the used-to-be-blonde to me. Savannah. Her hair is dark, but her stunning beauty is still shining through with or without the light tresses. I haven't seen or heard of her in years. Wait—she's pregnant?

"How's pregnancy going for you? I know the whole world has shown such excitement for your new bundle of joy!"

Thank you GMA host. My eyes remain glued to the television. No one is around to see this, right?

"It's going really well . . . I'm healthy and so glad I'm going to have my own family finally. My partner and I are both just extremely blessed and feeling the gratitude." She places her hand on her slightly poked out stomach.

"And is the world ever going to know this mystery man?"

"When the baby is born, yes. With everything I've been through I've been enjoying keeping this to myself." She's glowing. Darker hair makes her look so much younger, or maybe it's the baby. Regardless she's smiling so hard; I didn't think that was possible for her. The devil only smiles when people are in pain. Yet, she's smiling ear to ear at genuinely good news. The idea of Savannah being a cold-hearted snake had kept me sane for so long. She doesn't deserve Xavier, right? She's the manipulator and the villain. Yet, how is she coming off as America's Sweetheart right now? Can no one else see right through her?

My thoughts begin to drive me into a headache. The center of my forehead throbs uncontrollably as I finally take the time to scan my surroundings. Plain brown door, plain cream walls, boring. Empty. My right arm has an IV stuck in it that's hooked to a drip. The monitor is the most annoying part. Why the fuck is it beeping? Hand sanitizer dispensers. Rubber gloves. Soap. The world's most uncomfortable mattress. Hospitals and hell are the same exact place. No wonder I woke up to Savannah on the TV.

I'm in literal hell. I rip the annoying breathing tube out of my nose and try to zone out Savannah's laughter in the background. My tired eyes spot the remote, bingo. Quickly, I shut that noise off.

"Hello! I'm awake!" I shout, hoping anyone will hear and come to my rescue.

Immediately, Xavier comes bursting through the door. "Fuck . . . " His eyes are filling with water faster than I can process. Before I can utter a sound, he has me wrapped in his arms like a baby bird. "I'm so sorry . . . I don't . . . I don't know what I was thinking. I love you. I love you, okay? You hear me?"

My eyes widen, I'm blown away by his emotion. Truthfully, I haven't even processed how or why I'm here. Did I even want to? "I'm okay."

He finally pulls back to get a look at me. "I thought I lost you." Xavier's face is puffy and red, as if he's been crying for hours without a break.

"I'm here, okay?" My weakened hands attempt to grab onto his face and give him a quick kiss on the forehead.

He drops to his knees at the side of my hospital bed, hands still holding onto me. "I'm so fucking sorry . . . I'm a fucking piece of shit. I should have known."

"X . . . " This is all too much. It's like he's beating himself up so that I don't have to. But I don't want to. I can barely remember what got me here in the first place, and now I have this man collapsing in front of me. "Xavier, please get up. Look, this is no one's fault. I'm okay. Can we focus on that, for God's sake?"

He's startled by my calm energy, immediately rising at my demands. "I'm just glad you're okay, Kimber. This was a frightening night . . . "

"Okay." Without warning, the wave of emotion begins to run over me as well. "Come here."

"Yeah," he manages to say in between sniffles as he falls into my arms this time. As I hold him, I can feel his heart trying it's best not to burst out of his chest.

"We're okay," I whisper as I run my fingers repeatedly through his greasy hair.

"I don't want to do this anymore."

I freeze, completely unsure what *this* is. "Huh?"

"Drugs, Kimber. I don't—if it means losing you, I can't. I refuse."

I continue to rub his back. "Okay."

"You sure?"

His question almost makes me laugh. I never would have done any of this if it wasn't for him. "Yeah. I think we both could use a break."

"No, I mean, I'm quitting for life. I'm fucking done."

"Oh. Then yes. That's fine by me, trust me."

"Yeah."

"Now, can we get me out of here? This damn hospital gown has the air from the AC going up the crack of my ass."

He lets out a laugh before wiping his face with his shirt and standing. "I'll go get your nurse."

I watch as the man of my dreams walks out the door. Sober? I don't know if I'm excited or terrified. We tried this once before, about a year ago. I was tired of the party scene so we took a break from it, and Xavier thought that it would be best to take a break from the drugs as well. It wasn't fun. He was irritable the whole time and the only thing that would keep him calm was training. He spent all day, every day in the gym that week. I barely saw him. Could we do that again? Did I want to do that again? A happy Xavier had everything in order, from his drugs to me. Not one hair out of place. So why would he offer to disrupt his peace like that? Did he love me that much?

It dawns on me then. I have everything Savannah can't get.

Who cares if she's pregnant with a mystery man and glowing to the high heavens? The man of her dreams is now mine, and he's going sober for me.

Take that, America's Sweetheart.

Chapter

FORTY-NINE

I know it's been a while and I wouldn't be me if I didn't traditionally invite you to this. I could have texted but that's not very sincere, now is it?

Please join my family and me for my father's funeral on January 25th. I am inviting you because even though you never met him, you saw pieces of him in me, so I guess you knew him well enough. (Plus, I miss you.)

Address and all the other details are on the card behind this letter. Love you, Arlissa.

- Jerrica.

I read that letter maybe a million times, including on the way to the funeral. She invited Alejandra too. But alas, I had to be the bearer of bad news and let her know she was still on tour. Here's the thing: when you don't speak to someone for literal years you don't really feel bad about it, right? You're both busy, and as far as I know she's doing great becoming the next Confucius. But the guilt kicks in when they think of you when something really bad happens. Then, it's like *shit, why didn't I check in a week ago?* Now I look like the asshole who never called.

I sit there, alone, in a pitch-black dress that I have from one of the many times Xavier apologized for yelling too loud. What's appropriate to wear to funerals, anyway? Should I be covered head to toe or are my knees acceptable?

Due to having to drive myself, and the nerves, I'm late. So, I have to be the girl who takes the very last seat while a woman I can only assume is Jerrica's mom cries on the stand. Even in funeral attire, everyone around me is wearing things I'm sure I can't afford until I'm thirty.

I've been to a funeral once. I don't remember it well, but I remember Samantha's high school photo from that year being enlarged. Placed on a canvas for everyone to see—including her sad little sister.

I miss her.

For a majority of it I tuned out. This man and I had never met, and now we never will. But Jerrica is the most genuine person I've ever had the pleasure of knowing, and if he's responsible for raising such a gentle soul, then I have to pay my respects. I continue to zone out and count the crystals on the heels of the woman in front of me until I see Jerrica and a familiar brunette appear on the stand. My heart jumps out of my chest as I place my eyes on a pregnant Savannah. I'm just coming off an overdose that I'm trying desperately to forget, and there she is, glowing. Not even showing, but glowing. It's like she does it on purpose. She has a habit of coming into my life at all the wrong times but it's always the right time for her.

"I have Savannah with me, today. And if you guys know me, then you know her. She has been my sister for so many years." I

297

watch as Savannah squeezes Jerrica's hand in support. "Um, so she's just going to stand here and be that rock for me, if you guys don't mind."

"I love you, Jer-bear!" a random voice screams.

She smiles. "My father was a master, to say the least. He mastered the art of kindness and vulnerability. He mastered any task he set his mind on. Whereas I picked up and dropped hobbies all the time."

My mind trails off to a speech I don't even remember from my sister's funeral until now. I was a kid, but I tried my hardest.

I don't know what to say but . . . I miss you and I love you. I miss when we used to have TV time together.

"He taught me discipline. He was an amazing teacher who taught me more than the things that matter in this 3D reality. He taught me the power of routine and strength, and not only that but the power of people. And that's why I brought Savannah up here with me. She's not just here to say her piece since she was as much of a daughter to him as I was, but she's here because my father would frown on me if I tried to pretend like I'm stronger than I am sometimes. Sometimes, you need people. Sometimes, the people around you may need you more than you think. It's okay to tell people that you can't do things alone."

Mom told me that you're up there somewhere enjoying pumpkin pie because that's your favorite. I hope you don't meet anyone else you love more than me up there. I know Jesus is pretty cool, but . . . I'm cooler.

"I also want to say that even though we all feel we've lost him, we didn't. His energy is still around us. So, when people pass, all we did was lose them in the physical realm of things, right?"

Come back, Samantha, please. You were the bestest big sister ever. And school sucks now because we don't walk home together anymore. I can ride a bike, though. Your old bike! But it's not the same. Mom isn't the same. We miss you this much.

"Hi, guys."

My train of thought is interrupted by Savannah's shaky voice. She and Jerrica had traded places, and now I'm really interested in what the she-devil has to say. "We lost an amazing man. I love you so much, Elijah. Um, I thought I'd tell you guys a story. When I was in high school my life wasn't the best. I was saved by Jerrica and her parents. I mean that in every single way possible." Now Jerrica is squeezing her hand. What the hell did she need support for? This isn't her dad. "He was my father." Well. "I know a lot of you know me personally. And my biological dad and I are amazing right now. But, when I didn't have a dad, I had Elijah. He bought me clothes so I wasn't embarrassed at school, he taught me how to drive and lord was I bad at that. But there was one time in specific that I want to share with you. When I found out I succeeded in having a baby he was actually the first person I called. We went to a little pizza shop, you know, a whole in the wall. I just really wanted some darn grease, you know?"

Everyone laughs along with her.

"Anyways, we sat there together over twelve slices of a meat lovers' deep dish pizza and before I could spit it out, he said, 'is it a boy or a girl?'" She begins to choke up, her glistening green eyes becoming clouded. "He—he was a wizard, man. And I looked at him. And I said—I said, 'who knows, but I am so happy.' And he got up and he gave me the biggest hug I've ever experienced. And he said, 'no matter what it is I know in my heart that that baby will experience the love of a thousand parents from just you.' He didn't care about the conditions or even the father. He just trusted me. I got the news that he didn't have much time a bit after that. I want you all to know that if it's a boy I will be naming him after the beautiful man we all got to experience. The man that guided me and made sure I had a clear path."

The silence after Savannah steps back from the stand isn't a scary one. Instead, it's comforting. My index finger pats under my eye as a warm liquid sits there. Shit, shit. I cannot be sympathizing with Savannah right now. She and Jerrica entangle themselves in a long hug as the audience rises and begins to cry or hug one another. I stand there awkwardly while everyone makes movements around the church.

My eyes locate Jerrica, and I know there's no way I can talk to her without Savannah. But maybe, I should say hi to her at least. It's been years, right? There's a glow about her that's brand new; maybe she's okay now. My tiny feet quickly pass through the crowd of people. I have to get to her before anyone else does, or else I'd be waiting in a mile long line.

"Arlissa!" Jerrica calls out as her eyes watch me peel from the crowd.

A small smile graces my face while I hold the brunette's hand. "Hi. I'm so sorry for your loss."

"Thank you. Savannah, you met Lissa, right? My memory is shit these days."

The question makes my heart skip but Savannah's seemingly genuine smile calms it back down. "Don't worry about it, love. You've gone through a lot. It's nice to see you again, Arlissa."

Huh? How? "You, too. Jerrica—"

"Jerrica!" her mom calls, waving from the far end of the church.

"I'll be right back. Savannah, keep her company please." Before I can even blink Jerrica is lost in a sea of black attire.

"So . . . congratulations. You're pregnant, that's amazing."

"Yes, thank you. How are you?"

"I'm . . . amazing." I'm lying and somehow I feel like she can tell.

The green-eyed beauty lets out a deep sigh before smiling at me again. "I want to apologize."

"Huh?"

"I just, I want to apologize."

"For what?"

300

"What a broad question. Just know I'm sorry." She lets out a soft giggle. "Have an amazing life, Arlissa. Remember you deserve that." She gives me a slight nod before leaning in to kiss me on the cheek and walking away. The whole thing is so cryptic, and I'm left standing alone.

My thoughts eat me up for the rest of the day. Whether it's going over the funeral speeches in my head or what Savannah had said, I know I needed to hear it all. But I also come to the conclusion that it making sense of it all won't happen today.

Chapter
FIFTY

"Make sure you go and grab your first week free trial with the code 'Lissaxo' because you will not regret it! Love you!"

My finger releases the record button before I step back into the condo from the balcony. Work these days seems to be getting easier and easier. I can wear pajama pants and a nice top to promote some product to my willing and eager social media followers. And I can also stay out of away events that might remind me of my hospital visit. Working from home, something we all should do. A knock on the door takes me out of my zone as I quickly save the video into my gallery and head to the huge entrance.

"Who is it?" I call out as my brain scans the possibilities.

Xavier's voice transfers through the thick metal to my ears. "Open up!"

Brow furrowed in confusion, I swing the door open to my

boyfriend bent over something small and furry. "Is that a mouse? What the hell, X?"

He lets out a laugh before fully showcasing the animal that can practically fit in his hand. "I got you something. A friend of mine just got some puppies and I thought . . . my girl would literally eat this shit up."

I stand there caught off guard trying to understand what the hell is going on. Sobriety had put him in a mood lately, but things might be looking up. "That's . . . that was your exact thought process?"

He chuckles again before attempting to slowly put the puppy in my palms. "Yes. Plus, I know you had that funeral shit, so I just wanted to see you smile."

The small animal melts into my touch. I can't help but pout. "He's absolutely precious," I whine while Xavier brings in some shopping bags and shuts the door.

"He's a she."

I focus on the tan fur and huge black eyes that are barely opening. "Oh. Well, I'll name her . . . Dixie."

The warmth of Xavier's embrace overcomes me as his arms slowly wrap around my waist. "Well, Dixie. Welcome home. We're your parents."

I freeze up like a child who just walked in on their parents wrapping Christmas gifts. I pushed the idea of moving any further with Xavier out of my mind a long time ago. We moved in together, I'm nowhere near my thirties, there's no need to rush. Aly and Greyson have their own thing going, and I swear I'm okay with that. Those two are going to have a baby by next week, and that's okay. She's meant to have it all—the family and the career. Xavier and I aren't. Well, there were times where I'd fall asleep to the idea of us parenting a girl or a boy—or both. But that's it.

Hm, if Savannah can have it, why can't you?

"Parents, huh?"

He plants a quick kiss on my neck before backing up off of me. "Yeah, dog parents."

Rolling my eyes, I turn to him while also keeping Dixie close to my chest. "Right."

Xavier raises a brow before shaking his head. "Right. Anyways, I got something else."

"Oh, what is it?"

The man's large hands ruffles through his bookbag for a few minutes and still, all I can think of is the idea of us being parents. "Guess who is the new face of Nike?"

"Oh my God, you!"

"This calls for a motherfuckin' celebration."

"Are you serious? That's fucking awesome, Xavier!"

He pulls out two small green pills in a Ziploc bag. "With these."

"Xavier . . . "

"Come on! We're finally getting over all the drama. Let's do it."

"Fine. But Dixie gets put safely in our room first."

"This is your world, princess, I'm just living in it."

"Did you buy her anything?"

"Oh, shit. Yeah. I walked into a Petco and went fucking wild, those two bags over there are hers."

"Petco?"

He laughs, "Petco, where the pets go!"

I bend over and slip my wrist through the handles and head back to the bedroom. Dixie has a cute pink bed that's so small I'm convinced she can sleep on the TV stand. He also got her some toys, a bottle, and soft food. After everything is set up and she's safe and sound, I shut the door and head back to the living room where Xavier awaits.

We get as high as we used to over the course of the last few years. We'd take a pill, he'd probably take more than just that and a few shots to chase it down. My heart pounds out of my chest for the first five minutes, but one tablet of molly shouldn't kill me, right?

Last time was just a super bad trip. This is going to be different, Arlissa.

Xavier keeps himself composed for the most part but he's so out of it he can't tell that I'm losing my mind. Taking several deep breaths, the drugs finally take their toll on me, and I can calm my spirits. My body lays lazily on that marble floor, hair sprawled out every which way. Xavier joins me, intertwining his long fingers with mine as we both take in the infinite white space that's our ceiling.

"All right, everybody! Great shoot! Let's wrap it up and get home to our couches."

"Or our families!" one of the stylists shouts.

There's a roar of laughter as I tiptoe over to the photographer. "Hey, can I see those last two shots?" I inquire, adjusting my annoying blue top.

"Yeah, no problem." Her slim fingers click through the photos as my eyes follow. One with my head down, one with my head up, one straight ahead. I glare at the one straight ahead—Jesus, my cheeks have gotten fat. I need to lose weight, and I need to do it now.

"Uh, can we use the other angles, not the straight-ahead ones? That won't be a problem, right?"

"Yeah, I'm sure that would be cool."

"Okay, thank you so much. You did amazing today, by the way." I flash the woman a smile before skipping off to Holly, who's standing casually with my boyfriend.

Her smile expands as I approach the two. "Hey superstar, why the long face?"

"How long until the next shoot?"

"Right, about that."

I'm half focused, trying to gather my things. "Go on."

"I mean, since you asked, I guess I can tell you now."

"Holls, you're giving me an anxiety attack here. When is it?" Xavier smirks. "Go on, tell her."

"No, no. You did all the heavy lifting. You tell her."

"*Vogue*. Right after my birthday."

"You must have said rogue because I—"

"I got you a *Vogue* shoot. British *Vogue*, but I like them better anyways."

I rest my hand on my chest in a desperate attempt to stop my heart from falling onto the floor. "Oh . . . Oh my God."

Holly gasps, placing her hand on my shoulder, "What? What's wrong? Why are you not smiling?"

After a couple deep breaths, I try my best to give him the best smile I can muster. "Thank you, thank you so much—both of you."

Xavier wraps his arms around me and immediately my entire being calms. "Of course, baby."

"There's a tiny issue, though."

His hazel eyes look down at me. "Okay."

"I need to lose weight ,and I need to do it now. Or else I'm gonna lose my fucking marbles."

"I got you."

Holly raises a brow. "No, no. I don't need her on an athlete's diet, Amari."

He chuckles before shaking his head. "I promise she won't be."

Chapter
FIFTY-ONE

"Head down. Squeeze my hand if anything, okay? Be cool."
I nod, adjusting my yellow leather dress as the limo driver parks in front of the club. Xavier is turning twenty-four tonight, and I'm one hundred percent positive I'm more excited than he is. "This isn't my first rodeo."

When the limousine comes to a complete stop, he waits a few seconds for the driver to open the door, then slides out of the car with his head down and pulls me behind him. I follow the instructions, head down, and squeeze his hand like someone is trying to kidnap me. Paparazzi have a habit of getting too close if you engage with them in the slightest way. So, the best we can do is act like they aren't there and speed walk into the nightclub.

"Amari," Xavier says to the bouncer before he quickly lets us in. Next, we head up to VIP before anyone else knows we're there. Of course people noticed, but if you walk fast enough they might be too intimidated to speak. Plus, we always make sure our security is present whenever we're around a ton of people. Xavier rented the whole upstairs section of the biggest nightclub in California. All of his friends are coming and some of mine as well. Yet, this only left one question lingering in my mind.

I stretch upward so that I can whisper in his ear as we get comfortable in our booth. "Xavier?"

"What's up?"

"Who all is gonna be here?"

"You know, everybody."

"Max, Gregory, Ellie . . . " I pause, wondering if I should mention her name at all. "Willow?"

"Yeah, all of them. Why, what's up?"

I'm fucking starving since Xavier's idea of a fast diet was one meal a day and a lot of cocaine. Sure, my energy is through the roof, but the last thing I have time for is the girl who gets way too giggly around Xavier and tries to take him away with corny remember-the-time commentary. "No reason."

"Cool, because I'm just trying to have a good time tonight. Stay in your lane, yeah?"

"Yes, sir. You're the boss."

An instant wave of annoyance fills my system; I definitely need a drink now. My eyes remain glued to the entrance. If she's coming in, I have to make sure I have a thirty-second notice at least. With every person who enters and high-fives Xavier or offers me an awkward side hug, I take a shot. I'm about eight shots in before my eyeballs practically jump out of my head. There she is. She looks so tiny down there as she happily waves to everyone on the ground floor while making her way through the club. Her normally curly hair is now straightened for the occasion. Great, we practically have the same hairstyle. She's wearing an all-black dress with just enough cleavage to catch Xavier's attention. With every step Willow takes up the stairs, I take another sip out of my glass.

Once Willow arrives in Xavier's sights, I feel a gush of air as he rushes past me and wraps her in those huge arms of his. I hate it. Those hugs are meant for me, and me only. I know, they're friends. That's what Xavier says but it still doesn't feel right. Their chemistry is undeniable, and it is driving me crazy. I've spent the last two years being a "cool" girlfriend. Trying my best to be the total opposite of Savannah. But good God, I cannot take the way he lights up whenever she's in the room. Why the hell isn't he letting go of her? I slam my glass down onto the table, the sound masked by the unbearably loud music, and take fast-paced steps over to them. Maybe it's the intense amount of alcohol in my system, or it's the cocaine we snorted in the limo. But something's giving me the confidence to nip this situation in the bud once and for all.

You will not end up like Savannah.

"I'm so glad you could make it, man!"

"Anything for you, X."

I roll my eyes before tapping him on his shoulder. "Babe, I think Travis needs you. He was just saying he had something for you in his car, I think. Might want to go check that out."

Xavier releases his grip on the small woman and nods. "Shit, yeah. Let me go take care of that. You two have fun. Drinks on me! I'll be back."

Just like that, it's Willow and me. "Nice party, huh?"

I nod and hesitantly rub the side of my neck. "Yeah, I organized the whole thing for him. It is his birthday after all."

"Technically it's tomorrow."

My eyes practically roll to the back of my head. "Okay, Willow. What's the deal with you?"

The words that slide out of my lips catch her off guard as she looks at me in shock. "What are you talking about?"

"You and Xavier!" I scope my surroundings once I realize my voice is getting a bit too high. "Why are you guys so close?"

310

"Look, I've known Xavier since we were kids. We held hands in, like, second grade, but girl, I am nothing to worry about."

"Somehow I don't believe that," I snap.

"Well, you should. I'm not even into guys."

I facepalm right in front of her in order to hide the bright red my cheeks are turning. "You're kidding."

"No, not at all. Xavier's just a really good friend of mine, okay? I'm into chicks. Don't worry. He's all about you as far as I'm concerned."

"I'm so, so sorry. I . . . I've just been under a lot of stress these days."

She places a hand on my shoulder. "You're too pretty to be stressed about anything. It's a party, enjoy it. And maybe grab a cracker or something. You look out of it."

Willow flashes a cheeky smile before walking past me and beginning to engage with the other guests. And just like clockwork, the birthday boy comes back up the stairs. "What'd I miss?"

"Nothing," I quickly respond, wrapping my arm around my waist. "I just love you. Now can we enjoy your night?"

"Fuck, yeah, we can."

My worries about Willow wash away as we enjoy the rest of the night. There's no reason not to trust him. History isn't going to repeat itself because I'm so much better than Savannah ever will be.

We dance on top of tables, blow out the candles on his giant birthday cake, take blurry Polaroids, and spill champagne everywhere. If anyone can throw a party where people attempt to spend the night on the floor of a dirty nightclub, it'd be Xavier.

Chapter
FIFTY-TWO

ogue. I can now say that I posed for *Vogue*. My mother has been calling me all morning and demanding that I get the images blown up so she can hang them in the living room. This feels good; better than sex, maybe. I adjust my sunglasses on top of my head as my excited hands fumble with the door knob. Once that reassuring click fills my ears, I quickly push it open to reveal Xavier sprawled out lazily on the couch.

"You're home!" we both exclaim in unison as he jumps up.

"I thought you'd be at the gym."

He walks toward me and places a quick kiss on my lips. "I couldn't focus."

I raise a brow, wanting to be concerned, but the smile plastered on his face says otherwise. "Well! I'm just—I'm so happy! Like, over the moon happy! That whole shoot was amazing. I can't wait for you to see the shots and, ugh, the snack table? Let's talk about it. It's only up from here, though. And you're right, I couldn't have done it without you. Speaking of, we need to go to the UK now. Next vacation, maybe? How come we haven't done that yet?"

"I told you."

"Where are we going from here? Wow, I love my life. I need to get my Instagram insights up so when I post the shoot it does something, you know? That's the goal."

Xavier watches as I pace back and forth. "Great, very happy for you, but—"

"Wait! So, I went in, right, and they gave me this robe, and it was fluffy and warm and—"

"Kimber, I really need to get this out now or it'll probably never happen."

The tone in my boyfriend's voice automatically adds weight to my ankles as I slowly put my purse down in a nearby chair and make my way to him. "Okay," I mutter before placing my hands onto his. "I'll sit then."

Xavier slides over to make room for me. "There's nothing wrong, okay. So let's wipe that look off your face." He lets out a chuckle before lightly pinching my cheek.

"Okay, talk. I can't take the suspense."

"Right." He adjusts himself, completely unable to keep eye-contact with me. My heart begins to race as I try my best to guess what he could possibly say. The shortness of breath that I've been experiencing lately returned. I scan the room desperately as I try to find something to distract me.

"Okay . . . "

"You okay? I think I should be the nervous one here."

I nod, still looking past him for something to focus on. "Oh! Dixie baby!" I leap up and run over to the other side of the large room to place my new puppy in my arms. "Okay, talk." Dixie calms my entire being while I make my way back to the couch. I'm not going to say I have anxiety. There are real people who really suffer with these issues. I'm sure I'm not one of them. I get nervous like everyone else in this world. No big deal.

"Right, okay. Are you going to get up again? Should I do this standing?"

Every word he says tugs at my heart. What could he possibly be talking about? "Just talk."

"I love you, and—"

His tone alone is enough to spike my blood pressure. "If you're breaking up with me, can you just start with that?"

Xavier sends a confused look in my direction and shakes his head. "What? I told you this was nothing bad. Are you good, babe?"

A deep breath exhales from my mouth while my hands subconsciously pet the puppy. "Sorry. Sorry. I'll shut up."

"All right, well. I love you, and I'm in love with you, and I've been thinking about this a lot lately, especially since getting Dixie, but . . . I want a baby."

Once the words register, I immediately put Dixie down as I begin gasping for air. I don't know what heart attacks feel like, but I'm ninety percent sure I'm having one. Within moments, an intense feeling of pain spreads through my upper body and down to my left hand. "Xavier."

"Are—are you okay?"

"I think I'm having a heart attack." *What an awful way to die.*

He watches for a moment as I gulp for as much air as I can gather. I rest on the couch once holding my body up on its own just feels like too much work. "No . . . I think you're just having a panic attack, shit."

"Oh. Cool," I force out in between gasps. "Help me, then."

"Uh. Right, okay. Close your eyes."

I do what he says without a fight and waits impatiently for my next instruction. "Now what?"

His large hands hold mine, already bringing a sense of peace

314

into my system. Yet, it isn't enough to calm the pain. "I need you to take deep, slow breaths. And while you're doing that focus on . . . I don't know, a happy place. A dream or something. Anything that can make you happy enough to ignore the pain. I think."

The shakiness in his voice is a clear signal to me that he's feeling a large sense of regret over his proposal. I feel bad, but it's not something I can think about right now, clearly. "Okay."

My thoughts begin to drift, so I continue to focus on his thumb slowly caressing my palms. Shopping, hosting award shows, visiting my family a lot more often than I do now. Nothing is working, I'm still struggling to breathe, and it's only getting more painful. My throat closes up as if someone's fist is wrapped around it, I need to go deeper. Xavier. He's a happy place for me. The iron grip on my throat loosens up, but this isn't enough. I give my imagination permission to run wild and suddenly—there we are. A future version of myself is standing in a yard way too big for one person to maintain, but I'm not alone. Xavier is in swim trunks sipping lemonade and reading some sports book. I glance to my left to see a toddler tugging on my sundress. As the imaginary scenario continues, the tenseness of my entire body calms. *Mom, Justin won't let me play with the ball.* Future me knows exactly where to look. Her eyes focus past the little girl to reveal a slightly older boy playing on his own just a few feet away. She calls out to him, and he apologizes and runs through the vibrant green grass to play with his sister. Future me looks to her left, a curly-haired woman who is a bit older standing there, smiling. Samantha. We hug, and it's the warmest hug I've ever felt.

They look just like you.

"Must be some happy place," Xavier mumbles. It's at this moment that I check back into reality and realize that not only has the pain stopped—but I'm smiling.

I get control of my body back and quickly sit up. When my

eyes rest on him, I allow myself to see him like my future self clearly does. I kept the idea of moving any faster out of my head because I didn't want to bother him. But, if I'm being honest, I wanted this a lot longer than he did. "Oh. Yeah, thank you."

"Look, I'm sorry. I didn't mean—"

A loving kiss from me interrupts his sentence. "No need to apologize. I want to."

"What?"

"I want to have a baby."

On normal days, his smile can light up a room. But at this very moment it's blinding. The larger male wraps me up in his arms and places me onto his lap. "I fucking love you."

A giggle escapes my lips. "I love you more."

"I promise you don't."

"I swear I do. Now, don't we have something to be doing?"

"I am kind of hungry, isn't it dinner time?"

"Xavier!"

"I'm kidding, come on."

Sometimes life is an utter mess. Sometimes you spend days on end wishing you took the chances life gave you when they arrived. My career is peaking, yes. But with Xavier by my side there's no need for it to end now. I can balance having a family and work, sure. The man of my dreams wants to take that next step with me—no one else. And that in its own means the entire world to me.

Chapter
FIFTY-THREE

Receiving the call felt like a blur, honestly. Me? Hosting the Billboard Music Awards? The idea in itself is enough to take me back a few steps. There's truly nowhere but up from here and no one can convince me otherwise. My career, my personal life, I'm on top of the world. Plus, the rush of satisfaction I get from seeing strangers on the internet praising me is truly more than enough.

"I can't believe it!" I blurt out as Xavier mindlessly walks through the fifth designer store of the day.

"Shit, I'm proud of you. I never got an award show offer or no shit like that, so go you."

"Hey! You could."

He side-eyes me before rolling his eyes and letting out a low chuckle. "Yeah, in what world? They don't ask boxers to do those things."

"Don't be such a party pooper, okay?"

"I'm not. Hey, what do you think about this?" He holds up a hideous designer shirt for me to see.

"No. I will not walk around with you in that."

We both chuckle as he puts the clothing back down. "You are a very rude person, Arlissa Benson."

"Me? You're snorting crack!" I reply jokingly.

"Shit, I might be."

My smile quickly shifts into a pout. "Not funny. We're expecting a child now."

"We are?"

"I mean . . . " We both make slow strides through the store. "We could be, I think it's too early to tell."

Xavier pauses, placing his hand on my stomach. "Well, I've got faith."

I playfully roll my eyes before giggling and pushing his hand away. "We're in public!"

The rest of our afternoon consisted of a romantic lunch date at Subway that the paparazzi couldn't get enough of and even more shopping. For him, at least, I only found a pair of Prada sunglasses I liked and that was the end of that.

"Can you pass me that other bag so I can put this shirt on the hanger?" Xavier calls out, half of his body deep into our walk-in closet.

I jump up off the bed and get what he asked for. "You need help?"

"Nah, I'm good."

"Okay—" The interrupting ring of my phone cut off any remaining thoughts I have.

"Who is that?"

"Alejandra, hold on." I quickly press the green answer button that's lighting up my screen, my feet happily taking me to the other side of the room. "I missed you! It's been days since you last called!"

"You're fucking pregnant?" Her words blare through the speakers, but time has already stopped for me. "Hello?"

"Where did you hear that?"

"It's all over the fucking blogs! Now answer me!"

"I—I'll call you back." My fingers quickly press the bright red button on my phone. My body is still; focus remaining on the carpeted floors.

"You good?" Xavier calls from the closet.

"Check your phone."

"It's on the bed, what's going on?"

No words are leaving my mouth at that moment. My fingers move faster than my brain can process. I Google my name. *Arlissa Benson*. A few pictures of me, cute. I click the News tab in hopes that Alejandra is pranking me. Once the drop-down menu appears, the normal stupid headlines like *Arlissa Benson In An Itty-Bitty Crop Top At Venus Beach*, have disappeared. Instead, it's replaced with paparazzi photos of Xavier and I today and *They're Expecting* worded a million different ways. My heart completely drops, unsure of who was possibly close enough to us today to even hear.

We just planned this. There's no confirmation, and yeah, maybe we had a few hopeful conversations but that's it. For someone to be so cruel that they felt they *had* to let the whole world know whatever they heard or saw, it's heartbreaking. Not only did we have no privacy, but we have no respect. Anger, disappointment, and the grief of not being able to break the news on our own consumed me. Red-hot tears fall from my eyes while I remain motionless.

"Hey, hey. What's wrong?" Xavier asks, finally climbing over the bags and heading toward me.

I shake my head, handing the phone to him without even making eye contact. "I just . . . I don't get it. How are people so evil? Anything for a dollar, right?"

There are a few moments of silence, the only sound filling

my ears being Dixie rummaging through the bags and Xavier's fingers making contact with my phone screen. "Well."

My brow furrows in anger at my boyfriend's response. "Well? Are you serious?"

"Look, this stuff happens. I learned not to cry over spilled milk a long time ago."

"This isn't just stupid secrets, Xavier! This is our child. And we didn't get to announce it on our own. Hell, I don't even know if I'm pregnant. What if I'm not?"

"Hey . . . " He places my phone down before grabbing both of my hands. "They didn't take that from us. For all they know it's gossip, and we can deny it if we want. You don't have to tell anyone anything you don't want to."

My eyes roll so far back, I'm convinced they're stuck in the back of my head. "It's just sick because we don't even fucking know. Just feels like a fucking jinx now."

"Look, we can make this work for us."

"How? Since you're so full of ideas."

"We announce it at the award show. Well—you do. I'll be there but, you know. That'll give people something to talk about, and you can tell the publications to suck a dick."

The thought of using my unborn child as a career boost isn't settling well with me. But the longer I sit with the idea the longer I realize that my boyfriend is one hundred percent correct. I announce it on my own terms, and what's a better platform to use than an award show?

Chapter
FIFTY-FOUR

Time seems to drag on when you're actually waiting for something. Yet, when you want it to slow down it seems to zip by. The last few years had zipped by faster than I could really put in one sentence. But waiting for my period to come feels like an eternity. I guess I should say waiting for it not to come—but regardless, it took for-fucking-ever. But the end of April comes and my body doesn't suffer from not a cramp or cravings. Maybe, just maybe, it's actually time.

I sit on the edge of the toilet seat as the moments tick by ever so slowly. Maybe it's been ten minutes, maybe it's been only three. The blue and white stick that sits still on the sink is practically mocking me. We didn't do this the way smart couples do and look at my cycle, see a doctor, and blah blah blah. We're twenty-something-year-olds who are deciding to have a baby and did the dance that's required. The end. Easy, free, and not time consuming.

When those two blue lines pop up, am I going to be happy? Or will the sudden responsibility of carrying a child begin to overwhelm me? Am I going to immediately regret this decision and wish I waited just a bit longer? Or am I going to run to the closest bookstore and buy up every last parenting book? But, if there aren't two lines at all. If only one goes straight down that fingerprint-size screen and says, *ha, try again next time*. Will I break down in tears? Will I mourn something that doesn't even exist, yet? Or will I release a sigh of relief that I still have some time to just live for me?

What is living for me, anyway? My whole life I haven't had a clue what to do or where to go and I wouldn't even be here if it wasn't for other people. I'm not saying I haven't tried or worked, that's not true. But, this life, these ideas, none of them were mine. Knowing this has caused quite the imposter syndrome, but hey, at least I do my job. I guess, maybe being a mom will be really good for me. It's the one thing I know I always wanted—a family of my own. Maybe, I can really put my heart into this. Maybe, this could be my passion.

I slowly avert my gaze from the tiles on the floor, hesitant to make eye contact with the test that's practically mocking me at this point. *Just get it over with, come on, Lissa.* With one eye open, I make contact with the test. The lines on the tiny screen are practically glowing. Pregnant.

You're having a baby. I'm going to be an auntie!

Time freezes for just a moment. I can't feel a single thing—for just a moment. There's a person growing in this shell of a vessel that I am. A whole person. Dizziness washes over me, I don't know anything right now. It seems as if this test alone has shoved me into a black hole where nothing else existed but it and I.

Come on, Lissa . . . You're pregnant.

My heart races with excitement as I hop off of the toilet seat and hold the pee test in my shaky hands. I want to frame it. I want to take a picture of it and send it to every contact on my phone. There's no doubt, just pure joy overcoming my spirit as I take in the sight. This is happening. Every daydream, every wish upon a star to finally be the one that Xavier will come home to forever— is happening.

Immediately, I grab my phone and pull up Xavier's contact.

I write, *We did it. I'm pregnant.* I insert a photo of the test, and press send.

"Where's my beautiful girl?" Xavier's tone is the most pleasant sound I've ever heard. Just from the way his words ring through the condo alone, you can tell he's smiling from ear to ear.

"In here!" I call out, curled up in the thousand thread count bedsheets.

It takes a few moments before Dixie comes running in moments before Xavier. In his hand is a huge black box. "I got you something."

I slowly sit up. "You got me a pregnancy gift?"

"Eh. The timing is just fucking sweet, so sure."

"Why didn't you just say yes?"

He let out a chuckle before placing the obnoxiously large box on the bed. "Come on, look."

"I'm scared."

"Then I'll do it for you." His large hands begin unwrapping the ribbons before pulling the top off. Blue, puffy fabric basically pops out of the box. "Surprise."

"Oh my . . . " My pupils expand and all I can do is slowly pull the dress out of the box. "This is a ball gown."

"For your big night. I thought, why not get you something

special and way too expensive to wear. Plus, now that I know we're actually having this baby . . . it felt right."

My eyes begin to water, which only makes sense since my emotions have been sky-high all day. I wrap my short arms around Xavier's neck, not wanting to let him go for a moment. "I love you so much . . . and I'm so happy this is happening for us."

"This is all I've ever wanted."

"I didn't know that . . . "

Xavier pulls back from the hug for a moment, his brown locks falling down onto his forehead. "I never told you."

"Why not?"

"I've been there before, didn't go well . . . And after that, I was terrified to try again. But I'm not scared anymore with you." His eyes make contact with mine before he smirks. "My Cinderella."

My plump lips form a smile as I place a quick kiss on his forehead. "You're going to get the family you deserve, I promise."

He clears his throat before backing up from me completely. "Before I forget, I know you've been asking to go back to brown or a brown-blond thing . . . I don't know how that shit works so—"

"Oh my God, I can stop bleaching my fucking scalp?"

He nods. "I think it'd be best, yes. Another hair change would be perfect for the event. Wear it curly, too."

"You are truly a Prince Charming, Xavier Amari."

Being on top is nice. It's rewarding, and most importantly, it means God always has your back. At any point where I'm worried or scared, none of that matters. Because at the end of the day—I always win.

Chapter
FIFTY-FIVE

Two months of planning and rehearsals had passed before I was finally about to take that stage and announce our baby. My stomach is in knots as I keep my grip on Xavier's hand. This ball gown I have on is gorgeous, but it's also a bitch to walk down the carpet in. The flowy, baby-blue fabric follows me down the red fuzzy rug as Xavier and I keep each other close. We pause every moment or so for a camera flash, but keep going. One foot in front of the other. I've done this before, but every single time I have on a different kind of shoe or an incredibly difficult dress and spend seventy-five percent of my time praying I don't collapse.

We're one of the last ones to walk the carpet. So, once that anxiety attack is over, I'm being rushed by a team of people down a long corridor backstage. Xavier had taken a seat somewhere in the crowd and all I can focus on is trying to get my nerves down as much as possible. I don't have anything to numb my increasing

heart rate; I just have to go for it. We've practiced this for days on end—over and over again. The only difference now is that this was on live television with thousands of people in the crowd.

"You okay?" one of the staff members asks as they place a microphone in my hand.

"Eh," I start, practically jumping up and down. "You know."

"You got this, kid."

I nod, before my attention turns to the woman counting down to me by the stairs. Her fingers went from three, to two, to one, and before I can whine some more, my legs are making long strides up the stairs. The lights are blinding as I step onto the stage, waving at the audience, who are already eagerly clapping. The set design and the logo that screams "Billboard Music Awards" is even more intimidating now than it is during practice. It's my job to remember everything I'm told during rehearsals.

Smile and wave, Lissa. Just keep smiling and waving until you get to the center of the stage.

"What is up, Billboard Music Awards? I'm your host, Arlissa Benson. And it is so amazing to be here with you guys. Can we give it up for everyone in the building tonight?" The words flow out of me. I scan the crowd for Xavier—nothing. "We have so many amazing presenters and performers tonight, and I was so pumped watching them rehearse. Y'all do not understand what they have in store for you!" The cheers cut me off, so I keep a Malibu Barbie smile on my face. "I am so excited because this is my first time hosting this show, and tonight you're going to hear some great performances by the hottest artists of the year." My eyes finally land on my boyfriend sitting casually in the front row. A sense of calm runs over me as I continue to talk. Everyone is watching. Now is the time to make the announcement. "Are you guys ready for the first award?" The crowd roars as I stand there confidently. "Well, the amazing woman presenting has three Grammys to her name with a diamond record to match. Not only is she successful in the workplace but she is also a mommy to be—like me." Before I can continue I watch as people begin to stand and applaud, Xavier included. "Thank you everyone, really. And thanks to the press for trying to take this moment away from me. Well! Welcome to the stage Kendall Hudson."

My feet carry me quickly off of the stage and to the back to change into my second outfit. Crew members pass me by shouting congratulations so many times that "thank you" becomes more of an automated reply.

"Come on, come on," my stylist calls as she beckons me into the dressing room. I quickly step out of the blue cotton candy dress and it feels like time is running against me instead of for me. I catch a glimpse of myself in the mirror—two months pregnant. Wow. The little pouch isn't too obvious, but it's clear to me. My body is making room for someone else, someone who is going to kick me, beg for my food, and tell me they love me. And I'll love them. More than anything else.

"Knock, knock." Xavier slowly slips through the door and shuts it behind him.

"Hey! Can you help me pull this on, I'm bloated as hell."

"Yeah."

"You okay?" I softly ask in hopes my stylist is minding her business.

"Just not feeling too well."

"I mean, my back has been killing me, but I'm still here."

Xavier releases a soft sigh. "I know, and you're killing it, but I think I should get out of here."

"Huh?"

"Look, Greyson and Aly are coming tonight, and I know how bad you want to go out with them, so I need to rest or else I won't be able to make it."

I turn to completely face him. "But . . . what's wrong with you?"

327

"Just not feeling too hot. I just need to go back to the crib and take something."

"Xavier . . ."

"I meant like cold medicine."

"Okay . . . okay, I'll see you at home then."

He places a soft kiss on my forehead. "No, I'll pick you up. Text me."

I watch as he slowly walks out of the room. Something is off, something bigger than him just not feeling well. I know he's a bit jealous of me getting this position so early in my career, but that can't be it. Can it? I watch sadly as the door shut and he's gone. *He just got sick, that's all.*

"Come on, Arlissa. We have about five more minutes to get you all changed," My stylist interrupts. Back to business I go. But this time, it's bittersweet. No one important to me is here to watch me in my biggest career moment, yet. Not one person.

"Cheers to my best friend being a fucking Billboard host tonight. Like, holy smokes! And cheers to my husband and me finally being off of tour and back home in LA." Alejandra's wide smile graces the dinner table as she holds her wineglass high in the sky. "Oh! Oh! And cheers to the beautiful baby that I just know will be a girl and named after moi."

A laugh releases from my lips while I playfully shake my head. "You're a mess."

"The mess you love."

"And how was tour life?" Xavier interrupts.

Greyson chimes in, "I had a personal goal to try a cheese in every state and country we stopped at. I did that. And guess where my favorite was?"

Aly rolls her eyes. "Please ignore him."

I try to laugh again, but a sharp pain in my stomach says otherwise. A low grunt leaves my lips as I try my best to ignore the constant pinching in my stomach. "Jeez . . . "

"I'll guess. Uh . . . Greece? I know you guys stopped there for a holiday," Xavier responds, smiling more now than he did at the show.

"Nah, man. New York. I don't know but the way they just slather cheese on literally—"

"Ouch," I whine, holding my eyes shut for a moment.

Xavier leans in to whisper in my ear. "You okay?"

"Um . . . " My gaze settles on the four water glasses that reflect the candlelight dinner we're all attempting to experience. "Alejandra, can we go to the bathroom?"

The Latina scrunches her eyebrows up before nodding and standing from her seat. "I'll be right back, Grey. Just . . . you know what I like, order for me."

I turn to Xavier, trying to force a smile and hide my clear discomfort. "Same."

"Okay," both men say at the same time.

I grab Alejandra's hand as I take quick but painful steps to the ladies room. I can't say a word, my stomach feels like it was receiving small pinches from the inside.

"Do you need to talk or something?" Alejandra finally speaks once we found ourselves safely in the restroom.

Silently, I push into a stall and try to ignore the increased wetness in my underwear. Then, down my leg. I don't look. Hastily, I shut the stall with no concern about locking it and pull up my little black dress. Eyes straight ahead. I don't want to come to terms with whatever is slipping down my calf right now. The black thong I have on is completely soaked, but I can't tell by what. I sit on the toilet, praying that maybe I just have to pee and pregnancy is weird and causes you to have random nasty-ass leaks. But for the past two months I haven't had an issue with my baby at all. She's healthy, I'm sure of it. Plus, the doctor said that I'd be smooth sailing when it comes to work for at least another few months. I remain silent, focusing on peeing the best I can and ignoring the pain as much as possible. When the sound of drops come down in the toilet, it's heavier than I remember peeing usually being.

"Seriously, you just had to pee? So why the silent treatment?" Alejandra shouts from outside the stall.

Something still doesn't feel right. My body steadily rises from the seat before I take a peek at what laid in that porcelain bowl. What dripped down into the bottom of my shoe. Scarlet liquids and wine-colored clots ruin whatever happiness I have left inside of me. I stand there, blood-soaked panties at my ankles and just try to understand why. This has to be what I think it is. It's too graphic not to be. My mind searches for a reasonable explanation for this much blood—but the truth is right here.

"Okay, I'm coming in, you're being weird." Before I can react to Alejandra's words she's hovering over me. "Lissa . . . "

All it takes is her hesitant hand on my shoulder before I crumble down on that cold bathroom floor. Tears with no concern of my forty-five-minute makeup look rush down my face as I rock back and forth, desperately attempting to hold myself together.

But I can't. Blood curdling screams fill the entirety of this restroom—I kick feverishly at the air. Unbearable pain seeps out of my pores while my eyes refuse to break contact with that crime scene of a toilet seat. She's gone. My baby girl is gone.

Alejandra is quiet for maybe the longest time since I've known her. She bends down next to me and cautiously cradles my body in a warm embrace, neither of us worrying about who might come in either now or later. I keep screaming, enough to make a few staff members come inside. My audible sobs begin to soak my chest. With every tear that drops, I can feel a piece of my heart breaking off and falling onto this dirty bathroom floor. What an awful place to die. I wish I could have at least taken her home.

"I hate this! I fucking hate everything! Everything that I love dies, Aly. Why?" I yell, before Aly moves my head into her chest in an attempt to mute my screams. "I love her . . . I love her so much. I just want her back. I want her here." I break my grip from her, trying hard to take in the air that's currently escaping me. My heart beats, but I wish I could transfer it to her. I wish my little girl would have held on.

"Arlissa . . . " Aly tries but her sad eyes already know they can't make the words to fix this.

I bang my head against the stall, once, twice, three times. Begging for mercy. I can feel Alejandra trying to get me to stop, but I don't.

Please, God, just end it here. Please.

Exhausted, my eyes slowly start to close. I can see Xavier pushing through the staff members—I think. Then darkness.

Chapter
FIFTY-SIX

You can clean up the blood, wash the laundry, and wait for your body to rejuvenate like it usually does. But this isn't the common cold. I can change the bandages and wait for the stitches to get removed from when I banged my head against the stall, but it's not going to make me forget. Even though my entire system pressed "restart" and decided to act like nothing happened a week or so later, minus the spotting——the harsh reality is that it still did. I wake up in the middle of the night with the image of that moment branded in my head. My dreams are soul-ripping nightmares where I relive it over and over again, but each time it's worse.

Lying next to Xavier these past few days feels lonely. I can't really tell anyone how he reacted because I don't know. From the moment I woke up from that restaurant, there's a metal box that encased him inside of it. The person that became Xavier Amari is one I never met before. I don't know where he's been as I sulk in this bed, and I understand we cope in different ways, but—I need him. I fucking need him here.

With all the time I've spent at home with the emotions that come in waves, the only thing that becomes clear is that I need to talk to Xavier. The random disappearing act is getting old. This was his child too. The more time I have to think, the more it becomes clear that making excuses for how fucked up his life was (minus the recent event) isn't going to solve anything. He needs to stop running.

The sound of keys unlocking the door fills my senses as I quickly step out of the kitchen and into the living room.

Xavier takes a quick glance at me before completely blocking my presence out once again. "You're up."

"We need to talk," I mumble, holding my throw blanket as tightly around my body as possible.

He begins to make his way to the bedroom. "Tomorrow."

"No. Because knowing you these days I'll wake up and you'll be gone until God knows when."

"I'm not in the mood right now, Arlissa."

I follow him through the condo. "I don't care!" I instantly become blurry-eyed as I stomp my feet like a toddler. Would she have had an attitude like me? Or been more nonchalant and colder like her dad? At least, I hope it was a girl.

Xavier quickly turns to me in the darkened bedroom doorway and lazily wipes his eyes. "Fine."

"Are you sober?"

"You said you wanted to talk."

"Answer me."

"No. Okay? Is that what you want to hear?"

"Why can't you just—"

"What? Sit around here and sulk all fucking day? I can't, Arlissa. I fucking can't."

I'm taken aback by how easy it is for him to be so cruel to me right now. Why is it so hard for him to acknowledge anyone other than himself? "You know what . . . I can't. I can't keep doing this!"

He rolls his eyes so hard I only see the white part for a moment. "Doing what, Arlissa?"

"You're barely home because you're out getting high like you're the only one who lost something! You think you can fix everything by letting it just pass by, and that's not how shit works, Xavier. You can't just become a walking thunderstorm whenever bad shit happens."

His whole face becomes red with every word I throw at him. "You don't get to tell me how to cope with the shit that I go through. This is like the first time anything bad has ever even happened to your happy-go-lucky ass. Cut me a break."

"So I'm clueless to the fact that you're a fucking wreck? You get high not because it's fun but because you need to, and you think I don't see that? You drink so fucking much that we're restocking the bar more than the fridge. There is something seriously wrong here!"

Xavier throws his hands up before pushing past me and heading back toward the front door. "Oh, now there's something wrong with me? Because when we met you were basically on your fucking hands and knees begging for this. Cut me a fucking break. The only problem here is you suddenly trying to change who I've been. I'm fine."

"You're fine?" I call out as I chase after him. "You're fine, but you let a man who beats you to a pulp every day be your manager."

The silence is eerie, but it only lasts a moment. Before I can even understand what's occurring, the force of Xavier's heavy hands are pressed against my chest while my back hits the hard brick wall. Our faces are only an inch apart, but not in the way

I'm used to. Anger fills his eyes as he breathes heavily onto my skin, keeping his forearm across my neck.

"Don't you ever speak on my fucking dad, you got that?"

Before my petrified brain can even muster up a response, he releases his grip of me and allows my body to drop to the floor. My back aches in pain after being pushed so aggressively against one of the many walls that encased me in this condo with him. If these walls could talk, they'd be screaming, telling me to leave. Rushes of tears fall down my cheeks as I watch him move throughout the unlit room. The only glimpse of light is coming from the front door when he opens it to leave. I remain seated, too terrified to move. He didn't punch me or slap me, but I'm shattered, nonetheless. As my bare skin sits on that cold and dusty floor, my entire being feels worthless. The person I love the most was this close to hurting me—even more. I pushed him a bit too far and for a split second I didn't recognize who he was anymore. Has the love between us died along with our child? Or is the passion and pain just not a good mix? I'm trying to be there for him, help him; express how I'm feeling. I've dealt with the walls for too long and as soon as I try to break them down he becomes someone who puts the fear of God into me.

From dusk to dawn, to dawn to dusk. An entire weekend had passed with no word as to where Xavier is. It takes me an hour to get off that floor; and every time I shut my eyes I relive it all over again. I have no motivation to turn on any of my shows, no want to use more energy than what's necessary to feed and let Dixie out to use the bathroom. I drift off into my fifth nap of the day, praying that my nightmares won't haunt me this time.

"Shit . . . I didn't know you were sleep." The voice comes as a shock to my entire system as it rises me out of my slumber. Eyelids struggle to open and I try my best to come back to reality.

When my vision finally settles on Xavier, I can tell the monster is gone. His whole demeanor is softer—kinder. "You're home."

"Uh—yeah. I got you something."

I adjust the pillow under me before sniffling while he quickly walks away. I wait, not saying a word until he comes back. When he makes his way through the doorway again, he's holding a jet-black dog carrier. My mouth hangs open while I scramble to get out of the bed. "You didn't . . ."

"I thought . . . you'd like him. And—" He pauses while his long fingers fiddle with the lock in our dark space. "I want to say I'm sorry. I flipped out, and you were right, I haven't been doing well or handling shit well. And I—"

The large brown dog who's now slowly escaping from the carrier is the least of my worries. "Xavier . . ."

He walks over to me, causing my whole body to tense up. But it quickly releases once his soft hand lands on mine. "I will never ever ever act that way toward you again. I was out of my fucking mind, I'm sorry. Okay? Please just forgive me. I don't want to be this way with you."

"And you think I want to be this way with you?" Silence. The dog rubs against my ankles causing a rift between the tension.

"He likes you."

"It's a boy? Oh."

"What are you going to name him?"

"Bear."

"I like that. And I love you."

"I love you more. You know that . . . but I don't love being alone."

"I know, AK. I know."

My head rests on his chest and before I know it every negative emotion I had toward him has melted away. His strong arms wrap tightly around my frame as we calmly rock back and forth. This is the love, the support, and the energy I had needed all along. I just wish it didn't take this long to come to me. But loving someone unconditionally is a part of the love game, right?

Chapter
FIFTY-SEVEN

For a model I spend a lot of time on the couch. I try my best to do the normal things I see my friends doing on Instagram: tai chi, yoga, thirty-minute face masks, tea with almond milk in it. But the reality of it is—all I want to do is pet my dogs and watch *Master Chef*. Some things don't change. I surely never do, right? Maybe I don't fit into this world at all. Maybe I'm an imposter. Afterall, I do still trip on red carpets. Did I even want to model at all anymore? Did I ever want to be one to begin with? The rush and excitement of going to shoots is quickly evaporating. The only thing pushing me out of the door these days is keeping Xavier proud and the healthy paycheck that kept me from depending on him entirely.

Truthfully? It's all getting exhausting. I barely even wash my hair anymore. The idea of a family was so exciting to me because maybe—maybe that was all I ever really wanted to do. Having a child would have given me the perfect excuse to back out of taking pictures for the rest of my life. Look, I can handle it, okay? I can handle the Instagram sponsorships but I am so tired of waking up at five in the morning to pose for some overweight white man, or if I'm lucky, a really nice black woman who brings snacks. Imposter syndrome is a bitch.

But I know one person, one person who always put the idea of family before anything. *Jesus, Arlissa. Don't do it, not now.*

"Do you need anything before I go?"

I shake my head, further covering myself with an immense throw blanket. "He'll be back soon. I'll be fine."

Alejandra sighs, her hand resting on the door handle. "Is this your first time apart since—"

"Yeah."

"Why the fuck did he even leave?"

I shrug, "it's his big match . . . He can't miss it."

"That asshole. Well, call if you need anything, okay?"

"'Kay."

"Or I can stay."

"Go. You have stuff to do."

Her lips form a soft smile as she pulls the front door ajar. "Okay. I'll call you. I love you."

Within moments the only company I had that didn't bark is gone. I sit there, wondering how bad it would be to text the one person who cared more about another human life than itself. No, it's been too long. Texting him would be insensitive. I turn my phone over in my lap, before unlocking it and pressing the green call button. Scroll, scroll, scroll. "DO NOT DELETE."

I release a deep sigh, before hitting the highlighted call button. It rings, over and over again. My heart beats harder every single time. Voicemail. *Fuck.* I clear my throat, waiting for the hellish beep that'll tell me to start talking.

"Hey. I know this is weird and random. This is Arlissa, by the way. I just . . . I don't expect you to answer. I don't deserve it.

But, um, hey! How are you? Fuck, let me just make this quick. I need you right now. Everything is going to shit. I love you, C. So please . . . just call or text. Bye."

The buzzer on my phone goes off in a distinct manner as soon as I hang up. It's not a text or a call; it's one of my tweet notifications. When Xavier and I first started dating I thought it'd be a good idea to make sure I'm one of the first to know how his matches go when I'm not there.

So, I found the best boxing pages on Twitter and put on their alerts before every match. It's stupid, though. He never loses. So, the updates at this point are getting repetitive. But it's a tradition. It continues to vibrate, causing my whole hand to feel like an earthquake. I allow my thumb to slide down on my notification bar. Tweets flood my home screen with Xavier's name being the highlight.

Xavier Amari loses first fight in Las Vegas match.
Xavier vs. Leo. Leo wins.
Two undefeated young fighters go against each other, the underdog won.
Xavier Amari, losing his touch?

My mouth hangs open as I scroll through the tweets. No, there's no way in hell he lost. It's clear the miscarriage and our crumbling relationship made things a bit tense, but he's not a loser. He's a hard worker who doesn't let stupid personal issues get to him. This is going to destroy him. I know how Xavier works, calling him right now would only make things ten times worse. My body begins to tense up as I try my best to ignore the screaming voice in the back of my mind. He's going to come home angry, in a way that I had never experienced before. Or maybe he'd come back sad and in need of my presence. Part of me wants to pack up and run to anyone's house but this one. The other part of me knows if I'm not here when he gets home, he'll only react ten times worse. I can calm the fire, I know I can.

Silence fills the apartment after the heavy door slams shut. The sun peeks through the window and ushers the morning in. He's home. I couldn't get any sleep last night as the thoughts of how he could react to losing for the very first time in his entire career rushes through my overly occupied mind. I can hear minor things from the bedroom, like his footsteps or him putting his bags down, nothing too serious. Yet, there's no clear sign that he's in a good or bad mood. I'm not coming out of this room until I know exactly how bad it is. I lay there, quickly checking my phone for the time: 6:25. He had to have gotten an early flight, but he usually never steps foot on a plane early unless he has to. Or, unless he wants to get away from people as fast as possible.

The shattering sound of broken glass startles my ears as my instant reaction is to jump out of bed. I scatter around the bedroom as the sound repeats over and over again. I can only imagine how he's destroying our living room—his grunts are scarier than the glass breaking. My feet take baby steps out of the room, every time an object hits the floor it sends a razorblade like sensation down my spine. As I come to sights with the distraught man as he launches a bottle of white wine over his shoulder, fear has stricken me entirely. When we make eye contact, I pray to God that I won't become one of those shattered bottles. I pray he'd just continue to take his anger out on them, and that I'd just be the bystander who has to clean it up later. It's probably not a good idea to pray five seconds before the encounter.

His eyes pierce my soul. There are no tears to be found, just bloodshot holes in his face that are ice cold when they land on me. In that moment I know the Xavier I can trust is nowhere to be found. This is going to be new territory, a Xavier I've never seen before. A man that makes me automatically wonder if the doors are locked. Panicked eyes scan around the condo; I can already kiss anything breakable goodbye.

"You can just fucking go," he roars.

The words take me by surprise as I stand there frozen in fear. "Go where, sweetheart?"

"Leave. I see you looking at the door. You're dating a fucking failure now, so . . . you can get the fuck out. I know you want to." His words slur as he rolls his eyes repeatedly. Xavier had to have gotten wasted on that flight back, and probably in the cab ride home too.

"I don't . . . want to leave."

"No!" The volume in his voice heightens, sending shivers down my entire being. "I know what you think of me now. You don't have to fucking lie. You're a fucking liar!" Xavier charges to the TV in a drunken rage, only to punch it square in the center.

I gulp hard, the moisture in my mouth completely evaporating. "Xavier, you're drunk. Maybe you should—"

He steps toward me. "I should what? Rest? How can I rest when I'm fucking losing everything!"

"You—you—it was one fight."

He lets out a sarcastic laugh. "Yeah, yeah, one fucking fight. Shut the hell up, Arlissa!" His hand slightly raises as he speaks, causing me to wince in fear while I stand there with one eye open. "Oh, so now you're scared of me?"

I try my best to straighten my stance but it's nearly impossible. "No."

Xavier's large hands grab onto my arms as he shakes me feverishly. "So fucking look at me!"

My body stands frozen there, hands held up in front of my face as an instinctual reaction. "X—"

"You think I'm a fucking loser too, don't you? Don't you?" he roars.

I shake my head feverishly, fiery hot tears flowing down my cheeks. "No! No! I don't."

His grip on my arms only tightens with every whiskey-scented breath he takes. "You do. You're just like the tabloids and Savannah and all of them."

"What in the world does she have to do with any of this?"

He looks around frantically for a moment. "What?"

"Savannah."

Xavier raises his eyebrows in surprise only to lower them in anger just as fast. He hits my face with such force, a force I've never felt before. "Don't you fucking say her name."

My mind has yet to process the throbbing pain of my cheek before he strikes me again, and again. It's all happening so fast that I can't even register where; I just know it's happening. Next thing I know, I'm being pushed against the hard brick wall—for the second time in our relationship. This time hard enough to send my head flying backwards. Slowly but surely I feel the back of my head become more and more damp. My hesitant hands reach to where the pain is showing itself the most. Strands of hair guard the injury as I push past each one and press gently on what's obviously an open wound. A small one, I hope. Blood coated the tips of my fingers as I shakily bought my hand back in front of my face.

"Xavier."

He releases his grip of me, taking several steps back in fear. "I—"

"Xavier, I need to go to the hospital."

He aggressively shakes his head as the cold look in his eyes quickly thawed. "We can't."

"What?" I exclaim.

"I can't."

"I need to go. To the hospital."

"If we go to the hospital then we have to tell them what

happened, and my reputation is fucking finished." He runs his hands through his oily locks and his eyes start to water.

He doesn't care about me, he only cares about him. I could be suffering from a brain injury for all we know, and he doesn't give a shit. I look at how pitiful and small he appears right now, I just stand there in awe. This was never about me, this was about getting one up on her or whoever else he had to prove himself to. This isn't about love. This is about an image.

"Wow. I have to . . . I have to go."

"No!" he screams, stepping in front of the door.

"Xavier . . . I could really be hurt right now. I need you to move." This fragile, crying version of Xavier is someone I can work with. All fear aside I have to put my big girl pants on and be nice or I am never going to make it out of this house; not alive at least.

"Okay, okay, just . . . You can't tell them what happened."

"I won't. I promise."

My body tries its best to make it to the bedroom while Xavier crumbles in my peripheral vision. I can't go anywhere without my keys, my phone, or my purse. But how the hell am I going to get to the hospital? Xavier is no help and clearly isn't coming with me. The throbbing multiplies from my cheek to the back of my head as I quickly attempt to gather my things and slide some flip flops on. By the time I'm heading back toward the door, Xavier is seated on the floor; audibly sobbing. The dizziness is settling in and settling in fast, my health is on the line here. I swing the door open and quickly close it, hoping that no one will come out into the brightly lit hallway and see my neck dripped with blood. Or the swelling that I can only assume is getting worse by the second.

I'm losing a lot of blood, I think. *I'm not going to die*, I think. But goddammit, it hurts. I scroll through my contacts before settling on one person— the only person I know I can trust.

344

"Hello?" the gravelly voice says on the other line.

"Hey, Aly . . . you're awake. Is Greyson around?" My words slur as I tried to form a proper sentence. "Could you pick me up? I need to go to the hospital."

Chapter
FIFTY-EIGHT

I lay there lazily in the hotel room, hiding from anyone who could even say Xavier's name around me. It's all over; at least, it feels over. My mind has yet to process what's going on, and it's been days. I'm swollen, lying to doctors about how I ended up in their room looking like a rag doll. It's all too much.

The click of my hotel door turning open causes me to jump before I realize who it is.

"Turn on the TV!" Aly screams before slamming the door shut.

"Can you please text before you just barge in?"

Aly nods before taking a seat next to me. "Did I give you a headache? Are you okay?"

"No. But . . . yes. What am I turning on the TV for?"

"I guess . . . Look, I think . . . " She sighs before grabbing the remote and flicking through the channels. "Xavier is covering his ass in case anyone sees you like this."

Before I can even react, Xavier is on my TV screen looking more put together than he has in months. America's poster boy was smiling and doing an interview with one of the biggest TV hosts that I knew of.

Shit.

"I'm in an amazing mood, man. You know, there's a first for everything, and I'm solo now, and——"

"So, Xavier Amari is back on the market?"

"Yes, sir. Have been for some time now."

"What happened there? And how long exactly? You guys were just together at the Billboard Music Awards."

"We just didn't work out, that's all. I'm back to focusing on myself. We broke up a bit after that night, actually. No hard feelings, just a lot of heaviness in the relationship."

I sit there in shock, as he goes on and on about how long he's been single. We didn't break up because we lost the child, and I didn't even know we were broken up. I can't even focus on Alejandra's look of worry coming from my peripheral vision. My blood boils as I watch him giggle and laugh on TV about how much better he's been without me—when in reality, all I did was give him everything. He doesn't deserve me, he doesn't deserve what I gave him for almost three whole ass years.

No, I'm not going to let him get away with this. Not now.

"Where's my phone?"

Alejandra rises before helping me scan the sheets. "What are you doing?"

Once the technology is in my possession, shaky hands head to Instagram before quickly heading to the LIVE button. The first glimpse I catch of myself in days is a terrifying one. My once smooth brown skin is now covered in stitches and bandages, my dry curly hair with a bit of blood still in it, swollen and bloodshot eyes. I'm not the girl my followers are used to seeing.

As the viewers come in, I wait.

"Lissa . . . Don't do this," Aly warns.

I look up at her, then back at the phone, fifty thousand viewers already. They want to hear what I have to say, and I'm going to give it to them.

"Well, good fucking morning. I know I look a mess. But that is the cause of Xavier Amari. You say I'm the issue? You say I'm the fucking problem? You motherfucking spoiled brat."

"Lissa, close that," Alejandra whispers.

"You gave me stitches on my fucking head, you bastard! I have bruises, and let's not act like this is the first time. You cannot make me feel like the problem when you sit there and lie your way through everything. We were just together days ago! And then you say the day we lost our child was your last straw? I'm so glad I got away from you. You're the monster. You fucking treated me like property until I ran out that door. And I am so glad I never had a baby with you, because we did not have a home in that condo. It was a prison. So burn in hell, Xavier. And the fucking gossip blogs can too."

Alejandra snatches my phone and ends the live. "What the fuck is wrong with you?"

"What is wrong with you? Like you wouldn't do the same shit?"

"Lissa, that was before I knew what this industry is like. What people are like. What his fucking family is like. Do you know what you started? Reacting like this won't end well. Xavier has a very fucking powerful family. Ruining his reputation isn't the best choice."

"So let him ruin me?"

"No—that's not what I'm saying, I—"

"Go home to Greyson. To your perfect life. I am going to sit and sulk about what the fuck comes next. Because you know what? You didn't get beat on by the man you love. You can go home and lay with yours, so don't ever tell me how to react again."

"Lissa . . ."

"Go!"

Tears fill my burning eyes as I try my hardest to process everything while Alejandra makes her exit. I know she's just trying to help, but no one can help me right now. I've taken the only thing Xavier cares about—his reputation. And now I just have to wait to see his entire world crumble. Just like mine is.

Night turns into day, day turns into night. And for the first time in years I'm completely alone. Just me, this hotel bed, and the crumbs and wrappers I'm too tired to clean up. No one I met in this city wants to talk to the girl who Xavier's family is probably already fighting hard to call crazy. I wouldn't know; no one's phone call is getting an answer from me. Not now, not today, maybe not ever.

I'm turning into an empty vessel of a woman. Maybe a few days had gone by, maybe a week. It's all been blending together, and I don't even have the energy to put my phone on the charger anymore. I lay here in this bed, praying for someone to give me the strength to get up and show face.

Why?

Why me? Why is it the first time I ever find love I fuck it up? I tried with Xavier, I really did. And I couldn't break through. Well, I did for a moment, and we lost the baby. We lost the one thing that could have fixed it all between us. It's my fault. The one thing I was born for I can't even do. I can't even be a woman, so how can I be a friend or a girlfriend? Everything I love crumbles at my feet. I can't shut my mouth and keep my sister home, I can't carry a child, and I can't keep one guy happy. He's never going to talk to me again.

No, Lissa. He hurt you. You didn't do anything . . . Except you did.

Oh quiet, Samantha. This is your fault too.

Who would be there when you needed a shoulder to lean on? After every fight, he'd always apologize and explain himself. Jesus, you're such a fucking idiot. Why didn't you let him explain? He just lost the same baby you did—how can you be so selfish? How?

Maybe . . . Maybe if he'll forgive me—I can still call. Apologize. Explain that I understand that he went through two terrible losses at the same time. Maybe, then I'd get my appetite back. My glamorous life back. I'll have the energy to comb my hair. I'll shower. The whole world wouldn't want my head on a stick and my friends wouldn't ignore me.

I could get it all back. I could get us back.

My fragile body slides out of the BO scented sheets and scans the dark room for my charger. Dresser? No. Floor? No. My purse? Bingo.

Now we hook it up and wait.

What am I even going to say? What if he doesn't answer? Would I leave a voicemail? Jesus Christ, what if there's already another girl in his bed. Or, maybe, he's just as broken up about this as me. God, I hope I can fix this. I can't live without him. I won't live without him.

As my phone screen lights up, all I can do is watch the plethora of notifications come in.

Xavier Amari: A Monster?

Fuck, I forgot I have his notifications on for any press about him. The public isn't against me, they're against him. I ruined him. Everything I said . . . I need to fix this. After losing a child, his title, me—his reputation is the last thing he could afford to lose.

You're such a selfish idiot. He lost control one time, and here you go . . . Making a mess of everything he worked so hard to create. And his dad too. He's probably pounding the shit out of him right now.

Shit. I quickly clear all the stupid notifications before clicking his number and hitting the green call button that's basically jumping out at me.

It rings once. Twice. Maybe four times before my heart feels as if it's completely beating out of my chest. *Pick up . . . Please. I just want to make this right.*

"Hey—"

"Xavier . . ."

"You've reached Xavier Amari's voicemail, I can't get to the phone right now. Leave a message with your name and number and I'll try and get back to you."

My heart sinks but now is my time. "X . . . Xavier, hi. It's Arlissa but I'm sure you know that. That's why you didn't answer. I . . . I don't know how to start this but I want to apologize. I overreacted, I fucked up. But we can fix this. I'll do anything—say anything. Let me fix this. You said you'd die without me, remember? I do. So, if you felt this way once then I know you will again. We can fight this together. I love you, and I want to build a family with you, Xavier. I'm so sorry. I didn't mean anything I said." My throat choked up as the tears overwhelmed me. "X, please. I don't know who else to turn to. You've been everything to me . . . You introduced me to this world, and I can't be in it without you."

Please, just call me back.

Chapter
FIFTY-NINE

"Xavier, Arlissa! This way!"

"How are you two back together? Tell us everything!"

Xavier and I take quick steps down the LA streets that are flooded with paparazzi since they got the word we were back from our latest vacation. Xavier wanted privacy, that was all. If we were going to work this out, then we needed to go away. Then, deal with the press later.

He squeezes my hand twice, my cue to suck up to the paparazzi. "I'm happy, the happiest I've ever been. Thank you."

I step aside as our security pulls open the front door to our condo, letting us both in and keeping the paparazzi outside. While we wait for the elevator, he leans down to give me a kiss on the cheek—kisses I've grown quite used to again over the last week.

This is right. This is the way things have to be. I'm fixing everything for him, and he's loving me again. We're going to have this family, I have hope for it. He promised me.

"You okay, love?"

I nod as we make our way upstairs. "I just . . . I'm glad we're okay."

He smiles, becoming the prince charming I once knew again. "Me too. We fought, it got—ugly. But you're mine, and we're going to fix this. Together."

"Together."

When those elevator doors open, the familiar ding fills the space, and I try my best to not fall to my knees. I'm home. I spent so many days in that hotel room—dreading the idea of going back to Carson City with my tail between my legs. My life was over for a moment, and now it's back. My control, my power, my status—it's all slowly returning. Just one rule: Don't Google yourself. At least not yet.

The condo is just as I remember it, large and spacious, in desperate need of a houseplant or two. I drop my luggage down on those hardwood floors, Dixie and Bear come racing from their respective rooms—straight to me. My eyes swell as I kneel down to kiss on my puppies. My babies, the closest thing Xavier and I have to creating a family.

He hovers over me. "They missed you."

"I missed you all . . . I'm just so sorry, okay?"

"Lissa, we've been through this. You don't have to keep apologizing."

I rise from my kneeling position, fighting every urge to drop to my knees for him. "I told you I'd do anything . . . "

"I know, and I told you we'll play it by ear."

"Yeah, and I don't get how that makes sense, X. Your entire—"

"Stop. I know. And there's nothing we can do but move forward."

I sigh before slowly unbuttoning my sweater. It feels so good to be home. "So I can't even make a statement? I'll say I was losing my mind, or—or that I was just upset—"

"Kimber, stop." His stern voice catches me off guard as he walks over to help with my buttons. "If we release a statement that just makes it easier to pick apart your words. Both of ours. The best option is just to let them come to their own conclusions. What's done is done."

If this was an open-shut case, it would make it easier to not follow him wherever he went. It would make it easier to not get confused by every word he said—because the more he says the less I know.

With careful hands he helps me slide the layer off of my arms, my skin dances as his thumbs slightly brush against my forearm. Our love is electric, intoxicating and vulnerable. There's nothing anyone can do to make me afraid of him—again. Nothing he can do. I made a mistake but I'm ready to beg to keep my man.

"Hey . . . let's order a pizza and stay in. Watch one of those Adam Sandler movies you love."

A slight smile appears on his face as he begins to clear off the sofa. "Yeah?"

He's trying to be happy, our whole vacation I could see that he was trying his best but—I hurt him. I knew what mattered most, and I acted out of anger. The best I can do is see this through, make it up to him, get him to smile from ear to ear again.

I wrap my arms around his waist, resting my head on his back, "Mm-hmm. Whatever you want."

He turns, forcing me to release my grip of him and stand there defenselessly. "I love you."

The words drip out of his moisturized lips like pure liquid ecstasy. He hadn't said it since I've been back. To be honest I thought he didn't feel it anymore. The rush of emotion from the words alone causes blurry vision as I melt right there in front of him.

"I promise I love you more."

354

Xavier bends down, placing a kiss on my forehead. "We'll see about that."

"Hm?"

"Yeah, when we see what Adam Sandler movie you're choosing."

We both chuckle as I try to keep my thirsty hands to myself. A movie night isn't enough. We're home again. We need to celebrate. We need to start back where we left off. It's only right.

It took the pizza maybe half an hour to get there and Xavier refused to start *Click* until we had food in front of us. I watch him carefully; something's different. It's how calm he seems to be. How he has so little to say. Our love should be celebrated, and it seems like I'm the only one ready to buy a cake and do a toast for the occasion.

He's just tolerating you.

I lean over, letting my head rest on his shoulder. He doesn't put his arm around me like he usually does. *God, please just tell me this is all in my head.*

"Hey."

"'Sup?"

I sit up from the couch cushions, fully facing him. "I want to restart."

He raises a brow. "Isn't that what we're doing?"

"I want to try again . . ."

His eyes softened while he took a moment to take in what I was trying to convey. "Oh."

"I know it seems reckless, and we're just now getting this thing back on track but . . . I promised you I was here forever, and I am. I love you, and I want us to try again. I failed once but I'll do better this time, okay? I just want our family."

That's where it all went wrong, the day we lost that baby. So maybe, if we just started from that spot, started from square one, we could get back on track, we could be America's favorite couple all over again. The world will forgive him, and I'd play the crazy bitch in the media if I have to. But I'd be able to come home to him—to our child.

He brings happiness into the bleak life I've been trucking through. He's the reason I can see color through my pupils again. That winning smile, the charm. Xavier has his issues, but who doesn't? I have a spot next to him, a permanent throne that no other gullible fool is taking. Our love is beyond the curses and screams, more than the blood and bruises.

Xavier places his cold hands on my cheeks before nodding. "I'm down."

I let out a sigh of relief. "Really?"

"Arlissa, I love you. And I meant it when I said it'd be us forever in some way shape or form. I'd rather this than anything else. I fucking promise."

When he places his lips on mine, I can't help but completely come to his every demand. The sweetness of passion radiates between us as our bodies intertwined on that couch. Every happy moment we had flashes through my memory like a full-length feature film. Except, this time, the ending is so much brighter than I could have ever imagined.

The ending is happiness.

Chapter
SIXTY

My peaceful sleep is interrupted by an abrupt moisture that found itself on my thigh. With everything that we did that night, it could have been a million different liquids. I lay there, too lazy to get up and get a piece of toilet paper to wipe down my legs. My body melts into the mattress, the mattress that my back had missed. Hotels have nothing on this California King bed or the thousand thread count sheets that it's dressed with.

Peace. I smile as I lay there, thinking of the baby we probably just created. What would we name her? Lord, I wish I can tell now. I wish someone would just give me a sign. The excitement rushes through my entire being as my heart jumps out of my chest.

A baby. We were really going to get our do-over.

My eyes slowly open to reveal the pitch-black room. Nothing is out of place. Everything is as I remember it—even in the dark.

Slowly, I creep out of the bed on a mission to take care of whatever is currently drying up on my leg so I can get back to sleep. My silent toes creep across the hardwood floor until I reach the bathroom. I don't want to wake him. I'm sure he has a busy day ahead, so I quietly shut the door and flick on the light. My naked body stands in the mirror as I try my best to adjust my weak eyes to the alarming white light coming from the bulb above me.

My attention falls to my nails to see some reddish-brown splatters covering my nail beds. My heart skips a beat as my eyes scan down to my legs, blood that's beginning to dry is plastered over the bottom of my white nightgown and my thighs.

I can't be getting my period right now. No. This doesn't make sense. My breaths begin to mimic rocks skipping over open waters as I rip the bathroom door open and make quick steps to the bedroom.

Shit, I still can't see anything. He's probably still asleep, so let me just grab my—bingo! I dig my phone out from under the bed and quickly click the flashlight. Slowly, I rise and shine a bit of the light on the still body that had a place besides me.

No. No. A hard gulp makes its way down my throat. He's pale. Bloody, so bloody I can't find the origin of it. The pit in my stomach is tight as breathing becomes more of a chore than a mindless task.

"X . . . " I murmur, blurry vision making it harder to shakily climb back onto the bed. He's still, there's no movement—no breath. I think. Once I reach him, my body numbs entirely. There's no way. There's no way I'm going through this again almost two decades later. No, that would be just cruel, right?

Why would he do this? Life is perfect, we're perfect. I shake his shoulders vigorously as shock quickly transfers to anger.

"You bastard get up! You cannot do this to me, I will—you said——"

Oh my God, he probably didn't believe me.

I'll die without you.

The words ring through my ears—I did this. He did this because he thought I wasn't serious. Why didn't he just give me time? We just needed more time. The light tears turn into sobs and ear bursting screams. My voice almost gives out as the rush of tears completely overwhelms me.

He can't be gone.

"I'm sorry, I'm so fucking sorry, Xavier. Just please for the love of God come back!" I shout as I straddle the lifeless being that causes my entire lower body to make friends with the blood. My fists beat his chest repeatedly in hope for a response, anything. As more tears fall, my fire-red cheeks start to sting from the aggressive rubbing and sobbing I've been doing.

"Fuck! Why are you doing this to me? What did I do to deserve this?" I shout, anger building up in my entire being the longer I stare at a sickly-looking version of my lover.

No. No. This can't be real life. I can't lose someone else, not here. Not like this. Why? Why does everything I love get ripped away from me like I did something wrong? I'm not the problem. I can't be the problem.

Pain flows out of every pore, and I can hear my heart shatter bit by bit. It's not a silent shatter, no. It's the kind that makes you want to grip at your chest and rip that very organ out. I wish I'm looking down at someone else other than him. Anyone. It could be anyone else—just not Xavier. I rest my head on his still body, the blood on my hands beginning to dry up now as I trace my fingertips down his chest. Is he breathing, or am I just shaking?

I'm numb. Maybe if I just lie back down, close my eyes, I'll wake up and this will all be a dream . . . right? I can wake up and none of this will be happening right now. He'll be smiling at me before running out the door for a meeting. It'll be okay. The pools of blood soak into my white nightgown. None of that concerns me.

At least wherever I go after this I can take a piece of him with me.

"You can stop joking now," I whisper to what's left of the man I gave everything to. A laugh escapes my chapped lips as my melting brain tries its best to process what's happening in these four walls. "You won . . . You fucking won."

The sarcastic laughter continues as the guilt of my entire life piles up inside. My sister, now this. I take notice of the sunrise coming up gently, shining light on everything that was once hidden in darkness.

"I did it! Okay? I fucking did it! I killed him. I killed her. I killed my daughter," I shout as if the sun is going to give me a round of applause for confessing. My vision trails off, and so does my voice, cracked and going in and out from the countless screams I've been vocalizing all night. "This is all your fault, Lissa . . . You ruin everything you touch, you worthless piece of shit."

My spiral is interrupted by a bright light and heavy footsteps pushing through our bedroom door. I jump up, both hands covered in half-dried blood as I hold them up in fear.

"Arlissa Benson, I'm going to need you to step away from the body."

I vigorously shake my head, overwhelmed by the number of armed officers that are now surrounding me. Every time I blink, a new one shows up.

"What's going on?" I scream.

"Ma'am, please slowly get off of the bed and step away from the body."

No, no, no! They are not going to take him from me. "No—"

Before I can finish my thought, two large hands are yanking me from the sheets, revealing all the blood that I had let soak up in the fabric of my nightgown. "Get off me! You can't do this! You can't take him!"

"Calm down, Ms. Benson," one of the officers calmly says

with what I'm sure is a gun pointed right at my face. But his flashlight is so blinding there's no way anyone could see anything clearly. The coat of one officer catches the light, revealing the three letters printed: FBI.

"I want to stay with him! Leave me alone! Let me stay with him!" I fight with all my might and scream until my throat burns, salty tears dripping onto my nose. I holler as if my brain is on fire.

I try kicking, I try scratching--biting. But before I know it the right side of my face is pressed against the stone-cold wall and my hands are tied behind my back, a metal-binding locking them together.

"Arlissa Benson, you are under arrest for the murder of Xavier Amari. You have the right to remain . . . "

Every cell of my body feels as if it's melting while I try to make sense of the words that are being sent in my direction. What did I do?

How did I even get here?

Before I know it my curly locks are falling in front of my face as I'm getting yanked out of my condo.

"I did it . . . I did it . . . " I mumble.

"Ma'am you have the right to remain silent." The office reminds me as he guides my bare feet across the cold floor of the complex we lived in. I watch as neighbors slowly begin opening their doors and peeking out to see my distressed body being tugged through the halls.

"But I did it . . . "

My eyes feel as if they're rolling back behind my head as the cold California air hits my bare bloodstained legs. The cop doesn't try to be gentle at all when he shoves me into the back of the car.

The ending is supposed to be happiness.

ACKNOWLEDGEMENTS

Thank you first and foremost to me for completing something for once in my life. For two entire years without dropping the ball no matter how difficult (or expensive) it got. Thank you to my parents for letting me spend two years pouring all of my energy into this unconditionally. Of course, thank you to the angels watching over me for pushing me through this even though I really wanted to quit six months in. Thank you to Sean for reading every single draft and sharing even the gritty parts of this process with me. A special round of applause goes to the amazing team at Enchanted Ink Publishing for caring for my baby as much as I did, because trust me I was terrified to have anyone else but I read it. Kylee & Angie, you're getting a thank you as well because you guys showed excitement over this project before I even really knew what to call it. To Jean, and Lourdes; thank you for letting me yell my ideas at you until my head fell off. And thank you for never letting me give up. I'm really tired now, and it's all of your faults for pushing me through. Shame on you.